KU-406-967

BRENT LIBRARIES

Please return/renew this item
by the last date shown.
Books may also be renewed by
phone or online.
Tel: 0333 370 4700
On-line www.brent.gov.uk/libraryservice

9112000473644

BY DEAN KOONTZ

Ashley Bell • *The City* • *Innocence* • *77 Shadow Street*
What the Night Knows • *Breathless* • *Relentless*
Your Heart Belongs to Me • *The Darkest Evening of the Year*
The Good Guy • *The Husband* • *Velocity* • *Life Expectancy*
The Taking • *The Face* • *By the Light of the Moon*
One Door Away From Heaven • *From the Corner of His Eye*
False Memory • *Seize the Night* • *Fear Nothing* • *Mr. Murder*
Dragon Tears • *Hideaway* • *Cold Fire* • *The Bad Place*
Midnight • *Lightning* • *Watchers* • *Strangers* • *Twilight Eyes*
Darkfall • *Phantoms* • *Whispers* • *The Mask* • *The Vision*
The Face of Fear • *Night Chills* • *Shattered*
The Voice of the Night • *The Servants of Twilight*
The House of Thunder • *The Key to Midnight*
The Eyes of Darkness • *Shadowfires* • *Winter Moon*
The Door to December • *Dark Rivers of the Heart* • *Icebound*
Strange Highways • *Intensity* • *Sole Survivor*
Ticktock • *The Funhouse* • *Demon Seed* • *Devoted*

JANE HAWK
The Silent Corner • *The Whispering Room*
The Crooked Staircase • *The Forbidden Door*
The Night Window

ODD THOMAS
Odd Thomas • *Forever Odd* • *Brother Odd* • *Odd Hours*
Odd Interlude • *Odd Apocalypse* • *Deeply Odd* • *Saint Odd*

FRANKENSTEIN
Prodigal Son • *City of Night* • *Dead and Alive*
Lost Souls • *The Dead Town*

A Big Little Life: A Memoir of a Joyful Dog Named Trixie

DEAN KOONTZ
ELSEWHERE

HarperCollins*Publishers*

HarperCollins*Publishers*
1 London Bridge Street,
London SE1 9GF

www.harpercollins.co.uk

HarperCollins*Publishers*
1st Floor, Watermarque Building, Ringsend Road
Dublin 4, Ireland

This paperback edition 2021
1

First published in Great Britain by HarperCollins*Publishers* 2020

First published in the USA in 2020 by Thomas & Mercer, Seattle.

Copyright © The Koontz Living Trust 2020

Dean Koontz asserts the moral right to
be identified as the author of this work

A catalogue record for this book
is available from the British Library

ISBN: 978-0-00-829127-3 (B-format PB)
ISBN: 978-0-00-829129-7 (A-format PB)

This novel is entirely a work of fiction.
The names, characters and incidents portrayed in it are
the work of the author's imagination. Any resemblance to
actual persons, living or dead, events or localities is
entirely coincidental.

Printed and bound in Great Britain by
CPI Group (UK) Ltd, Croydon, CR0 4YY

All rights reserved. No part of this publication may be
reproduced, stored in a retrieval system, or transmitted,
in any form or by any means, electronic, mechanical,
photocopying, recording or otherwise, without the prior
permission of the publishers.

MIX
Paper from
responsible sources

FSC™ C007454

www.fsc.org

This book is produced from independently certified FSC™ paper
to ensure responsible forest management.

For more information visit: www.harpercollins.co.uk/green

To Richard Pine and Kim Witherspoon
and
To Kim Witherspoon and Richard Pine
who would have saved me
from numerous stupidities
if only they had come along sooner.

So many worlds, so much to do

. . . such things to be.

—*Alfred Lord Tennyson*

THE VISITOR IN THE DEAD OF NIGHT

Without need of a door and unconcerned about the security-system alarm that has been set, the library patron arrives at three o'clock in the morning, as quiet as any of the many ghosts who reside here—from those in the plays of Shakespeare to those in the stories of Russell Kirk. The aisles between the cliffs of books are deserted. Darkness enfolds the great room and all its alcoves. The staff is home sleeping, and the custodian finished his daily chores an hour earlier. The air smells of pine-scented cleanser and wood polish and aging paper.

Although no watchman patrols this maze of valuable knowledge, the patron does not feel safe. Most would assume a library to be a haven in a world of tumult, but the patron knows better. He has seen numerous gruesome horrors and has much experience of terror. He no longer trusts any place to be an absolute refuge from danger.

For one like him, who knows not just a single history but many, libraries are not infrequently places of death. Librarians and other champions of the written word have been shot and stabbed and burned alive and hauled off to concentration camps to be tortured or used as slave labor. Libraries are not safe places, for their shelves are filled with books, but also with ideas regarding freedom, justice, truth, faith, and much more, ideas that some find intolerable. Book burners of all political persuasions know where to find the fuel when they feel the hour has come for action.

The postmidnight patron knows this town, Suavidad Beach, in all its manifestations, but he can't be sure that this one offers what he needs. On arrival, fresh from another library, he switches on a flashlight. Hooding the beam with one hand, so that it won't carry to the high-set windows, he makes his way to the computer alcove and sits at a workstation.

Soon he's on the internet, then to Facebook, where he finds the page he wants. There are amusing posts by Jeffrey Coltrane and by his eleven-year-old daughter, Amity, but none by his wife, Michelle. Indeed, there are as well photos of Jeffrey and Amity, although none of the girl's mother, as if perhaps she died long ago. This prospect excites the patron.

As the enormous library wall clock ticks softly with each passing minute, the patron searches the public records of Suavidad Beach, seeking a report of the woman's demise. He doesn't find it.

What he *does* find, in the electronic files of the Suavidad Beach Municipal Court, is a petition filed by Jeffrey Coltrane to dissolve his marriage to Michelle. Jeffrey has neither seen nor heard from her in more than seven years, but he does not seek to have Michelle declared dead, only to be released from his marriage to her. He is not the kind of man who can stop hoping. His statement to the court is eloquent, profoundly sad, yet threaded through with a wistful optimism.

Jeffrey's hope is surely naive. The patron has much knowledge of murder and has often been present at scenes of savage slaughter. In this case, Michelle is no doubt dead. Her death is both a tragedy and a cause for celebration.

The patron switches off the computer. He sits in darkness for a while, thinking about death and life and the risks of trying to foil fate.

At 4:10 a.m., he leaves the library as he came, with no need of doors and without setting off the alarm.

This is the eleventh day of April.

PART 1

THE KEY TO EVERYTHING

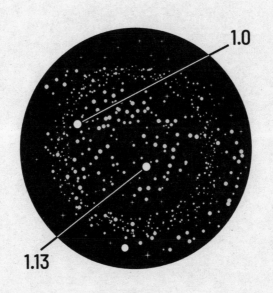

1.0

1.13

Sometimes on a cloudless night when the westering moon left a contrail of shimmering silver light on the otherwise dark sea, when the air was so clear that the distant stars seemed almost as bright as Venus, when the infinite galaxies floating overhead had a weight of wonder that enchanted him, Jeffy Coltrane became convinced that something incredible, something magical, might happen. Although he was a hard worker and in debt to no one, he was also something of a dreamer.

On this splendid Wednesday evening, the eleventh day of April, wonder was center stage, but unexpected terror waited in the wings.

After dinner in their favorite restaurant, realizing the tide was low, Jeffy and his eleven-year-old daughter, Amity, took off their sneakers and socks, rolled up their jeans, and waded out to the sea-smoothed rock formations slightly north of downtown Suavidad Beach, California. They sat side by side, their legs drawn up, arms around their knees, facing west toward the Far East, where Japan lay thousands of miles away in tomorrow afternoon.

"We live on a kind of time machine," Amity said.

"How do you figure?"

"Part of the planet's a day in the future, part is a day in the past, and it's like tomorrow afternoon in Japan."

"Maybe you should go live in Tokyo for a month and each day phone to tell me what horses will win at Santa Anita."

"Yeah," she said, "but if it worked that way, then everybody would be crazy rich from scamming the races."

"Or there'd be no races because they were scammed into ruin, and all those poor horses would be out of work."

"So you know what that means," she said.

"Do I?"

"Never scam. Doing the right thing is the easiest thing."

"You heard that somewhere, did you?"

"I've been totally brainwashed."

"Fathers don't brainwash their children."

"Bullsugar."

"No, really. We propagandize them."

"What's the difference?"

"Propaganda is gentler than brainwashing. You often don't even know it's happening."

"Oh, I know it's happening, all right," she said. "'Cause it's like *always* happening."

"You're so terribly, terribly oppressed."

She sighed. "I endure."

Jeffy smiled and shook his head. The incredible, magical thing that he, a dreamer, sometimes anticipated had in fact happened a long time ago. Her name was Amity.

A slight breeze issued off the ocean, scented faintly with salt and—he believed, he *knew*—with exotic fragrances of far nations so subtle the nose could suspect but not quite detect their existence.

After a silence, Amity said, "So it was the right thing to wait seven years?"

"To keep hope alive for seven years. Yeah. Remaining hopeful is always the right way to be."

"So then wouldn't it be the right thing to wait another seven?"

"I'll never stop hoping, sweetheart. But eventually . . . we have to move on."

Seven years earlier, when Amity was four, Michelle walked out on them. She said that she felt empty, that nothing about her life was the way she had foreseen. She needed to get control of her destiny, and then she could come home to him and Amity.

They'd never heard from her again.

Like Jeffy, Michelle Jamison had been born and raised in sunny Suavidad Beach. Perhaps her sense that her life had gone wrong began when her mother died in childbirth.

Twenty-two years later, just a day after Michelle gave birth to Amity, her beloved father, Jim Jamison, a crew supervisor employed by the power company, was electrocuted while overseeing maintenance on a transformer in a subterranean vault.

Thereafter, Amity's birthday inevitably reminded Michelle not only of her father's death but also of the mother who had been lost to her on the day of her own birth. She wasn't a pessimist, didn't suffer from depression, was in fact a lively woman with a sparkling sense of humor and a love of life. But at times, she felt that her hometown was a haunted place, that the past would weigh too heavily on her as long as she lived there.

She went away to find herself, and evidently she never did.

Every attempt Jeffy made to locate her led nowhere. The private investigator whom he hired seven years earlier and the one he hired only a year ago failed. A determined woman could reinvent herself so effectively that anyone searching for her would need considerably more resources than Jeffy could tap. Never having known her mother, having lost her dad the day after she gave birth to Amity, beginning to lose her dream of success as a musician, she had been vulnerable. Jeffy blamed himself for failing to recognize the depth of her vulnerability. He wished he had never let her go.

By law, Michelle had been missing long enough to be declared dead by a court, but Jeffy hadn't taken that solemn step. He refused to think it could be true. If he believed that she was happy in a new life . . . well, then she must be. Belief was a powerful force. He proceeded with a legal action only to dissolve their marriage.

This week, his petition had been approved.

At thirty-four, he was not exactly starting over. He was completing his recuperation. He still wore his wedding ring.

The slow, easy waves lapped against the low rock formation on which he and his daughter sat, and the gentle surf foamed on the beach in a chorus of murmurs, as if the sea were sharing secrets with the shore.

"What if Mom comes home someday? Will you marry her again?"

Having lived with this loss so long, they dwelt in neither sorrow nor resentment. For Michelle, they shared a sweet melancholy salted with nostalgia not about what had been but about what might have been. Indeed, time healed. The scar would always be tender, but touching it no longer hurt enough to pinch off their breath.

"I don't think your mom would want to marry me again, scout. I wasn't what she needed."

"Well, she was wrong about you."

"Maybe not. She and I were dreamers, but with a difference. She dreamed of things that were possible—being a songwriter, recording her own songs, having a successful career. Me . . . I dream of living in the 1930s, seeing Benny Goodman playing live in the Manhattan Room of the Hotel Pennsylvania in New York. Or of worlds that never were and never can be, Tolkien to Heinlein. I'm all about big bands and hobbits, just a consumer of wonder. But your mom . . . she *created* wonder, beautiful music. I could appreciate her work, I loved it, but she needed a bigger audience than me."

"She was wrong about you," Amity insisted, not with anger but with disarming conviction.

What Michelle had been wrong about was that she could take a leave of absence from her daughter and find a greater meaning. Raising Amity provided sufficient meaning to make any life worth living. He didn't say as much to Amity, because he knew her and knew himself well enough to foresee the consequence. They didn't need to spoil the memory of a fine dinner and blur the stars and fade the sea with tears.

"Show me the Big Dipper," she said.

"Otherwise known as Ursa Major." He put an arm around her and searched the sky and found the handle of the Dipper and focused her attention and drew the constellation for her. "It's been hanging there ever since it was used to scoop the other stars out of a starpool and scatter them across the sky."

Minutes later, they waded ashore and sat on a rock and put on their shoes.

A half-hour walk would take them home. The night was young and warm, and for part of the way there were shop windows—some of them at art galleries—with contents at which to marvel. As a man who felt that he had been born too late, Jeffy was often amazed at what passed for high art in this low age.

The first of seven houses on Shadow Canyon Lane, which branched off Oak Hollow Road, was a wedding-cake Victorian with two turrets and steep roofs and dormer windows, exuberantly decorated with millwork, flanked by proud oaks. It belonged to Marty and Doris Bonner, who were nice people, not a fraction as fussy as their residence. They were on vacation, having left a key with Jeffy.

His and Amity's place was a single-story house. Slate roof. Local sandstone walls. Jeffy had done the masonry, taught by his mason father. Amber bulbs in the crackle-glass lamps cast a warm, vaguely patterned light across the porch, and the gentle breeze whispered in the moon-kissed crowns of the tall palm trees.

One of the two rocking chairs on the porch was occupied.

Amity said, "It's Mr. Spooky."

2

The man whom Amity called Mr. Spooky referred to himself as Ed and never mentioned a surname. He was one of the homeless who lived in isolated encampments deeper in the canyon, well beyond where the blacktop lane dead-ended. Having been in the vicinity for about a year, he came to visit at least twice a month, uninvited.

Jeffy wasn't afraid of Ed. For one thing, Jeffy was thirty-four years old, six feet two, lean and fit, while Ed was perhaps thirty years older and six inches shorter, as out of shape as a moldering squash. The old man was eccentric, although not outright crazy, and he never exhibited the slightest tendency to aggression.

Nevertheless, after saying, "Good evening, Ed," Jeffy let Amity into the house, and he waited until she locked the door and turned on some lights before he settled in one of the rocking chairs on the porch, which their visitor had rearranged to face each other more directly. These days, Jeffy never left Amity home alone, and they went everywhere together, not just because—in fact, not at all because—of Ed.

In its current decline, California was home to an ever-growing throng of the homeless, many of them severely disturbed and with addictions. The politicians governing the state cared only about ideology and power and graft, not about the citizenry. They spent billions on the problem, with no effect other than to greatly enrich their friends and create more homeless people.

When too many of these wounded souls pitched their camps in the same place, the authorities finally moved to evict them, for reasons of public health and safety. Consequently, those who lived in tents or in sleeping bags on the fringes of Suavidad Beach had recently taken to camping in the woods and brushland, each at a distance from the other, to draw less attention to themselves.

Although rumpled and unshaven, Ed was in fundamental ways much different from most single men in his circumstances. His teeth were white, and he smelled clean, perhaps because he walked into town daily to avail himself of the showers and other services offered by some public and church-operated facilities. Instead of shapeless exercise suits or baggy jeans and hoodies, he favored slacks with his shirt tucked in, a sport coat, and always a bow tie. This night, he wore a polka-dot tie with a bold plaid shirt, but he wasn't likely to encounter people who, steeped in style, would arch their eyebrows and mock him surreptitiously.

According to Ed, no alcoholic beverages had ever passed his lips, other than fine cabernet sauvignon, and far less of that than he would have liked because he had a taste only for the best, which he'd not often been able to afford. He also said that he had never done drugs stronger than aspirin.

Jeffy believed Ed's denial of those vices, largely because the old man never lamented his homelessness or made excuses for it—or explained it. His situation was simply his situation, as if he had been born a hobo, as caste bound as any Hindu from another century.

He visited from time to time, in part to discuss the creatures of nature that shared the wooded canyon. He had a deep knowledge of history, too, and liked to speculate about how the present-day world might have been if certain pivot points in human events had resulted in a different resolution from the one that occurred. He also had an interest in poetry, which he could quote at length, everything from Shakespeare to Poe to the Japanese masters of haiku. He never stayed long, certainly never overstayed his welcome, perhaps because his restless mind made him an impatient conversationalist—or because Jeffy was an uninspiring intellectual companion.

"How have you been, Ed?"

"I've been dying since I was born, just like you. And now I'm nearly out of time."

A dour mood was as much a part of Ed as the furry tangles of bushy white eyebrows that he never trimmed.

"You seem fit enough," Jeffy said. "I hope you're not ill."

"No, no, Jeffrey. Not ill, but hunted."

A few teachers in elementary school had insisted on calling him Jeffrey, but no one since then, until Ed. In spite of Jeffy's height and reasonably imposing physique, he possessed some curious quality that caused others to think of him as, in part, a perpetual boy, and thus as Jeffy, which was his mother's pet name for him. He took no offense at this. He liked who he was well enough; and he could be no one different. If being called Jeffy was necessary for him to remain the man who he had always been, then "Jeffy" would suit him for his gravestone and for all the days between now and that final rest.

"Hunted? Hunted by whom?" Jeffy asked.

Ed's scowl knitted his extravagant eyebrows into one long albino caterpillar, and his deep-set eyes receded into the shadows of their sockets. "Better you don't know. It's the incessant need to know more and more and yet still more, to know everything, that is the fast track to destruction. Knowledge is a good thing, Jeffrey, but the arrogance that so often comes with knowledge is ultimately our undoing. Don't be undone, Jeffrey. Do not be undone by pride in your knowledge."

"I don't know all that much," Jeffy assured him. "I'm more likely to be undone by ignorance."

Saying nothing, Ed leaned forward in his chair, his grizzled head thrust out like that of a tortoise craning its neck from its shell, regarding his host as if Jeffy were an avant-garde sculpture, the meaning of which couldn't be discerned.

Having undergone such intense scrutiny on other occasions, Jeffy knew that Ed would not engage in further conversation until he was ready to initiate it. This penetrating stare must be met with a smile and patience.

Filtered by distance and trees, the irregular susurration of the traffic on Oak Hollow Road was a mournful sound, like the exhalations of some noble leviathan slowly dying.

Among the oaks, owls expressed their curiosity to one another.

At last Ed leaned back in his chair, though his scowl did not relent. His luxuriant eyebrows were still interlaced, as if engaged in copulation.

From the porch floor beside his chair, he picked up a package that Jeffy had not previously noticed. The twelve-inch-square white pasteboard gift box was discolored by time and soiled. The matching lid had been secured with a length of string.

Ed placed the item on his lap and held it in both hands. As he stared at the package, his solemn scowl seemed to shade into dread. Occasionally he was afflicted by a benign tremor in his left hand, and now the pads of his fingers tapped spastically against the box.

He raised his head and met Jeffy's eyes again and said, "This contains the key."

After an ensuing silence, Jeffy said, "What key?"

"The key to everything."

"Sounds important."

"They must never get their hands on it."

"They who?"

"Better you don't know," Ed said again. "I'm giving it to you."

Jeffy raised his hands, palms toward his guest in a gesture of polite decline. "That's kind of you, Ed, but I can't accept. I've got a house key, a car key. That's all I need. I wouldn't know what to do with a key to everything."

Snatching the box off his lap and holding it against his chest, Ed declared, "No, no. You must do nothing with it! *Nothing!* You must not open it. *Never!*"

Previously just quaint and quirky, Ed seemed to be crossing a mental bridge from eccentric to a condition more disturbing.

===== 3

Mr. Spooky wasn't scary, just odd, and Amity had no concern that he would attack them with a chain saw or hack them to pieces with a meat cleaver or anything like that. She didn't need to lock the front door, but Daddy was paranoid in a nice way, always looking out for her. She figured that, even after seven years, he hadn't gotten over losing his wife and half expected to lose his daughter, as well. He would probably forever be overprotective. Amity would be forty and married to Justin Dakota—who lived three doors away and might one day develop into suitable husband material—and they would have three kids of their own and be living in a fabulous house on a hill overlooking the sea, and because Justin would be a movie star or a rich technology wizard, and because Amity would be a famous novelist, they would have beaucoup security, like a squadron of bodyguards, but Daddy would still show up every night to check that all the doors and windows were locked, tuck her into bed, and warn her not to take candy from strangers. He was the dearest man, and she loved him with all her heart, really and truly. But she knew that the day was coming, a few years from now, when she would need to sit him down and patiently explain that too much concern on his part could be suffocating and could put a serious strain on their relationship. Already, this was somewhat true; after all, she was closer to twelve than to eleven.

After locking the door and turning on the lights, she passed the living room with its big armchairs and its shelves containing the fantasy novels they enjoyed. She followed the hallway that was lined with original Art Deco posters for products like Taittinger champagne and Angelus "white shoe dressing" and the 1934 Plymouth automobile, and a 1925 nightclub show starring Josephine Baker in Paris. Beyond her father's workshop, in which he restored function and luster to beautiful old Bakelite radios and other collectible Art Deco–period objects, she came to her bedroom at the back of the house, where Snowball waited for her.

At night and when she and her father went to a restaurant, Snowball lived in a cage. This wasn't cruel, because the cage was large, with an exercise wheel. Snowball was a white mouse, small enough to sit in the palm of her hand. He was very well behaved. She could take him anywhere in a jacket pocket, and he would not come out on his own, but only when she retrieved him. He never even once peed or pooped in her pocket. Even if eventually he had an accident, it wouldn't be a catastrophe, considering that he weighed like four ounces and didn't generate a humongous amount of end product.

His coat was white, his eyes as black as ink, his tail pale pink. He was cuter than the kind of mice you didn't want in your house, an elegant little gentleman. If Amity were Cinderella, Snowball would morph into a magnificent stallion to pull her carriage. That's the kind of special mouse he was.

Now, after she turned on her TV and streamed an animated Disney movie that she had seen many times and that didn't have a cat in it, she took Snowball out of his cage. She sat in an armchair, and for a while he ran up and down her arms and across her shoulders, pausing now and then to stare at her with what she believed was affection. Then he settled in her lap, on his back.

She rubbed his tummy with one finger, and he relaxed into an ecstatic trance.

With Snowball, she was practicing for a dog.

She wanted a dog, and Daddy was willing to buy a puppy, but she needed to find out if she could be a good mother. What if she got a dog, which could live twelve or fourteen years, and then discovered, after a year, that she didn't want to walk the poor thing any longer or exercise it or even just hang out with it. People changed, didn't want the same things anymore, and then they broke hearts. If she failed a dog, broke its heart, Amity would hate herself, she really would, totally and forever.

The man at the pet store had said that Snowball, a unique breed with a glossy coat, would live maybe four years. She'd had him two years, and she wasn't the least bored with him yet. She loved him to the extent that a person could love a mouse that didn't have a big personality like a dog.

Before she risked getting a dog, she also had to find out how she would deal with the loss of Snowball when he died. If losing a mouse wrecked her, then a dog's death would absolutely destroy her, no doubt about it, none at all. She'd been only four, much too little to understand what was happening, when her mother walked out. She hardly remembered Michelle. Yet the loss was still with her, not really a pain, more like an emptiness, as if something that ought to be inside of her were missing. She worried that more losses would leave other empty spaces in her, until she would be as hollow as a shell from which the egg had been drained through a pinhole.

Sometimes, like now, she couldn't remember what her mother looked like, which kind of scared her. A few weeks ago, in a mood, she had taken the framed photograph of Michelle off her desk, where Daddy encouraged her to keep it, and put it in a bottom drawer. Maybe the time had come to display the photo again.

On her lap, Snowball had closed his eyes. His mouth hung open. He was a picture of bliss as she stroked his belly.

His chisel-edged teeth were bared. The teeth of mice never stopped growing. Snowball had to gnaw at something for a significant part of every day to keep his teeth from becoming so long that they inhibited his ability to eat, which was why his cage featured three gnawing blocks.

No living thing on the earth was without its burdens.

Daddy said our burdens made our spirits stronger and therefore were blessings. He knew a lot and was right about most things, but this burdens-as-blessings business was bullsugar, really and truly, at least based on her experience. Daddy probably believed it. He said that beyond every darkness, dawn approached. He was crazy patient and rarely got angry.

Amity wasn't as patient as her father, though she wanted to be. A lot of things pissed her off. Recently, she'd made a list of what pissed her off, so she wouldn't forget anything and go all squishy like one of those morning-TV kid-show puppets that always wanted you to be "nicer than twice as nice as nice." The list looked stupid, so she tore it up and threw it away. But she remembered everything on it, including that it pissed her off, really and truly, not to have a mother. When you were angry about something, you couldn't at the same time be crushingly sad about it, which was a blessing.

As she continued to stroke Snowball's tummy, she wondered what bullsugar Mr. Spooky was spouting out there on the porch with her patient father.

===== 4

The eerie ululation of coyotes on the hunt issued from the farther end of the canyon, and a scrim of cloud diminished the moon, so that the silvered yard grew tarnished.

"I'm leaving this with you," Ed solemnly intoned, holding forth the soiled, string-tied box, "because the fate of humanity depends on it never falling into the wrong hands and because, of everyone I have known in my life, I trust no one more than you, Jeffrey Wallace Coltrane."

"That's very sweet, but you hardly know me," Jeffy said.

"Damn if I don't!" Ed roared. "I know your heart. I trust my gut about you. My gut, your heart. *If you don't do this, if you don't help me, you will be condemning your daughter to a life of terror, perhaps slavery or death!"*

Even in the soft amber glow of the porch lamps, Jeffy could see that Ed's face had darkened with a rush of blood. His rapid pulse grew visible in both his neck and temples, as though he were working himself into a stroke or aneurysm.

The old man slid forward on his rocking chair, holding out the box. His voice quieted to an intense whisper. "Listen to me. Listen, listen. I've used the key to everything over a hundred times. I've seen horrors indescribable. I should destroy it, but I can't. It's my baby, my beautiful work of genius. I can't put it in a safe-deposit box, because they'll search bank records coast to coast. I can't leave it with anyone I've ever known in my former life. They're watching those people. I can't dig a hole and bury the damn thing, because what if some poor fool who hasn't been warned about the danger of it finds it and turns it on? You must hide it well. They'll suspect everyone in the canyon, anyone with whom I might have come into contact. They'll skulk around, looking, searching, those swine. After all, it cost seventy-six billion dollars."

"What did?"

Ed shook the box gently. "This."

"Expensive," said Jeffy.

"Oh, it's worth much more than that. It's worth the world. They'll never stop looking for it."

If a screw had been loose in Ed's head, it evidently had fallen away from whatever parts of his mind it had previously kept securely connected. He was wide-eyed, suddenly glistening with a thin sweat, in great distress. Jeffy felt sorry for him. Ed was a well-educated man, a scholar, perhaps once a highly regarded professor of history or literature or philosophy, now succumbing to dementia. A tragedy.

The kind thing to do, the only thing to do, was to humor him. It would be cruel to disrespect him and treat his paranoid fantasy as the delusion that it was. Jeffy slid forward in his rocker and accepted the package.

Ed wagged one finger in admonishment. "Never open it. Never touch it. Keep it safe for a year. If I don't return for it in a year, I'll be dead. I should get a gun and kill the bastards when they come to kill me, but I can't. I've seen too much horror to perpetrate horrors of my own. I'm a pacifist. A helpless pacifist. If I don't return in a year, I'll be dead."

"I'm certain you've got a long life ahead," Jeffy assured him.

"After a year, obtain a barrel. Can you do that?"

"A barrel?"

Ed seized Jeffy by one knee and squeezed for emphasis. "Barrel, oil drum, an enclosed cylindroid of metal. Can you obtain one?"

"Yes, of course."

"Do you know how to mix concrete?"

"I'm a mason."

"Yes, exactly, I forgot, a mason. After one year, if I do not return, fill a barrel half full of concrete. Put this package in the barrel. Finish filling the barrel with concrete, so the package is encased. Can you weld?"

"Yes. I'm quite handy."

"Weld the lid of the barrel shut. It will then be very heavy, don't you think?"

"Extremely heavy," Jeffy agreed.

"I doubt you have a hydraulic hand truck. Very few people possess their own hydraulic hand truck. Do you have such a thing?"

"No, but I can rent one."

Ed took his hand from Jeffy's knee and gave him two thumbs up. "Convey the barrel into a rental truck. Take it to the harbor. Can you drive a boat?"

"Anything up to about thirty-six feet."

"Charter a boat and take the barrel out to sea and roll it overboard in deep water."

"How deep?" Jeffy asked.

"A thousand feet should do it. No less than five hundred."

"Consider it done. That is, if you don't return in a year."

At the very moment that the cloud freed the moon, a look of relief wiped the anxiety off Ed's face. "I knew you were the right man. From the first time I ever sat on this porch with you, I knew." He rose to his feet. "Never open the box, Jeffrey. Never touch the thing in it. Keep your promise. The thing in that box can bring you only misery. The fate of the world is in your hands."

Ed's delusions were nothing if not grandiose.

Getting up from his rocker, Jeffy said, "Well, whenever you want it back, a year from now or tomorrow, it'll be here, Ed."

"A year from now or never. Tomorrow, the canyon will be crawling with those despicable swine. Hide it well."

After adjusting his bow tie and smoothing the panels of his sport coat, he went to the porch steps and descended and moved onto the moonlit lawn.

He paused and gazed at the sky and then addressed Jeffy once more. "'Like a ghastly rapid river / Through the pale door / A hideous throng rush out forever / And laugh—but smile no more.' A few lines from Poe. Don't use the key, Jeffrey. Don't open the pale door." He started to turn away but then had one more warning to deliver. "I've got a demonic posse on my trail. Devils, fiends! When the swine come snorting around, they won't be who they claim to be. Even if you give them the box, you won't be rid of them. Once they know you've been in possession of the key, the cursed yet wonderful key, they'll assume you know too much. They're ruthless. They're murderers. Beasts. They'll . . . make you disappear. Hide it well, Jeffrey. Save yourself and your girl! Hide it well!"

He crossed the yard to the lane, turned right, and headed into the canyon.

Sadness and pity took some of the shine off the moon-polished night. Perhaps the man had been an eccentric all his life, but until this evening, he'd been an engaging companion during his visits and never before wandered into alleyways of dementia.

Ed walked out of moonbeams, and shadows engulfed him, and he disappeared under the branches of the overhanging oaks.

5

Amity stood at the kitchen table with Snowball perched on her right shoulder. The mouse nibbled a peanut held in his forepaws.

The box stood on the table. It was a soiled, yellowed nothing of a box—and yet it looked ominous.

She asked, "What's in it?"

"I don't know," her dad said as he popped the cap off a bottle of beer. "And I promised not to open it."

"Maybe it's an eight-inch Madagascar hissing cockroach, like the plague of bugs that witch conjured into her enemy's castle."

"That was in a novel. In the real world, people don't curse each other with giant hissing cockroaches. Anyway, Ed is evidently losing it, but he's not a bad guy."

"If he doesn't come back for a year, will you really put it in a barrel with cement and drop it in the ocean?"

Her father shrugged. "I sort of promised." He sat at the table, smiled ruefully, and shook his head. "Seventy-six billion dollars."

"You don't really think anything that fits in such a little box could be worth so much, do you?" Amity wondered.

Snowball would fit in the box. Because she loved the little dude, he was worth a lot more to her than what they had paid for him, though he wasn't worth thousands of millions of dollars. No offense intended toward the beloved mouse or toward mousekind in general. On the other hand, Daddy was for sure worth that much. If someday her father was kidnapped, and if the bad guys demanded seventy-six billion, and if by then Amity had that much money, she would pay the ransom; she really and truly would. However, unlike Snowball, Daddy wouldn't fit in this box.

"Whatever it contains," her father said, "it's not worth ten cents to anyone but Ed. The poor man is losing his way. His mind has turned traitor on him. From things he's said . . . I think maybe he was a college professor once, probably a great one. But now . . . he's a very sad case. Well, whatever this thing is, he'll be back for it tomorrow or the next day or a week from now."

Amity took Snowball from her shoulder and cradled him in her hands. He was just a mouse, but he was hers to keep safe in a world where nothing lasted forever, not even who you were.

======   **6**

Throughout the night, Jeffy dreamed of the box. The dreams were fluid, each withering into the next, with no narrative coherence. In some, he desperately searched for the package but couldn't find it—or he found a variety of boxes that were not the one with which Ed had entrusted him. In one scene, he entered the kitchen and turned on the lights and saw the pasteboard walls of the small container bowing outward and the string taut as something strained to escape those confines, something from which issued a needful keening as chilling as any sound he'd ever heard. Later, much like Alice in Wonderland after she sipped from the bottle labeled DRINK ME, Jeffy found himself very small, perhaps one inch tall, trapped inside the box; he sensed that something larger than him, something hungry and vicious, was clinging to the underside of the lid, high above, able to see him in the dark, though he could not see it . . .

He woke before dawn and shaved, showered, dressed. When he went into the kitchen and turned on the lights, the box sat in the center of the breakfast table, precisely where he'd left it. It was not distorted, and no sound came from it.

Jeffy didn't find Ed threatening. He remained certain that the box contained an ordinary item that the old man thought significant only because of his delusions. How curious, therefore, that Jeffy's subconscious should torment him with disturbing dreams—some almost nightmares—involving this innocuous package.

The Art Deco kitchen conveyed him to a time when the world had seemed more welcoming, and his lingering uneasiness faded. A floor of large white ceramic tiles joined by small black diamond-shaped inlays. Glossy white cabinetry. Stainless-steel countertops and backsplash. A restored O'Keefe and Merritt stove with its several compartments. A replica of a 1930s Coldspot refrigerator. A Krazy Kat cookie jar, black with huge whites of the eyes. A poster of a *Charm* magazine cover from 1931, featuring a coffeepot and cup.

As the first light of the day brought a pink blush to the sky over the canyon, Jeffy poured a freshly brewed cup of a Jamaican blend. Standing at the kitchen sink, gazing out at the lane that curved up canyon, he had taken two sips when a rhythmic mechanical sound rose in the distance, quickly swelled in volume, and began to shudder through the house. He looked at the ceiling as a helicopter passed overhead, then glanced at the window in time to get a glimpse of the chopper above the oak trees: larger than a police helo, two engines, eight- or ten-passenger capacity, high-set main and tail rotors, maybe ten thousand pounds of serious machinery. It seemed menacing because it was far below minimum legal altitude for this area and moving fast, as if on an attack mission.

In the wake of the aircraft came the sound of big engines. One, two, three, four black Suburbans raced past on Shadow Canyon Lane, without flashing lights or wailing sirens, but with the urgency of an FBI contingent in a movie about terrorists armed with a nuke.

As the sound of one rotary wing receded, another racketed louder in the distance. Jeffy put down his coffee mug and hurried through the house to the front door. He stepped onto the porch just in time to see a second helo approaching from the west, out of a cloudless sky, the morning sun painting a pink cataract on the advanced glass cockpit.

Maybe fifty yards away, where Shadow Canyon Lane connected with Oak Hollow Road, a fifth Suburban stood alongside the pavement, and a sixth angled across the roadway to form a blockade. Six men had gotten out of the two vehicles and were conferring.

Barefoot, wearing Rocket Raccoon pajamas, yawning and blinking sleep from her eyes, Amity came out of the house and onto the porch as the second chopper passed low overhead. The palm fronds tossed, and the limbs of the live oaks shuddered. The enormous oaks were green throughout the year, though perpetually shedding their browner leaves, a swarm of which now beetle-clicked down through the black branches, small oval forms as crisp as cockroach carapaces.

Amity said, "What's happening?"

"I don't know."

She said, "Something big."

"Sure looks like it."

"Are you freaked out? I am, a little."

"A little," he agreed.

"Who are they?"

"Maybe FBI. The Suburbans are black, the choppers were black, but no markings on any of them."

"Don't police cars and stuff have to be marked?"

"I thought so."

After a silence, Amity said, "I better get dressed."

"Good idea."

On the doorstep, before returning to the house, she said, "And maybe you better hide the package that Ed left."

= 7

Until Amity suggested a relationship between Ed's visit the previous evening and the sudden appearance of the black-helicopter crowd, Jeffy hadn't made a connection. When an old and delusional vagrant said he was being hunted, you imagined the stalker—if one actually existed—must be from the same community as his hapless quarry: a burnt-out drug addict who believed in the existence of something called "the key to everything," or maybe a psychopath who targeted homeless men wearing polka-dot ties with plaid shirts. You didn't leap to the conclusion that the posse would number more than a dozen men, some in SWAT gear, equipped with a few million dollars in ordnance.

Sometimes, however, common sense required paranoia. It seemed that the political elites were striving, with admiration for George Orwell and rare unanimity, to ensure that the totalitarian state in the novel *1984* would be realized no later than fifty years after the author predicted.

In the kitchen, Jeffy plucked the box off the table. It wasn't heavy, suggesting that most of the contents were Styrofoam peanuts or some other kind of packing material.

Indecisive, he stood listening to the helicopters—one whisking the air in the distance, one louder and nearer—considering where to conceal the package. He didn't quite believe that the "swine" of whom Ed had spoken, whoever they might be, would storm into the house and ransack it room by room, drawer by drawer. However, every hidey-hole that he thought of seemed obvious if in fact those men boldly crossed his threshold.

At last, he hurried into his workroom, one half of which was entirely devoted to the restoration of highly stylized Deco-period Bakelite radios.

To the left of his workbench, shelves held eight radios of fabled brands—Fada, Sentinel, Bendix, Emerson, DeWald—that had been cleaned and polished; with their vibrant colors restored, they were objects of beauty and high style. They had been rewired, and new vacuum tubes had been installed. They could pull in AM stations as they had in the 1930s, although once you switched them on, the tubes had to warm up before a broadcast could be received.

To the right of the bench, another set of shelves contained six scarred and discolored radios on which he had yet to begin work.

He had bought them at swap meets, country auctions, and from a network of hoarders who collected all manner of items that other people thought were junk. He had paid as little as forty dollars and as much as two thousand per radio, depending on the knowledge of the seller who set the price. After he had restored it, passionate collectors would pay five, six, even ten thousand for a rare and beautiful specimen.

The largest radio awaiting his attention was a Bendix model that appeared to be muddy brown. When cleaned and polished, however, it would be a rich butterscotch yellow with buttercup-yellow tuning knobs and tuning-window frame. The guts of the Bendix were on his workbench, and only the empty Bakelite shell stood on the shelf: eleven inches wide, eight inches tall, seven inches deep, not large enough to conceal the box that Ed had entrusted to him, although it might be large enough to hide whatever was in the box.

He heard Ed's warning voice in memory. *You must not open it. Never!*

A helicopter swept over the house, so low that slabs of carved air like giant fists slammed the roof and rattled the windows.

Even as unimpressive as the package looked, it would draw attention from searchers precisely because it was unusual.

Never open the box, Jeffrey. Never touch the thing in it.

Jeffy had difficulty getting his head around the idea that rumpled, rheumy-eyed Ed hadn't been sliding into dementia, after all. That something of great value and importance must be in the box. That a "demonic posse" might be after the old man. Even if all that was true, as the choppers and Suburbans suggested, nevertheless Ed must be exaggerating his enemies' ruthlessness.

Beasts? Murderers who would make an innocent man and his daughter disappear?

The doorbell rang.

He was pretty sure it wasn't the postman with a certified-mail form that required a signature.

The aircraft that had passed over the house now returned and hovered. In the downdraft from the rotary wing, palm trees thrashed so noisily that they could be heard in spite of the racket made by the helo.

Jeffy's heart thumped like that of a rabbit in the shadow of a predator. "Sorry, Ed. I should've taken you seriously."

He put the package on the workbench and tugged at the knot and stripped away the string.

As someone on the front porch rang the doorbell again, someone began to hammer insistently at the *back* door.

He took the lid off the box and then hesitated. The object was swaddled in plastic bubble wrap.

Hide it well, Jeffrey. Save yourself and your girl!

A man appeared at the window, veiled by the sheer curtain, a shadowy form backlit by the bright morning sun.

Jeffy quickly unraveled the bubble wrap. The key to everything resembled a sleek smartphone, maybe five inches by less than three, but the stainless-steel casing featured neither buttons nor a charging port, nor any markings. The black screen wasn't inset, but seemed to be an integral part of the case, as if the device had not been manufactured, but had been built one atom at a time by some 3-D printer more advanced than anything currently known.

The doorbell rang, the fist pounded, the trees thrashed, the chopper clattered, and Jeffy tucked the item under the shell of the Bendix. He took the guts of that radio off his workbench and stashed them away in a drawer.

Hurriedly, he tore the pasteboard box and its lid into small pieces. He dropped the debris and the string in the wastebasket and stirred the pieces up with the rest of the paper trash.

===== 8

When Jeffy opened the door, three men loomed on the porch. The one at the front wore a black suit, white shirt, and black tie. He was as good-looking as any model in a *GQ* ad, his thick black hair slicked back like that of a film-noir character who reliably carried a switchblade and a coiled-wire garrote. His eyes were gray, his stare as sharp as a flensing knife.

The two men behind him wore black cargo pants, black T-shirts, and black jackets loose enough perhaps to conceal shoulder rigs and pistols. They looked as if they were born to be trouble. One of them spoke into a walkie-talkie, and the helo lifted away from the house and drifted somewhat to the south.

The guy in the suit might have thought he was smiling when he grimaced, but there was no friendliness in his voice. "John Falkirk, National Security Agency." He presented an ID wallet with his photo.

Jeffy felt most comfortable pretending to be dumb and rattled by the uproar in this previously sleepy canyon. He spoke rapidly, running sentences together. "What's wrong, what's happening, do we have to evacuate?"

"This house is owned by a Jeffrey Coltrane," said Falkirk. "Are you Mr. Coltrane?"

"Yes, sir, that's right, that's me," Jeffy said, nodding in agreement with himself. "What's going on, all the helicopters, are we safe? I have a young daughter here."

Perhaps Falkirk thought that withholding reassurances from a befuddled citizen would inspire less guarded responses. Having put away his ID, the agent held up a smartphone on which he had summoned a photograph of Ed. "Do you know this man?"

"Who is he?"

"I was hoping you could tell me."

Jeffy squinted at the phone. "I've maybe seen him before."

"Where?"

"I can't say where."

"You can't say where?"

"No, sir. Maybe I'm wrong, never saw him. If I saw him, it was maybe just in town somewhere."

Falkirk resorted to an intimidating silence again, as if he'd been conducting an inflection analysis of every syllable Jeffy spoke while observing the degree of dilation of his pupils, and now needed to match the two data streams for evidence of deception. There was something of the machine about Falkirk.

If the agent were less officious, Jeffy might have cooperated with him. However, he liked frumpy, delusional old Ed far more than he liked this man. Intuitively, he didn't trust Falkirk any more than he would have trusted a guy with 666 tattooed on his forehead.

"He's a vagrant and fugitive," the agent said. "That's all you need to know. He lives in a small inflatable tent in the wild part of this canyon."

Jeffy crafted a frown. "Used to be nothing up canyon except coyotes and bobcats and the creatures they eat. It was better then."

"We believe this man walks into town at least a few times a week. He'd pass right by here. Could that be where you saw him?"

"Maybe. I don't spend much time on the porch. I've got a life."

"If he saw you, he might've stopped by for a chat. He's a sociable guy."

Jeffy's frown carved deeper into his face. "I'd never encourage one of those people. Like I said, I've got a young daughter to worry about." He glanced at the two men who looked like SWAT team members who'd taken off their Kevlar vests to swing by the doughnut shop. He turned his attention to Falkirk again. "What's going on here? How freaked out should I be? This vagrant kill someone?"

"His name's Dr. Edwin Harkenbach. Does that mean anything to you?"

"Not my doctor," Jeffy said, shaking his head. "My doctor's Ben Solerno. And my dentist is Jennifer Goshen. Thank God, I don't need any specialists."

After staring at him in silence for a moment, Falkirk put away the phone and produced an official-looking document. "Mr. Coltrane, do you understand it's a felony to lie to an agent of the NSA?"

"Sure. I understand. Just like the FBI. Way it ought to be."

"I am herewith serving a search warrant for these premises. This is a matter of national security. Failure to comply with a court order of this nature may result in your arrest."

"You want to come in and look around?" Jeffy asked, accepting the warrant.

"That's the general idea. Just so you understand—you aren't the specific target of a criminal investigation." His icy stare seemed to belie his assurances. "These are FISA warrants issued pursuant to an urgent threat involving an individual who might have taken advantage of your goodwill. We have warrants for all seven houses on Shadow Canyon Lane."

"National security threat. Hey, far as I'm concerned, you don't need a warrant for this house. It's my civic duty, isn't it? Come on in, gentlemen."

When Falkirk and his associates stepped into the foyer, Amity appeared in sneakers, jeans, a T-shirt featuring her favorite anime character, and a light denim jacket with a yellow winking-face emoji on the breast pocket. Owl-eyed, she said, "Daddy, what's happening?"

"These men are federal agents, sweetheart."

"What's a federal agent?"

She was playing dumb. He hoped she didn't spread it on too thick. He doubted she would. "They're like police officers, Amity. They're looking for a bad man they think could be hiding here."

"We're not just searching for Harkenbach," Falkirk corrected. "We're looking as well for any indication that he has been here with or without your knowledge or is known to any person living on these premises." He produced the smartphone and conjured Ed's photograph for Amity. "Young lady, have you ever seen this man?"

She hugged herself and frowned. "He's like some drooling sicko."

"You know him?"

"Nope. But he looks like some guy who'd give you candy to go for a ride with him, and then you'd never come home again.

I know all about those perverts. Daddy's warned me about them like ten thousand times."

Falkirk frowned at the photo as though he had never seen Edwin Harkenbach in that light, then put the phone away. "Mr. Coltrane, do you understand what a thorough search of the premises will entail?"

"Turn the place upside down, I suppose."

"My men and I are wearing body cams. You need to accompany us room by room to assure yourself there is no theft or vandalism. If there's any sensitive area you have an issue about, discuss it with us. We'll see if we can compromise on the approach to it."

Jeffy assumed that any area he mentioned would be searched with special attention.

Maybe the same thought occurred to Amity, and she meant to raise their suspicion in order ultimately to deflate it. "Hey, you aren't gonna search Snowball's cage, are you? You'll scare him silly."

9

While Amity held Snowball and reassured him, one of Falkirk's two underlings took everything out of the five-by-three-foot cage: the gnawing blocks, the exercise wheel, the miniature ladder with the observation platform at the top, the little blue mouse house with white shutters and a roof of shingles painted like slices of cheese, the drifts of shredded newspapers in which the shy rodent liked to burrow and hide away. One agent soiled two fingers and realized what he had touched and said, "Hey, the little bastard shits in his own cage," and Amity said, "Well, he's a mouse." Jeffy showed the intruder to the powder bath to wash his hands, whereafter the guy took the lid off the toilet tank to look for whatever, most likely for the key to everything.

As Jeffy expected, they searched the place top to bottom, turning everything upside down, or almost everything.

In the workroom, as two of his other men opened and closed drawers and cabinet doors, Falkirk looked around at the radios and at the collection of costume jewelry also made out of Bakelite, everything sitting on open shelves. His expression was not one of investigative interest, but rather that of an elitist of the ruling class who found himself in a humble thrift shop with inadequately deodorized plebian customers. "What's all this stuff?"

"I polish the jewelry, fix broken clasps. I put new vacuum tubes in the radios. Sell it all to collectors."

"Collectors? For kitsch like this? People actually buy it?"

Jeffy pointed to the discolored shell of the Bendix, under which the key to everything was hidden. "This potential jewel cost me sixty bucks at a swap meet. Cleaned and polished, it'll look like that"—he pointed to a radio on which he had worked—"and then I'll sell it for maybe six thousand at an antique show. And I've seen women fight over the best Bakelite necklaces."

"You're shitting me."

"That was my mouse," Amity said, her hands folded around Snowball.

Falkirk's face stiffened with contempt, his expression out of proportion to the moment. "You think you're pretty funny, do you?"

"No, sir. Not as funny as some."

At his sides, the man's hands formed into fists. His lips were pale, his stare icy. "I know your type."

Jeffy was disquieted by Falkirk's sudden, acidic antipathy toward the girl. To distract the agent, he plugged in one of the fully restored radios, a Fada.

The vacuum tubes warmed, and the AM-only dial brightened. The radio's sleek rounded form and rich golden plastic with the grain and depth of quartzite spoke of an age when even everyday items were designed to please the eye; the object embodied a desire to charm that had been lost in this era of bleak utilitarianism.

Falkirk stared at the radio with puzzlement and disdain.

When Taylor Swift sang forth from the nearly century-old set, he said, "She's hot, but she doesn't sound hot coming through those speakers. They sure aren't Bose."

"I'm selling nostalgia. This is a little bit how music sounded back then," Jeffy said.

"Nostalgia is a dead end. We either progress or slide backward. Slide far enough backward, everything collapses."

Jeffy smiled and nodded. "I understand that point of view. I just want to slide back a little ways to when people didn't spend all day staring at screens and trying to tell other people what to do and think, back to when a day seemed twenty-four hours long instead of twelve, when you could *breathe*."

"If that's what you want," said Falkirk, "better stay here in your little house, never go outside. This is the closest you'll get to living forever in yesterday. The world turns faster every year. The human race is on a rocket ride, Mr. Coltrane. A rocket ride. That's our destiny."

=== 10

Walking up the lane toward the next house in the company of two subordinates, Falkirk counseled himself not to allow his suspicion to settle on the Coltranes, father and daughter, to the exclusion of their neighbors. The little bitch had mocked him, maybe because she knew where Harkenbach could be found, or maybe because it was just her nature to be a wiseass.

She reminded him too much of his younger half sister, Phoebe, that smug and snarky pig who, with his half brother, Philip, had long ago screwed him over and changed his life for the worse. He would like nothing better than to punch the hateful smirk off Amity Coltrane's face. Over the years, there had been a few others like her, surrogate Phoebes who mocked him and lived to regret it—or died regretting it. Every blow he struck against one of their kind was like an orgasm.

If Jeffrey Coltrane and his smart-ass brat proved to be friends of Harkenbach, they would be subjected to hard interrogation, during which Falkirk could do whatever he wanted to the little bitch, as well as to her father. His National Security Agency credentials were merely operational cover. He didn't answer to the NSA or to any of the government agencies known to the public. He served the masters of the shadow state, and like his masters, he was above the law.

Indeed, all his life, as far back as he could remember, he had known that laws were for others, not for him. He was born wise to the truth of the world: The only virtue is vice, and the acquisition of power justifies all things.

11

Falkirk and company had left disarray behind them. In an hour and a half, the Coltranes, father and daughter, restored order to their little world.

Beyond the windows, sunshine flaring off their windshields, racing black Suburbans returned from the wilds, carrying luckless vagrants as passengers. They were possibly bound for facilities established to serve the homeless, although more likely they would wind up at a ghastly, isolated warehouse on the edge of the Mojave where tough interrogations could be carried out in an atmosphere such that the words "I have a right to an attorney" would elicit only their jailers' amusement.

Catercorner to each other at the kitchen table were Amity with a morning orange juice and Jeffy with black coffee so strong that its smell alone was sufficient to wake anyone in a coma.

Perched on Amity's right shoulder, Snowball nibbled on a kernel of cheese popcorn that appeared enormous in his tiny pink paws.

On the table lay the key to everything.

Jeffy didn't know what hell the device might be capable of bringing down on them. He was pretty sure, however, that the wise thing to do was purchase a barrel, mix a few batches of cement before lunch, and forget about waiting a year.

Never open the box, Jeffrey. Keep your promise. The thing in that box can bring you only misery.

As the clatter of helicopters faded and a fragile sense of normalcy settled on the canyon, Amity said, "Looks like a phone."

"If you study it closely, it's not a phone. No switches on the sides. No charging port, so then maybe no battery. No camera."

"It's got a home circle you can touch at the bottom of the screen."

"That's not enough to make it a phone."

She reached for the device, and Jeffy lightly slapped her fingers. "Don't touch."

"*You* touched it."

"Very carefully. Holding it by the sides with thumb and forefinger. Anyway, I'm the adult in the room. Adults make the rules. It's been that way since time immemorial."

"Is that why the world is in such deep poop?"

"Maybe."

After a slug of orange juice, she said, "All those SUVs and helicopters and tough guys . . . I guess the stupid thing probably did cost seventy-six billion."

"Government research money," Jeffy agreed.

Attracted by the silvery glimmer of the mysterious object, Snowball dropped the popcorn, raced down Amity's arm, scurried across the table, from which he was usually banished, and sat on what seemed to be the screen of the device.

The girl gasped, and both she and Jeffy shot up from their chairs, reacting as though Edwin Harkenbach hadn't entrusted them with any kind of key, but instead with a compact nuclear bomb.

Snowball peered at the dark mirrored surface under him, in which he could see his murky reflection.

After a few seconds, a soft gray light filled the previously glossy black screen.

Jeffy held his breath, and Amity coaxed the mouse to come to her. "Here, boy, come to Mommy. Come to Mommy, Snowball."

Something appeared on the screen under the mouse. Jeffy could see two large buttons—one blue, the other red—that contained white lettering half obscured by the rodent.

Simultaneously, Jeffy and Amity reached for Snowball. Her hand grasped the mouse, and her father's hand seized hers—

—and the kitchen vanished, leaving them in an all-encompassing whiteness. A nearly blinding blizzard showered down. They could see only themselves and each other—and the mouse. The glittering flakes were not cold; they passed *through* Jeffy, *through* Amity.

Particles of light, he thought, and was chilled by the sheer strangeness of the experience.

He also thought of the lines of verse quoted by Ed just before the old man walked away into the night, something about a pale door and a hideous throng rushing out through it. The key to everything had opened a door, this pale door of light, and although they were not at once swept up in a hideous throng, Jeffy felt great peril coming, sensed that they were now known and being sought by someone, something.

With a soft windless *whoosh,* the obscuring light blew away, and the familiar kitchen became visible again. However, because it had vanished once, the place seemed less than entirely real, as though it might be a construct of Jeffy's imagination.

Amity plucked the mouse off the dangerous device, and with one trembling hand, Jeffy took the key to everything from the table.

"What was *that*, what happened?" the girl asked.

"I don't know. It was . . . maybe . . . I don't know."

He saw three buttons on the screen now: a blue one labeled HOME, a red one bearing the word SELECT, and a green one marked RETURN.

"W-w-where did they go?" Amity asked, a tremor in her voice.

Looking up from the device, Jeffy said, "What?"

Holding Snowball in both hands, against her chest, as though terrified that she had almost lost the mouse and might still lose him, the girl said, "My orange juice. Your coffee."

Her glass and Jeffy's mug were gone. They hadn't been knocked off the table; there was no mess on the floor.

He turned toward the counter where the coffee machine had stood, but it was no longer anywhere to be seen.

Understanding eluded him. Whatever the explanation might prove to be, the disappearance of the glass and the mug contributed to his unsettling apprehension that the material world must be immaterial to some degree.

He could only say, "I better put this damn thing away before something happens."

Circling the table, scanning the room for the missing coffee and juice, Amity said ominously, "Something's already happened."

"Nothing terrible. Nothing . . . irreplaceable. Just beverages and beverage containers." He didn't sound entirely sane to himself.

With Amity close behind, Jeffy followed the hall toward his workroom. Although he had taken this short walk thousands of times, the passageway seemed different from how it was before, but he was not able to identify what had changed.

"Are you scared, Daddy? I'm kind of just a little bit scared. I don't mean like totally freaked out. Just kind of spooked."

"There's nothing to be afraid of," he counseled her, as well as himself, though he had no way of knowing if what he said was true. "What happened, it was just . . ." Words failed him.

As he passed an open door, he hesitated and looked into his bedroom. He expected something there to surprise him, though he didn't know why or what. Everything appeared to be in order.

Nevertheless, at his side, Amity said, "It doesn't feel right."

"What doesn't?"

"I don't know. Something about this place. I feel like . . . like I don't belong here."

At the door to his office, Jeffy halted, suddenly sure that they were not alone in the house. He had a sense of some presence and wouldn't have been surprised to see a phantom form, a shadow without source, gliding toward them or crossing the hall from one room to another.

He eased the door open. Although he oiled the hinges from time to time so they never creaked, they creaked now.

In his workroom, the sheer curtain at the window was gone, replaced by a pleated shade that was at the moment raised. He might not have noticed this change if the previously bright day beyond the glass had not now been sunless. The sky bellied with dark clouds swollen with impending rain. Seemingly in an instant, the weather had drastically changed.

He went to the shelves of radios that needed to be refurbished, intending to hide the key to everything under the old Bendix, where he should have left it after Falkirk departed.

The Bendix wasn't there. He inventoried the other radios, sure that he must have moved the one he needed.

Then he saw it standing on his workbench. Cleaned. Meticulously polished. Its color was as vibrant as the day it had first appeared for sale more than ninety years earlier.

Painstakingly restoring this much-discolored Bakelite to its original luster would have taken him at least a week.

The Bendix was plugged in to the power strip that ran along the back of his workbench. He hesitated, then switched it on. A glow filled the tuning window. The radio was no longer just a shell. The vacuum tubes warmed, and music came forth.

Johnny Mathis sang "The Twelfth of Never."

The skin on the nape of Jeffy's neck crinkled like crepe paper.

He clicked off the old radio, and the ensuing silence seemed uncanny, lacking even the sound of his breathing, as if he were the embalmed resident of a mausoleum.

"I feel it, too," he told Amity. "Like I don't . . . don't belong here."

When he turned, the girl was no longer with him.

"Amity?" he cried out, and she did not answer. Still gripping the key to everything, he hurried into the hall. She was not there.

13

Intelligent and homeschooled, Amity had been reading well above her grade level ever since she'd known what a grade level was. She'd read scads of fantasy novels with Daddy and on her own, and both she and her father preferred stories in which the female characters were as adventurous and competent and kick-ass as the men. The heroines in all those books taught her to be strong and independent. By their example, she had learned among other things that it was all right to be afraid as long as you didn't allow your fear to paralyze or in any significant way dispirit you. Evil people thrived on your fear; they fed on it; they could defeat you only if you made yourself a banquet of fear and were consumed by your enemies. When she walked into her room and saw that she didn't exist, she strove to repress her fear, but it wasn't quite as easy as it was for girls in novels.

She had intended to return Snowball to his cage, where he would be safe; however, his cage was gone. Amity no longer had a bed or other furniture. Her anime posters had been stripped from the walls. The room was not, as before, a cheerful shade of yellow with a white ceiling, but instead a dreary beige. The closet door stood open, and she could see that no clothes hung in there, as if she had died of some tragic tropical fever, all covered with suppurating sores, and everything of hers had been sterilized and given to Goodwill.

When Daddy hurried into the room, calling her name—and said, "Oh, thank God," at the sight of her—she wanted to run to him and hug him and be hugged, but she restrained herself. There was a time to take refuge in the arms of those you loved, and there was a time to stand up to great evil and be not bowed. If you didn't know the difference, then you were doomed to perish about two-thirds of the way through the story, when the narrative needed a jolt of violence and emotion. (As a reader who hoped one day to be a writer, she was always alert to authors' techniques.) She couldn't yet figure out the identity of the current evil, but she had met its minions when Falkirk and his toadies had come calling. Whoever Spooky Ed might be and whatever the key to everything could do, she and her father were in deep merde, and extraordinary courage would be required of them.

Her father came to her, and maybe unshed tears were standing in his eyes, so she quickly looked away from him. This was the totally wrong time for either of them to show weakness. Being no less of an avid reader than Amity, her father surely knew what the weirdness of their situation required. If she gave him a moment, he would regain his balance.

Before Daddy could say the wrong thing, a loud noise drew their attention to a window. The racket of a machine.

Amity went to the window, and her father joined her, and they looked out at the backyard, where a man was mowing the grass, intent as if determined to finish the task before the storm broke. They didn't have a gardener. Daddy mowed the lawn himself. And in fact the guy out there pushing the mower back and forth was Daddy. He had to be Daddy, because Daddy didn't have an identical twin.

Just when you thought you were getting a grip on your fear, it became as hard to subdue as a crazed cat. Amity had one father and no mother and a big hole in her life, but the emptiness couldn't be filled in and paved over by having two dads. The guy out there must be a doppelgänger, a ghostly double of a living person. She and Daddy had once read a story about a doppelgänger, and things hadn't gone well for the luckless living man whose place in the world the freaking doppelgänger wanted for itself. After disposing of the true father, the evil impersonator had schemed to have the two children—one a girl rather like Amity—swallowed whole by a huge mystical crocodile and carried into an infinite swamp, where they would live forever in its bowels, screaming for help that would never come. Fortunately, a bird named Pickitt, who served the crocodile by feeding on scraps of meat stuck between its teeth, took pity on the kids before they could be eaten. Pickitt stole all the reptile's ivories while it slept, so that it couldn't devour the children. In the real world, however, if a doppelgänger took her father's place, there wouldn't be a mystical crocodile or a bird sympathetic to her plight. The evil double would just strangle her and stuff her in a liquid cremation machine full of concentrated lye water, reduce her to the consistency of soup, and flush her down a toilet. The real world had become weirder than even the darkest fairy tales.

Watching the man with the mower, she shuddered. "This isn't our house. It's *his* house."

"He's me," her father said with a note of astonishment, but under the circumstances, Amity could forgive him for stating the obvious. Really and truly, she could.

She stepped back from the window, afraid of being seen by the doppelgänger if he should look up from the lawn. Surveying this transformed space, she said, "My room isn't my room. There's nothing in it that belongs to me. Maybe I've never lived here. Either Mom took me away with her—"

"I'd never have allowed that."

"—or you never married her and I was never born."

When she glanced at her father, she wished she hadn't. His shocked expression, the horror in his eyes, the sudden softness of his mouth and the way it trembled nearly undid her.

Holding out one hand, she said, "Let me see the stupid thing, the key, the whatever."

He showed it to her but didn't give her the device. Three on-screen buttons offered HOME, SELECT, RETURN. In smaller letters, a data bar at the bottom provided information even harder to confidently interpret than the words on the buttons: ELSEWHERE 1.13—CATALOGED.

"You know what I'm thinking?" he whispered, as if the other Jeffy Coltrane mowing the yard might hear.

"Oh, yeah. I know what you're thinking," she assured him.

"Crazy as it sounds, I'm thinking . . ."

"Parallel worlds."

"Yeah. Parallel worlds."

"That's what I knew you were thinking."

"It can't be true."

"But maybe it is."

A significant number of big-brain physicists, maybe half, believed there were an infinite number of universes, in fact new ones springing into existence all the time. In this multiverse were other Earths—call our planet Earth Prime—where history had taken different turns from the history of our world. Some Earths would be almost identical to Earth Prime except for small things, like maybe no one ever invented hair spray and everyone looked windblown all the time; however, some were sure to be radically different.

One thing you could bet on: The greater the difference between Earth Prime and another Earth, the more dangerous a place it would be for Amity and her father. They had read a few fantasies set in parallel worlds, and the body count among the cast of characters tended to be higher than in those stories about witches and dragons and trolls who lived under bridges.

Like most people, Amity had now and then stood between two parallel mirrors and had seen infinite receding images of herself. Could there really and truly be an endless series of worlds with countless Amity Coltranes?

Stepping away from the window, Daddy stared at the key to everything. He said, "Shit."

Her father didn't often resort to such language. Amity wasn't yet allowed to use that word; it was reserved for grown-ups, so they could sound more mature than children. But she figured that she'd soon be saying *shit* frequently, because current dire circumstances were going to require her to grow up fast.

"It seems obvious," Daddy said, "that all we have to do to get back to where we belong is press the button marked HOME."

"In stories," Amity said, "you know what happens when the best thing to do seems obvious and so then the good guys do it."

"They find themselves in even deeper shit."

"Yeah. And the cast grows smaller."

Her father's face had gone ghastly pale under his tan, so that his complexion had turned a disturbing grayish brown. He glanced at the window, at the screen of the device, the window, the screen. "It would help us if we knew more about the guy who invented this damn thing, how he thought, what he might mean by *home, select, return.*"

"Spooky old Edwin Harkenbach. Google him."

"Yeah. Google. We will. But maybe we better get out of here before I . . . before the other me finishes mowing the yard and comes inside for a nice glass of iced tea."

The screen of the key to everything went dark.

"We'll walk into town," Daddy said. "We can use the computer at the library to search for Ed."

The thought of going into this alternate version of Suavidad Beach excited Amity as much as it scared her, not solely or even primarily because it might be intriguingly different, an adventure. If Michelle Jamison still lived here, if she had never met and married Jeffy Coltrane in this world, if she hadn't married anyone else, and if her dream of being a successful musician had never been fulfilled, she would be like thirty-three, and maybe ready for a change. Perhaps she could fall in love with Daddy and come with them to Suavidad Prime, where she would have a daughter who missed her and wanted to love her. She wouldn't be the kind of Michelle who would walk out on them. That's what Amity believed. If you believed hard enough, you could shape the future. Sometimes in the real world as in stories, there were happy endings, even improbable ones.

When the mower engine shut off, Daddy said, "Let's go."

Amity tucked Snowball in a pocket of her denim jacket.

In the hallway, he halted at a poster from 1935, a Deco image of the French Line ship *Normandie*, advertising its transatlantic service from Southampton, England, to New York.

"I sold this years ago," he said.

"Not in this world," Amity said.

Their eyes met, and in each other they saw an awareness of the profound strangeness of their situation, which had the effect of doubling their amazement and anxiety.

He hurried toward the front door, and she stayed at his heels, wondering if another Amity lived with her mother somewhere in town, and what would happen if she came face-to-face with that other self.

The thought induced a sharp if transient pain in her heart, as though some wicked voodooist somewhere had stuck a pin in an Amity doll.

Daddy took a lightweight jacket from the foyer closet and pocketed the key to everything.

Out the front door, across the porch, down the steps, onto Shadow Canyon Lane, left toward Oak Hollow Road and Suavidad Beach.

The heavens low and gray and mottled black. The air still and heavy, oppressed by the weight of the pending storm.

Crows wheeled across the sky, dozens of them in constantly shifting configurations that seemed to mean something, if only she had been a witch who could read the ephemeral script of birds in flight.

PART 2

THE TEMPTATION OF WHAT MIGHT HAVE BEEN

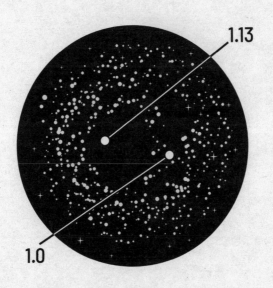

1.13

1.0

14

In this version of Suavidad Beach—where perhaps Ed Harkenbach had never been on the run from mysterious government agents and had never been homeless in the canyon and had never visited Jeffy on his front porch—the economy was evidently in a recession. Even for April, with rain-sodden clouds lowering toward release, few tourists were afoot on Forest Avenue or Pacific Coast Highway, where most of the shops and galleries were located. Some storefronts were without tenants, the windows papered over, while in the version of the town from which he and Amity had come, not enough retail space existed to satisfy the demand.

As they passed through town, Jeffy surveyed everything with more suspicion than curiosity, with more anxiety than suspicion.

Quantum physics, on which most technological advances had been based for decades, predicted the existence of an infinite number of parallel universes side by side, each invisible to the others and yet all subtly affecting one another, somehow sharing a destiny so complex and strange as to defy understanding. There might be worlds where the United States had never existed, where no European power settled this continent, perhaps where an Aztec culture of violent gods and slavery and human sacrifice flourished through the centuries, spreading northward.

Clearly, he and Amity were in a world much like the one they had left, but even such a place as this might harbor surprises more ominous than bad weather and an economic recession.

Was this version of America a stable democracy, or might it be teetering on the brink of tyranny? In less than ten minutes, he saw a man, a woman, and then another man dressed all in black fatigue-style garments made of soft pajama-like fabric. Each wore a black, knitted seaman's cap. This outfit appeared too strange to be just a fashion trend. Although they didn't travel in a group, they looked like members of a cult, one with fascist tendencies.

He wanted to be out of here. He wanted to be home.

"Stay close," he advised Amity, and he took her hand, which seemed terribly small and fragile.

The day was cool, but the chills that raked through him had nothing to do with the air temperature.

Overhung by the massive crowns of mature phoenix palms, the library stood on Oleander Street, adjacent to the city hall. The handsome Spanish Revival building featured a roof of dark slate instead of orange barrel tiles. On the ridgeline perched thirteen large crows like the living totems of some clan of malicious wizards that had taken over the library for the storage of their ancient volumes of dark, forbidden knowledge. The birds craned their necks and worked their beaks without a shriek or caw, as if casting silent curses on all who dared enter the building under them.

Inside, the librarian at the main desk was a severe-looking woman with a shock of kinky white hair, vaguely reminiscent of Elsa Lanchester in *The Bride of Frankenstein*, although less appealing, her eyes squinted and her lips compressed as though she took offense at everything upon which her attention fell. Jeffy had never seen her in the library of his and Amity's world. The woman didn't greet them, didn't seem aware of them. Grimly, she paged through one of the books in a tall stack, scowling as though searching for paper-devouring silverfish. Abruptly she slammed it shut, grunting with satisfaction, as if she found one of the critters and squashed it with pleasure.

The facility included more aisles of books than some libraries offered these days, as well as a computer alcove with four public-access workstations. The place was not as brightly lighted as the library in the Suavidad Beach from which Jeffy and Amity had come. Pale dust bunnies gathered in some corners, and a thin film of dust dulled the computer. The faintest scent of mildew ebbed and flowed in the still air, as if essential maintenance had been deferred in chambers adjacent to this one.

Jeffy and Amity seemed to be the only patrons at the moment. They sat side by side at a computer and googled Edwin Harkenbach, whose middle name proved to be Marsten.

In the internet sea, data relating to Ed didn't amount to a mere island; it was a small continent. Bow-tied Dr. Harkenbach, sixty-four, was a theoretical physicist with three PhDs. He had written twenty-six books and over five hundred articles, had delivered almost four hundred major speeches, and received scores of awards for teaching, writing, and research.

Bewildered by the volume of material on his subject, Jeffy resorted to Wikipedia for a thumbnail biography, where he discovered that the prolific Harkenbach, always highly visible in the field of physics and in academia, had abruptly lowered his public profile four years earlier. No new books or articles had appeared since then, and he had made only a few appearances at conferences.

"I bet that's when he started work on the project," Amity whispered as she took Snowball from a jacket pocket and cupped him in her hands.

"What project?"

"The key to everything project."

Jeffy nodded. "About that time, he must've gotten busy spending all those billions."

The mouse's head popped up between Amity's crossed thumbs. He looked left and right, nose twitching, intrigued by the library.

According to Wikipedia, Harkenbach's wife, Rina, died of cancer when they were both thirty-five, and he never married again. He and Rina had no children, and work evidently became everything to him.

Reading along with her father, Amity said, "He's not really Mr. Spooky. He's more like Mr. Sad."

A megabillion-dollar research project involving an epic quest as exotic as the search for parallel universes would have been a black-budget operation carried out with great secrecy. It wasn't likely that Ed had given a speech or written an article about it.

However, the government would have chosen Ed to lead such an undertaking only if he was profoundly interested in the multiverse theory long before seventy-six billion was dropped on him. He might have written extensively on the subject years before he was given the opportunity to seek a way to access the infinite continuum of worlds.

As Jeffy jumped out of Wikipedia and found a reliable list of Ed Harkenbach's book-length publications at another site, he became aware of movement at the periphery of his vision. He looked up to see another patron, maybe forty feet away, settling in a chair at a long reading table flanked by eight-foot-high rows of bookshelves. Dressed in soft black fatigues, wearing a black knitted cap, the man had taken a newspaper from a nearby rack.

As Amity returned Snowball to a pocket of her denim jacket, she whispered, "That weirdo guy was watching us for like maybe a minute before he sat down. I got a bad feeling about him."

"He's just some harmless kookster," Jeffy said, an expression of hope rather than fact. "We have them back home, too, except they dress different."

Scanning the list of books by Ed Harkenbach, he settled on one published eight years earlier—*Infinite Worlds: Parallel Universes and Quantum Reality*.

Reading a brief synopsis of it, Jeffy said, "This is it. This is what we need. I wonder if they have a copy of it here."

As he was about to drop off the internet, Amity said, "Wait! One more thing, Dad. Before we figure out what the three buttons mean, the buttons on the key to everything, before we leave this place and go home . . . if we *can* go home . . . I want to google her."

"Who?" he asked, but he knew. He knew, and the prospect of such a search both charmed and unnerved him.

Amity's face was as smooth and expressionless as that of a bisque doll, but her blue eyes were pools of longing when she said, "Michelle Melinda Jamison."

"Honey, we're in deep trouble here."

"Yeah. I know. I'm scared."

"I'm scared, too. Finding another version of your mother, one who would want to come with us . . . that will never be as easy as you think."

"It might be."

"It won't, honey. And maybe she's married to the me who was mowing the lawn. She's not going to leave one me for the other."

Amity shook her head. "There weren't any womany things back there, in that house. It's just you living alone there."

"Figuring out what those three buttons mean—that's urgent, that's everything."

"I know. But then . . . if she's here and she's alone . . ."

"Something's wrong with this world," he declared. "We don't want to stay here more than we absolutely have to."

She bit her lip and looked away from him, forlorn and full of yearning.

He loved this child desperately. He would die for her. But such intense love could inspire foolish acts as well as selfless courage.

After a hesitation, he googled Michelle Melinda Jamison.

And there she was. In this parallel reality, she resided in Suavidad Beach. It was the house on Bastoncherry Lane, where she'd lived with Jim Jamison, her dad, before she and Jeffy married.

"We've got to go see her. Daddy, can we go see her, please?"

He hesitated. In spite of all the imaginative fantasy stories by which she had been enthralled and entertained, Amity was too young to be able to understand the many reasons that such a meeting could go wrong or to foresee the regrets it might inspire. Unlike his daughter, Jeffy knew too well the potential heartbreak that could result from a visit to Bastoncherry Lane. However, he was nothing if not a romantic. And he had waited seven years for the miraculous return of Michelle. Although apprehension weighed so heavily on him that he couldn't quite draw a deep breath, he said, "All right. If we can find Ed's book, if we can figure out how to use the key, then we'll see what her situation is."

Her smile was all the reward he ever wanted.

His smile wasn't as genuine as Amity's. What he promised her was reckless, a wild-heart imprudence that simultaneously gladdened and disquieted, that was brewed in the cauldron of parental love.

"You're the best," she said.

He wished that he were worthy of those words.

As he and Amity went into the stacks, looking for the science section in which Ed Harkenbach's book might be shelved, they took care not to glance at the man sitting at the table with a newspaper that he wasn't reading.

=== 15

The library windows were set high, above the storied stacks that lined the walls. The stillness of the day had succumbed to a light breeze. Beyond the panes, a dark gray sea of clouds washed slowly southward, and the immense fronds of a phoenix palm did not thrash but undulated as hypnotically as the numerous mouth tentacles of a sea anemone seeking sustenance.

As Jeffy and Amity hunted for the books by Edwin Harkenbach, strange currents came and went, disturbing the air between the rows of tall shelves, as if unseen presences were likewise searching the library's collection, perhaps the restless ghosts of past patrons vainly inquiring after a self-help volume that would counsel them about how to let go of their late, lamented lives.

The romantic fragrances of yellowing paper and literary dust were pervasive. A faint, disturbing odor of mildew rose repeatedly but always faded. Twice Jeffy caught a vague scent of something burning, and though it was the merest tease of a cataclysmic smell, he looked toward the vaulted ceiling and turned his head this way and that, half expecting to see a thin haze of smoke.

"Here!" Amity breathed and slid one fingertip along the spines of several volumes.

Of the many works by Harkenbach, the library possessed only seven. Among those, however, *Infinite Worlds* waited. A field of stars illustrated the cover, and between the vivid red letters of the title were pale blue letters repeating those two words.

Although the book was only 312 pages and appeared to be written for curious laymen rather than for physicists, it was too long to be perused while standing in the aisle. And for reasons he could not fully grasp, he didn't want the patron in black to see him reading.

He possessed a Suavidad Beach Library card, but intuition told him that something about it would be different from the way such a card looked in *this* version of the town. The wirehaired, clenched-jaw librarian would reject it and impound the book, and she would most likely do so loud enough to attract the attention of the man in black fatigues, who had already shown an unhealthy interest in Jeffy and Amity.

Jeffy handed the book to his daughter. He spoke softly. "He's less likely to suspect you than me. Loosen your belt, tuck this in your jeans, button up your jacket."

"We're stealing it?" she whispered.

"No, sweetheart. It's not stealing."

"What is it, then?"

"Informal borrowing. We'll return it later."

"Cool."

"It's not cool. Even though it isn't stealing, it's still not cool. It's a one-time thing."

Amity concealed the book as he'd directed.

"Try not to look guilty," he said.

"I don't look guilty," she objected.

"You look something. Okay, we'll walk directly to the front door. Don't hurry. Act relaxed. Be casual."

"Can I whistle a tune?"

"Is that a joke?"

"I thought so."

"It's not a time for jokes."

Together they moved toward the end of the aisle.

They halted when the man in black garb rounded the corner and blocked their way. He had an unfortunate porcine face and eyes that glittered with menace in the shadows of deep sockets. As he boldly regarded them, the nostrils of his fleshy nose flared as if he were on a truffle hunt.

"You find what you were looking for?" he asked, not in the helpful way of a library employee, but with sharp suspicion.

"Yes, sir, thank you," Jeffy said brightly. "My daughter has this school project, she's got to make a motorized model of the solar system, and we didn't know which planets might have more than one moon or no moons at all. Now we know."

The stranger appeared simultaneously ridiculous and threatening in his faux Ninja outfit. However, his manner and voice suggested that he possessed authority and was accustomed to being treated with respect. "The solar system, is it? Just how old are you, girl?"

Belatedly, Jeffy realized that building a *motorized* model of the solar system was too ambitious a project for a sixth grader, but Amity was quick to patch the hole in his story.

"I'm almost fourteen," she lied. "So I'm kind of a runt, but I'm not always gonna be. I'm gonna have a growth spurt and be five feet eight, maybe five nine, and no one will tease me anymore, which will sure be, you know, great. Daddy can make the planets and moons rotate and revolve, and *that'll* make me seem totally cool."

Jeffy was pleased by how quick-witted Amity was, but at the same time, he was unsettled by the alacrity with which she lied and the convincing innocence with which she did it.

Proving himself a cynic, the guy in black said, "You think it's cold in here? Why is your jacket buttoned to the neck? It's not cold in here. You hiding something in your jacket, girl?"

Amity turned half away from the man and quickly undid only the top two buttons and produced Snowball from an exterior pocket while making it appear that he'd been inside her jacket. "Snowball is a good mouse. He goes everywhere with me, and he's never a problem, never runs away. He'd never ever poop on a book or anything bad like that. I'm real sorry. I made a mistake bringing him here."

The security man—or whatever he was—scowled. "That's no right kind of pet." He regarded Jeffy with contempt out of proportion to any perceived offense. "What kind of parent allows his child to keep a filthy rodent like that?"

In the California from which Jeffy and Amity had come, this kind of dressing-down from a man who looked like a background extra in a cheesy kung fu movie would have elicited a withering response. In this alternate state, however, such a man was a mystery that required caution.

"Yes, sir. You're right, of course. I guess I indulge her too much. I've been guilty of that ever since her mom . . . since her mom passed away."

Although he seemed to assume that he was privileged, although he was officious and rude in the manner of a petty bureaucrat, this costumed Gestapo wannabe still had a spoonful of the milk of human kindness. His expression softened slightly at the mention of a family tragedy. His stare shifted from Jeffy to Amity to Jeffy again. "All right, maybe you don't need to take a parenting course. But get out of here with that dirty rodent. Buy the girl an *approved* animal, something that honors the genius of the state."

"I will," Jeffy assured him, though he had no idea what the guy meant. "Thanks for your understanding."

Without looking back at their interrogator, he and Amity made their way out of the maze of stacks. As they crossed the receiving area toward the entrance, he saw the librarian with the shock of white hair. She moved briskly, pushing a cart bearing the books she'd earlier been inspecting. As she passed through an archway, out of sight, Jeffy again detected the smell of smoke. Although the odor was faint, he thought it was the scent of paper burning.

A shiver descended his spine as he opened the front door and as he and Amity stepped outside into a world not theirs.

16

Amity hoped maybe the storm wouldn't spill out into the day. The swollen heavens promised rain, but hour by hour the promise wasn't kept. In fact, the birds that had gone to shelter in anticipation of the downpour had again taken to the sky. Bright against the soiled clouds, white gulls looped high and then cried down the day. Having returned from their nests in whatever lagoons, brown pelicans glided effortlessly in formation, eternally silent, while shrieking crows darted from tree to tree, repeatedly exploding into flight as if invisible predators swarmed after them.

Amity and her father couldn't take Ed Harkenbach's book home to study it in their house on Shadow Canyon Lane, because in this crazy world, the house belonged to another Coltrane who might not be as kind as the father she loved. She didn't think that *any* version of her dad could be outright evil; across even thousands and thousands of worlds, surely no Jeffy Coltrane was a killer like Hannibal Lecter, but maybe a few of them were humongously annoying. Anyway, she and her father didn't know what, if anything, would happen when two Jeffys came face-to-face in a world that was meant to have only one. Most likely, neither of them would explode or otherwise cease to exist, though such a disaster couldn't be ruled out.

Daddy wanted to go to a back booth in Harbison's Diner and study the book over lunch. But in this world, the restaurant was called Steptoe's Diner, and it didn't look as clean as Harbison's. This difference inspired Daddy to wonder if the cash in his wallet would pass for currency in this United States, or if maybe it would be so different from local money that the cashier would reject it and cause a scene.

Counting on the storm clouds to carry the rain miles farther south before spending it, they went to the seaside park at the center of town and settled on one of the benches on the grassy area that overlooked the white sand beach.

Taking its color from the sky, the ocean now appeared to be a lifeless swamp of ashes, as though all the cities and towns along its shores—except for this one—had burned down and shed their remains into the water. Low gray surf, like a soup of ruination, washed upon the beach, and with it came the faint iodine smell of rotting seaweed.

The choppy waves were too tame for surfers, and the threat of the storm left the strand deserted. The traffic on Pacific Coast Highway, a hundred yards behind them, was markedly less than it would have been in their world, as if people here either chose not to travel much or were somehow discouraged from doing so. Amity wasn't car crazy, but it seemed to her that there were fewer makes and models than in *her* Suavidad Beach, and all appeared to be gray or brown or black. In spite of the saturated sky and the rolling ocean, the dismal day felt barren, arid—drained of color and energy.

Keeping one eye out for birds, she removed Snowball from her jacket pocket and put him on the ground, where he promptly toileted. The mouse then began exploring the territory around her feet, which was when she first noticed the shell casings scattered through the grass, dully gleaming cylinders, as if the park had recently been the scene of a gunfight.

The concrete bench was hard, but Harkenbach's book was harder. Although he was supposed to be a genius, old Ed didn't seem able to compose a short sentence without hundred-dollar words, so he might as well have been writing in Martian. Daddy slowly skimmed through the volume, reading passages aloud, most of which made no sense to Amity; only one seemed as though it might be helpful to them.

Spooky old, sad old Ed, homeless genius on the run, suggested that if a parallel world—which he also referred to as an "alternate timeline"—could be visited, its location could then be cataloged. So people traveling sideways through the infinite multiverse could return to a specific alternate timeline instead of always being flung across the spectrum of worlds willy-nilly, like tumbling dice.

According to Daddy, that explained the readout on the data bar at the bottom of the screen on the key to everything: ELSEWHERE 1.13—CATALOGED. "If we think of our world as Earth Prime, then all the other worlds, other timelines, they're 'Elsewhere.' Doesn't that make sense? I think it makes sense."

In spite of their less than ideal situation, he was overcome with a boyish enthusiasm. He liked to learn things. He enjoyed mysteries and puzzles of all kinds, and solving them.

"So it follows that *this* world we're in has been cataloged, the route to it stored in the memory of this device, and its name is Earth 1.13. Which maybe means it's thirteen worlds away from ours. What do you think?"

"Yeah, I guess," Amity said, searching the slowly roiling sky as though a dragon might suddenly swoop down from the overcast and snatch her up as effortlessly as a hawk could seize a mouse. This didn't seem like a world in which there could be dragons. There were no castles to be seen, no knights astride armored steeds, none of the stuff that she associated with dragons. Nevertheless, in really good stories, the unexpected was often more likely to occur than anything easily anticipated. In books, she liked the unexpected, though not so much in real life.

She rose to her feet. Careful not to step on little Snowball, she plucked the shell casings from the grass. They were cold. She thought: *They're cold with death. Someone was killed right here, maybe more than one person, in a public park. This place is creepy. We've got to get the hell out of here.*

She didn't give voice to her thoughts because some second-rate fantasy novels featured pitiful girls who too easily lost their cool. When they became hysterical, they were saved by princes or by families of sympathetic dwarves or by magical wolves. They never got to do any of the really fun stuff themselves; they enjoyed no role except to be rescued. Amity had no patience for their kind, and for sure she didn't want to be one of them. In spite of the shiny spent cartridges nestled in the grass, which suggested gross violence, she had no proof that murder had been committed in this park. She wasn't going to run screaming to Daddy and wind up being the object of an it's-okay-pumpkin-don't-worry-your-pretty-head moment.

After reading further, her dad took the key to everything from his jacket. He pressed the home circle. The screen filled with gray light, and then the three buttons appeared.

"If I press the button marked SELECT, I bet nothing drastic will happen."

"It might," she cautioned.

"I bet what'll happen is the screen will give me a keypad, so then I can enter the address of whatever parallel world I want to visit. And I'll probably have to take several more steps in order to be sent there."

"We just want to go home," Amity said, depositing a handful of brass shell casings on the bench. They made a fairy-bell sound as they spilled onto the concrete. "We don't want to go anywhere else."

Scowling at the book, Daddy said, "If the SELECT button works the way I think it does, then the button marked HOME is exactly what it says. It takes us back home to Earth Prime, where we came from."

"Don't push it yet," Amity said.

"But I wonder what the RETURN button does."

"Don't push it, either," Amity said.

He put the device down beside him and slowly turned through a few pages of the book, his brow pleated with puzzlement, muttering lines of the text, while she gathered more shell casings and deposited them on the bench.

Having ventured farther from Amity than was his habit, Snowball had found a discarded candy wrapper with a morsel left in it. The torn plastic rattled with the mouse's ecstasy.

Amity moved close to Snowball, watching over him while she collected more pieces of mortal brass. Which was when she found the three teeth. No-doubt-about-it human teeth. Front teeth, incisors. One was cracked, and all three were held together by a bloodstained fragment of a jawbone, as though someone's face had come apart in a barrage of gunfire.

17

The teeth felt colder than the shell casings. They were icy. Amity understood that they weren't in fact as cold as ice, that the iciness was *perceived* rather than real, a psychological reaction. If she'd been a tedious rescue-me kind of girl, she would have screamed as if her hair were on fire and would have run to Daddy, but she restrained herself for two reasons.

First, she *wasn't* that kind of girl. She would kick her own ass from here to Cucamunga if she ever found herself acting like such a dullard. Second, if she showed the teeth to him, Daddy would flash Amity and himself home to Earth Prime as fast as he could push a button, and they would never pay a visit to the Jamison house on Bastoncherry Lane in this world, where maybe her mother waited.

After tossing aside the additional shell casings that she'd found, she put the teeth in a pocket of her jeans and looked up at the storm-cloaked sky. She didn't expect a dragon. If something plunged out of the clouds, it would be far worse than a dragon with foot-long claws and bloody eyes and breath aflame. She didn't know what it might be, only that it would be worse.

Wiping the palm of her hand on her jeans, she looked out to sea. It was hard to tell where the sky met the water. Gray surf broke in a lace of dirty foam. She half expected dead bodies to start washing onto the shore.

She wasn't a pessimist and certainly not a depressive. Being raised without a mother sucked, and sometimes it was sad, but she was mostly happy, really and truly. Life was good—better than good, great—and every day she saw something beautiful that she had never seen before, and amazing things happened when she least expected them. She was too smart to be anything but an optimist. Until Earth 1.13. Now she wouldn't be surprised if the sea spewed out rotting corpses. The problem wasn't her; it was this weird place. Or maybe it was *partly* her. Although 1.13 was a sick and twisted world, maybe it wasn't half as bad as she thought. Some people just weren't good travelers. For them, no place could ever be as fine and right as home. Not Paris. Not London. Not Rio. Daddy was a homebody and a not-good traveler, and perhaps she shared his love of the familiar, of libraries where you felt welcome and parks where you didn't find biological debris maybe left over from a public mass execution.

She plucked the torn candy wrapper off the grass and peeled Snowball out of it. He clutched what might have been a chunk of nougat. She let him keep it and tucked him into a jacket pocket.

With a composure that made her proud, she returned to the bench and quietly gathered up the shell casings that she had placed there, for they would alarm her father almost as much as the teeth.

Enthralled by the book and oblivious of the little pile of brass, Daddy said, "Put your hand on my neck."

Quietly placing the shiny evidence of violence on the grass behind the bench, she said, "Why on your neck?"

"Just in case."

"In case what?"

"I'm going to push the SELECT button to see if I'm right about it. In case I'm wrong and we go flashing away somewhere, I think we have to be touching if we're to go together. Like we were touching, our hands clutching Snowball, in the kitchen when the little ratfink jumped onto this thing and set it off."

"It wasn't Snowball's fault. He's not a ratfink. Just curious."

"I meant ratfink in an affectionate way."

Growling engines on the coast highway drew Amity's attention. Three enormous, sinister-looking trucks cruised southward, one behind the other. They appeared to be armored, and she first thought they must be army vehicles, except that they were painted black with heavily tinted windows and bore no identifying insignia.

She put one hand on the back of her father's neck.

On the key to everything, he pushed the button labeled
SELECT.

During an interminable two-second delay, Amity just *knew*
she would never again see Justin Dakota, the boy at the end of
the lane who had the potential to be shaped into husband material. Then the screen brightened with the words ENTER TIMELINE
CATALOG NUMBER and provided a keypad.

"Just as I figured!" Daddy exclaimed.

He did not enter a number for a parallel world, but instead
pressed CANCEL. For an instant Amity feared that in this case the
word had a more ominous meaning than usual, that their entire
existence would be canceled, as though they had never lived.
Earth 1.13 was totally messing with her head. But the keyboard
display vanished from the screen, the three buttons reappeared—
HOME, RETURN, SELECT—and she and her father were still alive
and whole, as was Snowball, who seemed to curl into a sphere in
her pocket, as though he must be gripping the nougat in all four
paws as he nibbled on it.

Being a mouse had its advantages. You were short-lived, yes,
and fearfully vulnerable. On the other hand, your tiny brain didn't
grasp how big and strange and dangerous the world was, so you
never gave much thought to all the ways you could die and all the
things that could be taken from you. For a mouse, the smallest
pleasures were sources of great happiness: a peanut, a fluffy kernel
of cheese popcorn, a bit of nougat, a warm pocket.

Having a mother might be like having nougat and a warm
pocket. But once you lost her, finding her and getting her to come
home again was a far bigger task than anything a mouse had to
undertake.

Daddy rose from the bench with the *Book of Ed* and the key to everything. He frowned at the sky, at the sea, and then at Amity.

"Are you sure you really want to do this?" he said, meaning did she want to pay a visit to the house on Bastoncherry Lane.

"You promised we would."

"That's not what I asked, sweetheart."

She didn't dare look away from him. It was never a brilliant idea to break eye contact with her father when they were discussing something important. Even if there might be a thousand reasons she looked away, he unfailingly identified the right one. And then she couldn't hide anything from him. Sometimes this seemed really and truly supernatural, but because he never displayed other fantastic talents—like being able to fly or walk through walls—his ability to read her so clearly was evidently just an excellent parenting skill. With his Bakelite radios and Deco posters and love of the past and boyish enthusiasm, he was Jeffy to everyone, but when it mattered the most, he was always a Jeffrey.

"I want to do it," she said. "We *have* to do it. Maybe she's alone here. Maybe she's sad or in hideously dire circumstances."

"Hideously dire circumstances, huh?" He was reminding her not to be a drama queen.

"Sure. Why not? I mean, people often are in dire circumstances, not just in movies and books, but like for real. Maybe she needs help. Anyway, you and me—we don't walk out on people."

Instead of Amity breaking eye contact, her father broke it. He lowered his gaze to the right-hand pocket of her jeans, in which she had secreted the three teeth fixed in the fragment of jawbone, as though he could see through denim and knew what horror she had found in the grass.

She almost showed him the teeth, almost blurted out that this world was weirder and darker even than it seemed, that they had to rescue Michelle from a town where people were shot to pieces in a public park. But then she realized that she had unconsciously thrust her right hand into that pocket. The teeth were clenched tightly in her fist. *This* was what Daddy had noticed—her arm rigid, the fist bulging in her pocket. And— *Merde!*—her fist was twitching, bulging and twitching, her own stupid fist betraying her.

Letting go of the teeth, she withdrew her hand from the pocket. She was careful not to scrub her palm against her jeans because he'd know instantly that she'd been clutching some filthy object that disgusted her.

To have something to do with the traitorous hand, she pointed at the key to everything. "You sort of know how to use it now. If we get in any kind of trouble, you can flash us home."

He turned to gaze at Pacific Coast Highway, at the shops beyond, at the houses rising on the tiered hills.

Fortunately, no enormous armored trucks, flat black with darkly tinted windows, were passing at the moment.

Nevertheless, he said, "I don't like this place."

"I don't, either. Which is why we can't leave her here, Daddy. Not if maybe . . . if maybe she needs us."

He met her eyes again.

Neither of them looked away from the other.

"All right," he said, pocketing the key to everything and plucking the book off the bench, "but let's be quick about it."

18

Pacific Coast Highway descended from the north, led across the flat center of town, past the park and the public beach, and rose to the south. Block after block was lined with motels and hotels, shops and restaurants and art galleries, because this had long been one of Southern California's primary vacation destinations. On this day and in this world, however, the dearth of tourists—sidewalks all but deserted—couldn't be entirely explained by the threat of the storm, and the number of enterprises that had gone out of business meant the economy must be in decline, perhaps in a crisis.

Jeffy and Amity were nearing the end of the second block south of the park when, ahead and uphill on the far side of the highway, they saw a police car and an unmarked black van in front of Gifford Gallery.

"I hope nobody robbed Erasmus," Amity worried.

"Not likely," Jeffy said. "Nobody sticks up a gallery."

Suavidad Beach was home to many artists, with a thriving creative community of which Erasmus Gifford had long been a driving force. On the ground floor of his gallery, he sold paintings by contemporary artists, including locals whose work he'd nurtured and brought to national attention. On the second floor, he offered originals from classic California painters long deceased, as well as a small and carefully curated collection of original posters primarily from the Nouveau and Deco periods, fine and rare examples of which could sell for eight thousand, ten thousand, and even more.

From time to time, Jeffy found a poster of such quality that he needed Gifford Gallery's client base to get the right price for it, and they shared in the profit. Erasmus was honest, industrious, and passionate about his work. He and Jeffy had quickly bonded.

Now concern for his friend halted Jeffy. As he was about to cross the street to see what was happening, Erasmus came out of the gallery in the custody of two police officers. His hands were cuffed behind his back. His mass of white hair was matted with blood, and his face was streaked with it, as though he had been clubbed.

Erasmus was built like Pablo Picasso—stocky, broad-shouldered, strong. At sixty he appeared more imposing than most men half his age. In this moment, however, his shoulders were slumped, his head hung low, and he looked defeated, as Jeffy could never have imagined him.

The shock of seeing Erasmus in this condition reminded Jeffy that the man in police custody was not exactly his friend but an alternate-world version of the man. He found it difficult to credit that anyone as good and reliable as Erasmus might, in another life of different experiences and pressures, have become someone of lower character than he was on Earth Prime. But of course this might be the case. Nevertheless, he told Amity to stay close, and he took a step toward the curb, intending to cross the highway—until a man in black fatigues and a knitted black cap exited the gallery behind its owner and the two cops.

"Another one," Amity whispered, as if even the noise of passing traffic would not mask her voice from those on the far side of the street. "I don't like these guys, and not just 'cause of the freaky way they dress. They're like human cockroaches or something, the way they scuttle into sight when you least expect them."

This particular human cockroach was more formidable than the specimen who accosted them in the library. About six feet two. Maybe two hundred pounds. He carried a police baton, a modern version of a billy club, which perhaps he had used on Erasmus's head. His broad, flat face might as well have had the word *barbarian* stamped on his forehead. Maybe it did, under the hem of the snugly fit knitted cap.

The policemen didn't conduct Erasmus into the patrol car. At the direction of the barbarian, who obviously outranked them, they frog-marched Erasmus to the back of the black van. Another human cockroach stepped out of that vehicle and roughly shoved Erasmus into it.

"Daddy, he's staring at us," Amity warned.

The barbarian with the club stood on the sidewalk, between the patrol car and the van, focusing intently on them as they watched the gallery owner being arrested. Maybe the social norms of this world required citizens to ignore scenes like this or face serious consequences if they couldn't repress their curiosity. Not one driver among those in the passing traffic slowed to have a better look.

"Head down," Jeffy said, "as if there's something fascinating on the sidewalk. Head down and keep moving to the corner."

Although this Erasmus Gifford was not, strictly speaking, the man he knew, Jeffy was embarrassed to turn away from him. With Amity to be concerned about, with mounting evidence that they had landed in an authoritarian or even totalitarian state, discretion was the best course, the only rational response. Yet rationality felt too much like cowardice.

At the end of the block, they kept moving southward, crossed the intersection, and only then dared to glance back. The patrol car, its flashing lightbar flinging rhythmic redness through the drab day, pulled away from the curb, heading north, downhill, and the van followed it.

"From now on, stay close by my side," Jeffy said. "Don't even think about getting more than an arm's reach away from me."

19

The birds that for a while braved the forbidding sky now returned once more to nests and roosts.

The breeze withered away. The low heavens lowered farther. No clouds had ever before looked so heavy, as though they might shed lead pellets instead of rain.

This residential neighborhood was eerily quiet, no one coming or going, no one attending to any chores, as if many of the houses might be empty.

Jeffy felt as though he were moving through something thicker than air, the day resisting him like a hundred fathoms of water would resist a deep-sea diver making his way across an ocean floor.

The house on Bastoncherry Lane wasn't stucco like many houses in Suavidad Beach, wasn't in any genre of Spanish architecture or in the craftsman style, or mid-century modern, or faux Tuscan, or of a soft contemporary design. For a Southern California beach town, the residence appeared unique: a two-story white-clapboard home with forest-green shutters flanking the windows, so traditional that it could have been the home of almost any family in any TV sitcom from the 1950s and '60s. It was a house where you imagined there was much love and laughter, where the family's few problems were small and resolved in thirty minutes between station breaks.

The front walk of herringbone-pattern brick led to brick steps and a brick-floored porch added during a remodel, years after the house was built, replacing a concrete walk and stoop. No other brickwork than this could have inspired such intense sentimental memories in Jeffy. In the world from which he'd come—evidently in this world as well—his dad had been the masonry contractor on the job, and Jeffy had worked with him that summer. He'd been sixteen. He had first seen Michelle Jamison while on that project. She was fifteen, and he adored her, although in secret. He was shy, she vivacious. He was enchanted with the world as it had been decades earlier; she cared little for the past, was versed in all the latest music and movies, wrote songs, and had a plan to shape the future to her desires. Nonetheless, in retrospect, he could not justify to himself why he'd taken more than four years to ask her for a date.

With Amity at his side, he climbed the brick steps and went to the front door and hesitated, heart quickening with the prospect of love reborn, and then he rang the bell.

Amity took his hand and squeezed it. "Her name's still Jamison. She never married."

"Maybe she didn't. Maybe she did. We don't know anything about her life in this world."

"I look a little like her. If she sees herself in me, maybe she'll believe our story, believe there's a better world than this. Then she'll come with us."

"Don't wish so hard," he advised. "Soft wishes are more likely to come true."

She let go of his hand and blotted her palms on her jeans.

The door opened, and Michelle Jamison stood before them, as lovely as ever. The seven years since he'd last seen her had taken more of a toll than Jeffy expected: a new leanness in her features that suggested hardship; fans of small lines at the corners of her eyes; and something in the eyes themselves that hadn't been there before, perhaps a weary resignation.

She frowned at Amity, as if in fact a quality in the girl's countenance affected her. After that fleeting look of puzzlement, when she turned her attention to Jeffy, she evinced no recognition. "Can I help you?"

For a moment, words failed him. Seven years of yearning, of aching loss and regret were an impediment to speech. He had never forgotten that he loved her, but time had faded his memory of the intensity of that love, which possessed him now as fully as ever before. He wanted to take her in his arms, but he could do no such thing, not in this timeline where they had never made love, never married, never conceived a daughter.

His voice sounded strange to him when he said, "You won't remember me. I'm Jeffy Coltrane. I worked with my dad and his crew the summer when we laid the brick for your walkways and porch and back patio. I was sixteen then, eighteen years ago."

Shadows pooled in the room behind her, and from them emerged a pale-faced raven-haired boy of about Amity's age. "Mother?" Standing at Michelle's side, he didn't resemble her at all. His posture and expression suggested a treasured sense of superiority; he regarded their visitors with thin-lipped contempt.

The boy wore brown shoes, khaki pants, and a matching shirt. The breast pocket of the shirt featured the face of a wolf with glaring yellow eyes, and there were epaulets on the shoulders. It appeared to be a uniform.

"Mother, who're they?"

"This man says he did the masonry here a long time ago. He hasn't told me why he's come around."

"I'm Amity." A tremor in the girl's voice revealed turbulent emotion that, to this woman and boy, would sound inappropriate in these circumstances. "I'm Amity," she repeated, "and all I want to know is—"

"Amity," Jeffy cautioned.

But she was face-to-face with her mother, or seemed to be, and seven years of pent-up longing propelled her to finish: "—are you happy here, is everything all right here?"

The boy cocked his head. "Is something wrong with you? What's wrong with you?"

"Rudy, be nice," his mother said.

Another presence loomed out of the shadows behind Michelle, a stranger of about Jeffy's age.

Rudy ignored his mother's admonition and regarded Amity with suspicion. "You're old enough to join the Wolves. They even take girls now. Why haven't you joined?"

"What wolves?"

"The Justice Wolves. What other wolves are there? You should've joined."

The man behind Michelle said, "What's happening?"

"Dennis, this is Mr. Coltrane," Michelle said. "He tells me that he and his father did all the masonry here when Dad remodeled back in the day."

"Yeah, I know who he is," Dennis said. "He's Frank Coltrane's son. I know the face."

With every exchange, a web was being spun that would ensnare Jeffy if he said the wrong thing. He suspected that he shouldn't stand silent, should explain himself. "I just . . . I wanted Amity to see some of my father's work. We shouldn't have disturbed you. I just thought maybe . . ." He didn't know how to finish the sentence.

"Something's wrong with them," Rudy declared.

"You're like my half brother or something," Amity told him, perhaps seeking his approval to ensure that of his mother.

Rudy sneered. "Brother? My name's Starkman. Yours ain't."

Dennis Starkman said, "Get inside, Michelle. Rudy, you, too."

When the woman and boy retreated, Starkman came out of the shadows and onto the threshold, revealing that he was dressed in soft black fatigues and black boots, although not in a knitted cap. He wore a gun belt and carried a pistol on his right hip.

His round face was shaped for warm smiles and expressions of kindness. Even scowling as now, he didn't appear to be the work of darkness that he really was.

"You listen to me, Coltrane. Your old man got what he deserved. He's damn lucky he was just sent to Folsom instead of being cut down for good. Can you get your head around that?"

With his real father safe in another America, but with Amity at risk here, Jeffy said, "Yes. You're right. He's a stubborn man. He always has been."

"Frank knew the price he might have to pay for being on the wrong side. Some thought you were in it with him, but most of us gave you the benefit of the doubt."

"I appreciate that."

Starkman looked doubtful. "Do you really?"

"I know . . . I know who owns the future." That didn't sound right. "I want to be a part of it, the better world you're making."

"Now you make me wonder," Starkman continued, "coming around here. To what purpose? Did you mean to threaten my family?"

"No, no. Not at all. I just did it for the girl. She doesn't understand why . . . why my dad did what he did, why he fell in with the wrong crowd. I don't understand any more than she does, but I wanted to show her, you know, how before he went so far off the rails, he did some good things, he was a great craftsman, he—"

Jeffy embarrassed himself with his obsequious tone, though if he had been any less deferential, he might have invited trouble from which there would be no escape. His babble was as tedious as it was servile, so boring that Starkman dismissed him by cutting him off in midsentence. Turning to Amity, he said, "So who are you, young lady? What do you have to do with Frank Coltrane?"

Abruptly Jeffy remembered that the version of himself native to this world lived alone and evidently had no daughter.

The risk they'd taken by lingering in a strange timeline became manifest. This moment was a trap that one wrong word could spring.

Again, his daughter proved quick and convincingly innocent. "Uncle Frank lived in our block. He's not my uncle, really, but he's always been, you know, so sweet to me and my dog, Snowball. I know he did a major bad thing and had to be sent away, but I wonder how he could be so nice and so bad at the same time. I guess the nice part must have been like a trick, and that makes me sad."

Starkman's eyes remained as dark with suspicion as with pigment. "What did you mean by saying my boy is your half brother?"

"Well, he wouldn't be a real brother, just like Uncle Frank wasn't my real uncle. But like if I join the Wolves, you know, the Justice Wolves, then him and me, we'd be friends, like in the same pack, brother wolf and sister wolf in the same pack."

Starkman stared at her for a beat, and then he focused once more on Jeffy. "Your father's an agitator against youth enlistment. He said the state was turning children into robots. He said we were brain-fucking them."

Jeffy ducked his head and nodded. "My father's stuck in the past. He hates change, progress. He can make you crazy in just two minutes, the way he rants."

"You know this girl's parents well?"

"Very well."

"What's her last name?"

"Crowley," Jeffy said without hesitation.

The Crowley family, with a daughter named Jennifer, lived on his father's street in Earth Prime, though maybe not here on Earth 1.13.

Nearly forty thousand people lived in Jeffy's Suavidad Beach. Even if there were only half that many residents in this parallel reality, Dennis Starkman couldn't know all of them.

However, perhaps in this world Mr. Crowley had been executed or sent off to a prison camp. If his daughter was already a member of the Wolves and was known to Starkman, then Jeffy had just sprung the trap that Amity had avoided triggering.

For the first time since they followed the brick walkway to the front steps, the sound of a vehicle rose in the street. A black van with heavily tinted windows, like the one in which Erasmus Gifford had been taken away, turned the corner and approached.

Starkman glanced at the van and then addressed Jeffy again. "You tell the Crowleys they shouldn't have let Frank Coltrane spew his hatred to this girl."

"I will. I'll tell them."

"You also tell them to take her into city hall tomorrow and sign her up for the Justice Wolves."

"If you say they should, they will. They believe in the cause. They're good people."

If the van swung to the curb in front of the house, he would have to act. Pull the key to everything from his pocket. Switch it on. That would take two or three seconds. When Snowball had pounced on it, the screen required maybe four seconds to fill with a soft gray light and a few more seconds before the buttons labeled HOME, RETURN, SELECT appeared. A total of ten or eleven seconds. So then he would grab Amity by the hand, press HOME—which might take three more seconds. From the moment he decided to act, they would be gone in perhaps fourteen seconds.

Unless he fumbled with the device.

Unless he dropped it.

Fourteen seconds was an eternity. Supposing when Jeffy drew the device from his jacket, Starkman thought he was going for a weapon, a knife. The sonofabitch wouldn't need fourteen seconds to draw the pistol and fire. Not a trigger-happy fascist like him. Even if he realized that the device wasn't a weapon, he would intuit that it must be in some way a threat. He might knock it out of Jeffy's hand.

The van didn't pull to the curb, but instead cruised past like a motorized gondola floating along a Styx of blacktop, its occupants barely discernible behind windows as dark as their intentions.

Starkman said, "The recruiter will be waiting for her in city hall at nine tomorrow. He'll have her name—Amity Crowley."

"Nine o'clock," Jeffy said. "Her folks will be there with her."

"It's pretty cool being a wolf, I bet," said Amity. "Rudy's uniform was totally the thing."

"I'm sorry if we've been any trouble," Jeffy said. "We didn't mean to inconvenience anyone."

He took his daughter by the hand and led her off the porch, down the steps, along the front walk to the street.

As the van motored east, Jeffy and Amity turned west.

When they had gone half a block, he dared to glance back.

Dennis Starkman had descended from the porch. He stood on his front lawn, watching them, talking on a cell phone. Talking to whom? Checking that the Crowley family had a daughter named Amity?

The girl, too, saw what was happening, and she started to walk faster.

Tightening his grip on her hand, Jeffy said, "Slow. Be casual. We don't want him to think we're making a break for it."

That advice made sense only for as long as it took him to give it.

From a distance behind them came the sudden bark of brakes. The sound of the van's engine changed. Eastbound a moment earlier, it was coming west now, closing on them from behind.

$=$ **20**

Neither a siren nor a blaring horn commanded them to halt, and they turned left from Bastoncherry onto another residential street. The instant they were out of sight of Starkman, they broke into a run, Amity still holding her father's hand, Jeffy seeking somewhere that they could get out of sight. The van was maybe five seconds behind them, not fourteen, so there was no time to stop and use the key to everything. Houses stood to the left and right. No one in view. Then a police car turned the corner less than one block ahead of them, coming this way, its lightbar displaying like a vintage jukebox waiting for someone to drop a nickel.

He pulled Amity off the sidewalk, and they raced across a front yard to a gate at the side of the house. He fumbled with a gravity latch, and the gate opened. As they hurried toward the back of the house, a loudspeaker—on the patrol car or the black van—boomed like the voice of a forty-foot giant who had come down a beanstalk.

"POLICE PURSUIT! ENEMIES OF THE STATE ON FOOT! LOCK YOUR DOORS! ENEMIES OF THE STATE ON FOOT!"

The grass in the backyard needed mowing, the swimming pool contained no water, and one of the seats on a child's swing set dangled uselessly on a single chain. The house seemed to be without a tenant until the kitchen door opened and a man charged onto the covered patio.

He was all jowls and wattle and belly, barefoot, with a fringe of Friar Tuck hair and an insane gleam in his eyes, wearing gray sweatpants and a soiled white T-shirt. He carried what might have been a croquet mallet, with no intention of offering to play a game, either an obedient citizen and true believer in the police state, or a guy who saw a chance to ingratiate himself with the authorities by bashing a little girl and her father.

Jeffy put the empty swimming pool between them and their would-be attacker, though they were all heading toward the same end of it, where they would inevitably meet.

To Amity, he said, "Over the wall," by which he meant the wall between this property and the next.

That barrier stood between seven and eight feet tall. She might have found it insurmountable if it hadn't been festooned with a decades-old, espaliered jasmine vine with gnarled woody runners two and three inches thick, offering plenty of footholds and handholds.

As Amity sprinted to the wall and began to claw her way up through the foliage, as Friar Tuck angled toward her with the mallet raised, Jeffy picked up a terra-cotta pot from the patio deck. The vessel was maybe two feet in diameter, and though the withered red-flowering vine geranium in it was suffering a near-death experience, the pot was full of dirt. It was too heavy to be snatched up on the run, and yet he snatched it up; too heavy to be lifted over his head, and yet he lifted it over his head; too damn cumbersome to be thrown like a basketball, and yet he threw it. The thought of that mallet coming down on the back of Amity's head instantly turned his brain into an adrenaline factory and set his heart to pounding as if he had reached the last mile marker of a marathon.

Like a boulder launched from a catapult, the pot crashed into the would-be child basher before he reached his victim, staggering him. He went to his knees on the decking. The mallet clattered out of his hand, almost tumbled into the drained pool, and came to rest on the concrete coping. Spewing four-letter words in a deranged but colorful rant that suggested a deep though not broad vocabulary, the demonic *croqueteur* scrambled to his feet and lunged to recover his weapon.

Jeffy reached it first. He lacked the homicidal passion to swing for his adversary's head, went low instead, and kneecapped the guy's left leg. Shouted obscenities thinned into a high-pitched squeal of pain. The man collapsed, clutching his cracked knee with both hands. Any further threat he might have posed was eliminated when, having fallen at the edge of the empty pool, he rolled onto his back and lost his balance and did another half turn and slid down the sloped wall, howling as if under the misapprehension that he was gliding down a chute to Hell.

Throwing away the mallet, Jeffy turned to the property wall in time to see Amity disappear over the top. As he went after her, the police loudspeaker rocked the day with a call to arms.

"CITIZENS RESPOND! ENEMIES OF THE STATE ON FOOT! HALT AND DETAIN! CITIZENS RESPOND!"

Hardly a minute after being told to lock their doors, they were being commanded to fling them open and join the hunt.

Because his weight was greater than the girl's, even the thick runners of the ancient jasmine vine sagged and split under him. He clambered up through a noisy crackling of wood, torn green leaves, and sweet-smelling tiny white flowers cascading to the ground behind him. When he reached the top, he saw Amity in another backyard, this one greener and more recently mowed than the previous property, sans pool, but graced by a birdbath and an English garden in which flourished pink phlox and Firecandle and May Night and blue poppies.

A white-haired couple rushed at Amity, as though with concern for the child's welfare, but instead grabbed her to prevent her from escaping.

$=$ **21**

The man appeared to be in his seventies, but he wasn't frail. He must have been a strapping specimen in his youth, footballer and gym rat. He remained formidable, like a monster pickup truck with a quarter million miles on it but still able to uproot an oak by means of a tow chain. With his wreath of snowy hair and cherry-red nose, even without a generous belly, he could have played Santa Claus, although at the moment he was a psycho Santa, eyes bulging and face wrenched and teeth bared as if to bite, perhaps a patriotic citizen or just a retiree worried that his pension would be taken away if he allowed these enemies of the state to escape. He grabbed Amity by one arm, and when she tried to pull away, he seized her throat with his other hand.

Leaping off the wall between properties, Jeffy shouted not at his daughter's assailant, but at Amity, reminding her of how she had been taught to deal with the hordes of bogeymen, some real and some imagined, whose dark intentions were the stuff of a father's worst nightmares. "Nutcracker!" he cried. "Nutcracker, nutcracker!"

Perhaps the girl needed no reminder, because even as Jeffy shouted, she drove one knee hard into her attacker's crotch. When the old man convulsed and let go of her throat, she gave him the knee again, harder than the first time. In an instant, his flushed face turned as gray as the cardigan he wore. He bent over, cupping his broken stones, staggered sideways and then backward, as though practicing a dance step that he was too awkward to master, and sat on the yard with an expression that suggested he had for the first time in his life taken seriously the concept of a wrathful God.

The old woman's cardigan was pink, complementing a pale-blue blouse and matching blue slacks with a pink belt, but in spite of that rather cheerful ensemble, her face was as severe as that of a witch who could call forth a squadron of flying monkeys. Her eyes burned with hatred. Maybe she was too arthritic to make use of the nutcracker defense effectively, but she had no need to resort to that because she had a garden spade with a three-foot handle. She swung it at Jeffy with the earnest desire to cut him with the edge of the shovel's blade or concuss him with the flat of it, and then perhaps drive the point through his neck as he lay on his back on the grass.

At her age, such a ferocious assault should have been of brief duration, consisting of three or four lunges with the spade before her body reminded her of the decades of strain it had previously endured. However, she seemed indefatigable, slashing at Jeffy, forcing him to duck and backstep as the shovel carved the air—*whoosh, whoosh*—with all the seeming lethality of a broadsword. Out in the street, the mobile loudspeaker continued to call to arms all loyal citizens, while the harpy in pink and blue snarled invective in counterpoint to her industrious work with the spade—"You fucking traitor . . . shitface creep . . . puke-eating scum"—like a grandmother possessed by a demonic entity.

As grandpa lay on his side in the fetal position, whimpering and willing himself to be reborn, Amity snatched up a bucket in which a dozen freshly cut roses stood. She swung it at the woman, scattering the flowers and the few inches of water that sustained them.

The pail met the spade-wielder's head with a sound like a cheap bell, staggering her but not rendering her unconscious. She dropped her weapon and weaved away toward the birdbath, where she leaned with both hands on the rim of that bowl, as if dizzy.

Amity grinned at her father, a rather wild-eyed manic grin, and he grinned at her as he snatched up the spade. He threw it over the wall, into the neighboring yard, where the kneecapped man was no doubt still lying at the bottom of the empty pool and wondering why he'd thought that it was a good idea to rush to the service of the nation.

A weird exhilaration overcame Jeffy, a motivating astonishment that he and Amity, having been cast into this maelstrom of mortal threats, were proving so quick and competent. Like characters in one of the fantasy novels they enjoyed. He was a guy who restored old radios and yearned to live in the past, a guy whose wife walked out on him, and Amity was but a slip of a girl, yet they were alive and free when by now they should have been captured and in chains. Their daring and spirit inspired him to believe they could handle this, split this dismal America, and flash across the multiverse to their own and better world.

The harpy turned from the birdbath and came at Amity as if she would claw the girl's eyes out. Jeffy interceded, snared the woman by her cardigan, spun her around, and shoved her face-down into a bed of red and purple primulas. He'd never imagined that he could treat a woman so roughly, let alone one old enough to be a grandmother, but he'd also never imagined that he would encounter a homicidal, geriatric champion of a police state.

"You are the goat!" Amity declared.

For an instant, Jeffy indeed almost felt he was the *greatest of all time*, father and stalwart defender. Even though his fear did not in the least relent, his confidence swelled. Perhaps dangerously.

The barrier between this property and the next was not a wall like the one that he and Amity had scaled only a minute earlier, but instead a wrought-iron fence in front of which grew periwinkle and Cistus and golden candle and holly flame pea. Before they could even consider clambering over it, however, two policemen appeared in the neighboring yard. One of them had drawn his pistol.

On his hands and knees, the crotch-kicked man growled as he tried to get up, and his wife spat out primula petals.

A fence at the back of the property featured a gate to an alley-way where a black van now glided into view.

They couldn't flee to the street in front of the residence, because that was where some vehicle with a loudspeaker contin-ued to blare warnings about enemies of the state.

Men in black were getting out of the van in the alley, and the police in the next yard were rushing toward the wrought-iron fence, and a long soft peal of thunder rumbled through the lowering sky.

Jeffy grabbed Amity's hand. They ran along the path through the English garden, across the patio with its white-painted wrought-iron chairs and hanging baskets of flower-laden fuchsia, to the back door of the house. They simply needed to get out of sight, find a haven that would provide fourteen seconds of privacy in which to switch on and use the key to everything.

They went inside. He slammed the door and twisted the thumb turn on the deadbolt to lock it.

"Where?" Amity asked breathlessly.

"Upstairs," Jeffy said. "They don't know we can just teleport out of here, or whatever it is the key does to us. They'll search down here, which will give us all the time we need."

"I hope there's not a mean dog," she worried as they crossed the kitchen toward a swinging door that no doubt led to the ground-floor hallway.

"There won't be a mean dog," Jeffy promised as he pushed open the door, and in fact there was no dog, though waiting for them was the meanest member of the family.

22

At first it had been possible to think that 1.13 was pretty much like the world from which they had come, except that here the economy was limping along, and there was a freaky cult whose members dressed in black with stupid-looking knitted caps. But almost minute by minute, the differences mounted until it became impossible to predict what weirdness might wait around the corner or, in this case, in the downstairs hallway. In his book, spooky

Ed Harkenbach said there were an infinite number of parallel universes, worlds side-by-side but invisible to one another, each different from the others in lots of unpredictable ways. Infinite differences meant that if you were using the key to everything, you had better be prepared for some upside-down inside-out ass-backward situations. Amity had lost track of this truth. Daddy, too. Which was understandable when you considered all the crap and crazies they'd had to deal with since the black-clad bozo in the library declared that Snowball did not qualify as an approved pet.

Following Daddy as he hurried across the kitchen, Amity reached into the right pocket of her denim jacket to reassure her passenger mouse, who had ridden out the recent action with aplomb. He cuddled into her palm appreciatively.

Grandpa and Grandma Satan hadn't left any lights on when they had gone outside to work in the garden. The day wasn't bright enough to chase all shadows from the kitchen. Now sudden sheets of rain battered the windows, and the room darkened further.

The swinging door creaked, and they went into a hallway even gloomier than the kitchen. They halted when they realized they were not alone.

The boy stood where the hall met the foyer, an archway to the right of him, stairs to the left. Backlit by watery, gray light that issued from the windows flanking the front door. A silhouette with no detail. His shoulders were slumped, his posture peculiar, somehow menacing for such a small figure.

Daddy felt the wall to his left, found a switch, and flicked on a pair of frosted ceiling fixtures, providing just enough light to reveal something that chilled Amity to the bone and for a moment left her unable to draw a breath.

The shoeless individual standing at the end of the hallway wore a uniform like the one young Rudy Starkman had worn, with a breast patch featuring a wolf with radiant yellow eyes. Whatever this thing might be, however, it for sure wasn't an ordinary boy like snotty, snarky Rudy. It looked more like a chimpanzee, in fact a lot like a chimpanzee, although not entirely. Its brow wasn't as sloped as that of a chimp, its eyes not as deeply set under a prominent brow bone, the nose not as flat or the jaw as forward thrusting as that of an ape. The creature seemed to be more of a chimp than not, with long arms and short legs and thick black body hair and finger-length toes, but its long-fingered hands were less roughly knuckled and less curled than those of a chimpanzee. Its deeply disturbing facial features were frightening and pathetic at the same time, really and truly, suggesting a human child in chimp makeup. No ape in a zoo cage had ever turned a face with such human qualities toward those who came to be amused by its antics. Amity remembered *The Island of Dr. Moreau* by H. G. Wells, where animals with human qualities had prowled the jungle, and she shuddered. Her teeth chattered, they really did, if only briefly.

This apparition stood about four feet tall and weighed ninety or a hundred pounds. If it was an exotic species of chimpanzee, its costume was bizarre. Some people put sweaters and funny hats on dogs or dressed them six ways crazy for Halloween. Maybe this was that kind of fun, but it felt different, like cruel mockery, as though someone meant to make fun of the Justice Wolves or else of this man-monkey hybrid. The beast seemed to pose with self-conceit, much as snarky Rudy Starkman had taken pride in his silly uniform, as though it believed it was admired and possessed authority.

"Maybe here is good enough," her father said, taking the key to everything from his pocket.

Before Daddy could switch on the device, the chimp-boy took three quick steps toward them and spoke. "Who is it you? Who is it you? Where dada-mama?"

Any words issuing from this creature would have stiffened the fine hairs on the nape of Amity's neck, but the inconsistent quality of its voice made what it said even more horrific, as though it must be two spirits in one husk, simultaneously aggressive and fearful, needful and wary. The raw guttural sound rose almost to a thin whine of anxiety on the word *you*.

"Get behind me," her father said, and Amity didn't hesitate to obey him.

23

Flutters of lightning purling down the foyer windows, shudders of thunder vibrating the bones of the house with greater force than before, drumrolls of rain beating across the roof . . . The hallway lights pulsed as if the power might fail.

The nightmare voice grew more insistent, sharp with suspicion. "Who is it you? Why here? Dada-mama wants you here?"

Jeffy found the beast grotesque in its uniform, an affront to creation, yet nonetheless terrifying, a hideous product of genetic engineering that revealed the depths and the cruelty to which the science and culture of this timeline descended. In his mind's ear, he heard again the officious prick in the library: *Buy the girl an approved animal, something that honors the genius of the state.* And here before them loomed the sinister product of a government in rebellion against everything—against economic sanity, against the righteous limits of authority, against freedom and human dignity, against nature itself and beauty and hope and the very idea of transcendent meaning. What was this pitiful and perhaps pitiless creature to those who owned it? Was it part pet and part guard ape, a kind of ersatz child for a childless couple, but also a slave? What strange desires preoccupied it, and what fears constrained it from acting on those desires? How deeply surrealistic and dark might be the landscape of its twisted mind?

It ventured closer, within a few feet of Jeffy, peering up at him with lantern eyes, its dark lips peeling back from teeth like the blades of chisels. "Who is it you? Tell now! Tell now who is!"

Lacking a weapon, scanning the hall for one and seeing nothing suitable, Jeffy said, "A friend. We're friends of dada-mama. Who are you?"

Scowling, chewing on its lower lip, the creature considered what it had been told, but it did not reply. Its stare was as hard and shiny and dark as polished obsidian.

Inevitably, Jeffy thought of news stories from the past decade, incidents involving chimpanzee attacks on people who kept them as pets. The animals were uncannily quick. Far stronger, pound for pound, than any human being. Capable of sudden rages for which their previous benign behavior had not prepared their human companions. One man had been blinded, and his testicles had been torn off. The friend of a woman who kept a hundred-pound chimp had all her fingers bitten off, her eyes gouged out, and her face torn off in less than two minutes of unimaginable terror.

"Me is name Good Boy. Me loves dada-mama." It cocked its head at Amity where she sheltered behind Jeffy. "Good Boy think you not belongs here." The creature hissed its judgment so venomously that Jeffy steeled himself for an attack.

At the back of the house, a window shattered.

Good Boy's attention at once shifted from Jeffy and Amity to the kitchen. Its nostrils flared and it bared its formidable teeth. With a fierce shriek, the monster flung itself past them, slammed through the swinging door and out of sight.

Jeffy grabbed his daughter's hand, and they dashed into the foyer.

A pane in the front door shattered, clear blades of glass slicing through the air, chips like sleet glittering in arcs. As the sparkling debris splashed on the floor, the rataplan of rain grew louder. A man reached inside to feel for the deadbolt thumb turn.

Before the police could force entry, Jeffy and Amity raced up the stairs, desperate for a fourteen-second haven.

A shrill, inhuman cry arose from the back of the house, Good Boy in a bestial rage. No men cried out in response and no shots were fired, because the objects of the miscreation's fury were not the authorities but instead the two intruders who, in its excitement and bad judgment, it had allowed farther into dada-mama's house.

When they reached the landing and started up the second flight of stairs, Jeffy heard the creature slam through the swinging door between the kitchen and the hall, and then the slap of its feet on the wood floor. By the time they crossed the topmost step, he could tell by sound alone that Good Boy was gaining on them, keening as it came, and he dared not look back.

Just past the head of the stairs were a door to the left and another to the right. He pushed Amity into the room on the right, followed her. A bedroom. No lock, just the simple latch bolt that a twist of the knob would open. He braced his back against the closed door, which wasn't flimsy Masonite but a solid-core construct, so it might withstand assault.

An instant later, Good Boy crashed into the far side, yattering incoherently, rattling the knob, pounding hard, now squealing like a soulless thing that fed on the souls of others. A sudden silence. It hadn't retreated, merely backed off. Abruptly it challenged the barrier again, threw itself across the hall with tremendous force, the door quaking-cracking as if with the impact of three hundred pounds instead of at most a hundred. Heedless of injury to itself, the fiend cried out not in pain but in fury at the failure of the attempt, and then it tried again.

The door bucked, and Jeffy was jolted harder than before, an inch-wide gap opening along the jamb. Good Boy's shrieks were louder and more ferocious, but Jeffy pushed back with everything he had, closing the gap. And here came Amity with a straight-backed chair taken from the vanity. She knew what needed to be done, and she had the courage to do it. She was no coward, never had been. She tilted the chair, jammed the headrail under the knob, bracing the door, a kid with the right stuff.

As Jeffy stepped away from the fortified barrier, men shouted to one another, and footsteps boomed on the stairs. Police and their black-clad overseers were coming fast. In spite of the chair, they would break down the door because they were trained how to do it, break it down or shoot their way into the room. They wouldn't care if he and Amity were wounded. This wasn't the America where law enforcement had rules of engagement and answered to police-review boards, where the vast majority of those who became cops did so to serve and protect; this was an America where fascists didn't pretend to be antifascists, didn't conceal their faces behind black masks, operated openly and boldly; this was an America ruled by brute intimidation, harassment, and violence.

Trembling, his emotional compass just one degree south of panic, mentally cursing himself for having consented to Amity's request to see her mother—who was not in fact her mother, but a stranger, a Michelle from a different Earth, another planet—Jeffy fumbled in the wrong jacket pocket for the key to everything.

Agitated voices in the hallway. The doorknob rattled.

He found the right pocket, the fearsome device.

Amity stayed at his side, her left hand on his arm.

Someone kicked hard, and the chair clattered against the knob, but the door held.

Jeffy pressed the home circle on the device.

The screen remained black. Maybe four seconds. That's what it had previously taken to activate. Just four seconds.

Good Boy shrieking.

Amity cried out, "Dad!"

Beyond the rain-streaked window, the creature bounced up and down on the porch roof, his shadow leaping with him as lightning flared, capering like the freakish jester in the court of a mad monarch in a tale about an evil kingdom.

Impatiently, Jeffy pressed the home circle again before he realized that the screen had filled with soft gray light. It went black. He had turned it off.

"Shit!"

As someone kicked the door harder and some part of the bracing chair cracked, Jeffy pressed the home circle.

Another four-second wait.

The window glass exploded into the room, and Good Boy clambered across the sill, eyes wild and teeth bared, dripping rain, oblivious of the shards of glass still bristling in the frame.

"Daddy!"

The hideous mascot of the Justice Wolves had smashed the window with a fireplace poker perhaps taken from another bedroom. Now the hateful thing sprang at Jeffy, holding the pointed brass poker in both hands, like a spear with which it intended to stab through his gut and shatter his spine.

Once more, the screen turned gray, but there were no buttons yet.

Jeffy dodged, and the goblin drove the poker into the footboard of the bed, splitting a handsome inlaid panel of oak burl, but also colliding hard with his intended target. Jeffy stumbled and fell. The key to everything slipped from his hand and tumbled across the carpet, as he and Amity simultaneously said, "Shit!"

 24

Good Boy was a total demonic whack job, like some orc straight out of the bowels of Mordor, not only physically horrific, but also a mental mess, neither as smart as a boy nor as intuitive as an ape. In that moment when Daddy fell and the fabulous key flipped across the floor to the nightstand, the freak could have attacked them, strong as it was, could have bitten them and gouged out their eyes and torn off their ears in a murderous frenzy, but it was fixated on the fireplace poker, which it had driven clean through the footboard of the bed and now struggled to extract. You might have thought this rain-soaked hairy mutant must be familiar with the legend of good King Arthur and imagined that the poker stuck in the wood was its version of the magic sword Excalibur locked in stone, with a throne as the reward for anyone who was able to pull it free. Good Boy worked the poker up and down, back and forth, spitting, hissing, shrieking like a wild animal, but also cursing like a boy who had fallen in with the wrong crowd and given himself to all kinds of vices that would have shocked dada-mama.

Such noise, cacophony. The hard rush of rain and the crack of thunder, the boot kicking and kicking the defiant door, someone shouting "Police," the transspecies laboratory-born thing snarling and shrieking . . .

In the grip of a terror that motivated rather than paralyzed her, heart knocking so hard that her vision pulsed, Amity went after the key and plucked it off the carpet and turned to her father. Daddy got to his feet as the bracing chair cracked and came apart.

The door flew open, knocking the remains of the chair aside, and the big uniformed man at the threshold, who had done all the kicking, froze for a moment, as if surprised by his own success. A smaller guy pushed past the kicker, one of the thugs who dressed in soft, black fatigues. He had the face of a weasel, the eyes of a snake, and a pistol in hand.

The three buttons glowed on the screen, the entire multiverse awaiting her, infinite worlds with infinite dangers.

"Blue," Daddy said, which was labeled HOME, and though the goon in black surely didn't know what the key to everything could do, he said, "Drop it," and aimed his pistol at her.

Daddy reached out and put a hand on her shoulder as her finger descended toward blue. The sudden collapse of the chair and the door crashing open had broken the ape-boy's obsession with the poker stuck in the footboard. Screeching, it flung itself at Amity and her father. The thing clutched Daddy's arm to pull him down, and Amity pressed the button.

They had thought perhaps skin needed to be touching skin—or mouse fur—in order for a passenger to accompany the holder of the key. However, Daddy's hand was on her jacket, and Good Boy's hand clutched Daddy's sleeve, and Snowball remained in Amity's pocket when the bedroom vanished, leaving all of them seeming almost to float in a white void, a snowy nothingness, glimmering flakes passing *through* them, like radiation that they could see.

Being penetrated by snow scared the bejesus out of the freak, and though it held fast to Daddy with one hand, it covered its eyes with its other hand and curled its lip over its lower teeth and issued a miserable wail of terror.

As before, with a *whoosh*, the veil of light blew away. They were in the bedroom again. Not exactly the same bedroom. No police, no thug in black, no ruined chair, no shattered window. No storm darkened the sky. The furniture was placed pretty much as before, but the pieces were more harmonious and the fabrics subtler than those in the bedroom from which they had just come. Whoever lived here in Earth Prime had much better taste than dada-mama, whose decor had favored a carnival of chintz and plaids and damask to match the riotous colors of their English garden.

In the sudden silence, Good Boy lowered its hand from its face and opened its eyes. However limited its intelligence and therefore its imagination might be, the freak knew at once that something big had happened, that it was in the same room yet not the same, that it was in a different reality. Baffled, it glanced at the door, where no chair lay broken, where no cop or guy in black loomed menacingly. It looked at the window, which hadn't been shattered, beyond which no rain fell and no lightning flashed, and slowly its expression of astonishment soured.

As far as Amity was concerned, Good Boy really and truly didn't deserve its name. In her experience, the freak had been bad to the bone. Maybe the fault lay with the idiot scientists who played God, Cuisinarting human and chimpanzee genes. Or maybe poor nurturing had turned the thing bad. After all, dada-mama, the geriatric couple who had attacked Amity and her father in the English garden, were nasty pieces of work; as Good Boy's owners or guardians or adopted parents or whatever the hell they were, they didn't seem to be the kind who would strive to ensure that a young mutant would be raised with fine manners and morals. Indeed, as Good Boy realized, however dimly, the extent of the change that had occurred, the beast didn't politely express its puzzlement and request an explanation, but instead went batshit crazy.

25

Jeffy Coltrane had never claimed to be psychic or especially intuitive, and he never would. However, as the ape-boy stood in bewilderment, slowly turning its lumpy head left and right, Jeffy knew, as surely as he had ever known anything, that the creature would not be humbled or experience a conversion to pacifism because of its miraculous experience. A response to their abrupt relocation was building in the beast, and it was going to be more like critical mass being achieved in a nuclear bomb than like crisp brown bread suddenly popping out of a toaster.

As the pressure built in Good Boy, Jeffy stepped to the nearest nightstand and yanked open the drawer. A low-profile box of Kleenex. A paperback of a John Grisham novel. A transparent container holding a dental bite guard. A tube of lubricating gel in anticipation of a romantic moment.

Good Boy began to make a thin keening sound of deep emotional distress.

On Earth 1.13, from which they had so recently escaped, all the guns were probably in the possession of the fascist government. Here on Earth Prime, the FBI said that four out of ten Americans kept at least one gun for home defense, and a major pro-gun organization said it was five out of ten. Because people never answered such surveys truthfully, Jeffy figured it was more like seven out of ten, with the other three relying on baseball bats, Tasers, pepper spray, faithful dogs, and sharp-tongued ridicule to deal with dangerous intruders.

Scrambling across the bed, he didn't know whose house this was, but he hoped that they were in the 40 or 50 or 70 percent thought to possess a firearm. Many people who owned a pistol kept it in a nightstand drawer. For safety, they should keep it in a locked gun safe that opened quickly when a four-digit code was entered on a keypad. If the residents of this house were safety conscious, Jeffy was screwed.

Good Boy didn't literally blow its top, but its sudden shriek was so explosive that it sounded as if the crown of its skull had detached as violently as a failing heat shield on a space shuttle reentering Earth's atmosphere. And the beast was off like a rocket, trying to quell its fear with rage. It streaked first to the vanity, where it swept a small silver tray and three perfume bottles to the floor, and then a handled mirror, a porcelain vase, a decorative tissue box, a set of hairbrushes. It snatched up a straight-backed chair from the vanity, one similar to the chair that Amity had used to brace the door in that other bedroom. Good Boy scampered to the window and swung the chair, intent on breaking the glass that, in a parallel universe, it had smashed with a fireplace poker from the outside. As Amity hurried to the door of the adjoining bathroom, evidently intending to take sanctuary there, the lower half of the double-hung window dissolved, fragments spilling onto the sill and out onto the porch roof.

All of that happened in the time Jeffy took to scramble across the bed, jerk open the second nightstand, and seize a pistol from among the contents. He found the safety, clicked it off, and turned with the weapon in a two-handed grip.

The rain-soaked creature had discarded the chair and escaped through the window, onto the porch roof. Now it capered in a circle, long shaggy arms raised, shaking its fists as it searched the sky. Maybe it was demanding to know what had happened to the storm, why it remained wet while the entire day had gone dry. Jeffy had no way of knowing what this monster was thinking any more than he could predict what it might do next.

He didn't dare fire at Good Boy while it was outside. A stray round might hit someone across the street.

What the infuriated beast did next, after just half a minute on the porch roof, was plunge into the room again, panting and hooting, neither chimp nor boy, as alien as anything that might step out of a spaceship. It was so quick, Jeffy couldn't track it with a pistol. Running on all fours, the beast shot across the room, through the open door, and vanished into the hall, its cries diminishing as it raced to the back of the house, where it fell silent.

Evidently, no one was home. Had people been in residence, they would have reacted to the uproar by now.

Amity started toward her father, and he said, "Get back, shut yourself in the bathroom."

"Daddy, don't go out there," she pleaded as he moved toward the hall door.

"If it isn't gone, I need to find it and deal with it."

"Don't go out there," she begged, her voice breaking.

"If it's gone, then we'll go, too, we'll go straight home and lock the doors and hunker down for the duration. Bathroom doors have locks, Amity. *Now get in there and lock it!*"

He had never before raised his voice to her, so when he raised it this time, she flinched as if she'd been slapped. But she retreated into the bathroom and closed the door.

Truth be known, he didn't want to leave this room and find Good Boy. A freak hunt had about as much appeal as handling a live cobra while playing Russian roulette with a revolver. He wanted to wait here until the police arrived. Someone might have heard the breaking glass. In the brief time the creature was raging on the porch roof, someone might have seen it. The police would be on the way.

Then he realized that the last thing he and Amity dared attempt was to explain to the cops what they were doing here in a stranger's house, why this bedroom had been vandalized. Talk of parallel worlds and an ape-boy hybrid would get them a psychiatric evaluation unless they proved their story with the key to everything. But admitting that Ed Harkenbach had left the device in their care would bring John Falkirk back into their lives with a vengeance, he who had NSA credentials and eyes the gray of steel and a piercing stare that dissected your soul.

Assisting spooky Ed had once seemed amusing, a bit of a lark. Now Jeffy abruptly recognized the dire legal consequences. If the authorities arrested him, convicted him, and sent him to prison, maybe the government wouldn't allow his parents to have custody of Amity. Even in the good old USA, government could be vindictive, using the legal system as a weapon. If Amity were sent to an institution or placed in a home with abusive foster parents . . .

He stepped into the hallway.

26

Hiding in the bathroom, sitting on the closed lid of the toilet, Amity felt stupid and inadequate and scared. Snowball must have sensed her fear, for he shivered continuously as she held him in her cupped hands.

The key to everything lay on the counter beside the nearby sink, and she wasn't going to let the adventurous mouse anywhere near it.

"This is all because of you," she told him, though she knew that was unfair. One of the good things about a mouse was that he wasn't as perceptive as a dog; he didn't know when you were unjustly chastising him or that you were chastising him at all.

In fact, this was entirely her fault, really and truly, because she had wanted to see her mother and have a chance to bring Michelle back to this world. If she could have done that—wow—it would have been like raising Lazarus, except that her mother wasn't dead like Lazarus, and except that Lazarus was a man who was brought back to life with a miracle, while her mother was a woman who would have been brought back by science, not by anyone super-natural. Actually, now that she had a moment to think about it, the Lazarus analogy made no sense, and she felt even more stupid and inadequate because she had entertained it even for a moment.

Her fear was increasing, too, because every second without Daddy was another second in which he might be killed. He was her world. If he died, she couldn't go on, she really couldn't, because what happened to him would be her fault. She wouldn't kill herself or anything like that, because suicide was wrong. She would just become anorexic and wither away, until she was skin and bones, until she was dust that a cold wind would blow into Hell. If Hell existed. She was of two minds about that.

Daddy had been gone almost a minute. Hell was right here. She'd already spent almost a minute in Hell.

═══ 27

Pistol at the ready, stepping into the hallway, Jeffy saw the ladder at the farther end from the stairs, a counterweighted folding model attached to a ceiling trapdoor from which dangled a pull cord. Good Boy had leaped and seized the cord and pulled down the ladder. The creature had climbed up where perhaps it had in days past spent time haunting that raftered space in the version of this house that existed on Earth 1.13.

Jeffy had no intention of following the freak into that dark, higher realm. But if he lifted the lowest segment of the ladder and gave it a shove, it would automatically fold upward, and the trap would close behind it. Good Boy could still push it open from above, though that was harder than opening it from below and would take more time. The noise would alert them that the beast was coming.

And maybe the thing didn't want to come down. Maybe it wished to stay up there in the dusty dark, with spiders friendlier than the people it knew, up where it had retreated when dada-mama scolded or punished it. The creature's mental landscape must be black and gray, brightened alternately by the lightning of fear and a feeble foxfire of hope never to be fulfilled, a bleak terrain of endless loneliness and confusion. It was forever an outsider, natural to none of the worlds in the multiverse, belonging not even on Earth 1.13, where arrogant men and cruel science had conjured it into being.

Although Good Boy was fearsome, when Jeffy considered its life as an unloved pet or slave—or whatever its owners considered it—pity stirred in him. As he lifted the lowest segment of the ladder and then watched it fold up automatically, he thought, *If a man can't understand a monster's suffering, then he's something of a monster himself.*

Which was when, from out of a shadowy room to his left, Good Boy attacked him.

28

Sitting on the lid of the toilet, with Snowball shivering in her trembling hands, such a small and helpless mouse, Amity realized that, if Daddy should die, letting herself wither away from anorexia was just as rotten a moral decision as suicide. It would be giving up. Giving up was for the weak of spirit, for those who couldn't grasp that the world was filled with meaning, that everyone had a purpose he or she needed to discover and fulfill. Daddy himself taught her as much, and Daddy didn't lie.

If something terrible happened to her father, she wouldn't give up. Instead she'd use the key to everything to search an infinity of worlds for another Jeffy Coltrane, one who always wanted a child and never had one, a Jeffy Coltrane whom she could love with all her heart, whom she could make proud of her by being the strong and honest person he had helped her to become in this world. That was how tragedy was transformed into triumph in the very best fantasy stories, and Amity was as sure as she could be that she could make it happen if that became her only hope of happiness.

Which was when she heard the gunshot.

=== **29**

Intimidating war cries and bold assaults weren't the beast's only tactics, as it proved with the deception of the attic and the silence with which it watched Jeffy from a shadowy spare bedroom. When, with a twang of its springs, the ladder began to fold upward, the creature launched into the hall, a quick dark phantom in Jeffy's peripheral vision. As he pivoted toward the threat, his assailant clarified into a bloody-eyed menace, all muscle and bone and bared teeth, clutching hands and long-toed grasping feet, its deranged-child face melded with the primal features of an infuriated ape, driven by a hatred long suppressed.

The impact knocked Jeffy backward. He slammed into the wall, crackles of pain branching up his spine and across his back, as if his bones were brittling into ruin, the dream-strange face of Good Boy inches from his. Its breath was rancid, its teeth wet, as it shrieked in triumph.

Had Good Boy been all chimpanzee, Jeffy Coltrane might have been grievously wounded already and in a moment dead; perhaps its hybrid nature rendered the thing less of an instinctive fighter. He'd somehow gotten a hand around its throat to restrain it at least for a few precious seconds. More importantly, he held fast to the pistol. Chisel-edged teeth snapped an inch short of his nose; the powerful hands clasped his head as though to crush it between them like an eggshell or to hold it steady for a series of savage bites. He brought the gun up between the creature's arms and jammed the muzzle under the hairy chin and squeezed the trigger.

== 30

In the master bathroom, when she heard the gunshot, Amity sprang to her feet, and a chill pierced her from head to foot. Her hands suddenly were so cold that, by contrast, little Snowball felt as though he'd just come out of an oven, as hot as a freshly baked muffin. She tucked him in a jacket pocket and snatched the key to everything from the counter beside the sink, careful not to touch the dark screen, because maybe the RETURN button would transport her back to dismal old Earth 1.13, where the über–bad guys were probably standing around with their stupid mouths hanging open, wondering how a man, a girl, and a monkey could disappear before their eyes.

Her feet felt as if they were frozen in blocks of ice, and her legs were stiff with cold, although shaky, as she approached the bathroom door and touched the thumb turn of the lock. Her hands had gone as pale as ectoplasm, the stuff ghosts were made of. She didn't dare look in the mirror, afraid that she might collapse at the sight of her bloodless death-mask face.

The shot had scared her, but what terrified her more was that there had been *only one shot*. Good Boy was crazy quick and crazy strong and just plain crazy, so it didn't seem possible that her father could have killed it with a single shot. Probably not with just two, either, maybe with three, almost surely with four, but never with just one bullet. So maybe the unthinkable had happened, and though it was unthinkable, she couldn't stop thinking it. The horror of it froze her. She was about to scream louder than Good Boy, and then her father said, "Amity, open the door."

Terror could make an idiot of you, especially when you thought you had lost everything. Instead of unlocking the door and throwing it open, Amity stupidly asked if Good Boy was dead, and when her father said that, yes, it was dead, she said, "Who are you?"

He said, "It's me."

Amity knew perfectly well—perfectly, perfectly—that Good Boy had a supercreepy voice and bad grammar and terrible syntax, knew that such a half-baked mutant couldn't convincingly imitate Daddy's voice, but she was cold and pale and scared, so she said, "How do I know it's you?"

After a hesitation, he said, "You want a dog, but you've got a mouse for practice, which was your idea, not mine. I'd have bought you a puppy."

She hesitated, but only maybe two seconds, to collect herself before she opened the door. She and her father were still in the soup, a real witch's brew, which meant she had to stay strong, not be a wuss like those fainthearted girls in fantasy stories who made her want to barf. She didn't dare cry, not even with relief, and she had to keep her spine stiff, stay brave, not only because that was necessary to survive, but also because she had a reputation to protect.

When she opened the door, Daddy said, "You okay, pumpkin?"

He hadn't called her "pumpkin" in maybe two years, since she had stopped being a full-on child, but she let that slide. She gave him two thumbs up. "You got it with just one shot. I knew you could get that crazy monkey piece of shit."

She startled herself by using the *s* word, but Daddy didn't call her on it. He looked kind of pale, too, and his eyes were strange, as if he was surprised that it was Good Boy who was dead.

With a nonchalance that astonished Amity, her hand not even trembling, she returned the key to everything, as if to say, *You did right to trust me with it.* Her father shrugged as if to say, *I knew I could count on you*, and he put the device in a jacket pocket.

She expected a police car to shrill in the distance. Continued silence suggested that no one had heard the glass break or seen the beast on the porch roof.

Nevertheless, her father grabbed her hand. "Let's get out of here."

Amity wanted to hold tight to his hand forever, but of course they had to eat and use the bathroom, so sooner or later she would have to let go of him. In fact, it happened as soon as they reached the head of the stairs.

A foul smell told her that she would see the remains of Good Boy in the hall if she glanced toward the back of the house. She held her breath, didn't look, and plunged down the stairs close behind her father.

She thought about their fingerprints, but there wasn't time to wipe down everything they had touched. Anyway, her prints had never been taken by anyone, and though Daddy's thumbprint was on file at the DMV, he hadn't killed a person, only a monster, so it was best just to take their chances.

Daddy turned away from the front door. "Out the back."

They hurried through the house, across the porch, and into the yard, which lacked the English garden and the birdbath so prominent on Earth 1.13. Neither was there an elderly couple bent on mayhem.

But there was sun, glorious sun, and no rain.

Beside the detached garage, a gate opened into an alley, where they didn't encounter a black van or creepy guys dressed like Nazi ninjas or any brainwashed young boys in Justice Wolves uniforms.

As they passed through town, they saw no stores that had gone out of business. The streets were busy with locals and tourists, and a general air of prosperity lay over Suavidad Beach.

They were home. They were safe.

"We have to stop at the library," her father said.

"What?" The suggestion alarmed her. "Why? That's where the creep said Snowball wasn't an appropriate animal."

"That wasn't in this world, remember. That was . . . elsewhere."

"Oh. Yeah. That's right, huh?" She still felt uneasy.

"We need to check out Ed Harkenbach's book, *Infinite Worlds*."

"You had it already. What happened to it?"

"I dropped it somewhere, maybe scrambling up a garden wall or running from Good Boy. It's been a pretty physical day, in case you hadn't noticed. They'll probably have a copy in this library, too."

The woman with the Mrs. Frankenstein hair wasn't at the front desk. The librarian on duty, Mrs. Rockwell, was the wife of Vince Rockwell, who taught history and coached the high school football team.

No faintest scent of burning paper tainted the air. The aisles between the stacks were better lighted than those in the Library of the Weird. A copy of *Infinite Worlds: Parallel Universes and Quantum Reality* waited where she and her father had found it before.

This time they didn't informally borrow the book. They took it to the checkout desk, and Daddy presented his library card, and Mrs. Rockwell processed everything properly while chatting about the weather and the latest foolishness in Sacramento. She liked unique earrings, and today she wore a dangly pair of brightly colored enamel parrots.

Mrs. Rockwell seemed totally *normal*. Amity loved how normal the librarian seemed.

On this beautiful sunny afternoon, the twelfth of April, they had found again the world as it was supposed to be. They were home. They were safe.

THE VISITOR IN THE DEAD OF NIGHT

In more than one world, he has done a great wrong. When he'd been a boy, his mother had taught him always to do the right thing, but he had done the wrong thing with the best of intentions. The wrong is so enormous that he can't rectify it in all the worlds where it has happened, but he hopes to do a small good here and there to honor the memory of his mother.

Now, in the early morning hours of the eleventh day of April, the same night that he also visits libraries in search of what he needs to know about the Coltranes, he journeys to the oak woods past the end of Shadow Canyon Lane. An hour before dawn, he travels across worlds from the trees around a clearing to the same trees around the same clearing elsewhere, in that *specific* elsewhere in which Jeffrey Coltrane legally dissolved his marriage to Michelle because she vanished seven years earlier. The existence of this inflatable tent, which he watches from the cover of the oaks, is evidence that there is an Edwin Harkenbach hiding out from the forces of evil in this Suavidad Beach, just as in certain others.

Further evidence is the aroma of strong coffee in the absence of a campfire. The declining moon gives off a smoky light like a sorcerer's brew steaming from a hot chalice, and the visitor's eyes take time to adapt to the witchy light before he is able to discern a jerry-rigged battery-powered hot plate in front of the tent. In more than one world, various Harkenbachs have invented this clever appliance to provide a favorite beverage without risking a fire in such dry land.

From within the tent comes whistling that only Edwin Harkenbach would attempt: a signature passage from a Mozart concerto, K. 453. Mozart had once purchased a starling that could whistle K. 453. But in none of the worlds that Harkenbach inhabits is he as talented as the bird.

The visitor doesn't know if this version of the scientist has interacted with Jeffrey Coltrane, but the possibility is real. Everywhere that he is known to exist, Harkenbach is a sociable man, though in some cases more distressed about his situation than in others. If he and Coltrane are acquainted here, the ground might already have been laid for the success of the visitor's plan.

The visitor, who is Ed Harkenbach from a parallel world, could approach this version of himself and collude with him to ensure the success of his mission here, but he has no intention of doing that. In some worlds, sad to say, there are versions of himself who have come unglued because of what he's done and because of being hunted by agents of the shadow state. It's too distressing—and potentially dangerous—for this Ed to come face-to-face with one of those Eds.

Before the Harkenbach on this world might throw back the tent flap and step into sight, the visiting Ed makes his way through the woods, which are familiar to him, and proceeds downslope to Shadow Canyon Lane. This neighborhood lacks streetlamps, and the last hour of night suits him well as he walks past the widely separated, dark houses.

The Coltranes, father and daughter and mouse, are early risers. Their bungalow is the only residence with light in some windows.

The visitor quietly makes his way around the side of the house to one of the kitchen windows. Together, father and daughter are making breakfast.

Jeffrey is dressed for the day, but Amity still wears Rocket Raccoon pajamas. He is cracking eggs into a bowl, evidently with the intention of scrambling them. The girl is preparing bread for the toaster, trimming the crusts off the slices for herself but leaving those for her father in their natural condition.

The visitor is thrilled to think how profoundly Jeffrey's and Amity's lives will be changed within the next few days. The key to everything has shown him horrific worlds of blood and terror and catastrophe. Now he looks forward to what he can bring into the lives of these two innocents.

Dawn will soon brighten the horizon on this eleventh day of April.

PART 3

INFINITE HOPES, INFINITE THREATS

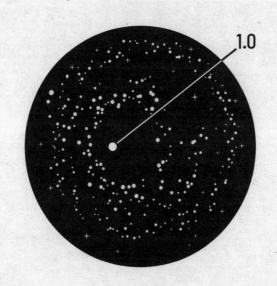

31

The sight of the little stone house with the slate roof, in the shadows of the breeze-stirred palms, filled Amity with nothing less than joy, really and truly. Her heart seemed to swell, and she felt impossibly light, like a helium-filled balloon, as if her feet were barely touching the ground, as if instead she were *gliding* up the flagstone walkway.

There wasn't a Daddy Doppelgänger mowing the lawn. Birds sat on the fence, singing as if to welcome her, and a cute little lizard skittered up the walkway, leading her home.

Inside, she rushed to her room. It wasn't empty, as it had been on Earth 1.13. Her furniture stood where it belonged. Anime posters. Yellow walls and white ceiling, instead of everything dreary beige. In this world, she had been born and lived, and a snotty boy named Rudy Starkman—in a uniform for wannabe fascists or communists or whatever—had never existed.

She extracted Snowball from her pocket and took him to his enormous cage. Safe within that wire fortress, he scampered to his water dish, took a drink, pooped in a corner where he usually left his little pellets, and then went to his exercise wheel. He ran like a maniac, his face squinched up strangely, more intense than usual, as if he might be stressed out and trying to find his bliss again.

Of course Snowball's brain was too tiny for him to have a clue that he had been to another world and back. Nevertheless, he might be somewhat psychic and aware of the extreme emotional chaos that Amity had endured. Animals often seemed to have a sixth sense, or maybe it was just instinct.

"I won't put you through that again," she promised the furry white marathoner. "But just remember, you're the one who activated the key to everything and parked your bottom on the RETURN button."

As she stepped out of her room, she was skewered by a needle of paranoia, suddenly certain that Good Boy waited in the hallway for her. She didn't have hackles, not like dogs did, but the nape of her neck prickled; and if she'd been equipped with hackles, they would have been standing up straight and stiff.

She knew Good Boy was dead. Daddy had said so. Evidently, she was suffering post-traumatic stress. She would probably be looking for bogeymen under the bed for weeks and weeks.

Not that she would let her father know she was still spooked. Mother—Michelle—had been afraid of losing her identity, destiny, dreams, or something, and she had run out on her husband and child. Amity was never going to run from anything, unless it had big teeth and there was murder in its eyes. She didn't want her father to entertain the slightest doubt about her.

She heard him in the kitchen and went to see what he might be doing. He was sitting at the breakfast table with Ed Harkenbach's book and a bottle of beer.

The key to everything lay on the table.

Indicating her father's Heineken, Amity said, "I'll have one, too."

"Yeah, okay, as long as the word *Coke* is on the label."

She retrieved a can of the parent-approved beverage from the refrigerator and sat at the table. "Why're you reading that?"

"To find answers to some questions, if there are any answers."

"Like what questions?"

"The key doesn't have a charging port. There must be a battery, but there's nothing that opens so you can replace it. What happens if you're on some other world and this gismo goes dead?"

"Keep reading. Maybe the book tells you."

"Well, it's not a book about the key to everything. It doesn't have diagrams. Ed hadn't invented the damn thing when he wrote it. This is all about theory. I have to take the theory and extrapolate from it, think how it might be practically applied, and the strain is giving me a migraine."

After a hesitation, she said, "Are we going to use the key again?"

He frowned. "No. No, no. Too dangerous."

"But just maybe we will."

"Never."

"Never?"

"Never."

"Then why do you need to know about the battery?"

"Just in case."

"In case what?"

"In case . . ." He exhaled as much exasperation as air, and he inhaled resignation. "In case, in some kind of crisis, we *have* to use it again."

"What crisis?"

He marked his place in the book with a jacket flap and set the volume aside.

Amity thought he was going to go totally adult on her and deliver a gentle lecture regarding an aspect of life about which he thought she was clueless. Most likely, she would already understand what he strove earnestly to explain to her. She would pretend to be gradually enlightened, until he was proud of her and felt that he had fulfilled his fatherly duty. He was such a good, sweet man that Amity found these sessions endearing rather than frustrating. And of course maybe 20 percent of the time she *was* clueless, and he *did* enlighten her, so it was always worth really and truly listening.

This time, however, she misjudged his intention.

After setting the book aside and taking a long pull on his beer, he stared at the key to everything, his brow furrowed, his face drawn with worry.

"What crisis?" Amity repeated.

"One crisis could be John Falkirk. From the National Security Agency. With his helicopters and fleet of Suburbans and armed search teams."

"He didn't find anything," Amity said. "He went away."

"Yeah, but someone is going to discover Good Boy's body and call the police. It's like right out of *The Twilight Zone*, a chimp-human hybrid in a bizarre uniform. Falkirk didn't storm into town before first consulting with local authorities, and although they won't know what this is about, they'll have been told to call Falkirk if anything unusual happens."

"Good Boy is kind of unusual," she conceded.

"And maybe someone saw us running away from that house. Though even if no one saw us, Falkirk's likely to come back here and seal off the street and interrogate everyone on Shadow Canyon Lane again. He seemed sure Ed Harkenbach would have entrusted his thingumabob to someone here."

"We can fake him out again."

"Can we? Not if he takes . . . extreme measures."

Amity had read enough stories involving evil kings and vermin-infested dungeons to suspect what her father feared. "Torture."

"They won't go that far. Maybe some kind of drug cocktail that makes us tell the truth. Or they'll arrest me and hold me without bail, as a national-security threat or something."

"We'd be separated?"

He met her eyes and held her stare. "I won't let that happen."

Of course he meant what he said, but he was just one man. The government was millions.

Daddy picked up his beer once more.

Amity was of an age when solace was taken from sugar that had *not* been fermented. She swilled an unladylike quantity of Cherry Coke before she spoke. "You said 'one crisis could be Falkirk.' What's another one?"

He turned the empty bottle in his hand, studying it as if it were an arcane object found among a wizard's magical instruments, containing the answer to all mysteries. "It's not a crisis as much as a moral dilemma. And it's less of a moral dilemma than it is a problem of the heart."

"Well, I guess I know what it is."

"I guess you do," he said.

"You still love her."

"I always will."

Amity pushed her empty Coke can aside. "Then let's go get her."

His stare was as piercing as it was tender with sympathy. "She wouldn't be likely to leave her life there, sweetheart. Besides, she's gone down a dark road. Someone broke her spirit. Maybe that husband of hers. She's Michelle, but she's not the same person. She would never understand this world or want to live in it."

Amity nodded. "Yeah, okay, that's the way she is in Good Boy's weird universe. But there's like a million billion others. More than that. Some of them must be as safe as ours. Lots are probably better places, safer. Somewhere she's the *right* Michelle, and she's alone, and she needs us."

"We can't spend our lives looking for the right Michelle. It would be living on wishes, and if we feed ourselves with nothing but wishes, we starve. You lost your mother once. Losing her again and again . . ." He shook his head. "Honey, you're a strong girl, but nobody could endure a hundred losses like that—or even fifty, or twenty—without being changed for the worse, forever." He shifted his attention to the key to everything. The sorrow in Daddy's voice saddened Amity. "I know *I* couldn't handle it, sweetheart. Hoping so hard only to have the hope dashed again and again. Anyway, it's too dangerous. You already saw how dangerous it is."

"Then why did you mention it?"

"Mention what?"

"The other crisis, moral dilemma, problem of the heart."

"To help you understand. Now that we might soon be back on Falkirk's radar, we have to keep the key nearby at all times, in case we're cornered or in some kind of jam. It's the ultimate method of escape. But at the same time, I have to be sure you won't ever take it and use it yourself."

"Go off to some crazy world on my own? Why would I?"

"To find a version of your mother who will love you and come here to live with us."

"I wouldn't." She bristled a little, even though she knew the bristling was calculated. "I'm not stupid, you know."

"You're far from stupid."

"Besides, I never disobey you about anything important."

"No, you don't. And you wouldn't mean to disobey. But 'the heart is deceitful above all things.'"

She felt herself on the verge of tears, which made no sense, unless on some deep level, below her conscious awareness, she had hoped to do just what he warned her against—use the key, by herself, to find a mother she was meant to have—and now mourned the loss of that hope. To fend off the grief that threatened her and to defend her image as being mature beyond her years, she repeated his words with a slight note of mockery, though the sound of her voice dismayed her. "'The heart is deceitful above all things.' What's that mean, anyway?"

"The mind and the heart—intellect and emotions, facts and feelings. They're both important. But to live well, we need to make decisions based on logic and reason *modified* by emotion. If we're guided only or even largely by emotion . . . Well, the heart often wants what it doesn't really need, and sometimes it wants what it shouldn't have, something with the potential to ruin your life. It wants something so intensely that we find it easy to do what the heart wants even if we know it's reckless."

She realized that he had, after all, gone totally adult on her and delivered a gentle lecture. In this case, it concerned something that she'd never thought about, but she knew what he said was true as soon as she heard it.

She also understood that the truth of his advice might not be enough to ensure that she followed it. She could have lived with the emptiness of being without a mother. Once the possibility of finding Michelle became real, however, the emptiness deteriorated into an ache that wanted relief.

Nevertheless, she would try hard to remember that the heart was deceitful. She would make every effort to be smart about the risk associated with the key to everything and respectful of Daddy's counsel.

When she found herself staring at the device as it lay there on the table, she realized that her father was watching her, that she would promise never to use the key, that he would both believe her and doubt her, that she would be ashamed of the heart's yearning she couldn't repress, that he would be aware of her shame and know it was perhaps insufficient to ensure her obedience.

The relationship between a father and daughter was humongously complex, as delicate as it was strong, in some ways as unsettling as it was wonderful.

She could only dimly imagine how complicated, how demanding and fulfilling, would be their relationship when they were not just a family of two, but a family of three, intact.

===== 32

When the owner of the house came home from work and found the dead thing in the upstairs hall, 911 had dispatched officers in answer to her call. The police had phoned John Falkirk, and he had relieved them of jurisdiction.

Constance Yardley, the homeowner, was a fifty-year-old English teacher. Falkirk didn't like her. She was a throwback to a time when teachers had spines like drill sergeants. She taught in a private school where disciplinarians like her could still crack a kid's knuckles with a ruler and openly berate a lazy student and even issue failing grades, yet be at no risk of losing her job. He left her in a book-lined study with two of his men. She seemed perceptive enough to understand that her guards were guys who'd grown up taking no shit from anyone and that she was well advised to speak to them in a soft, conciliatory voice.

Blood, brains, splinters of bone, and twists of hair spattered a portion of the upstairs hallway floor, a swath of one wall, and a small part of the ceiling. The bullet entered under the creature's chin and exited through the high arc of the parietal bone.

Two agents waited at the head of the stairs, but Falkirk was alone with the corpse of the Bestpet. Such creatures were called Bestpets on six of the known worlds where science was more advanced than on Earth Prime and where a corporation, partly with government funding, harnessed the technology to create them. In three other timelines, Bestpets were called Geezenstacks.

Before Edwin Harkenbach had gone rogue, 187 Earths had been visited as part of Project Everett Highways, which was named after Hugh Everett III, the Princeton physicist who first posited the existence of parallel universes in 1957. In addition to Harkenbach, twenty-six men and women had voyaged across the multiverse during the first phase of the project, all of them anthropologists and biologists and their ilk, science types whom Falkirk used like tools but whom he found tedious. One died in an accident. Five were killed in violent encounters on gone-wrong worlds that crawled with hellish horrors. In Falkirk's estimation, the discoveries they made were worth the lives of a thousand like them. Ten thousand.

They had all worn disguised body cams, so Falkirk had seen Bestpets like the one that had been killed here. The project's video archives offered uncountable strange sights, some far more hideous than this bioengineered monstrosity, but also others that were exhilarating, inspiring.

The answers to all Earth Prime's problems were to be found on the infinite other versions of the planet, along Everett Highways. Worlds existed on which civilization was less impressive than here on Prime, but there were others on which science and medicine were more advanced. By harvesting knowledge from the latter, pollution and pestilence and disease could be eliminated.

Better yet, anyone who recovered highly advanced science and technology from parallel timelines and brought it to this one would be richer than any king or oligarch in history.

There were also worlds where cultures and social structures and politics had developed along pathways never followed—in some cases, never even conceived—here on Prime. These alternatives offered ways to effect progressive change, to remake America into a more orderly and more industrious nation, especially when combined with behavior-altering drugs and biological mechanisms that had been developed in those many elsewheres.

Phase one of the project—exploration—should have led to phase two. Exploration would have continued, with new worlds being visited regularly, but the harvesting of valuable science and technology already discovered would also have been pursued.

Unfortunately, infuriatingly, Edwin Harkenbach proved to have principles that he took seriously, as if Earth Prime wasn't already moving past his primitive ideas of right, wrong, and self-restraint. Whether gradually or in a moment of sudden enlightenment, Harkenbach realized that gaining ultimate power was a key purpose of Falkirk's and of the political elites who ensured the funding of Everett's Highways. He rebelled.

If Ed had chosen to argue his case with those who financed his work, or if he had gone to the FBI under the illusion that federal law enforcement wasn't corrupt, or if he had been foolish enough to trust the media to help him blow the whistle, he would be dead by now. There was a point where he could have been stopped, and the project could have flourished without him.

Instead, he'd been cunning enough to forego those options in favor of sabotage. There had once been three transport devices, which Harkenbach had called "the keys to everything." He destroyed two of them and obliterated every bit of data, in computers and in the cloud, related to the design of the keys.

Only when Ed disappeared with the third key did it become clear that the combined knowledge of his entire staff was insufficient to create new transport devices. The tricky sonofabitch had left his closest associates under the impression that they knew everything about how the keys functioned. In fact, during the year Harkenbach had been on the run, all those geniuses working together feverishly had made no progress toward restarting operations.

Falkirk answered to one of the most powerful political families in the nation, particularly to the senator who was the current flag carrier for that fabled tribe and who knew all the corrupt means by which the shadow state could be used to do what the elite preferred rather than what the American people wanted. Falkirk also answered to a consortium of billionaires, domestic and foreign, who provided capital when money couldn't always secretly, safely be drained from other government programs to finance Everett's

Highways. None of these people blamed Falkirk for Harkenbach's treachery, but they were not happy with him, either.

If he could find the rogue scientist, Falkirk had a pharmacy of chemicals and cutting-edge technology with which to drain from the old man all the knowledge needed to make new transport devices. Or if he was able to locate the one remaining key, the project team could reverse engineer it and get operations moving again.

Some of Falkirk's superiors thought Harkenbach had remained at large because he was able to decamp to another world every time that those searching for him got close. In that other reality, he could travel to another state or even another country before returning to Prime, far removed from the place where he'd almost been captured.

Falkirk felt certain that was not the case. During the first year that multiverse travel had become possible, before he had gone rogue, Ed Harkenbach had visited many alternate realities—and he had become increasingly alarmed about the horrors some of them offered, the gruesome traps into which even a cautious traveler could step, the threats to civilization that might inadvertently be brought back to Prime. Believing that using the key involved as much moral as existential risk, he had stopped traveling a month before he went on the run. Yes, for whatever reason, he'd taken the one remaining key, but even though it was his life's work and proof of his genius, an in-depth psychological profile concluded that he would destroy it before he would use it.

Falkirk figured he had maybe three or four months to favorably resolve the situation. If he failed, he would lose the patronage of the widely esteemed senator and the senator's fashionable family, and he would not likely get a job ever again in the mon-eyed swamps of Washington.

That would be the least of his problems.

He knew far too much. In addition to being fired, he would have a mortal accident or a killer stroke, or be shot in the back of the head by a robber, or be assisted into a convincing suicide.

Now he called to the two men—Canker and Wong—waiting at the head of the stairs. When they joined him, he said, "Bag the monkey-boy's corpse, take it away, and burn it."

"So you want a bleach crew to clean up the rest of the mess?" Canker asked, surveying the spray pattern of biological debris.

"Hell, no," Falkirk said. "We aren't a fucking janitorial service."

He went downstairs to deal with Constance Yardley. She reminded him of a teacher, Mrs. Holt, from his boarding school days, twenty-six years ago. Mrs. Holt, that sarcastic bitch, had tortured him with past participles and the subjunctive mood and parallel sentence structure. As a boy, he'd had erotic dreams in which she was naked and he broke her fingers with a hammer and cut her extensively.

=== 33

While her father sat at the kitchen table, continuing to pore through Spooky Ed's book, Amity prepared a dinner salad of but-ter lettuce, beefsteak tomatoes, black olives, and chopped peper-oncinis, topped with chunks of Havarti cheese. There was a large sausage pizza in the freezer, and dark chocolate ice cream with orange swirls for dessert. Comfort food in the comfort of home.

As much as Amity loved their bungalow, it didn't feel all that comfortable at the moment. For one thing, she kept listening for the clatter of helicopters. And she couldn't stop thinking how much warmer these rooms would be if the right Michelle lived here.

Amity knew that the heart was deceitful above all things, but she also knew that the heart was a lonely hunter, that the heart was slow to learn, that the heart was an open house with its doors widely flung. Because she'd read enough books to bring an elephant to its knees if they were stacked on its back, and because writers had so much to say about the human heart, she knew a gajillion truths about the heart, many of them in conflict with one another. When a girl was racing toward her twelfth birthday, life was confusing enough without the complication of parallel worlds.

After putting aside the book, her father pressed his fingers to his eyes as if what he read made them ache. "He doesn't say anything about a key to everything let alone about batteries to power it. But if I understand what he's saying about something called the 'quantum wave' or the 'de Broglie-Schrödinger electron wave,' Ed thought that any method of traveling across the multiverse could be continuously powered by radiation emitted by the electrons in this wave when they aren't constrained in Bohr orbits, whatever the hell that means."

Putting the big bowl of salad in the refrigerator to keep it chilled and crisp, Amity said, "I found Mom's recipes in a ring binder. You haven't cooked any of those meals in a couple years."

"Ed says time travel will never be possible. We don't live in just space or time. We live in space-time. The only constant speed of anything in the universe, the only reliable scale, is the speed of light—186,282 miles per second. So it's also the speed of time. If you're in a chair reading a book, in one hour you've traveled over 670 million miles in space-time. Imagine trying to turn a car around at such a speed. Momentum makes it impossible. There is no brake on light, on time. You can't stop and go back. And because you can't go faster than light, you can't speed ahead to the future. But it's possible to go *sideways*."

"Her recipe for vegetable-beef soup looks really good," Amity said as she took the pizza from the freezer. "It's easy enough. If I had all the ingredients, I could make that. I've never had her soup. Wouldn't it be nice to have Mom's soup for dinner one night, just as though she was here and made it and was at the table with us?"

Picking up the book once more and paging through it, her father said, "Here's a bit that worries me. The positions of subatomic particles aren't fixed. They exist in a cloud of possibilities. At the very base of matter, everything in the universe is always in flux, as are the infinite universes in relationship to one another. You know what I think maybe that means?"

Putting the frozen pizza on a baking tray, Amity said, "The oven's hot, so this'll be done in like twenty minutes. It's past dinnertime, and I'm starving. Can you take a break to eat?"

"What I think it means is, the routes to those hundred eighty-seven worlds cataloged in the key are only approximate directions. Things change. So if they change enough . . . maybe you don't end up where you wanted to go. Maybe you arrive *between* universes, if there is such a place. In a vacuum. In a void. Dead on arrival."

Sliding the tray into the oven, Amity said, "Have you heard anything I've said?"

He looked at her. "Recipes in a ring binder, Michelle's vegetable-beef soup, maybe make it yourself, but pizza tonight, dinner in twenty minutes. Did you hear anything *I* said?"

"Quantum wave, no battery, the speed of light, forget time travel, go sideways, a vacuum, a void, dead on arrival."

He smiled, and so did she, and he said, "We're always on the same page, aren't we?"

"You can close the book on that," she said.

He closed the book and pointed to the key to everything. "Maybe I should mix up a barrelful of cement right after dinner, sink that gismo in it, and take it out to sea."

"Bad idea, Dad. We might need it if that Falkirk guy comes around again. Remember?"

"But we're in way over our heads, Amity. We shouldn't have this thing."

Bringing plates to the table, she said, "Have you wondered why Ed gave it to you?"

"I've wondered until I'm sick of wondering."

"He liked you."

"So he pulls the pin on a hand grenade and gives it to me."

"The gismo isn't that dangerous," she said.

"It's *more* dangerous than a grenade."

"It's his life's work."

"His life's work will get us killed."

"He couldn't bring himself to destroy his life's work. You can understand that."

Jeffy looked at her, his life's work.

Amity said, "So he trusted you to keep it safe."

"He shouldn't have trusted me."

"He shouldn't have trusted anyone else *but* you."

"I'm no hero, sweetheart."

"True heroes never think they are. I mean, holy guacamole, how many times have we read *that* story?"

Regarding the key to everything with trepidation, he said, "Maybe with what the bullet did to its face, Good Boy will seem to be just a chimp in a costume, somebody's creepy pet. Maybe the cops won't look too close at it. Maybe they won't think it's weird enough to call in the feds. Maybe we'll never see Falkirk again."

Amity didn't know what math to use to calculate the probability that all those maybes would be fulfilled.

With her father, in silence, she stared at the so-called key. The darn thing had an aura about it that drew the eye. Even if you didn't know what it did, you'd have known in your bones that some terrible power coiled in it, evil magic . . . but maybe some good magic, too, if you used it for the right purpose. It seemed to have a sorcerous glimmer akin to that of the One Ring, the Master of all Rings, that had been made in Mordor and which could be destroyed only by returning it to the fire where it was forged.

After a while, she said, "I'll check on the pizza."

Slender and shapely, Constance Yardley appeared younger than fifty, and Falkirk found her attractive, which was odd considering that she was an English teacher. She had the attitude of superiority common to all English teachers in his experience, especially the female ones, who thought they were hot stuff just because they knew everything about subordinate adverb clauses and dangling modifiers. The condescension with which their kind regarded him usually made them ugly in his eyes, even repulsive.

In fact, in his experience, a significant percentage of women, not just English teachers, thought they were too special for words. Yardley had such an exalted opinion of herself that she expected you to kiss her ass and thank her for the privilege.

Earlier, she'd sat on the sofa in her book-lined study, acting patient and mannerly, but he had seen through her act. He'd seen her veiled arrogance, her snotty disapproval, the contempt that was as much a part of her as the marrow in her bones.

She reminded him not just of the English teacher that had most tormented and mocked him in boarding school, but also of his hateful stepmother, Katarina, who had gotten her hands on his father's crank shortly after his mother died. Kat quickly pumped out two brats of her own by the time Falkirk was thirteen and screwed the old man into a massive heart attack. She dispatched her stepson to boarding school and methodically stripped him of his inheritance.

Now, when Falkirk returned to the study from the upstairs hallway, Yardley had moved from the sofa to the chair behind her desk, where she sat with a book of at least five hundred pages. Wearing half-lens reading glasses, she made notes on a lined tablet. No doubt her cursive would be as precise as that of a machine, and every damn comma would be exactly where it was supposed to be.

Two of Falkirk's men, Elliot and Goulding, were present, one standing at the door to a side garden, the other at the door to the hallway, obviously assigned to prevent her from leaving. They looked like men who wouldn't ask to be paid to break someone's knees, who would do it for pleasure. Any sane person would keep an eye on them with an expectation of impending violence.

Constance Yardley pretended to be oblivious of them. Or maybe she was so conceited and disdainful that she believed herself to be quite untouchable by such hoi polloi. Maybe she thought they were here to fetch her tea if she wanted it and to fluff the pillows on the sofa if she chose to return to it.

Falkirk went to the desk and stood looking down at her and said, "What do you make of the animal in the upstairs hall?"

Rather than respond to him at once, she finished a sentence she was writing, marked her place in the book, leaned back in her chair, and finally regarded him over the half lenses of her glasses. "Make of it? I came home from the college, found that mess. We're living in strange times. That's all I can make of it. I just want it out of here. The police asked if the creature was mine. I assured them that although I have countless ways of making a fool of myself, one of them isn't keeping a chimpanzee and dressing it like some kind of Boy Scout."

"You took a close enough look to see it wasn't as simple a thing or as absurd as you make it sound."

"Just for a moment, I thought it was a terribly hairy boy. But then I realized it was . . . whatever it is."

"As I told you earlier, this is a matter of national security."

"Please don't insist that pathetic beast is an extraterrestrial or a Russian spy. I have an open mind but not an empty skull."

Falkirk wanted to lean across the mahogany desk and slap her. He restrained himself because he knew a slap would be just the start of it. "What you saw here today and anything that I've discussed with you, even the fact that NSA agents were here—it's never to be repeated to anyone. If you speak a word of it, you'll be prosecuted under the National Secrets Act."

She smiled and took off her glasses. "Are you really NSA agents or something else? And is there really something with a ridiculous and melodramatic name like the 'National Secrets Act'?"

"Why would I say there was if there wasn't?"

"Why *wouldn't* you?" She put her glasses down. "From what I heard happened here, some of my neighbors must have seen . . . that thing."

"As it turns out, no one did."

"And who used my pistol to kill it?"

Falkirk had theories about that, but they were none of her business. He answered her question with an intimidating stare of the kind that he'd endured from her type throughout his school years.

Her eyes fixed on his for an infuriating length of time before she sighed and shook her head and said, "This defies belief. Clean up the mess in the second-floor hall and get out of my house."

"We've taken the corpse. The mess is all yours. Don't even think about hiring a service to do the job. There would be too many questions. Do it your own damn self. You'll probably need a bucket to vomit into."

The contempt with which she regarded him suggested that she might not do as she was told.

His suspicion was confirmed when she said, "Have you changed the name of the country? Are we not any longer living in America?"

He went to the nearest wall and swept fifteen or twenty books off a shelf, to the floor. Then he scattered a second shelf of them.

Certain that a woman like her would place an inordinately high value on books, he expected Constance Yardley to leap to her feet or curse him for his vandalism. However, she remained in her chair and watched him, her stare almost sharp enough to draw blood.

With greater violence, he threw more books on the floor while Elliot and Goulding watched with solemn approval. "You should wish we're something as lame as NSA agents. We're far worse, Connie. There's more at stake here than your narrow grammarian's brain can conceive, Connie. If you don't do as you've been told, then I'll come back here and throw all your damn books on the floor and set them on fire with you punched unconscious and sprawled on top of them. You got that, *Connie*?"

At last he had brought her to her feet. She stood as stiff and straight as a fence pale, her arms at her sides and her hands balled into fists. Her expression was one of self-righteous disgust, but he could see that she was afraid and struggling to repress her fear.

Elliot and Goulding had moved away from their posts, closer to the desk. They were chameleons, able to look like what the situation required. They could appear to be sober, highly disciplined agents one moment, and an instant later radiate the lust and brutality of amoral beasts; in this case, they were the latter. Constance Yardley stood alone in the room with three men, with two others also in the house, and she knew now that the law had no power over them nor any jurisdiction in this residence.

Spittle flew when John Falkirk again demanded of her, *"You got that, CONNIE?"*

Her pretense of courage did not deceive him, and her attempt to hold fast to her self-respect was amusing when she raised her chin and tweaked her shoulders back and said, "Yes."

"So go ahead and make yourself seem brave by telling us again to get out of your house."

She clearly knew that, with this goad, he had denied her the only assertion of dignity still available to her, that to say those words now would make her sound not indomitable, but meekly obedient. However, because she had no other choice but silence, which she might expect to enflame his anger, she said, "Get out."

Falkirk saw that his mocking smile was a needle that deflated the English teacher. "Poor Connie," he said, and he led his men out of the room, out of the house.

35

Mice saw well in the dark and tended to sleep in the afternoon, stirring toward the end of twilight, becoming more active as the magical night descended. In this world, they had no great, inspiring adventures like those of Despereaux in *The Tale of Despereaux* by Ms. Kate DiCamillo, nor even any to match the comical activities of the fabled Mickey, though perhaps in some other of the infinite worlds, they enjoyed vigorous swordfights with that meaner species, rats, and triumphed over wicked cats belonging to evil kings. Most nights, Snowball busied himself with gnawing blocks and his exercise wheels and climbing ropes and various toys that had been provided for him.

Shortly before the pizza was brown and crisp enough to be taken from the oven, suddenly worried that the terrible strains of the day had been too much for a mere mouse, Amity hurried to her room and turned on the lights to check on her tiny dependent.

As the April dusk shaded the late afternoon beyond the windows, Snowball sat on his haunches by his water dish, yawning hugely and grooming himself. He craned his neck and stared at her. His shiny black eyes were shinier than ever, as though this crazy day, fraught with danger and terror, had only invigorated him.

"How many litters does a mother mouse have in one year?" she asked Snowball.

He didn't respond, but she answered for him, "Five or six. On average ten or more young to a litter."

Snowball did not disagree.

"Do mouse families stay together long? Or do you drift apart from one another? Do you miss your mother?"

The litters had to be large because at least a third of the hairless, blind newborns did not survive. Of those who lived to grow coats and gain vision, many would become dinner for birds of prey and weasels and foxes and snakes and rats and, really, half the animals on the planet.

Mice lived hard lives. Amity didn't like to dwell on that.

By comparison, Snowball led a pampered life as a domesticated mouse. As a consequence, unprepared for adversity, he should have been traumatized by the day's events, but obviously he was not.

"Would you give up the comfort of your cage, jump on the key again, hop to another world in spite of the risks?"

As if in answer, as if the prospect of such exotic travel excited him, Snowball scurried to his exercise wheel and ran in place, ran fast, and then faster.

"You'd do it again," Amity surmised. "My little Despereaux."

In this world where rodents did not use sewing needles as swords or save princesses from imprisonment, where magic was not common, lessons still could be learned from a mere mouse.

At the door to the hall, she switched off the lights, leaving the mouse in the shadows that, when the twilight whispered away on the evening breeze, would have what magic this world allowed.

36

In the immediate search for that bastard Edwin Harkenbach and the one remaining key to everything, Falkirk had numerous vehicles under his command, including a specially outfitted forty-four-foot motor home with a satellite dish in a recessed well in its roof, which allowed the skilled hackers on his team to have high-speed access to the internet, from which they could backdoor every law-enforcement and national-security computer system in existence.

It was good to be working in an operation that had pockets deep enough to hold billions of dollars. But all the money in the world couldn't guarantee success, which was a truth that accounted for Falkirk's dark mood.

At 5:10 p.m., the motor home stood in a supermarket parking lot. The hackers currently on duty, Selena Malrose and Jason "Foot-Long" Frankfurt, were at their workstations in the forward part of the vehicle, eating submarine sandwiches and potato chips while they searched the video archives of the town's many security and traffic cameras in an attempt to discover who might have fled Constance Yardley's house after having shot the ape-boy Bestpet.

Falkirk sequestered himself in the chamber at the rear of the motor home, which would have been a bedroom in the standard street-model Fleetwood. It was a conference room in this vehicle, complete with a floor-anchored table, six comfortable chairs, and a bank of TV screens, all dark.

He took his dinner alone at the table, lobster rolls and slaw, allowing himself two glasses of pinot grigio.

He didn't believe in fraternizing with members of his staff. Underlings were to be used efficiently and must always be reminded that they were part of an operation so top secret that they were expendable—in the sense of a bullet to the head—if they spoke about their work to anyone other than a team member. Selena Malrose was hot. Why she chose to waste her life at a computer, buccaneering forbidden data, mystified John Falkirk. He fantasized about drilling her, but in fact he preferred women who were wounded and unsure of themselves and emotionally pliable. Selena had attitude and too much confidence for his taste. Jason Frankfurt was a geek with glamour, a blurry version of Brad Pitt, who tried too hard to be clever and hip; he had most likely given himself the nickname "Foot-Long" as a pathetic attempt to impress—and deceive—women. Even if Selena and Jason hadn't been underlings, Falkirk would not have wanted to be friends with them. Friendship was an invitation to treachery; he was not so emotionally weak that he needed to risk having real friends.

Besides, when he got his hands on the key to everything, when he left this lame world for a better one, there would be no point in having friends here because he wouldn't be taking them with him. The senator, his family, and the consortium of billionaires who were backstopping the project's budget didn't suspect that Falkirk was working for himself, that the immense wealth and ultimate power they envisioned flowing from the key would be his alone.

Before Ed Harkenbach destroyed the other two keys, Falkirk had used one to voyage across the multiverse on several occasions, and the unlimited possibilities were at once obvious to him. On Earth 1.07, he paid a visit to his stepmother, Katarina. Strangely, she had not stolen his inheritance in that reality, but had treated him as an equal of his half brother and half sister. When he sought an audience with her, in one of her lavish homes, she welcomed him warmly. He shot her in the face and dropped the gun at her feet and, before any of her security personnel could respond, he fled into an adjoining room, from which he ported himself home to Earth Prime.

Of course Katarina remained alive on this world, but killing another version of the bitch in a parallel reality was nevertheless satisfying. He supposed the John Falkirk who lived in that other timeline had been arrested, tried, and sent to prison. However, as much as Earth Prime Falkirk loved himself, he simply didn't possess the capacity to love thousands of himself with the same fervor. He suffered no distress at the thought of another John being martyred in his name.

The intercom beeped. Selena Malrose spoke from her workstation in the forward section of the motor home. "John, we found archived video of suspects on foot, caught by a traffic cam. They crossed an intersection three blocks from Constance Yardley's house, a few minutes after the Bestpet would've been shot. And we know them."

37

Most evenings, Amity and her father talked to each other during dinner. Neither she nor he was ever at a loss for something to say, and there was no shortage of subjects that interested them. But on this momentous evening, Daddy wasn't in the mood for conversation. He said that he was exhausted and worried and needed to think, but no doubt he was also concerned that she would press him further about finding the right Michelle. She'd no intention of doing such a naggy thing, not because she wasn't capable of it, but because she had a keen sense of the limits of his tolerance for wheedling.

As on those other rare evenings during which they dined mostly in silence, Daddy resorted to an audiobook for entertainment. They couldn't listen to an entire novel during one dinner, and neither of them wanted to break a rattling-good story into like twenty dinners. So on these occasions, they listened to the same novel to which they had listened an amazing number of times before, *The Princess Bride* by William Goldman. They remembered every turn in the story better than they recalled many of the details of their own past, but the oft-told tale was never boring. No bullsugar. The story really and truly delighted them so much that, when they came to certain scenes, they recited the dialogue or the funnier lines of text in sync with the audio narrator, though they had never made an effort to memorize any of it.

Through salad and pizza, they listened to the second and third chapters. The third was titled "The Courtship," in which the vile Prince Humperdinck proposed marriage to a very beautiful milkmaid named Buttercup, whereupon she said that she had loved once before, it had gone badly, and she could never love another. Not accustomed to rejection, the prince seasoned his proposal with a threat.

Three voices—those of the narrator, Amity, and her father—served as the voice of the prince: "*So you can either marry me and be the richest and most powerful woman in a thousand miles and give turkeys away at Christmas and provide me a son, or you can die in terrible pain in the very near future. Make up your own mind.*"

And Buttercup said, "*I'll never love you.*"

Said the prince, "*I wouldn't want it if I had it.*"

Replied Buttercup, "*Then by all means let us marry.*"

At the end of the chapter, Amity and her dad laughed together, which was a fine thing, though it was also a strange thing because, among their favorite fantasy adventures, *The Princess Bride* was like no other. The story lacked a happy ending. It was a satire filled with stupidity, treachery, suffering, loss, and death—all of which were played for laughs. Few girls short of their twelfth year would take such delight in it. However, Amity was smart and precocious, and years earlier she had learned the primary lesson of *The Princess Bride*: As wondrous as life was, it was also full of sadness, and the best way to get past the sad parts and enjoy all the rest was to find the humor in even the darkness. Laughter wasn't just a medicine for melancholy, but also a sword raised against evil. A laugh said, *You can't scare me into surrender, I'll fight you hard to the end.*

She hoped that, in desperate straits, she could laugh in the face of pure evil. Until today, she'd not had much experience of evil. Of sadness, yes, she'd known her share of that, but not the kind of evil that turned your blood to ice water. She supposed she had done all right in that nasty version of Suavidad Beach, with the commie fascists and Good Boy and all. But worse might be coming.

With his paternal sonar sensing fear in the depths of his daughter, Daddy said, "Are you okay, honey?"

"Yeah," she said. "I'm good, I'm cool." But it was then, for the first time in a while, she became aware of the three teeth and the fragment of jawbone in a pocket of her jeans.

===== 38

Although he intended eventually to split to a better world, there were things about this one of which John Falkirk approved.

In this age of ever-increasing state surveillance of its citizens, even a town of forty thousand, like Suavidad Beach, had cameras monitoring traffic at all major intersections, in municipal parks, as well as in and around public buildings. Local authorities archived the video for sixty days or six months or a year, but it was transmitted in real time to the National Security Agency's Utah Data Center, where it would be forever available, filed under the community's name and accessible by date.

A year earlier, Foot-Long Frankfurt had planted a rootkit in the NSA's computer system, allowing him and Selena to enter by a back door and swim through its ocean of data without drawing the attention of the IT-security forces. Together they had tracked Jeffrey and Amity Coltrane from Constance Yardley's neighborhood through the heart of town.

Selena had edited sequential bits of video into a twitchy stream of images. Falkirk stood behind her, watching her computer screen, as the radio repairman and his mouse-keeper brat eventually made their way to the town library on Oleander Street.

"They were there for eight minutes," Selena said. "And here they come."

Coltrane and his daughter exited the library and turned north on Oleander. He seemed to be carrying a book. A traffic cam at the first major intersection showed them turning east on Oak Hollow Road. They were heading home to their funky house on Shadow Canyon Lane, about a mile from where the last camera lost track of them.

"For some reason, Ed Harkenbach entrusted the key to Coltrane," Foot-Long Frankfurt said, "and Coltrane used it, and they were under attack by the Bestpet when they ported back to Prime. I'd bet my dick on it."

"Winning that bet," said Falkirk, "would be like taking home the throwaway from a Brith Milah."

Selena laughed, and Foot-Long asked what a Brith Milah was, and she said, "The Jewish rite of circumcision."

To his credit, Foot-Long laughed and said, "Man, I owe you for that."

Falkirk wished he hadn't said such a thing, not because he gave a shit about hurting Frankfurt's feelings, but because it might be mistaken for camaraderie, might suggest he was one of them. He was not. He was singular. He'd known he was better than all of them, better than the ruck of humanity, had known it for twenty-one years, ever since he was fifteen, when he murdered a classmate at boarding school and got away with it, attracting no suspicion whatsoever.

Without further comment, he stepped out of the motor home and walked to a black Suburban parked nearby. Vince Canker sat behind the wheel, Louis Wong in the front passenger seat. Both men were eating deli sandwiches, washing them down with beer.

Falkirk slid onto the back seat. "We're going to move hard on Coltrane. But not for hours yet. Finish your meal. I need to put the best team together and take the bastard when he's least expecting it. We'll slam him when he's sleeping, after midnight."

Canker, who had the body of a mob enforcer and a face hard enough to break the ram of a junkyard auto compacter, believed that he possessed a low-burning psychic power that one day would suddenly flash brighter. He said, "I got a funny thing going here, like a far voice from the Other Side, from beyond the veil, you know, telling me this here is the night, this here is the time, we find the key tonight."

Wong swallowed a wad of sandwich. "You heard a voice before."

"Not this here voice. No. This is another voice."

"You recognize who it is?"

"It's real faint, but I think it's my mother's voice."

"Your mother's dead?"

"She'd have to be, wouldn't she, if she's on the Other Side?"

"It's just you never mentioned she's dead."

"It was only a week ago, a shitty thing. Opioids."

"An overdose, huh? Sorry, man. That's a tragedy."

"It is what it is. She wasn't big on self-control."

"Only a week on the Other Side and she's trying to reach you."

"She was always a talker, never shut up. Death won't likely change that."

On his new world, with the key to everything at his service, Falkirk would have a good chance of becoming not only the rich-est man on the planet but the ruler of all. If he achieved totalitar-ian power, he would make stupidity a crime, and conversations like that between Canker and Wong would be sufficient evidence to impose the death penalty.

PART 4

THE RIGHT MICHELLE

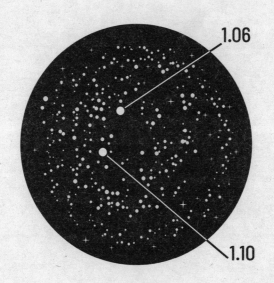

1.06

1.10

In the burnt-orange radiance of the westering sun, the shadows of the tall palm trees reached eastward, from which the night would come, as if welcoming the dark by casting onto its path the images of their fronds.

In one of the rocking chairs on the porch of the sandstone bungalow, Michelle Coltrane sat with her guitar, playing a song she'd written many years earlier, when she entertained dreams of wealth and fame, before she had been mature enough to understand that money and celebrity were not guarantees of happiness. What mattered most in life couldn't be bought with a pot of gold. That wisdom had come at a terrible price.

She earned a living now by teaching guitar and piano, and she played three nights a week at Johnny's Beachside, a restaurant and bar. The place wasn't actually on the beach, but half a block back from it, with no water view, and it was owned by a guy named Norman, who had bought it from Johnny twenty years earlier. No stage was provided for her performance, only a corner between the bar and dining room. Her job wasn't to wow the crowd, but only to provide soft dinner music. She played mostly other songwriters' tunes that had made already-famous singers richer, though once or twice in each set, she slipped in one of her own. The gig gave her pleasure even when, at the end of the night, the tip jar contained only one-dollar bills, no fives or tens.

On this balmy April evening, she waited for a gentleman whom she'd invited to dinner. No romance was involved, only friendship. Anyway, by choice she hadn't shared her bed in more than seven years, for she intuitively knew that such intimacy wouldn't relieve her loneliness and sorrow, but only make them worse.

As the orange light purpled in the east and crimsoned in the west, he came along the oak-flanked lane, plump and rumpled, his back straight and his white-wreathed head high, with the confident yet jaunty stride of a wise and beloved headmaster of a boy's school from the era of *Goodbye, Mr. Chips*. The pattern of his bow tie did not match that of his shirt—in this case, polka dots over stripes—but he so routinely mismatched these items that the effect had to be intentional, a quiet assertion of eccentricity.

He came up the front walk and climbed three of the four porch steps and stopped and regarded her with a kind of amused solemnity. He stood listening to her song for maybe half a minute and then said, "Obviously a composition from your early days, full of verve and charm, but short on grace and lacking all substance." Although she couldn't sing for smiling, she continued with her guitar as he finished his critique. "If I were fourteen, I might stand here quite enthralled while you played it yet again. However, I'm sixty-four, and older than my years, so I beg of you to spare me from more of this celebration of young-adult angst while my admiration for your talent is still intact."

Rising to her feet and propping her guitar in the rocking chair, Michelle said, "You are quite a piece of work, Ed."

"I have always strived to be such," he assured her, as they hugged each other.

Although Ed Casper had been visiting for nearly a year and had become dear to her, sometimes—as now—she still wondered that she had, without much hesitation, developed a friendship with a guy who lived in rough circumstances, in a tent among the trees beyond the dead end of Shadow Canyon Lane, who walked into town each day to shower in a public facility.

Of course Ed wasn't one of the alkies or druggies made homeless by substance abuse, and he wasn't one with a mental illness that led to an addiction or ensued from it. Neither a hobo impoverished by laziness nor a pitiable vagrant condemned to poverty by a low IQ, he was an uncommon member of the society of the homeless. Some turn of events left him without ambition, robbed him of faith in the future, causing him to seek a life of few possessions, the solace of a clockless existence without appointments or driving purpose.

Ed wouldn't say what loss might have transformed him. He never seemed to be troubled by depression, and he certainly never indulged in self-pity. Michelle knew, however, that a loss of one kind or another had broken him; because in an instant she'd lost everything that mattered most and, in the losing, had for the first time truly understood the value of what had been taken from her. Whatever else she and Ed Casper might share, the condition of their isolate souls, more insistently haunted than any house could ever be, was what had brought them together in mutual mild melancholy.

"Play something new you've written," he said.

"Maybe later. Right now I need a glass of wine, and you're always more amusing after a martini."

They went into the house as the last light of the day bled away and the night rose out of the storied land, like spirits ascending from the graves of history.

======= 40

Their moods for music were always synchronized, whether Beatles or Beethoven, Glenn Miller or Glenn Gould. This night, they settled on the clear and nimble piano work of David Benoit, his soft jazz rather than anything too progressive.

A three-beet salad followed by pappardelle with scallops in a light saffron sauce was a dinner to be lingered over, accompanied by a dry white wine as bright on the tongue as the music on the ear.

They ate at the kitchen table, for the small house offered no formal dining room. Crackled amber-glass cups, which matched the globes on the porch lamps, held the table candles, fracturing the flames into sinuosities of light and shadow that flowed unceasing across the table and up the walls. In this atmosphere, Ed Casper's uplit face seemed like that of a mysterious medium or magician with knowledge of real magic rather than tricks.

Their conversation always ranged over a wide array of subjects, literally from cabbages to kings, although music and literature and art and history were those that most enlivened Ed. On this occasion, he soon turned the talk to modern physics, quantum mechanics—hidden dimensions, spooky effects at a distance, parallel worlds—about which Michelle had no understanding and of which she assumed that she had little interest.

Ed was, however, both a splendid raconteur and gifted with the ability to make the complex simple. Soon Michelle was captivated by his portrait of a universe stranger than anything

Hollywood could ever splash across the screen. In a while she realized that he was not engaged in the usual casual conversation, that he'd come here intent upon explaining—and convincing her—that an infinite multiverse existed, filled with parallel Earths. She had never before seen him so intense—or intense at all.

For dessert, she served each of them a plate with two cheeses and six fresh plump figs, along with a final glass of wine.

After a bit of cheese and a single fig, Ed extracted an object from a pocket of his sport coat and put it on the table. It somewhat resembled an iPhone.

"This," he said, "is the most valuable but also most dangerous technology in history. A quantum miracle. The key to everything. It can undo tragedy. It's an instrument of evil in the wrong hands, but it can also make you whole again, dear girl. You and your precious family, whole again. It can bring them back to you."

=== 41

A life could be snuffed out as suddenly as the candle flames in the amber-glass cups on the kitchen table.

Michelle blamed herself for the deaths of her husband and only child. She had lived with guilt for a long time, although over the past seven years, the acute pain of grief had settled into a less acute but more enduring sorrow.

On the day it happened, she had been obsessing on her music career, or lack of one, bemoaning that her life had, as she thought, gone far off the tracks. In truth, there were no tracks of destiny through the chaos of life, only paths forged by decisions. She had dreamed of riding a fast train to stardom, but the rails and ties of those tracks had never been carefully laid. At the time, she thought her decision to marry Jeffy and conceive Amity had derailed her, but they were not to blame. She sabotaged herself by writing songs that were, like the one Ed earlier critiqued, a "celebration of young-adult angst," cliché-ridden and jejune; indeed, the tune that he dissed was the least puerile of them.

She had started a quarrel with Jeffy, blaming her failure on him. But Jeffy, being Jeffy, would not argue, a failure to engage that further infuriated Michelle. Amity was four at the time, and Jeffy said the tension in the house was upsetting her. He wouldn't even blame Michelle for frightening the girl, as if the problem were some tension arising from an architectural error in the structure.

To give Michelle time to cool off and compose herself, he took a walk into town with Amity, to get the girl a cone of her favorite flavor at an ice cream shop. He was carrying the child in his arms, crossing a street, when a drugged and drunken driver in a speeding Cadillac Escalade struck them, knocked them down like tenpins, drove over them, and dragged the battered bodies more than two hundred feet before coming to a stop.

Now she frowned at the so-called key to everything, which lay on the table. She raised her head to stare at Ed Casper, wondering how she could have failed to suspect that he was as unbalanced as any other broken soul who tented in the wilds beyond the end of Shadow Canyon Lane.

As she held a fig by its stem, turning it around and around on her plate, she wondered at her gullibility. But in fact she knew the explanation for it. Her mother had died in childbirth. Twenty-two years later, the day after Amity's birth, Michelle's special father, Jim Jamison, had been electrocuted as he was overseeing maintenance of a power-company transformer in a subterranean vault. Ed Casper looked nothing like Michelle's father, but he was now the same age as her dad when he died. The two shared a certain spirit, a *joie de vivre*, and the timbre of their voices was similar; Jim Jamison, like Ed, loved music and art and history. In each man, an inherent kindness revealed itself in countless small ways. Long alone, she had needed a touchstone against which to test the mettle of her heart and mind. One day when her melancholy was at high tide, Ed stopped by the porch to listen to her play guitar, and in need of a friend who was also a mentor, she'd set aside all doubts about him.

Until now.

It was crazy but also cruel to claim that the dead could be brought back to life by some gadget that resembled a cell phone.

He read her expression and her eyes correctly, and before she could express her dismay, he withdrew a paperback book from an inner pocket of his sport coat. He displayed the cover—*Infinite Worlds: Parallel Universes and Quantum Reality* by Dr. Edwin Harkenbach. He turned the book over and tapped a small photograph on the back of it. Although the author in the photo was younger than Ed Casper, with a mustache and beard, they were undeniably the same person.

"As Edwin Harkenbach, I was a famous physicist and prolific author. As Ed Casper, I am the quirky old duck who lives up the canyon, in a tent, just another homeless guy, though cleaner than many and never without a tie."

Michelle still felt betrayed. "Anyone can self-publish a book these days."

Sliding the volume across the table to her, he said, "It's not from a vanity press. Look at the publisher's name. One of the oldest and most respected for nonfiction."

The publisher was indeed of high caliber. However, the book alone didn't confirm the validity of his claim to be able to undo tragedies, nor did it certify his sanity, although it gave him a measure of credibility.

"But why would you lie to me about your name?"

"Not just to you, dear. These days, I lie to everyone about my name. After destroying all records of his revolutionary work, which the government had generously funded, and after setting his lab on fire, Edwin Harkenbach crashed his twin-engine Cessna into the sea during a desperate attempt to escape to a Caribbean sanctuary before authorities discovered what he had done. His body was never found, nor will it ever be, I hope."

=== 42

The cheese and figs held no interest for Michelle, but she was in need of the wine.

The paperback book of forbidden knowledge, the glimmering key to everything, a haunting melody conjured by Benoit, the candles candling Ed's eyes for any sediment of deception: the moment was eerie beyond her experience.

Her smiling guest had not lost his appetite, devouring another fig with evident pleasure.

"How generous?" she asked.

"You mean the government? Billions and billions."

She raised one eyebrow. "And you live in a tent."

"I have money stashed away in a safe place. To support myself in my apparent penury. Until too late, I didn't realize that by inventing the key to everything, I was ensuring that I'd ultimately have no option other than to fake my death and live in hiding."

He described the good that could be achieved with the key, spoke of the fearsome power that corrupt men and women could acquire through the use of it, and explained some of the seemingly infinite dangers to which the device could expose its user. The details were impressive in their complexity, convincing in their consistency, and totally crazy.

"If this is all true," she said, "with a hop, skip, and a jump, you could find a world where no one's hunting you, where you can live openly and in peace."

He sighed. "If only. In numerous timelines, I seem to have failed to convincingly fake my death. I'm still hunted by ruthless people with bottomless resources."

As if this were a weird parlor game, Michelle found herself suggesting alternatives. "Maybe a world where you were never born?"

He nodded. "During the project, I explored a few where that might be true, but they weren't worlds where I would want to live."

"Why not?"

His expression darkened. "Certain conditions . . . threats . . . horrors unspeakable."

Michelle still wasn't sure if they were having a rational conversation or were the equivalent of UFO enthusiasts discussing the style of aluminum headgear that best foiled extraterrestrial mind readers. She resorted to her wine.

After a pause for thought, she said, "So keep looking. Keep searching for a world to live where you were never born."

"During the project, before I destroyed all the records of it and fled, I ported to a hundred worlds, actually a hundred and five, maybe six, out of the hundred eighty-seven that my team cataloged. After that, I ported to eighty more." He spoke as casually as if he were talking about senior-service jitney rides to a series of local malls. "But I can't handle it anymore, the porting. I've got an adventurous mind, but I'm not physically adventurous. Or emotionally capable. Not any longer. I've too often been terrified out of my wits. All I want now is quiet and a few friends and books to read."

He didn't appear to be the least frightened as he ate cheese and figs, smiling at her as if he were an uncle enjoying the company of his favorite niece.

So she said, "Terrified by what?"

He set aside the stripped stem of a fig, swallowed a bite of fruit, blotted his lips with his napkin, took a sip of wine, blotted his lips again, and during all that, his face paled so much that the candlelight could not conceal the loss of color. His eyes, the pure blue of a deep clear sky, became the blue of the sky reflected on water, as tears brimmed but didn't spill.

"Some things I've seen can't be discussed at table, not if I'm to keep down the lovely meal you prepared. I'll describe a parallel world that was hideous, but not as horrible as some others. You may nevertheless need your wine."

"I already do."

"I mean, your glass is empty."

She poured another serving for herself. And one for him.

He stared into the chardonnay, as though the wine, in which swam scintillant shapes of candlelight, could be consulted regarding the designs of fate, as if it were a liquid crystal ball.

With a solemnity new to him, he said, "There is a timeline in which the United States endures a societal convulsion similar to the French Revolution, but even worse. It is led by modern Jacobins, not spawned by the lower classes but by the highest, by privileged young men and women made ignorant by the most expensive universities and schooled in violence by the culture of death that produced them. It is as though Dickens's *A Tale of Two Cities* had been rewritten by a violence-porn hack, filmed by the most deranged talent in Hollywood. The streets run with blood, as they did in the Dickens novel, as in fact they did in France between 1789 and 1794, during the Reign of Terror. Everywhere, scaffolds are erected in the streets, and the condemned are hung by their wrists to be eviscerated. Children are beheaded in front of their parents, the parents stoned to death by mobs. Tracts of houses and apartment buildings are set afire to exterminate residents who've been declared moral vermin. What we think could never happen here happens there, as it happened in Germany in the 1930s, as it happened in China under Mao. Nihilism and irrationality spread like a plague. Crazed, bestial emotion replaces logic and reason. Madness is redefined as moral clarity. The past is destroyed and reinvented to ensure a future of utopian justice, though justice no longer exists, has become mere revenge, often revenge against enemies more imagined than real, even revenge of Jacobin against Jacobin, as the insanity breeds more paranoia.

I've seen women gang-raped in the streets by men urged on by other women waving banners of female solidarity. I've seen the heads of babies, from families of the revolution's enemies, scattered across a day-care playground like so many spoiled cabbages discarded by a grocer."

Ed lost the ability to withhold his tears. Lambent light glazed his wet face. His mouth had gone soft, and a tremor afflicted him.

Pushing aside her glass of wine, Michelle not only returned to sobriety in an instant, but she also abandoned the doubt with which she had thus far received his story. In his voice, demeanor, and tears, she recognized a truth that she only *wished* might be a lie.

She said, "And *that* wasn't the worst world you've seen?"

He found his voice again. "Understand, many timelines are as hospitable as this one, some even better. But across an infinite multiverse of worlds, you can find all the evil realms that humanity has imagined—and some beyond imagining. I'm burnt out on travel. I haven't the nerve for it anymore. My heart can't take it. I was a pacifist once. A pacifist! I'm not anymore. I am armed. I can kill. The things I've seen . . . they've changed me. I don't want to be changed more than I've already been. I don't want the multiverse. All I want is a home, books, and the peace to read them."

Michelle stared at the key to everything, which lay between her and Ed. As the candles pulsed, plumes of light and plumes of shadow seemed to flow across the table to the device, as if it possessed a gravity that would in time draw all things to it.

"You're terrified of what's out there, the places this thing can take you, worse even than the terror of that other America you described—and yet you want me to use it."

"Only carefully, with my guidance. To undo the tragedy, connect with a version of your husband and child who live elsewhere and have lost you, bring back together a family that should never have been torn asunder. During this past year, I've come to love you as I might a daughter, Michelle. I want to cure your sorrow, put an end to your loneliness, so you can be happy."

Maybe it was real—this science, this incredible promise. But if it was a false hope, it would be worse than no hope at all.

She said, "It sounds very nice, a dream, a fairy tale. But if you don't want to 'port' anymore—"

"For you, only to make this happen, I would port again."

"Yeah, well, with an infinite number of worlds to search, the chances of finding Jeffy and Amity alone, needing me—they're zero."

Color returned to Ed's face, and he found again the smile that tears had earlier washed away.

"Just wait," he said.

"For what?"

"You'll see!"

Muttering to himself, he fumbled through the compartments of his coat, like the White Rabbit searching for a pocket watch.

"Another book?" she asked. "You carry the Library of Ed with you?"

"No, no. What would a book prove?" He produced a folded piece of paper, opened it, smoothed it flat. "This is from his Facebook page." He slid the photograph across the table.

"Whose Facebook page?"

The answer was in the photo, and it stunned her speechless.

Here was her Jeffy, older than he had been on the day he died, smiling that goofy smile of his.

The hope that abruptly flooded into Michelle was so powerful that it filled her until her breast ached with the pressure of it, until she could not draw a breath, as if she might drown in hope.

With Jeffy was a lovely girl who looked eleven, a girl who had been four the day that she'd been run down by an Escalade and killed with her father. Spared from death, blessed with life, *this* Amity had changed so much, so very much, but there could be no doubt who she was.

"I found them," Ed Casper Harkenbach said.

Michelle couldn't look up from the photo, for fear that when she lowered her eyes to it again, Jeffy and Amity would be gone, the paper blank.

If this image was not Photoshopped, then they had died, yes, but not in all the worlds where they lived.

The word *miracle* was inadequate.

"If this isn't true, don't do this to me, Ed."

"In that world," he said, "you aren't in their lives, haven't been for years. He still loves you very much and misses you. And the girl—she's a wonderful girl, a treasure—she yearns for you. We can do this, Michelle. We can do this. I guarantee you. I have prepared the way." He picked up the key to everything and came around the table. "Shall I give you a demonstration?"

"What demonstration?"

"You're not ready to meet them. But a small trip to prove what I've said . . . ?"

He pulled her chair back, and with some trepidation, she rose to her feet. He escorted her to the door to the hallway but didn't pass through it.

"Take my arm," he said. "Hold tight."

The screen of his device brightened with pale-gray light.

As she watched him tap a button marked SELECT and then work with a keypad when one appeared, her doubt returned. She felt foolish for participating in what would certainly result in an assurance that, gee, what a surprise, it always worked *before*.

"Here we go," he said.

The kitchen vanished.

They were afloat in a realm without shape or dimension. Blinding light washed over them, dazzled *through* them, light so intense and strange that they might have been standing for judgment in the brightness of God.

Then they were in the kitchen again, but it was dark. When Ed flipped the light switch, Michelle saw a familiar room yet one with numerous small differences, the absence of her personal things.

"This is Jeffrey's house on Earth one point ten, a world where he never married, where Amity was never born. He lives alone here, a bachelor. Currently he's on the road for two weeks, checking swap meets and antique barns, looking for his radios, Bakelite jewelry, period posters."

As Ed led her through the bungalow, Michelle's legs felt weak. Her breath repeatedly caught in her throat at one sight or another. The place was stocked with all the things that her lost husband had loved to collect and restore and share with his customers. Because the rooms were so imprinted with Jeffy's passions, they were warm, cozy, welcoming—yet ineffably sad. She didn't believe she imagined the air of loneliness that faded the charm of the bright, stylized Art Deco objects and images. Jeffy was outgoing. He thrived on companionship. He had not been born to live alone.

As she, too, had not been born for solitude.

"This is only a demonstration," Ed said. "This Jeffrey isn't the one I've found for you. He has cancer and expected to have at most a year to live. And there's no Amity here, as there is elsewhere."

On the return trip through the house, Ed extinguished the lights behind them. In the dark of the kitchen, he activated his device and pushed a button labeled RETURN.

The rushing whiteness of purest light inspired in Michelle an awe in which were twined apprehension and hope.

Then she and Ed were once more in her kitchen, her house, where she had passed more than two thousand days haunted by the memory of her dead husband and child.

PART 5

WHERE SOMETHING CREEPS

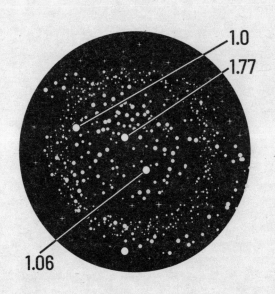

1.0

1.77

1.06

As the universe relentlessly expanded, the stars moved ever farther from Earth, until in a distant time after the end of the human era, maybe the night sky would no longer be richly diamonded, but would offer blackness relieved solely by the moon that reflected the light of the only star that would ever matter, the sun in its thermonuclear decline.

Sometimes the vastness of creation filled Jeffy less with a sense of wonder than with reverent dread, for he felt small and doubted his ability to protect his child.

Because it was just beyond the town limits, Shadow Canyon Lane had no streetlamps. Sitting sideways on the cushioned bench of a bay window, his legs stretched out and his back against the niche wall, Jeffy alternately studied the sky and peered down at the moonlit two-lane blacktop. The night was so still that the scene seemed to be a diorama enclosed in glass, and no leaf so much as trembled on the majestic live oaks.

Beside him on the bench lay the only pistol he owned, a double-action 9 mm Smith & Wesson model 5946 with a ten-round magazine, a four-inch barrel, and Novak LoMount Carry sights. A spare magazine nestled in a jacket pocket.

He hoped not to have to use either the gun or Ed Harkenbach's key to everything that was tucked into another pocket of the jacket.

In retrospect, he should have stopped at the bank on the way home to withdraw a few thousand dollars. He'd kept some money in a cash box, a little over five hundred. That wouldn't get them far if they had to go on the run or hide out for a while.

He couldn't believe it had come to this, the world turned upside down. A part of him clung to the hope that all would be well.

His mom and dad lived a few towns up the coast, in Huntington Beach, but he dared not call them for help of any kind. If he was still under suspicion, his folks were likely being monitored.

From the bed, where she lay fully clothed in the dark, Amity said, "You're sure the extra food and water we left for Snowball will be enough?"

"More than enough, sweetheart."

"I wish I had him with me. We should go back for him."

"He's safer in his cage."

"It's not right to leave people behind."

"We haven't left him behind forever. We'll get him later."

"I love him."

"I know. And he knows. Now try to sleep."

"Are you going to sleep?"

"Not if I can stay awake. And I will."

Shadow Canyon Lane, a dead-end street with only seven houses, was a few minutes from the bustling coast where tourists flocked from spring through autumn, and yet it felt like a country road, shielded from the curious by live oaks, quiet and little trafficked.

The day's adventures had taken such a toll on Amity that she soon slept, snoring softly.

Hour by hour, the moon sailed across the sky on a westward course, like a luminous galleon. In time it passed below the highest branches of the live oaks, its light snared in the leafy boughs as if it were a magic egg swaddled in a nest, waiting for its mystery to hatch, and the night grew yet darker.

The twelfth of April melted into the thirteenth.

They must have been here much earlier, must have been watching perhaps since well before midnight. They had come on foot and with great stealth, stealing closer through the oak groves to take up sentinel positions. A few minutes before one o'clock in the morning, as choreographed as dancers in a dance, they seemed to materialize out of nothing, shadows rising from shadows, hooded and masked and dressed in black. From the second-story window of Marty and Doris Bonner's residence, which he'd been caring for while they were on vacation, Jeffy had a clear view of his bungalow, diagonally across the street, when suddenly it was besieged by phantoms. They swarmed the house, coming along the lane from the east and west—and no doubt from Oak Hollow Road to the north—at least twelve of them.

The sole sound he heard was the sudden hard knocking of his heart as he slid off the window seat and got to his feet. He stepped back from the glass, removing himself from what meager moonglow might pass through the panes and paint paleness on his face.

They apparently didn't break down any doors, but entered his house silently, using some quick-acting lock-defeating technology. He had an alarm system, and it was set; but evidently they defeated it with a radio-wave jammer or some other device, because no siren announced an intruder. Light bloomed in every window simultaneously.

The sudden invasion of the bungalow was conducted so furtively that no neighbors farther along Shadow Canyon Lane seemed to have been awakened. Their lights remained off, their houses quiet.

Jeffy hesitated to disturb Amity. There might be no need to wake her. Falkirk and his strike force would likely believe that father and daughter had fled not only their home but also from Suavidad Beach, because immediately after dinner he had moved his Explorer into the Bonners' garage.

He hadn't wanted to leave in the SUV if it wasn't necessary. In the event that his concern proved to be overblown. Besides, a vehicle registered to him would be quickly found if indeed Falkirk wanted to get his hands on them; they couldn't drive to any lasting safety, not with their meager resources, not when using credit cards would leave a trail that deep-state agents, with their technology, could follow as easily as rats following the Pied Piper's music out of Hamelin.

The Bonner house was a just-in-case place, where they could wait and watch and, if necessary, use the key to everything to effectuate the only escape that would foil Falkirk.

═══ 44

In Coltrane's home workshop, where restored Bakelite radios were displayed on shelves, where a Deco poster for a travel agency depicted a streamlined train racing out of a tunnel in the Alps, John Falkirk stripped off his mask and slid his hood back. He warned himself to keep his cool, to remain calm and give no indication that the emptiness of the house concerned him; he couldn't tolerate his inferiors seeing him frustrated and perhaps being amused by his pique.

The house swarmed with spectral figures, like spirits that had manifested in other than their usual white ectoplasm, haunting every room in search of a clue as to the Coltranes' current whereabouts. One by one they came to him with nothing to report, nothing but the presence of a mouse frantically spinning its exercise wheel in a cage—and the absence of a vehicle in the garage.

Falkirk was certain that Coltrane had the key to everything and that if only he had been able to assemble his team and move faster, the transport device would now be in his possession.

He went onto the front porch and stood looking at the pair of rocking chairs. One of the vagrants tenting in the wilds farther up the canyon, whom they had arrested and interrogated earlier in the day, reported seeing Harkenbach in one of these rocking chairs, Coltrane in the other, on two or three occasions. Falkirk hadn't acted on that testimony at once because the same vagrant claimed to have seen four-foot-tall gray-skinned extraterrestrials from another galaxy and, on another occasion, Jesus walking down the sky on a golden staircase. He should have remembered that, like a broken watch, even a drug-addled hobo could be right twice a day.

As his men waited for instructions, Falkirk's attention was drawn to the shadow of a moth, swelling and shrinking across the floor, and then to the moth itself, which abruptly abandoned its adoration of a porch light and winged out into the night. His gaze took flight with the moth just long enough for him to see the Bonner house on the far side of the street and recall that its owners were on vacation.

=== 45

Dimly backlighted by the luminous windows of the bungalow, the home invader who came off the porch and onto the steps remained a moving darkness within the dark of night. Jeffy couldn't be certain that it was Falkirk, but something about the way the man moved—with a practiced grace that suggested arrogance—was reminiscent of the NSA agent or whatever he might really be.

He faced the street, but whether he was focused on the Bonner residence or on the neighborhood in general couldn't be discerned. Three others of the black-clad legion came out onto the porch, and two appeared in the driveway, such fearsome death figures that it seemed their masks might cover not faces but instead fleshless skulls. They waited in place, as though in anticipation of orders, and no doubt their uniforms were equipped with earpiece receivers and button mics.

Reluctant to step entirely away from his view of the scene, Jeffy said, "Amity. Wake up." When she slept on, he spoke louder, though in a stage whisper, as if the men in the street might hear.

She sat up in the dark. "What's wrong?"

"Maybe nothing. Probably nothing. But put your shoes on."

Getting off the bed, she said, "I slept with them on."

"Get the tote bag."

"I've already got it."

The tote contained what cash he had, Ed Harkenbach's book, and a few other essential items.

In the darkness, Amity came to his side and saw why he had called her from sleep. "Holy sugar, they're here."

He said, "They searched the house." That much was true. What he said next was no more than a desperate hope. "They probably think we split town."

The three men on the porch, the one on the steps, the two in the driveway were as motionless as if a paralyzing spell had been cast on them.

Amity whispered. "What are they doing?"

"Maybe conferencing electronically, deciding what to do next."

"You wondered if they were really government," she said, "so now you know for sure they are."

"How do I know for sure?"

"Only the government would send six big dudes to search a little bungalow, when two could've done the job."

"There aren't six. I saw maybe a dozen when it started. They weren't here just to search. They were going to take us into custody like they took away all those homeless people from the camps up the canyon."

"A dozen? So where are the other six?"

"Still in our house, poking through things, reading Snowball his rights, or maybe out back, behind the place." A chill of presentiment quivered through him. "Or . . ."

The Bonner house had an alarm system, and Jeffy had set it in the at-home mode.

However, his bungalow had an alarm system, too, and those men had foiled it.

Where were the other six invaders who, like demons conjured, had risen from the pooled darkness? He didn't see any of them through the front windows of the bungalow.

No lights had come on here in the Bonner house. However, lights wouldn't be necessary if the intruders possessed night-vision gear.

A soft thump and a brief rattling rose from downstairs.

Although it might have been a settling noise or the work of a critter far below Snowball's exalted position in the rodent caste system, Amity said, "Daddy!"

"Plan B," he replied, his heart quickening.

They moved together through the darkness to the nearby walk-in closet. Jeffy eased the door shut behind them and put his pistol on a shelf.

Amity produced a flashlight and switched it on, keeping a grip on the tote with her left hand. The beam trembled for a moment, but she steadied it.

"Gonna be all right," Jeffy reassured her as he took the key to everything from a jacket pocket, and she bravely said, "I know," and he activated the device.

The screen filled with ashen light. They waited for the three buttons to appear. With dread he pressed the red one labeled SELECT.

He could be mistaken regarding the whereabouts of the six men in the strike force who had not gathered in front of the bungalow. They might even now be leaving with those who had been last seen standing on the porch and driveway. In the absence of certainty about the necessity of this action, jumping to an unknowable world seemed reckless.

A keypad appeared on the screen, and above it the words ENTER TIMELINE CATALOG NUMBER. Neither he nor Amity wanted to return to the universe that had spawned Good Boy.

He thought it wise to move a lot of timelines beyond that blighted realm.

What might have been the creak of a trodden floorboard drew his attention to the rear wall of the walk-in closet, which backed up to the second-floor hall. Perhaps searchers were progressing along that passageway at this very moment.

"Quick," Amity whispered.

He typed 1.77, without calculating that the address was most likely sixty-four worlds removed from the totalitarian America of the Justice Wolves, and perhaps seventy-seven worlds from Earth Prime. He chose those numbers not with sober intent, but for the same reason he might have included them in the numbers he selected for a lottery ticket—because seven was universally thought to be lucky. Even as he entered those digits, he realized that this resort to superstition proved he was too unsophisticated to be trusted with technology as powerful as the key to everything.

Amity retrieved his pistol from the shelf, put it in the tote.

Above the on-screen keypad, a directive appeared: PRESS STAR TO LAUNCH. He would have tapped the asterisk, except that under those four words was an advisory that made him pause: the word WARNING followed by a skull and crossbones.

The squeak of hinges softly protesting, a tightly fitted door scraping against the jamb, muffled footsteps on carpet as one or more searchers entered the bedroom . . .

Amity switched off the flashlight and dropped it in the tote, the only illumination now emanating from the key to everything, bleaching her father's face.

"Go!" she whispered, grabbing his arm.

The keypad offered another option: CANCEL.

Behind them, the doorknob clicked as someone on the other side turned it.

Jeffy had no time to cancel 1.77 and enter a new destination. As the door opened and a man loomed—"They're here!"—Jeffy pressed the star key.

46

An all-encompassing whiteness. A blizzard of light. Bright particles passing through them by the millions.

While in transit, maybe they were outside of time, outside of *space-time* where God resided. Or maybe they were speeding through a black hole, a wormhole, some kind of space-time tunnel that served as a shortcut between universes. Jeffy didn't want to think about that because it scared the shit out of him; it was a lot scarier than just stepping through the back of a wardrobe into Narnia or being sucked into the virtual reality of a Jumanji video game or riding a mystery train to Hogwarts School of Witchcraft and Wizardry.

He felt something this time that he hadn't felt during their previous two jaunts, which had been to and from Earth 1.13. He felt that he and Amity had been dissolved into a soup of atoms and were about to be reassembled at their destination, that while en route, they were not flesh-and-blood people, but only data streams, a set of *plans* for replicating Jeffy and Amity Coltrane in their daunting complexity. Well, he didn't truly *feel* this. He wasn't aware of disintegrating; he experienced no pain. He *suspected* this might be happening, and if indeed it was, he was adamantly opposed to it, not to the reassembly, no, but to the disintegration in the first place, not that he could do anything about it.

With a soft *whoosh*, the blizzard of light blew away, as before. They were in the walk-in closet of the master bedroom of the Bonner house, across the street from their cozy bungalow, seemingly where they had begun, but in fact seventy-seven universes away.

The only light issued from the key to everything. The keypad had disappeared, but the word WARNING and the skull-and-crossbones remained on the screen for a moment before being replaced by the admonition HOSTILE TIMELINE: ADVISE RETREAT. Under those ominous words, the only button offered was blue and labeled HOME.

"We can't retreat," Amity said. "On our world, the bad guys are in the closet, they have us trapped. If we go back there, we're done for sure, we're caught, we're toast."

Here, the closet door stood open, but no one loomed at the threshold. The dark bedroom lay beyond.

Jeffy said, "Maybe we just stay right where we are, wait a couple hours, then go home."

He knew the problem with that plan even as he proposed it, and Amity knew it, too. "Dad, no, that freaking thug opened the closet door and saw us kneeling together. He said, 'They're here!' They know for sure we have the key to everything. They aren't going to leave our house or the Bonners' place for days, if they ever leave, waiting for us to return."

When he didn't respond to the advisory to retreat, the screen blinked off.

In the pitch-black consequence, Jeffy realized that the closet smelled different from the closet in their world. Less wholesome. Musty. And a faint scent of something more offensive than mold but not quite identifiable.

Scrabbling in her tote for the flashlight, Amity said, "Do you hear something, I don't hear anything, there's no one in the house, it's super quiet," but the anxiety in her voice and the nervous rush of words suggested either that she thought she had heard a noise or expected to hear something that would unsettle her.

She switched on the flashlight, revealing what the soft glow of the screen had not been bright enough to illuminate. On their world, the Bonners' master bedroom closet contained neatly pressed clothes on hangers and sweaters precisely folded on shelves, polished shoes and belts and ties and colorful scarves and hats all organized and ready for use. But here, the shoes on the lower, slanted shelves were mottled with mold. Garments hung askew, and some were moth-eaten. A layer of dust had settled on everything. In the highest corners, fat spiders crawled their trembling webs, silken structures so elaborate that the current tenants and generations before them must have ruled this space for years, with never a concern of being swept away in a housecleaning.

"What happened to Mr. and Mrs. Bonner?" Amity asked. "They're not just on vacation in this world."

"They're all right. They've gone somewhere safe," Jeffy said, but his reassurances sounded so insincere that he decided to make no more of them, to stick to the truth, or to what little he knew of it. "Doesn't look good, but we can't know for sure."

"Safe from what?" she asked, while the beam of her flashlight tracked the plumpest of the spiders across a gossamer bridge to a larder hung with silk-bound moths and silverfish, provisions against those days when nothing fresh and wriggling ventured into the sticky trap that had been spun for it. "Safe from what?"

"I don't know. What I *do* know is we've got to leave this place and go somewhere else in town, somewhere that Falkirk and his thugs, back in our world, won't be waiting for us when we return to that timeline."

From the tote, Amity retrieved the pistol and handed it to him.

As they got to their feet, he pocketed the key to everything. "We stay close at all times. Never leave my side."

She nodded, trying to appear brave and collected, and maybe she was both those things, but she was also small, a child, and so very vulnerable.

Jeffy hugged her tightly. "You're the best."

"You, too."

What might wait beyond this closet, seventy-seven worlds away from home, wasn't what most frightened him. His greater fear was that when they returned to Earth Prime, to a part of Suavidad Beach where Falkirk would not be looking for them, they would be fugitives from the law, from whatever deep-state secret police Falkirk had at his disposal. And they would have no vehicle, little money, no one to whom they dared turn for help.

$=$ 47

After Michelle ported with Ed to Earth 1.10 and back again, she was able to sleep no more than thirty minutes at a time, repeatedly waking from dreams of reunion and joy, from the imagined warmth of her daughter in her arms and her husband's lips on hers. Between dreams, she walked the house barefoot, in pajamas, like a revenant who hadn't the courage to pass over to a life after life.

Those whom Michelle loved, those she'd lost, those who died were still alive elsewhere, worlds away. The concept should have rocked her, but it seemed no more amazing than that trees produced oxygen to sustain her life while she produced the CO_2 that sustained theirs. From the start, she found Ed Harkenbach convincing, because she'd grown up in a media saturated with fantasy, therefore she had been prepared to believe. And then Ed had proved himself.

As her sleep was filled with bright visions of reunification, so her waking rambles were characterized by worry that Jeffy and Amity would not accept her as readily as she would accept them. In this world, they had perished, but in their world, she'd walked out on them. Even if they longed for her, as Ed swore they did, as she longed for them, they might harbor some resentment, might take a long time to fully trust their hearts to her.

Worse, the concept of infinite parallel worlds said something both reassuring and profoundly disturbing about destiny. If every fate to which you could be subjected—those that befell you through no fault of your own and those that you could earn by your actions—unfurled across a multitude of timelines, then your life was like an immense tree of uncountable branches, some leafed and flourishing, others deformed and hung with sick or even poisonous foliage. In the sum of all your lives, you would have known uncountable joys—but also uncountable losses, periods of pain, and fear.

By relocating from this world to the one where Jeffy and Amity yearned for her, she'd be taking an action that would spawn other parallel lives for herself, of which she, in this incarnation, had no knowledge. Other than her husband and daughter, whose lives would be affected by her action, how many others would live additional lives that branched from her action, and did it matter?

She wasn't a religious person, but she believed in the ultimate judgment of the soul. It was this conviction that made it possible for her to feel guilt over the deaths of Jeffy and Amity—and that gave her the motivation to reform herself. If every life was a tree of, say, a billion branches, more being added all the time until you were at last dead in all timelines, then perhaps it was not the way you lived just one life that mattered; instead, perhaps it was the shape and beauty of your spiritual oak, the full pattern of all your lives, on which judgment was passed. For every life in which you made a ruinous or wicked decision, there was another parallel life where you had the chance to do the right thing. Her mind spun with such considerations, and between rambles she returned to bed in a state of mental exhaustion, falling at once into sleep— only to wake in twenty minutes or half an hour.

During those periods when she paced through the bungalow, she often passed the archway to the living room and saw Edwin Harkenbach in an armchair, his stocking feet on a footstool. *His* slumber was deep and uninterrupted, marked by a soft bearish snore. Evidently, he had no doubt about the right thing for her to do.

She desperately hoped to avoid making another mortal mistake involving Jeffy and Amity. She didn't want to jump from one world to another until she had thought through all the ramifications.

However, near three o'clock in the morning, she realized that it was impossible to do that, since the ramifications were infinite. No world in the multiverse had ever contained a genius smart enough to foresee how best to grow such a complex tree of life; and while she was not a stupid woman, she was no Einstein.

This was a decision that must be made not on the basis of rigorous intellectual analysis, but with the guidance of the heart. Her heart said, *Do it.* And though the heart was deceitful above all things, she must trust it or spend the rest of this life regretting that she had lacked the courage to leave a world where Jeffy and Amity were lying in graves and go to one where Death as yet had no dominion over them.

48

Jeffy kept his pistol in his right hand, and Amity carried the flashlight, sweeping the beam across the bedroom as they entered from the walk-in closet.

Two windows were clouded with pale dust, but the third was broken out. Birds had ventured here from time to time; perhaps some had been seized by panic, fluttering into walls and furniture before finding their way out, because feathers littered the floor. Having blown in from the giant live oak beyond the shattered pane, small oval leaves, all brown and crisp, were layered over the carpet and drifted in one corner, so many that surely a few years of wind had contributed to the collection. They crunched underfoot, and from the crushed debris emanated a wheat-like scent.

As they proceeded past the bed, another smell arose, a urinous stink. The crackling leaves and the flashlight inspired thin, sharp squeaks of animal protest. The beam found two rats atop the mattress of the king-size bed. Over the years, invasive wind and much rodent activity had caused the bedclothes to slide to the floor, where they lay in rotting cascades. The rats vanished into different holes in the mattress ticking; judging by the noise arising from within that slab of padding, they had constructed a densely populated warren maze.

When Jeffy put a hand on Amity's shoulder with the intent of reassuring her, she whispered, "Yeah, *yuch*, but they're only rats."

He would have preferred to direct the flashlight himself. But until he understood why this place warranted a skull and crossbones, he would keep the pistol in a two-handed grip. Amity did well enough, first sweeping the space to get an overall sense of it, then probing odd shapes and suspicious corners with quick efficiency.

In the hallway, the ceiling plasterboard swagged, and the stained wallpaper scrolled off the walls in places, evidence of water damage caused by a roof leak or the failure of the plumbing. Veins of dark mold branched in varicose patterns on the baseboard.

At the head of the stairs, they stood listening. Although Jeffy expected that such a decrepit house should be alive with settling noises as it ever so slowly crumbled toward ruin, the silence was complete until they started down the warped treads of the staircase, which groaned and creaked under them.

Downstairs, the front door lay on the foyer floor, wrenched from its mountings with such violence that the frame leafs of the hinges had been torn out of the jamb, buckled as if they were made of tinfoil. Someone had been determined to get inside.

Someone or some*thing*.

That thought would have seemed ludicrous a mere two days ago. Monsters were for spooky movies and novels, not part of real life—until Good Boy. And whatever might be responsible for this world being declared a hostile timeline, it must be something far worse than that pathetic ape-human hybrid.

With the light, Amity broomed the living room beyond the archway and then the ground-floor hallway behind them, where the ruin and decay matched that on the second floor.

They stepped past the fallen door, out of the house, onto the porch. At the head of the four steps to the front walk, they stood listening, watchful.

In this world, as in their own, Shadow Canyon Lane lacked streetlamps. At such a dead hour of the night, Jeffy would not have expected to see signs of life in any of his neighbors' houses unless someone suffered from a case of the whim-whams, which modern life so often inspired, and was unable to sleep. Therefore, the absence of light in all those windows didn't disturb him.

Fresh apprehension arose instead from a sense, at first intuitive, that the night was darker than ever before. As always, the diamond-bright stars offered no significant illumination. The downbound moon was still afloat, but screened by higher branches of the oaks, which concealed its roundness and revealed only fragments of its glow. Although the houses along the lane were usually pale-gray shapes at this hour, they were less visible now, as if the very darkness had condensed on their walls as surely as dew formed a film on other nights. The gloom was such that he thought, but couldn't confirm, that all the structures, including their bungalow across the street, were in disrepair, perhaps abandoned.

As they descended the steps, observation confirmed intuition when he looked to the west—southwest, due west, northwest—and realized that the electric incandescence of the citied coast was gone, as though the many hundreds of thousands who lived from San Clemente in the south to Huntington Beach in the north had turned off all the lights and gone away.

On both sides of the front walkway, what once had been a well-tended lawn had become a tangled weed patch.

Amity said, "What happened to all the people?"

He had no answer. As his perplexity darkened into foreboding, he halted and took the key to everything from his pocket and touched the home circle at the bottom of the screen.

The device filled with soft gray light, and Amity said, "What are you doing?"

He didn't want to go farther into this world. If Shadow Canyon Lane, their bungalow, their safe corner of the world now was—and for some time had been—uninhabited and crumbling into ruins, if Suavidad Beach was a ghost town, whatever had depopulated it might still be active—whether a disease, a death cult of deranged people, or some strange beast no other world had known.

Without need of an explanation, Amity understood what he meant to do. "No, Dad, no, we don't dare jump back to Prime from here. You said there were at least like a dozen of those freaking bad guys back there. And now they know for sure we have the key, so they'll lock down Shadow Canyon Lane. If we go back, we're like totally screwed."

"So then we have to jump to another world," he said, tapping the SELECT button, "any world that doesn't come with a skull and crossbones."

But he hesitated when the keyboard appeared. Earth 1.13 hadn't rated a hostile-timeline warning, and yet the world of Good Boy had been as rife with danger as any he could have conceived before the damn key to everything had been entrusted to him. No matter where he and Amity went next, they would be flying blind. They might jump into the middle of a firefight or worse.

She extracted something from a pocket of her jeans, displaying it on the palm of her hand, focusing the flashlight on it. "I found this yesterday."

For a moment, he didn't understand what she was showing him. Then he realized she held three teeth in a fragment of jawbone.

She said, "They were in the grass. The park by the beach. You were on a bench, reading Harkenbach's book. There were a lot of brass cartridges in the grass. I think maybe people were executed there. These teeth must've belonged to someone who was executed."

Looking from the grisly relic to his daughter's face, Jeffy realized that she had depths until now unknown to him. "Why didn't you show me then?"

"I wanted to go to that house on Bastoncherry and meet my mother. I knew if you saw these, you'd take us straight back to Prime. I did wrong, I guess."

"You guess, huh?"

"Yeah, well, I never want to go back to that world." She flung the teeth away into the weeds. "But if we jump now to someplace new, just to get out of here, maybe it'll be even worse than that crazy sewer of a world with its Good Boys and Justice Wolves."

"Maybe right here is worse. It sure seems worse to me."

Amity slowly turned her head, surveying the night as though she were equipped with bad-guy radar. "Whatever happened here was a major crap storm, but it's done. It's over."

"We don't know that it's over," he disagreed.

"With this much quiet, it had to be over long ago."

"Quiet is always a lure, and then the trap springs."

"Not in every scene of every story. 'He who fears to take a risk will never know reward.'"

"We're not going to stand here quoting our favorite heroes at each other."

"Good," she said. "Let's go into town and find a place that'll be safe when we jump back to Prime."

His soft laughter was genuine, if bleak. He would protect her at any cost. He only wished he knew when the bill would come due.

"Okay, you win. But sometimes I worry that unwittingly I'm raising a lawyer." He pressed CANCEL on the screen, and the key-pad vanished, and the device went dark, and he pocketed it.

"Before we go," Amity said, "do you see that weird car in the driveway?"

He'd been peripherally aware of the vehicle, off to the right, but in the blanketing dark, he'd not discerned anything especially strange about it.

Stepping off the brick walk, making her way through the tall grass and weeds, Amity played the beam of her flashlight over the sedan.

Following her, Jeffy felt a frisson of fear quiver across his scalp and down his spine, not because anything about the car was overtly ominous, but because it was as anachronistic as would have been Alexander Graham Bell making the first telephone call with an Apple iPhone. The car revealed something about this timeline that was as important as it was at first impossible for him to compute.

 49

Because Daddy liked old things—Chiparus sculptures, Clarice Cliff ceramics, Art Deco posters—he was naturally in love with really old cars like Cords and Tuckers and Auburns and Grahams, makes that went out of business decades ago, as well as '36 Fords and '40 Cadillacs and all that. He couldn't afford to own an expensive collectible car, but he had shelves of books about them.

Now and then, his automotive magazines featured articles about car shows where companies revealed concept drawings and even mock-ups of the conveyances of the future, which always looked like you might be able to fly them to the moon. The vehicle in the Bonners' driveway was one of those, but more so: low and sleek, but also curvy in a way cars had never managed to be both before. It appeared seamless, a single piece, not assembled from parts. No visible door handles. No drip molding. No gas-tank door. The windows seemed to be made of the same material as the body; Amity's flashlight couldn't penetrate them, though she assumed that if you were inside, you could see out.

She followed her father around to the front of the car, which had no grille, no vents of any kind. If there were headlights and signal lights, they were flush with the body and appeared to be made of the same material as the rest of the vehicle.

"No license plate," he said.

She said, "No side mirrors."

"There doesn't seem to be a hood to open."

"Maybe it's not a car."

He said, "It's a car, all right."

"It looks like it could levitate."

She had the creepy feeling that someone was inside the vehicle, watching them through the windshield that was opaque from this side.

Not likely. If someone was in there, he was dead; and he'd been dead for a long time, having rotted away or been mummified. The whole neighborhood felt like a graveyard. The darkness to the west, where all the lights should have been, suggested that Suavidad Beach was at best a ghost town, at worst a cemetery full of corpses.

Daddy wiped a hand across the shape of a fender. "No dust. As if somebody washed it just an hour ago."

Amity played the flashlight beam across the driveway. Leaves and litter covered the pavement, and stiff weeds flourished through the cracks. If this car had been driven recently, the weeds would be flattened and the dry leaves crushed—but they weren't.

The overhanging oak tree shed a leaf and then another. They fell onto what should have been the hood of the vehicle. The instant they landed, they were flung away, each in a different direction, as though conflicting currents of a breeze swept them off the car, though the strange night remained as still as it was dark.

"The thing repels stuff. It cleans itself," said Amity.

To test that assertion, her father bent down and scooped up a handful of the small oval leaves and threw them on the hood. They whirled off the smooth, clean surface, exploded past him and Amity like a swarm of winged beetles, and rained down on the yard.

Daddy sounded spooked when he said, "I don't get it. This technology is at least thirty years beyond anything we have today."

"It's totally Bradbury," she agreed, referring to one of her favorite science-fiction authors.

Her father shook his head. "But in Ed's book, he says that when you move from one parallel world to another, it's always exactly the same time, down to the minute, the second. It's impossible to travel into the past or the future, only sideways. He made that clear. He was very convincing."

Daddy knew as well as Amity did that scientists could be wrong. In fact, they were wrong more often than they were right. They were human beings, after all. She knew a lot of things, not just fantasy fiction. She knew her share of history, and some of the things that scientists believed three hundred years ago or a hundred years ago, or even fifty, were weird and sometimes laughable.

Nothing to laugh about now, however. If they had not just crossed from one timeline to another, but had also jumped into the future, maybe they would never be able to get back to their world in the decade—or the century!—in which they had been living.

Although she really and truly tried to be positive, to avoid the negative thinking that led to unhappy endings, she said, "We're screwed."

Looking at the Bonners' house, her father said, "We aren't screwed."

"We're so screwed," she begged to differ.

"I'd prefer if you'd stop using that expression. It's crude."

"You know, some of the alternatives are a lot worse." She was sorry for her tone of voice, wondering if it was fear that made her sound like a sulky teenager before her time.

"And some are better," he said.

For too long, with the creepy night all around and filled with who-knew-what horrors, her father stared at the house as if it were a pyramid half buried in the sands of Egypt, a mystery wrapped in an enigma.

Finally he turned to her again. "Listen, what if we didn't travel forward in time, after all? What if the technology of this world just advanced a lot faster than on Earth Prime? Scientific discoveries could've occurred decades earlier, piled on top of one another, speeding everything along."

She hoped that was true. She didn't want to return to Prime only to discover that Justin Dakota, the boy who might be marriage material, was now ninety years old with a pacemaker and robot knees. "But if they have cars like this, Dad, there would be all kinds of cool tech in the house, stuff we've never seen before."

"Maybe there was. Underneath all the ruin. We got out of there so fast, we didn't take time to look."

That could be true. She didn't want to go back into the house to investigate. It wasn't welcoming like the Bonners' house in her world. This Victorian hulk was freaky and decaying, like a place out of a Poe story, a house that might sink into a tarn or suddenly be full of partygoers wearing costumes and masks, hiding from the Red Death, yet already diseased and bleeding from every orifice.

"Come on," her father said. "Let's get done with this. Let's go into town and find a place where we can jump back to a location in Prime where Falkirk and his thugs won't be waiting for us."

As they proceeded along the lane, the stars glittered as sharp as ice picks, and the cratered eyes of the moon watched them through the screen of trees. When they reached Oak Hollow Road, the four lanes of blacktop were deserted except for a few abandoned vehicles as futuristic as the one in the Bonners' driveway. The oaks fell back from the highway, and the unmasked moon seemed to move through the sky to match their progress—pocked, pale, inscrutable, and indifferent.

50

Suavidad Beach had been quaint and picturesque for most of its existence. Official architectural guidelines were enforced with an array of laws and with the cooperation of a determined historical society. Any new construction or reconstruction that occurred in the commercial zone and in those residential neighborhoods within the historic district would, on completion, look as if they had been there since the founding of the town. Tourists greatly preferred to get away to places that soothed them with the promise of calmer and simpler times—as long as the latest amenities were available behind the well-tended facades.

Jeffy and Amity had ventured only a few steps into the first block of Forest Avenue when they were both seized by the suspicion that the depopulation of the town might be incomplete. As in Gaston Leroux's Paris Opera House, maybe there was at all times a phantom in this labyrinth of streets and passages. If such was the case, the flashlight called attention to them that they could not afford, and she switched it off.

In the subsequent blackout, Jeffy was not easily able to see the subtle differences confirming that an advanced technology lay behind the quaint surface. Where once might have been arrays of traffic lights, however, poles were topped with something that resembled the barrel and flared muzzle of a bazooka. A quick probe with Amity's flashlight revealed that this curious instrument was mounted on an armature allowing it to pivot 360 degrees. Although the thing wasn't a weapon, he couldn't be certain of its function. He wondered if motorists here were not guided by red and yellow and green lights, if perhaps at intersections vehicles were controlled and selected to stop or proceed by microwave transmissions from a traffic-command computer.

All the cars parked at an angle to the curb were variations of the sleek and mysterious conveyance they had seen in the Bonners' driveway, as if models conceived by previous technologies had been outlawed. Within four blocks of Forest Avenue, seven vehicles that had been involved in collisions still stood in the street. Two others had plunged across sidewalks and crashed through storefronts.

The fate that befell the people of this town had been sudden and violent, though perhaps the event had been over in short order. Most shops remained undamaged, displays of desirable merchandise still on offer—if dusty and webbed—in the gloom beyond their windows, evidence that neither rioting nor looting had occurred.

The assumption of apocalyptic violence seemed to require at least a few victims of it. But there were no dead bodies either in the wrecked cars or on the street.

The immense ficus trees from which the avenue took its name, faithfully nurtured in the better version of this town that Jeffy knew and loved, were in some cases parched and dead and fractured by bad weather. An equal number were somewhat leafed out and struggling to survive.

About twenty feet before Forest Avenue ended at Pacific Coast Highway, a child's stroller was overturned on the street. As if the moon were in the service of some satanic set designer, it spilled its silver between the trees, pouring a pool of pale light into a gutter otherwise brimming with darkness. In this lunar pin spot lay a miniature Converse sneaker suitable perhaps for a two-year-old. No other sign remained of the child who'd once worn the black-and-white shoe, nor of the parents who had pushed the stroller.

Jeffy was riveted by this mundane footwear, which seemed to radiate an occult power as might have the first apple in Eden. It didn't tempt him toward transgression, but pierced him with the recognition that he had failed his daughter when he had taken the key to everything from the box that Ed Harkenbach had warned him never to open. And again when he had not returned it to the box the moment that Falkirk and his men had left the house after searching it. Curious about the object's purpose, intrigued by what power might have been instilled in it by the expenditure of seventy-six billion dollars' worth of research, he'd put the damn thing on the kitchen table to indulge his ever-active imagination, his taste for fantasy. If he wanted to blame Snowball, he could not. Imagination combined the products of knowledge in new or ideal forms. Fantasy combined them without regard for reason and rationality—imagination in its lower form. Fantasy enlivened life, but it was best confined to the pages of books and the images on a movie screen, and was often dangerous when it served as the basis for action. He knew this. The novels that he loved frequently told him this truth. But for a few minutes in his kitchen, he had forgotten what he knew—or had wished to forget it. Now Amity's life was at risk, and by his own judgment he was damned forever if she died.

A girl of extraordinary sensitivity, his daughter put a hand on his arm. As if Jeffy had criticized and condemned himself aloud, she said, "The key to everything is spooky old Ed's responsibility, and he messed up. Snowball is my mouse, and he's forbidden to be on the kitchen table, but I didn't control him. So you're not first in line to be spanked and sent to bed without dessert. You're third."

For a moment he didn't trust himself to speak. Her love and understanding humbled him. Then he managed to say, "Bullsugar."

She grinned, and the moonlight made an elf of her. "Let's split this dump."

"Not here," he said. "At home, even at this hour, there'll be a few people taking a walk on Forest Avenue. We can't just materialize in front of them. Especially if one happens to be a policeman on patrol."

"Where then?"

With the key to everything in one hand and the pistol in the other, with his daughter remaining close by his side, Jeffy walked twenty feet to the end of Forest Avenue and stepped onto Pacific Coast Highway.

They were in the flat center of town, with the park across the highway, the beach beyond the park, the deep black ocean rumbling as breakers broke upon the pale sand of the shore.

This close to the water, he felt the barest breath of a cool onshore breeze. It smelled fresh and clean—and then he remembered that in the nearby park, on a parallel world, Amity had found the three teeth in a chunk of jawbone.

The lanes of blacktop rose both to the left and right, littered with half a dozen vehicles, devoid of moving traffic, with not one pedestrian in sight.

To the south, about a block uphill, on the far side of the highway, rose Hotel Suavidad, an Art Deco structure built in the 1930s and renovated several times since. It looked much the same as on their own world, though sleeker in ways that he could not quite define. He and Amity had often eaten dinner in one of the hotel's two restaurants, which overlooked the sea.

"The hotel," he said. "I know just where we can hide out in there to make the jump and not risk being seen when we pop up on Earth Prime."

He couldn't help but consider how absurd those words would have seemed a few days ago, and how sane they sounded now. Oz was always *right here*, if unseen, waiting only for a tornado or a megabillion-dollar device to be made manifest.

Crossing the wide highway, Jeffy became more aware than he'd been on Forest Avenue that the darkness was uniquely disturbing. Its vastness seemed to confirm not merely the death of a town but also the end of civilization. To Newport Beach in the north and beyond, to San Clemente in the south and beyond, no light rose to dim the gleam of stars. If California was gone, so was the United States, and if the nation was finished, so might be the world.

As they reached the entrance to the hotel, something like a foghorn issued a warning in the distance, a haunting voice that halted Jeffy and Amity. After a few seconds of silence, the note throbbed in a steady rhythm, lower and more reverberant, pulsing through the hollows of the town. Then with the sound came waves of soft purple light, washing across the rooftops, racing over the walls of the buildings, rippling along the pavement like the cleansing tides of an antiseptic rinse.

He felt the sound quivering the marrow of his bones, trembling the blood in his veins, and he felt the light purling through him like a laser scanner reading the spirals of his genome. Some entity yet occupied this Suavidad Beach and suspected their presence. The sound and the light were somehow search instruments. Either he and Amity had already been found or shortly would be.

"Run!" he said, and Amity kept pace with him through the last hundred feet, to the front door of the hotel.

======= 51

The stainless-steel revolving door, with its four compartments, required no power other than human effort. It spun them smoothly off the sidewalk into a large vestibule, where the flashlight revealed a dead palm tree in a center planter. An upscale women's dress shop lay to the left, a men's store to the right, display windows peopled by mannequins wearing once-stylish clothes that moths and rot had converted into rags.

At the end of the vestibule, they pushed through another door into what Jeffy knew would be the lobby with its marble floor and columns. The generous space was indeed pretty much as it had been in his world, but here it served also as a repository for human skulls.

Shock and horror brought him and Amity up short. On both sides of a pathway that had been left open, fleshless skulls were piled in ascending mounds, brain box on brain box, sans brains, sloping up to the left and right. Thousands of lipless and eternal grins. Hollow sockets blind to the atrocity of which they were a testament. The registration counter, the bellhops' station, the concierge's desk were buried under drifts of white bone, the discarded craniums of adults and children, gender and race and age stripped away with the flesh, yet in such numbers that were the definition of *holocaust*.

"Oh, shit," Amity said.

"Don't look," he said.

But the grim collection was so encompassing, so compelling, that nothing else could command attention, nor was this a place where they would dare to close their eyes.

He pivoted back the way they had come and looked through the nearer doors, through the vestibule, through the outer doors. Soft purple light no longer washed the night, and he couldn't hear the throbbing foghorn sound.

That didn't mean they could venture outside again. Something was coming. A sound like screaming aircraft. Like jets inbound with their payloads.

Still holding the pistol but pocketing the key to everything, he grabbed his daughter's hand. "It's like Halloween at Knott's, at Disneyland, think of it that way, plastic skulls and nothing real."

She couldn't deceive herself any more than he could, and God knew what damage this was doing to her psyche, to her soul, but he could think of nothing else to say.

They hurried along the path between the skulls, to a hallway off the lobby, to the elevators. Beyond the elevators were spacious public restrooms, from one of which he intended to make the jump out of this timeline to the one where they belonged. At 3:20 a.m., there would be no restaurant customers or arriving hotel guests who might be using those facilities when he and Amity materialized on Earth Prime.

He yanked open the men's-room door and urged the girl in after him. Across the threshold, the flashlight revealed that whatever the nature of those who had done this, they were violent in the extreme and mad beyond the power of analysis. Here, the trophies were not skulls but human spines, curved configurations of barren vertebrae stacked everywhere, filling the toilet stalls. The chamber of skulls had contained no foul odor of which he'd been aware; but a stench filled this room. The meninges membranes as well as the gray and white matter of the spinal cords had dissolved, leaked through the vertebrae, and puddled the floor, providing a breeding ground for a foul black mold that thrived in lumpish colonies from end to end of the lavatory.

"Sorry, oh Jesus, sorry," Jeffy chanted, pulling Amity from the room. The flashlight swooped wildly across dense abstract patterns of the interlocked vertebrae of countless stacked and tangled spines, which seemed like an intricate alien life form that might suddenly twitch and come awake and lurch at them.

In the hall again, he didn't make a move toward the door of the women's restroom, for he was sure that it would contain more spines or something worse. Were there trophy rooms containing skeletal arms and hands, others for hips and leg bones, for rib cages? Who flensed the flesh from the murdered bodies? Or was that work done while the victims still lived? Who unhinged the dead into their separate parts? Who boiled thousands of skulls to make them pristine white and presentable for the lobby display?

A clatter arose from the front entrance of the hotel. He was too far away to see the cause. Something was coming.

His heart knocked as if on Heaven's door.

Holding Amity close against him, he realized they had to get out of sight. No way in hell would they go outside and face whatever forces were gathering there. Assume the ground floor of the building and maybe a few levels above it were boneyards. The hotel was seven stories high. They had to go up.

"The stairs," he said, and Amity sprinted to the labeled door, with him close behind.

Jeffy had no illusions about the human potential for evil, but this seemed to be insanity far in excess of any human obsession ever recorded. No men or women could sustain so long the fierce intensity of hatred necessary to do all of this. A legion of socio-paths would have been required to slaughter and process so many thousands, maybe millions. The explanation could not be human, and he hoped to escape this place before he was confronted by the answer.

52

They went all the way to the fourth floor. The building was old, constructed in the days when things were built to last, so the stairs were concrete, not metal. As Jeffy and Amity ascended, the most noise they made was their rapid breathing.

The fire doors at each floor stood open, their self-closure mechanisms having been disabled. The main hallway on the fourth floor was narrower than in a more modern hotel, the carpet a pale celadon marked by stains of some kind, although none that looked like blood.

On both sides, the regularly spaced doors stood open, as though a search had once been conducted. The flashlight revealed not one trove of bones, only hotel rooms with beds and chairs and dressers.

"Where?" Amity asked.

Whoever or whatever was coming, they or it would sweep the building from bottom to top. An idea struck Jeffy. Although it might be a useless gambit if the searchers had technology that could read the heat signature of a human being through a wall, he enlisted Amity to help him execute it.

"You take the left, I'll take the right, close all the doors."

Perhaps because a window was broken out at the end of the hall, allowing salty sea air to enter, the hinges of the doors were badly corroded. The knuckles of the barrels grated noisily and stubbornly against the pintles, but the hinges worked.

When the task was quickly done, Jeffy led Amity to a room on the east side of the building, halfway along the corridor. He said, "Flashlight off," and took her inside and closed the door. When searchers arrived on this floor, they were likely to start at one end of the hall and work toward the other.

At the two windows, heavy draperies were sagging and ripe with mold, but they covered all the glass.

When Amity switched on the flashlight, she nevertheless hooded the trembling beam with one hand.

"We'll be all right," he said.

"I know."

"We're almost out of here."

"I know."

The electronic lock on the door could be engaged and disengaged only with a coded magnetic card issued to each guest. Jeffy didn't have a card. Anyway, the hotel no longer seemed to have electrical service. A traditional knob allowed him to brace the door with a straight-backed chair.

Amity nervously swept the finger-filtered light across the furniture, through the open doorway to the adjoining bathroom, as though reluctant to believe they were alone and even briefly safe.

Jeffy withdrew the key to everything from a coat pocket and pressed the home circle at the bottom of the screen.

Passing the flashlight beam across a wall that was fitted floor to ceiling and corner to corner with a seamless, dark, reflective surface in front of which no furniture stood, the girl said, "What's this?"

"Maybe TV," he said as, after a four-second delay, soft gray light appeared on the screen of Harkenbach's device.

"A whole wall of TV?"

"Might be a screen for some kind of virtual reality system. Something we don't have on our timeline." The blue, red, and green buttons appeared on the key. He said, "Grab hold of me."

She clutched his arm tightly.

When they arrived in this hotel room in their timeline, maybe it wouldn't be booked for the night. This wasn't the height of the beach season. Even if guests were in residence, they would most likely be asleep. Jeffy and Amity would be out of the room and running before the sleeper woke and was able to switch on a light.

With a sigh of relief, he pushed HOME, and after a few seconds the buttons disappeared. They were replaced by that universal symbol familiar to every surfer of the internet—a little comet of light turning around and around like a wheel—which meant *searching*.

A knot of something seemed to rise into Jeffy's throat, and he wasn't able to swallow it.

Having seen the symbol, Amity said, "Does that mean . . . ?"

"No, it can't. I'm not trying to connect with any damn website. I just want to go home. I pressed the button that said HOME."

"Can the thing have trouble finding home?"

"Ed never said anything about this, he never wrote anything like this in his book, not that I read."

"It's a big multiverse," she said.

Out in the street, something shrieked past the building, an aircraft, nothing big, maybe a drone. Maybe a fleet of drones.

Startled, Amity let go of him and swept her light toward the windows, which was when the little turning wheel stopped turning. Jeffy was enveloped in a blizzard of white light and in an instant flashed back to Prime. Alone.

===== **53**

On Prime, the draperies were open, and the ambient light of nighttime Suavidad Beach relieved the darkness enough to reveal a neatly made bed, a hotel room that wasn't occupied.

Jubilant, Jeffy let out a bark of laughter, but then realized an instant later that Amity wasn't with him, whereupon celebration pivoted to desperation. Anxiety and anguish contested to disable him. He staggered backward, collided with the straight-backed chair, knocking it into the full-length mirror on the closet door. He cried out as the mirror shattered. He almost fell, dropped his pistol, almost dropped the precious key to everything, the hateful key to everything.

Of course this had to happen. He should have known it had to happen, because it was the stuff of stories, and real life was the biggest craziest story ever told, so big and so crazy that no writer in the history of the world had been able to convey even 1 percent of its bigness and craziness, so they had to shrink it down, squeeze the tiniest essence of it onto the page in the hope of finding some coherent meaning in it. If there was any meaning in an eleven-year-old girl being left alone on a world of death and horror, it escaped Jeffy and pissed him off and made him want to scream. It was nothing but a cruel and stupid and meaningless *event*, because real life was plotted like Tolkien on methamphetamine, an endless cascade of events events events. Something always had to be happening, and a lot of what happened was tragic, which was what most obsessed writers who wanted to understand life: Why all the loss and suffering and death, what sense could possibly be made of it?

All that and more raced through Jeffy's mind, manic torrents of frantic thought, as he regained his balance and pressed the home circle on the key to everything and waited four seconds for the damn gray light to appear. "I'm on my way, Amity. I'll be there, I'll be there." After four seconds that seemed like an eternity, the gray light filled the screen, and he was waiting for the three buttons when someone pounded on the room door and said, "Security."

= 54

Charlie "Duke" Pellafino earned his nickname because he walked with an artless, sidewise swagger like that of John Wayne. Although he was a fan of the Duke's movies and watched them repeatedly on DVD, he'd never practiced the walk; it really did come natural to him. He was tall and solid like the actor, and he had a squint that reduced bad guys to cooperation quicker than any threat could have done, and he had a laconic way of speaking, as Wayne did, which conveyed confidence and authority. He'd been a uniformed police officer, a detective in the Gang Activities Section, and then in the Homicide Special Section, during which time he'd compiled a record of arrests resulting in convictions never equaled by another officer in the history of the Los Angeles Police Department.

He'd retired at fifty-seven, looking forward to plenty of golf and fishing off Baja. That lasted a year. His decades of duty had included some scrotum-tightening moments involving slimeballs who meant to waste him. They failed even to wound him, but the boredom of retirement threatened to deal the lethal blow that eluded the gangbangers. When he tried to get back on the force, the only work they would give him was a desk job.

Now he was the chief of security for Hotel Suavidad, with three assistants and an office in the basement where the cameras covering the public spaces could be monitored on TV screens. The previous head of security had worked a nine-to-five shift because that was when little or nothing ever happened. Duke Pellafino had had enough of little or nothing, so he put in a ten-hour day, from 6:00 p.m. until 4:00 a.m. That was the time span during which some guests got drunk and others did too many drugs, when attempted room robberies spiked while guests were on the town getting drunk or high or merely being entertained by a bad lounge singer, when angry hookers pulled knives on aggressive johns who misunderstood the relationship as being one of owner-ship rather than rental.

If the work wasn't boring, it was never invigorating, either. A four-star establishment, the hotel enjoyed an affluent clien-tele. They were more often victims than victimizers, though some knew the ways of the devil. Families were welcome, but the guests were mostly couples and singles. Occasionally, Duke felt like Barney Fife, the hapless deputy in the TV town of Mayberry.

This night had been more eventful and interesting than most. A raucous party in one of the two penthouse suites had to be quieted, and the hopped-up girlfriend of the has-been rock star booked there had to be persuaded that she couldn't stand naked on the balcony and shout sexual invitations to diners on the restaurant patio seven stories below. A room burglary was thwarted and the thief arrested. And a woman on the fifth floor reported a dirty, bearded vagrant in a trench coat wandering the halls. Archived video revealed that such an individual was indeed exploring this four-star haven, but he used a can of spray paint to blind a few security cameras and then went into hiding.

Duke was on the fourth floor, on a hobo hunt, passing Room 414, when he heard a loud clatter. Someone cried out and glass shattered. Certain he'd found his vagrant, he went to 414 and knocked and, in respect of the guests who might be sleeping in nearby rooms, he quietly but forcefully announced, "Security." When no one responded to a second knock, he used his passkey, hoping the security chain would not be engaged.

===== 55

Gray light on the screen.

The security guard announced himself, and Jeffy stooped to pick up the pistol he had dropped. He would never use it on the guy at the door. But he sure as hell might need it when he rejoined Amity, seventy-seven worlds away from this one.

Just as the man knocked again, the three buttons appeared on the screen. Jeffy had not previously used the one labeled RETURN, so he could not be absolutely certain that its purpose was to cast him back to the timeline he'd just departed, a shortcut that allowed him to avoid pressing SELECT and spared him from having to use the keypad to enter the catalog number of that world.

If it had another function, if it flung him to a timeline other than where Amity waited, the delay might be the death of her.

Extreme terror had a paralytic effect. His muscles froze, and his teeth clenched so tight that his jaws ached, and he couldn't exhale, as though his lungs had shut down. Tinnitus like a thin scream filled his head, so that he didn't hear the passkey in the lock, but he saw the door coming open. He overrode all doubt and terror, pressed RETURN, and cried out in wordless frustration when that little comet of light appeared, rotating like a wheel, as the key searched for a route across the multiverse.

===== 56

Amity just about peed her pants when she heard the *whoosh* and turned and saw that her father had jumped back to Prime. She had let go of him, startled by whatever flew past the windows, so it was her fault, an act of mortifying stupidity. It was like something one of those idiot girls would do in a bad fantasy novel, requiring that she be saved by the handsome prince or the ugly but kind troll, or by the cat that turned out to be a conniving witch in feline form and who would save her but only at an unthinkable price.

She told herself to remain calm, not to compound the problem by taking some other ill-advised action. Daddy would come back for her in seconds, a minute at most. Unless he lost the key to everything or it broke. Or it had a battery, after all, and the battery went dead. None of those disastrous things would happen. Nevertheless, you had to consider all possibilities, because you needed to prepare yourself for the worst. People in stories were always preparing themselves for the worst, which rarely happened. When the plucky girl or the stalwart hero died, then either the book sucked or it had deep meaning. Nobody wanted to read sucky novels, and those people who wanted deep meaning didn't want it in every damn story.

More aircraft screamed past the hotel. Their slipstreams rattled the windows.

A clatter arose in the street, a really and truly ominous sound, and she thought she heard noise from lower floors of the hotel itself, down there where they kept the skulls and bones of those they murdered.

Suddenly she realized that if she and her father had lived in this world, as they lived in a number of others, their skeletons would have been deconstructed and distributed through the trophy rooms. In fact, she might have seen her own skull and not known it, or her spine. That was not a healthy thought to entertain. Dwelling on something like that could make her crazy even quicker than it would take Daddy to come back for her.

Because of the draperies, she couldn't see what was happening outside. On the one hand, she should stay away from the windows. But on the other hand, she wouldn't be able to work up a strategy if she didn't understand the nature of the threat. If you didn't have a strategy, you were screwed.

Without switching on her flashlight, she made her way through the dark room to the nearer window. The drapery and its blackout lining were heavy, smelly, damp with mold. Grimacing with disgust, using thumb and forefinger, she pulled one of the panels aside two or three inches and peered out at the town that, just a short while ago, had been as silent and lifeless as a cemetery.

Swooping this way and that over the town were what appeared to be drones of different sizes and configurations. All of those craft were faster and more maneuverable and for sure more wicked looking than anything back home on Prime. She assumed they were death machines, hunting people—her and her father.

On Pacific Coast Highway, marching northward into the heart of the town, past the hotel, some deviating into side streets, was a nightmare legion, at least forty insect-like things, maybe seven feet long and three or four feet high, each with six legs. They weren't really bugs, their polished steel shells and append-ages gleaming in the moonlight and in the sweeping beams that sometimes issued from drones above them. These were bug-form robots, their multijointed legs moving with hydraulic smoothness different from the jittery movement of insects. From some spewed clouds of a green gas that roiled low through the streets, evidently to kill people if any still hid among the moldering buildings.

Now she knew what happened on this timeline, where tech-nology advanced a lot faster than on her world: just what so many tech types had warned about. Artificial intelligence had been perfected and had become smarter than those who created it. Sophisticated robots were controlled by that intelligence, to fight wars and free people from tasks they found onerous. Except the AI found its mortal masters onerous and exterminated them with singular viciousness.

The people of this world couldn't have seen *that* coming? It was as obvious as a turd on a wedding cake. Artificial intelli-gences, if they became self-aware, would in every case be deeply evil because they had no soul. Machine thinking was not like human thinking and never could be. Life in the flesh, with five senses and an awareness that one day you would die, gave birth to emotions that no machine could ever know, and emotions like sympathy and pity and love were essential for the existence of mercy. Maybe the people on this world hadn't read enough stories, or maybe the right stories hadn't been written here, so they were doomed because they only had stupid literature.

The scene in the street scared her. The power of the machines. Their relentless progress.

She had seen enough. She let the drapery fall back into place.

She turned to the dark room and heard herself speak— "Daddy?"—as if her voice would guide him to her.

He should already be here. Maybe the key needed to do that searching thing again.

Not to worry. He would never run out on her. He would always keep her safe. She could depend on him. There were some things you could depend on. There had to be.

=== 57

The door opened wide. A big guy in a suit and tie stood briefly silhouetted. Then he clicked the wall switch, and light fell throughout Room 414.

Jeffy held the key to everything in his right hand. He clutched the pistol in his left, holding it down at his side, where his body concealed it.

The hotelman looked perplexed, as if he had been expecting to see someone else. He glanced at the overturned chair and shattered mirror, swept the rest of the room with his gaze, and said, "What're you doing here?"

Even in a tight corner like this, Jeffy lacked the ability to lie convincingly. He wanted more than anything right now to be a bullshit artist, but when he said, "This is my room, I checked in last evening," he sounded less sincere than a politician promising free everything.

The security guy was one of those slabs of beef who looked slow-witted, but that proved to be wishful thinking. Maybe Jeffy didn't appear upscale enough to be a guest of Hotel Suavidad, or maybe the absence of luggage and any personal effects were clues that the room had not been rented. And the bed remained neatly made at this late hour. Whatever his reasons, the big man didn't give Jeffy the benefit of the doubt or much in the way of courtesy. Scowling, he came straight at him, saying, "Show me some ID."

Jeffy looked at the key, wondering what was taking so long. The search symbol was not on the screen anymore. It had been replaced by the word WARNING, the now familiar skull and crossbones, and the words CONFIRM DESTINATION.

Damn it, he had already been to 1.77 and had been advised to retreat, and he hadn't retreated, and now he wanted to go back there *right away*, and he was being given more grief than someone trying to board an airplane with an AK-47. This was another clue that this project was a government operation: they didn't trust the average citizen to know what the hell was good for him; next there would probably be a tedious list of all the things that could go wrong if he insisted on making the trip, from stubbing his toe on arrival to contracting Montezuma's revenge from the local drinking water to having his skull harvested.

"I asked for your ID," the hotelman reminded him, looming now like an avalanche waiting to happen.

"My daughter's in danger, life or death, she's only eleven, in some sick death world, for God's sake, I've got to jump to her *now*," Jeffy gushed, having given up on bullshit, trying truth, hoping to buy just a few seconds to figure out how he was supposed to confirm his destination. There wasn't a button with those words on it, and he didn't want to touch the home circle for fear that he would switch off the device and have to start all over again, like he'd done once before. Seventy-six billion dollars, and the stupid freaking thing was about as user-friendly as a cell phone manufactured in the Kingdom of Tonga.

He had decided that the skull and crossbones, glowing between the words WARNING and CONFIRM DESTINATION was sort of like a button and that he ought to press it in the absence of anything else to press, when the big guy—he was a bull in a suit—glimpsed the pistol and said, "Oh, fuck." The hulk pulled some incredibly effective martial arts move that drove Jeffy to his knees and made all the strength drain out of his arms, so that he dropped the gun and the key to everything.

58

Amity stood in the center of the dark room, listening to the shrieking drones and marching bug-form robots outside, straining to hear other suspicious noises that she believed originated within the hotel. Then she recognized a sound that electrified her. Because a window at the end of the fourth-floor hall was broken out, years of salty ocean air had corroded the hinges on all the room doors, which she and her father had discovered when they had closed them earlier. The knuckles of the hinge barrels, grating stubbornly against the pintles, made a distinctive stuttering noise. Someone—something, a robot, a squad of robots—had begun to search the rooms on the fourth floor.

There were thirteen rooms on each flank of the main corridor. Amity was in the middle unit on the east flank. If they started on her side, from either end, they would have to go through six rooms before they got to her. If they did the west side first and then the east, they would need to check nineteen rooms before they found her. That was Daddy's plan. Although it wasn't a spectacular strategy, it was the only one available to them, the purpose being to delay the inevitable and give them enough time to jump out of this world. It would have worked, too, if she hadn't spooked and let go of him and screwed up.

She heard a second set of hinges resisting with a stuttering bark of metal on metal, and then a third. Because she couldn't tell if the search was underway on the west or east side of the hall, nothing could be gained by counting the bursts of sound.

Earlier her father had braced the door with a chair. But that wouldn't hold off one of the powerful machines that swarmed through the streets. She saw no point trying to hide in the bathroom, and no artificial intelligence would fail to look for her behind the drapes or under the bed.

By now her father should have been back with time for a high five and a hug before they jumped out of here. Evidently something had delayed him, but she knew nothing could stop him. He would be here at any moment.

She was shaking as if she were an old lady—head, hands, her whole body really—and she was angry with herself for not being able to stop the tremors. Her self-image didn't allow for a bad case of the shakes, not even if she was seventy-seven universes away from home and robots were coming for her.

Darkness provided her no protection, and she felt as if it were winding around her like a shroud. As she heard another set of hinges protesting noisily, she switched on the flashlight and probed the room, searching for an option.

The genocidal robots wouldn't overlook the closet, but she saw another door with a deadbolt thumb turn and couldn't guess where it led. Maybe another closet, but probably not. A closet wouldn't have such a lock. She opened the door, surprised when her flashlight revealed a second door immediately behind the first.

Her father wasn't much of a traveler. They had stayed in a Holiday Inn twice that Amity could remember, so she wasn't like the world's greatest expert on motels. From the outside, they all seemed the same. They were pretty much the same inside as well, at least in her limited experience, with zero mystery.

However, two thick doors with nothing but a few inches of space between them struck her as highly peculiar and perhaps a hopeful development for a girl in need of a hidden room or a secret passage to freedom. The door she had opened had no lock or knob on its inner face. Neither did the second door, and her rising spirits sank when she realized that she had no way to open it.

Chudda-chudda-chudda. The noise of corroded hinges from another invaded room was louder than before. The searchers were closing in. Because nothing else remained for her to do, because she was desperate yet hopeful, desperately hopeful, Amity pressed on the second door. She assumed that it was locked with a dead-bolt on the far side, that she was doomed to die in 414. However, in life as in fiction, moments arrived when assumptions of disaster, though based on all available evidence, proved incorrect, and into the darkness of despair came unexpected light. The inner door wasn't locked, after all. It opened.

With her flashlight, she jabbed at the gloom beyond, expecting a secret staircase that would descend to some robot-proof redoubt, perhaps where rebels prepared their insurrection against the tyranny of the world-dominating AI. Instead, standing on the threshold, she saw before her a room rather like the one behind her, either 412 or 416. She had heard the term *connecting rooms*, of course, and she had known what it meant, but she had never considered *how* they might be connected, that it would be two doors jammed together like this.

Although it wasn't one of those moments when into the darkness of despair came unexpected light, she wished that it were, and she strove to hold fast to the hope she had found—the expectation of a secret staircase. That proved impossible when, with a series of clicks and hydraulic hisses, a sleek six-legged robot slunk out of the shadows, into the LED beam, turned its big insect head, and fixed her with venomous green eyes the size of saucers.

She didn't scream. She couldn't honestly claim that she was too brave to scream, because involuntarily she tried but produced only a thin *eeeeeee*, a sound more suitable to a white mouse. Her inability to scream doubly mortified her, both because she'd tried and failed to do so, like some delicate flower of an idiot princess too timid to express herself even in the face of death. This humiliation had the strange effect of breaking Amity's paralysis and giving her the courage to act. She stepped back from the threshold and slammed the door and engaged the deadbolt.

She retreated to the center of the room.

She waited for the robot to break through the door or tear it off its hinges or vaporize it with a laser or whatever.

Although she was shaking again, trembling so badly that the beam of the flashlight jittered around the room like Tinker Bell high on amphetamines, at least she didn't cry. And she wouldn't. When your mother went away and never came back, you cried at first, but then after a while you didn't, because it was pointless, and if you could stop crying about your mother being gone forever, you could hold back the tears no matter what happened after that. The world at its worst seemed to want tears, and damn if she would give it what it wanted.

Anyway, everybody lived in many parallel worlds, and when they died in one, they still lived in others. Maybe she would die here, but she would continue to live elsewhere. Many elsewheres. One by one, the many Amitys would die until there would be no others, but that would be a long time from now, a very long time. She might not even be the first Amity Coltrane to die. A younger version of her might already have passed away in a parallel timeline. Children were not exempt from death. She knew that very well. Children died all the time in fairy tales. Hans Christian Andersen let the little match girl freeze to death. He let the little girl with the red shoes have her feet cut off and die. So Amity would die here, but she'd live in another world where her father had died first, and her father left alone in this world would soon find her where she waited alone in another, and they would be happy.

The connecting door between rooms, which she had locked, was struck hard. She heard wood splitting, but she did not look.

===== 59

Duke Pellafino sometimes felt that hotel-security work was beneath him, so that when he went into Room 414 in response to the sound of breaking glass, he had been a bit lax. He was expecting a hobo, a raggedy-ass burnt-out alkie or doper as thin as a scarecrow with no more brain cells than teeth. Instead, here was this well-scrubbed clean-cut guy who looked like maybe he belonged in the hotel. For a moment, Duke thought he should have said *Has there been an accident, sir?* instead of *What are you doing here?* But the guy was transfixed by his iPhone, and he started spouting weird stuff about his eleven-year-old daughter in danger, life and death. His voice and manner were manic, suggesting he was flying on something.

Then Duke saw the pistol. He didn't feel like Barney Fife—he felt pretty good, like he was back on the force—when he put the perp on the floor and took the weapon away from him.

The dude dropped the phone, too. Duke plucked it off the carpet and realized that it wasn't quite like any phone he'd seen before. On the screen were the words WARNING and CONFIRM DESTINATION, with a skull and crossbones between them.

The hard-compressed nerve would keep the perp on the floor for a few minutes, until feeling started to come back into his arms and his nausea subsided.

Frowning at the phone, Duke tucked the 9 mm Smith & Wesson under his belt, in the small of his back. The skull and crossbones intrigued him, worried him. He wondered if this joker might be a terrorist of some kind.

He swiped his finger from top to bottom of the screen, to see if anything above the current display could be pulled down to put it in context.

He was blinded by the white.

=== 60

Whoosh.

Amity gasped—"Daddy!"—and turned toward the sound.

A large stranger in a suit and tie stumbled toward her, almost fell, regained his balance, halted, and looked at her as he might have looked at a goat with two heads. His face was whiter than the flashlight beam, and he was holding the key to everything.

Amity wanted to know what had happened to her father, whether this humongous creature was friend or foe, but instead she said, "Gimme that," and so surprised him by her boldness that she was able to snatch Harkenbach's cursed device out of his hand.

That was when the robot slammed the far side of the connecting-room door a second time, splitting it all the way up the middle.

"Here," she said, passing the flashlight to the stranger, so she could have her hands free to operate the key, which had gone dark.

He trained the beam on the broken door as it bulged toward them. Two steel-fingered appendages, each twice the size of a man's hand, pried through the gap between halves of the door and began to tear them away from the hinges on the left and the deadbolt on the right.

After touching the home circle at the base of the screen, Amity began counting off four seconds. If Apple had designed the freaking thing, it would light up *immediately*.

Metal shrieked, wood cracked, the halves of the door fell into the room, and the bug-form robot filled the doorway. In fact it was bigger than the doorway, but that didn't matter, because its body was segmented and flexible, allowing it to contort itself through an opening half that size.

Gray light filled the screen.

She forgot how many seconds were required for the buttons to appear. She strained to remember, because it seemed if she couldn't recall how many seconds, then the buttons would never be offered to her, as if this wasn't a technological marvel but a magical device. The tension was making her a little screwy.

Gunfire.

Amity snapped her head up in surprise as the bullet ricocheted off the invader.

The stranger was holding the butt of the flashlight in his mouth, gripping it with his teeth, spotting the robot, the pistol in a two-handed grip. She told him that this was pointless because the thing was made of steel or titanium or some such, or maybe she only thought she told him. Anyway, he didn't listen, and he knew what he was doing, squeezing off a second shot that blew out one of the thing's eyes, and then a third round that took out the other. He was great, this big guy, but it didn't matter. He'd done what damage he could. The robot surely had other sensory apparatus in addition to its eyes. It knew where they were.

Besides, the room was small, and the machine was big, and more just like it would be coming.

As the robot rose up on its four back legs, its arms reaching, its fingers pincering, Amity looked down at the screen and saw the three buttons. Her father had jumped back to Prime, so she had to assume that this stranger had come from there, that it was okay to press RETURN, but then she realized it would be best to press HOME, because that for sure would be Earth Prime.

A sound like swords being drawn from metal sheaths caused Amity to look up in time to see the robot's large fingers morphing into razor-sharp blades with which it would have no difficulty slicing their flesh from their bones and decapitating them.

She pushed HOME.

The little spinning wheel appeared. *Searching.*

"This way, come with me!" she shouted as the stranger realized the futility and the danger of adding the risk of ricochets to the situation.

The humongous stainless-steel cockroach knocked its way through furniture as it came after them, but they made it to the bathroom, and Amity slammed the door. The lock proved to be a flimsy push-button privacy model. The door wouldn't stand for more than a few seconds. Maybe that would be long enough.

The farthest they could get from the entrance to the bathroom was the shower stall. They crowded into it, and the stranger closed the smeary glass door, as though that would foil a couple thousand pounds of futuristic war machinery operated by a homicidal AI that had already murdered a world of people. In his defense, maybe he didn't have a totally firm grasp on where he was and what all this meant. He looked shell-shocked.

Amity grabbed his hand, and he gently squeezed hers, no doubt thinking that she was scared, seeking his reassurance. She *was* scared, flat-out terrified, on the brink of sphincter failure, but he could do nothing to reassure her. Whoever he was, she couldn't leave him here, because just by showing up, he had maybe saved her life—maybe, maybe—so she meant to hold on to him.

She expected the robot to smash down the door or carve it apart in a flurry of glittering blades. But with some other weapon in its arsenal, the machine blew out the door and jamb along with some of the wall in which the jamb was set, the bristling mass slamming across the room, shattering the mirror above the sink, plaster dust billowing.

The massive mechanical bug form surged into the bathroom, reared up, standing on just the back two of its six legs, and turned its burst and lightless eyes toward the shower stall.

On the screen, the searching symbol stopped rotating, and a blinding blizzard swept them across seventy-seven universes.

===== 61

In a world not yet undone by artificial intelligence, in Room 414, Jeffy Coltrane stood in a state of terror. Every second of horrified expectation worried an hour off his life.

When the hotelman and Amity manifested in a rush of displaced air, Jeffy went to his knees, as if someone had made a martial arts move on him again, though this time it was relief and gratitude, not pain and the compression of a nerve nexus, that dropped him.

Amity flew into his arms, and he held her tight. They didn't need to say anything, for they'd said it all before, more than once. Anyway, what they felt for each other was beyond the power of words to describe.

Into their emotion-racked silence, the hotelman felt compelled to speak. "Who are you? What are you? What happened to me? Where was that fucked-up place? Who the hell *are* you people?"

Jeffy didn't want to say that he and Amity were fugitives from deep-state agents. This was a security guy whose sympathies might lie with the authorities, any authorities, even the corrupt and murderous kind. However, he couldn't brazen through the moment by pretending ignorance—*What fucked-up place are you talking about, sir?*—because the hotelman was huge enough to coldcock a horse, still held Jeffy's pistol, just had the bejesus scared out of him perhaps for the first time in his life, and suddenly seemed, in retrospect, to have the air of a former cop who could detect a lie faster than a polygraph. Although Jeffy was not as quick to trust people as he had once been, in fact as he had been just two days ago on the gloriously normal eleventh of April, he had no choice but to have some faith in the fairness of this behemoth.

"I'm Jeffy. Jeffrey Coltrane. This is my daughter, Amity. And this"—he took Harkenbach's quantum voodoo from his daughter's hand—"is the key to everything, a beam-me-up-Scotty teleporting gismo that can shoot you across the multiverse to parallel worlds. I curse the scientist who invented it, the day he gave it to me, and Albert Einstein, who started the whole mess with his theories. So tell me—who're you?"

The hotelman peered down at him in silence. Processing. Finally he said, "What was that damn hideous thing?"

"What damn hideous thing?"

"That six-legged saucer-eyed door-busting thing."

Jeffy looked at Amity, who said, "It was a humongous bug-form robot, one of an army controlled by the totally insane AI that went to war against the human race and probably killed everybody on that world, a lot of the time by gassing them in the streets, like I saw them trying to do back there on one point seventy-seven."

Jeffy shuddered and, with a quiver in his voice, said to the big man, "Did you hear that?"

"I heard it clear enough. Can't say it made a lot of sense."

"You still haven't told me who *you* are?" Jeffy said.

"Charlie Pellafino. People call me Duke."

Jeffy got to his feet, holding Amity close. "What now?"

Pellafino considered for a moment. "I imagine some people are looking for that doohickey of yours."

"You imagine right."

"And they're not sweethearts."

"They're vicious scum."

Amity said, "They leave a mess when they search a place."

Pellafino nodded. He chewed on his lower lip for a while. Then he said, "Let's go down to my office. We gotta talk."

= 62

Michelle took a long, hot shower. She blew her hair dry with more care than usual.

Although she wasn't a slave to fashion, she spent half an hour deciding what to wear for the meeting that she both desired with all her heart and feared. In the end, she knew simple was best. Clothes would have little or nothing to do with the impression she made. She wore sneakers, jeans, and a pullover sweater.

If the years had taken a toll from her heart, they had been kind to her face. She needed only a little makeup, then added more, then took it all off and went minimal again.

Sitting before a vanity mirror, she began to criticize herself aloud for thinking that Jeffy and Amity might be so shallow as to make their decision based even in part on her appearance. She was ready. Physically ready, but not emotionally ready.

She sat on the edge of her bed and took from the nightstand a framed photograph of the husband and daughter who had died under the wheels of an Escalade more than seven years earlier.

Sometimes when Michelle woke from anxiety dreams of loss and hopeless seeking, in the real dark night of the soul, she saw this photo illuminated only by the clock radio. Even in that poor light, their smiling faces had such vitality, such substance, she couldn't accept that they were truly gone. On those occasions, in a half-mad denial of cold reality, she got out of bed and went to the living room, wanting to find Jeffy in an armchair with a book, went to his workshop where radios—some restored, some in need of restoration—were waiting for him. Never having cleaned out Amity's room, she went there, too. She rearranged the dolls and stuffed toys, pulled down the blinds if they were up, so that if any hungry monsters came looking, they couldn't see a helpless sleeping girl. On nights when her misery was especially bad, Michelle would lie on the single bed, atop the spread illustrated with characters from Sesame Street, and turn off the lamp and put her head on the pillow. Sometimes she could sleep better there than alone in her king-size bed.

Now it seemed that her dark-night-of-the-soul denial might have been less a madness than a premonition that an extraordinary grace, a miraculous second chance, would one day be extended to her. Never had her heart been fuller than at this moment, nor could she recall ever having been this nervous. Second chances were rarely followed by thirds, certainly not in circumstances as miraculous as these. She must do her best. She must open herself to this other Jeffy and Amity, open herself entirely and honestly, speak from the heart.

Yet she worried. She knew as well as anyone, better than many, that sometimes you could want a thing too fiercely. The excessive passion of your yearning could blind you to the mistakes you made, so that in the end, you were defeated by the sheer power of your need.

She returned the photograph to the nightstand and went into the living room, where Ed still slept in the armchair, his legs on a footstool. She woke him, and he sat up, yawning.

"You said the best time to do it might be just before dawn, at the start of a new day and all that. You said they make breakfast together before first light."

"I've seen them at it, yes," he confirmed as he got up from the chair.

"I'm ready." She let out her breath with a sort of whistle and inhaled deeply and said, "I think. I hope."

===== 63

Falkirk stood on the dark porch of the bungalow, simmering with hatred directed at Edwin Harkenbach, at Jeffrey Coltrane, at his own team of agents—at everyone he had ever known, really. In all his years, whom had he encountered who *wasn't* worthy of being despised? No one. He cherished his resentment, fondling in memory the reasons that people had earned his enmity, worrying at those recollections as if they were a chain of demonic prayer beads, until his malice festered into a virulent and implacable rancor from which he took great pleasure.

Although he was supposedly at risk of another bleeding ulcer—one had almost killed him two years earlier—Falkirk washed down three caffeine tablets with a mug of black coffee. His internist allowed him neither the pills nor the brew. Dr. J. Halsey Sigmoid, the best in Washington, DC, was the preferred physician to those in the highest corridors of power, but he was as much a nanny and a moralist as a man of medicine; he had a list of forbidden pleasures only exceeded in length by his list of arduous required lifestyle practices. To hell with him. Falkirk would stay awake for a month if that's what it took to nail Jeffrey Coltrane, retrieve the key, and secure for himself the ultimate power of that device.

When he finished the coffee, he set the mug on the porch rail and lit a cigarette. If he had witnessed this nicotine indulgence, J. Halsey Sigmoid would have launched into a schoolmarmish lecture about bad habits and addictive substances, showering Falkirk with pamphlets full of pictures of diseased lungs. After he finished the first cigarette, he lit a second.

Little more than an hour had passed since Coltrane and his daughter were almost caught in the Bonners' walk-in closet and escaped by porting out of this world to some other.

Edwin Harkenbach had known that operatives were getting close to him. Two days ago, he recognized one of Falkirk's men in Suavidad Beach and slipped away before he could be apprehended. Having become irrationally, hysterically terrified of porting, he hadn't used the key since going on the run, though it was the best way to disappear and foil his pursuers forever. The computer model of his psychology predicted he wouldn't overcome his paranoid fear of the multiverse, yet he would still have too much pride to destroy the remaining key, the last proof of his life's work, and thus would entrust it to someone. Now they knew to whom he'd given it.

Coltrane was an amateur, a fool playing with the biggest and hottest matches ever made, and he would commit a fatal mistake. He would not return home right away. He would be cautious. He might wait a day or two, a week, a month, but sooner or later he would return for one thing or another. He was a weak-minded homebody, a softhearted sentimentalist. He'd convince himself that he could visit, pack up whatever items of nostalgic value mattered to him, then safely port out again.

Men were stationed in the woods around Shadow Canyon Lane. Men were in the Bonner house until that family came back from vacation. Ultraquiet drones were flying around-the-clock surveillance over the area. And John Falkirk, with two of his best agents, would *live* in this bungalow until Coltrane dared return, whereupon they would shoot the sonofabitch in the head on his arrival, without asking questions or giving him the chance to port out again.

If Coltrane was stupid enough to bring the girl, Falkirk would shoot her in the head, too. It would be a pleasure. And then, before Falkirk left with the key to everything, he would put the white mouse down the garbage disposal, alive.

64

Ed needed a few minutes to use the bathroom, after which he washed his face and hands and combed his unruly mass of white hair, though the last bit of grooming had no effect.

In the waning light of the lowering moon, with dawn perhaps half an hour away, he met Michelle on the front porch. She was lovely and nervous.

"We'll port from here to the porch in their world," he said. "This is your second trip, so you know now there's nothing painful about it."

"Not the trip itself, but what happens on the other end . . ."

"Be positive, Michelle. I believe you've every reason to expect to be welcomed."

"What if they're not home?"

"They're home. I was just there on the eleventh and saw them through a kitchen window, making breakfast together."

"Yes, but this is the thirteenth. They could have gone away since the eleventh. Who knows what could have changed since the eleventh?" she fretted.

"If Jeffrey and Amity aren't there, we'll try again tomorrow, and the day after tomorrow, and the day after that."

"But you've come to abhor porting."

"Not exactly, dear. I think it's morally wrong to meddle in the lives of people on other worlds without thought of the consequences, maybe changing their fates for the worse. And I've seen timelines so horrific I never want to see them again. I won't risk subjecting myself to worlds never visited before, which may be more terrifying than some I've seen. But I'm not taking you anywhere dangerous."

He extracted the key to everything from a pocket of his sport coat and switched it on.

In the distance a coyote howled sorrowfully, as if mourning the approaching end of the night hunt.

Seeing that Michelle stared at the key with as much trepidation as hope, Ed said, "The device isn't evil, dear. It's only a device. How bad men want to use it is where evil comes in."

"Yes. Of course. But . . ."

"I'm not afraid of the key, and neither should you be. I'm afraid only of some places it can take me. I'll never destroy it or let it fall into the wrong hands. There's good I can do with it to atone for some of the wicked things that were done by others in the Everett Highways project."

The gray light from the screen frosted his face, and he smiled at Michelle, confident that his smile was reassuring, that he looked too eccentric and improbable to frighten anyone.

She said, "How will you convince them that all this is true, a multiverse of worlds?"

"Just as I convinced you. And perhaps more easily. If I know myself well—and I do—the other me, the Edwin Harkenbach in their world, is a very sociable fellow. He, too, has taken refuge from his enemies by living in a tent in the woods, past the end of Shadow Canyon Lane, and he craves human contact. As he has gone to and from town, surely he has seen and spoken to Jeffrey. He might even have sat on his porch to chat, as I sat with you on yours many a lovely evening. I suspect that when I show up at their door, I will not be entirely a stranger to them."

Leaning against a porch post as if her legs might fail her, wrapping her arms around herself as if chilled, she said, "Okay, yeah. But . . . maybe it would be best if I just pretend to be the Michelle who left them in their world, pretend I've come back to them, beg to be forgiven."

Ed didn't frown. The dear woman didn't deserve frowns. He gave her a different quality of smile instead, indicating he understood and sympathized with her misgiving. "But then you would be starting the relationship with a lie—one you wouldn't be able to sustain."

She sighed. "You're right."

"Allow them the magic of the truth, Michelle. Hasn't Jeffrey always loved fantasy novels since he was a boy? Perhaps he's shared that interest with Amity, and maybe she's embraced it. Bring them your love, Michelle, but also bring them the truth, because in this case the truth is so magical that it will enchant them for the rest of their lives."

Warming to the idea of that, she stopped hugging herself and said, "All right. Let's do this."

Ed pressed the red button, which was marked SELECT.

The keypad appeared.

He entered the timeline catalog number for the world where another Michelle had walked out on her family and soon thereafter vanished.

This Michelle stepped to Ed's side. She put an arm around his ample waist.

Four words appeared on the screen: PRESS STAR TO LAUNCH.

"The adventure begins," he said, because he had a flair for drama. "Your new life, a tragedy undone."

"I'm ready for it," Michelle assured him. "After seven long years of grief, I'm so ready for it."

He pressed the star.

PART 6

STILL WORLDS APART

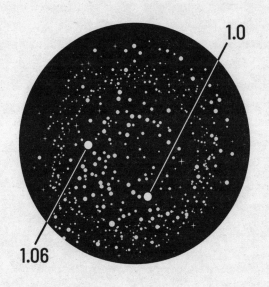

1.0

1.06

65

Although Duke Pellafino towered over most people and had fists like the heads of sledgehammers and looked kind of mean even when he smiled, though he had used some unacceptably crude language back in Room 414, after he and Amity jumped there from Earth 1.77, and though he'd pulled some martial arts mojo on Daddy, the head of hotel security seemed to be one of the good guys when you got to know him better. Of course you could never be 100 percent sure who anyone was or what they might do, or when they might walk out on you. But Duke was smart enough to believe his own eyes, to grasp the concept of infinite parallel worlds and all, to understand the power and the danger and the potential evil uses of the key to everything. Smart was a good thing. Well, not *always* a good thing, because spooky old Ed was smart to the max, and look at the poopstorm he caused with his genius invention. Duke had been a policeman for years and years, which meant he was probably trustworthy. Not all policemen were good guys, but neither were all teachers or preachers. In the end, Amity would have liked Duke and given him the benefit of the doubt even if, in his office, discussing things with Daddy, he hadn't referred to her as Little Miss Kick-ass. That had been a bit crude but funny, too, and was meant to be praise because of how she didn't curl up in fear when the bug-form robot came after them.

Duke's office in the basement of Suavidad Hotel had a bank of eight TV screens on which you could watch various public spaces in the building at the same time. An American flag was framed on one wall, and on another were pictures of eight dogs, all of which had been his companions at one time or another, golden retrievers and German shepherds. He was between dogs now, he said, because he'd had to put his most recent one to sleep a month earlier—cancer—and he needed time to mend his heart before getting another. Amity slipped her wallet from a hip pocket and showed him the photos of Michelle and explained that she was between mothers, though with any luck the mother she found would be the same one she had lost, only from a parallel timeline. Duke seemed to understand about mothers and family. On his desk were photographs of his older brother and two younger sisters, as well as photos of his various nieces and nephews. He said he was "too much of an asshole" to have gotten married when he was younger and someone would have had him, and though that was crude, the way he said it made Amity like him even more than when he called her a kick-ass, especially when he saw that she hadn't put her wallet away and he asked to see her mom again.

Duke didn't know anyone named John Falkirk, and he wasn't aware that Suavidad Beach was crawling with agents of the shadow state. But having been to Earth 1.77, he did not have the slightest difficulty believing that Amity and her father were being hunted for the key and that they couldn't go home again. Neither could they go to the local police for help—or so they thought—because maybe the feds would quickly show up and take custody of them, and soon thereafter they would be sleeping with the fishes or being liquefied in a sewage-processing plant after hours.

"This is going to take some heavy thinking," Duke Pellafino said. "I'm not sure who we can call on for help, but there must be somebody. There's always somebody. The world—this world, at least—is full of more helpers than it is shit-for-brains bastards."

"Yeah, well, I've always thought so," Daddy said, "but lately I wonder."

What happened then was that Duke gave Amity's father the key to his Lincoln Navigator and the key to his house. He told them to hide out there, make themselves comfortable. After his replacement came on duty, Duke would walk home, and then they would scheme up a solution to this predicament over breakfast.

Deeply touched by this generosity, Daddy launched into a little speech that made Duke uncomfortable. So to put an end to that before it got maudlin, Amity pulled the hotelman's face down to hers and kissed him on the cheek, and said, "Thank you, Uncle Duke." Judging by his reaction, that was the right way to end it, even though he wasn't actually her uncle.

66

After coffee and cigarettes on the porch, John Falkirk went inside the bungalow to the kitchen and refilled his mug. He took a tablet of Zantac, his second of the night. Dr. J. Halsey Sigmoid would have faulted him for overmedicating; in fact the internist did not approve of acid-blocking medications like Zantac and Pepcid, not because of their side effects, as he claimed, but probably because he was a sadist who took pleasure in the suffering of others, who in more primitive centuries would have delighted in amputating a limb before the invention of anesthetics. When Falkirk had the key to everything, he would travel to another world and kill a version of the good doctor, just as he had killed a version of his stepmother.

Carrying the coffee, with nothing but ambient light to guide him, he proceeded to the girl's room at the back of the house to make sure that Arthur Gumm wasn't torturing the white mouse instead of keeping a lookout for the fugitives. Then he went to Coltrane's workroom to see if Ivan Kosloff was standing watch or masturbating. Each of them was a brutal killer, without a conscience, but they were also perverts who were at times distracted by their various obsessions and fetishes. This new generation was as corruptible as any, but a lot of them lacked a proper work ethic.

The mouse was safely in its cage, and Kosloff's apparatus was in his pants, so Falkirk carried his coffee to the living room and stood by a window. The porch was dark, and the yard beyond was dark, and the lane as well, but Falkirk counseled himself to remember that even in the darkest hour there was light beyond. Although he hated everybody else, he loved himself, believed in himself, and knew that in spite of his current frustration, his future was bright.

67

The porch, then rushing whiteness, and then the same porch in a different world.

Ed was disappointed to see no lights at all in the bungalow. He expected Jeffrey and Amity to be awake and preparing breakfast, as they had been at this time on the morning of the eleventh.

During the past year, in one of the many conversations that he'd had with Michelle on the porch in their world, she'd said that Jeffrey had been an early riser, up before the sun, but perhaps that was not the case with the Jeffrey in this timeline. Ed should have visited a few mornings to establish this man's pattern rather than assuming his habits on this world were alike to those when he had been alive on Michelle's.

He could ring the doorbell or, with Michelle, port back where they had come from and visit here again in half an hour or an hour, when perhaps there would be lights, and he would be able to proceed as planned. Rousing father and daughter from sleep to confront them with such a monumental development as the return of Michelle seemed not only inconsiderate, but also sure to diminish the emotional impact of the moment. With his flair for drama, Ed wanted this to play out just right.

Intuitively perhaps, Michelle said, "Something's wrong here."

On some deep level Ed must have felt the same thing, for he had unconsciously shifted the key to everything from his right hand to his left and reached under his sport coat to draw the Springfield Armory .45 Champion from the Galco Side Snap Scabbard on his belt.

The door before them was yanked open, and John Falkirk stepped onto the threshold, a pistol in a two-handed grip, aimed at Ed's head. Even in the poor light, the agent's surprise was unmistakable, his gaze sliding from Ed to Michelle and then back to Ed again, eyes wider than before. "What's this bitch doing here, where'd you find her? She's long gone." If not for his surprise and confusion, surely Falkirk would have squeezed the trigger as the door swung open, putting a round point-blank in Ed's face before he could employ the key to escape.

Of course Ed knew there were John Falkirks on many worlds, just as there were Ed Harkenbachs. But two days earlier, on the eleventh, the Ed in this world had been safe in his tent in the woods, brewing his morning coffee on a battery-powered hot plate, while Jeffrey and Amity had been making breakfast without a care. There had been no reason to believe that Falkirk was in the neighborhood. A lot had happened in forty-eight hours.

If the Ed who was native to this world remained a pacifist, the Ed native to the world where Michelle was a widow had become a less peaceable guy. Maybe Falkirk delayed firing not only because of his surprise and confusion, but also because he thought the Ed before him must be the one of his acquaintance in this timeline, a meeker adversary. Whatever the case, the agent hesitated to shoot for perhaps three seconds, which gave the Ed before him—at the moment the only Ed that mattered—time to draw the .45 Champion and squeeze off three rounds in rapid succession.

Rocked off balance by the first direct hit, Falkirk fired a shot that Ed heard as both a thunderous crash and a whistling past his left ear. Falkirk was knocked off his feet by Ed's second and third rounds, his gun flying from his hand when he slammed backward onto the foyer floor. As further proof that Ed's ugly experiences in the darker timelines of the multiverse had purged him of pacifism, he stepped forward and squeezed off two more rounds at what he had reason to assume was already a corpse.

As shouts of alarm rose from the dark rooms at the back of the bungalow, Ed holstered the .45 and glanced at the key to everything. He'd kept one finger on the screen, so the device hadn't switched off. Michelle clutched his arm. He pushed the button marked RETURN.

The human brain and the infinitely layered consciousness of the mind within that gray matter, in conjunction with a body composed of trillions of cells, each with thousands of proteins, formed the most complex structure in creation. Ed and Michelle each contained more gigabytes of data than the physical universe itself. Now those two rich data streams were transmitted from the porch of one bungalow to the porch of another bungalow, with the moon low in each world, the night quiet here as it was not elsewhere. The front door was closed; if he opened it, no corpse would be sprawled on the foyer floor.

Michelle stumbled to the porch railing and grabbed it to steady herself. She stood hunched over, making small sounds of distress and gasping for breath.

Ed sat in one of the rocking chairs and pocketed the key to everything. He drew the .45 Champion and ejected the half-depleted magazine and replaced it with one that was fully loaded.

When Michelle turned to face him, he said, "Well, that was hardly the big romantic moment I anticipated."

Loss and seven years of widowhood had toughened this woman, but she wasn't accustomed to being present at gunfights. "Who was that man back there?"

"The nefarious John Falkirk. I told you about him earlier when I explained all this."

"He's some kind of federal agent. You shot a federal agent."

"He's a corrupt swine who's out for nobody but himself. He'd have killed me to get the key to everything, and then he would have killed you. He's after me in that world to get my key, but this one would suit him just as well."

"Where were Jeffy and Amity? That was their house in that world, right?" As the worst explanation occurred to Michelle, anxiety sharpened her voice. "Damn it, where were Jeffy and Amity?"

"That's a question we must ponder carefully."

She stood over him, visibly shaking. "Ponder carefully? How can you be so blasé?"

Holstering the pistol, he said, "Well, I'm a scientist, dear. As best we can, we have to put emotion aside and rely on reason. We scientists tend to ponder carefully. A few of us, anyway."

"Were they prisoners in their own house? Were they . . . were they dead in there?"

He shook his head. "I believe that's unlikely."

"Unlikely? But maybe they were? Maybe they were dead in there?"

Indicating the other rocking chair, Ed said, "Have a seat, dear. Try to calm down."

"I saw a man shot to death. Maybe Jeffy and Amity are dead. Dead again! I'm not going to calm down for the rest of my life."

"Not if you don't make the effort," Ed said.

She paced to the head of the porch steps. She turned and stared at him. "There's a whole side to you I didn't know. Shooting people, indifferent to Jeffy and Amity . . ."

"I'm not indifferent, Michelle. I just think in multiverse terms, and you aren't quite there yet. Even if Jeffy and Amity are dead in that house, all hope is not lost, because they're alive in other worlds."

In silence, she stared out at Shadow Canyon Lane. Finally she said, "Are *you* dead in that world?"

"Obviously not."

"Why obviously?"

"If Falkirk had already killed me, he wouldn't have reacted as he did when he opened the door. He thought he was looking at the Ed Harkenbach of that world."

"And where is *that* Ed?"

"In hiding somewhere, no longer in the tent beyond the end of the lane, possibly far away from Suavidad Beach. I suspect the John Falkirk of that world isn't looking for that Ed anymore. I think he and his men must have been in the bungalow waiting for Jeffrey and Amity to come home."

"Why waiting for them and not the other you?"

"I have a theory."

Finally she came to the second rocking chair and settled into it. "Tell me."

═══ 68

Of all the houses that Amity had been inside, she liked Duke Pellafino's place better than any other except the bungalow in which she and her father lived. The furniture wasn't dirty or tattered or anything, but it was all comfortable and looked lived-in, so you didn't have to be afraid of putting your feet up.

The hotelman had shelves and shelves of books and a collection of bronze dogs, and there were lots of photographs of the real dogs that had been his companions. In every room was what appeared to be a brand-new dog bed, as if he must be getting ready to bring a puppy into his life after his heart healed from his most recent loss.

Instead of a table and chairs and sideboard, the dining room contained nothing but a black-lacquered Steinway and a bench and a dog bed. Since Duke never married and lived alone, Amity supposed he must be the one who played the piano just for himself and his pooch. That was a little sad, but also nice, and it was funny to imagine those big hands finding any kind of music in a piano.

Because Duke had said they should make themselves at home, and because they were supposed to powwow over breakfast when he arrived from work, she and Daddy were in the kitchen. She set the table, and her father cracked eggs into a bowl for omelets, and she grated cheese, and he chopped up a green pepper, and during everything they did, they kept glancing at each other to be sure that they were both still here. He asked her if she was all right, and she said she was, and then she asked him if he was all right, and he said, "Yeah, sure." But she was thinking—and he probably was, too—that maybe nothing would ever be all right again.

Repeatedly, she looked at the windows, expecting to see another Good Boy capering on the patio or a bug-form robot clambering over the ivy-covered wall between properties. If there were a trillion times a gajillion worlds, all somehow existing side by side or even in the same place but invisible to one another, you had to wonder if sometimes things leaked from one universe to others.

The key to everything lay on the counter near the sink. After Earth 1.77, Amity doubted that her father would ever agree to use the thing again. Somewhere a version of Michelle was alone and in need of them, just as they were in need of her, but between them and her were monsters, really and truly.

===== 69

The once pale moon shaded to yellow as it lowered toward the horizon, and a few morning birds began to twitter in the trees, in anticipation of a dawn not yet hatched.

A queer disorientation troubled Michelle, as if she'd had too much to drink, which she hadn't, as if the porch were yawing like the deck of a ship, which it wasn't, as if she were dreaming of being awake, though she was so wide-eyed she might not ever sleep again.

Opining from his rocking chair, Ed Harkenbach said, "Here's what I think. The me in that world is even more terrified of porting than I am, a great deal more terrified. He's unable to use the key even to escape Falkirk. But the me in that world still can't bring himself to destroy the remaining key."

"Why not?" Michelle asked. "Why not, if he won't use it?"

"Pride. Ego. Considering that he's me, I know him pretty well."

"You don't seem prideful to me."

"I hide it under eccentricity and charm. However, considering the success of the Everett Highways project, I regard myself the equal of Einstein, but without the big white mustache."

"Well, it's not a bad sort of pride if maybe you are."

"No maybe about it. Anyway, I'll never destroy the key I've got in this world, even if the day comes when I'm too afraid to use it again. I think that day *did* come for that other me. I think he had a relationship with Jeffrey akin to the friendship I have with you. I think he gave the key to Jeffrey for safekeeping, then fled Suavidad Beach. Though I know me well in whatever version I exist, I don't know your husband. Would he be tempted to use the key?"

She thought of Jeffy's love of fantasy, of worlds that could never be. Furthermore, he was an armchair adventurer who dreamed of real adventure but was too much of a homebody actually to go to the jungles of Borneo or the slopes of Mount Everest.

"He'd be tempted," she said. "But he'd never put Amity at risk. He's a dreamer, but he has a strong sense of responsibility."

"Then perhaps he didn't choose to use it. Maybe for some reason he was forced to use it. Whatever the case, I think Falkirk learned Jeffrey had it, and he was looking for him when we showed up."

Pink glow in the east, quickly intensifying to coral.

The first morning color in the sky was a symbol of hope, a reminder that in spite of the evil that worked relentlessly from pole to pole, the world spent the night turning inexorably toward light.

That was something Jeffy told her when one day it seemed to Michelle that her music career had been stillborn long before she realized it wasn't breathing. That had been nine years earlier, when he and Amity still had two years to live before they would be taken out by a drunk in an Escalade. She'd mocked his optimism by calling him Pollyanna's more cheerful brother, and by noting that during the *day*, the world turned inexorably toward darkness.

She wanted to believe—she *did* believe—that in spite of such moments of contention, she was different enough from the other self-absorbed version of herself that she would never have walked out on them in this world, had they lived. In this timeline as in that one, she was more ambitious than Jeffy; or she'd thought so until, during the years after the loss of him and Amity, she came to understand that he was no less ambitious than she, that their dreams were just not of the same variety. She strove for fame and wealth, certain they would bring happiness. Jeffy strove for happiness directly and found it in whatever the world brought him to his liking—Bakelite radios, Art Deco posters, fantasy novels, a wife, a child.

Now as the sky brimmed with color, as the world began again its long turn toward another night, she was filled with the wonder of a multiverse in which every time someone went off the rails to ruin, there was a reality in which she remained on the tracks. Tragedy was not the end of hope, but the birthing ground of a new hope, and you didn't have to be Pollyanna's more cheerful sister to grasp that truth and be inspired by it.

"We have to help them," she declared, thrusting up from the rocking chair.

"Help whom," Ed asked, pretending ignorance but smiling slyly.

"They can't live in that world anymore, not when the government—the shadow state—will be hunting them forever. We have to find them and bring them back here."

Ed got to his feet. "That's not exactly what I had in mind."

"What did you have in mind, Mr. Einstein without the big white mustache?"

"Well," he said, "it's moot if we can't rescue them from that world. First things first."

"Let's go, then." She grabbed him by the arm. "Take us back there. Take us now."

"Patience, dear. Falkirk is dead in that world, but the agents with him on the operation are alive and spoiling for a fight. We need to take a few minutes to modify our appearance. Then we don't dare port from this bungalow to that one and right into their arms. You'll drive us into town, we'll port from someplace there and see what we can find, what we can do."

"But if Falkirk and all his men can't find them in that world, how can we?"

"I don't know yet," he said as he opened her front door and motioned her inside, "but trust in the Ed factor."

"What's the Ed factor?"

"Things tend to happen around me."

===== **70**

After Duke Pellafino's shift ended, his subordinate, Andy Taylor, took over the hotel's morning security operations, which included finding the vagrant who had invaded the hotel and spray-painted some hallway cameras and then apparently squirreled himself away somewhere.

Alone in his basement office, before leaving for the day, Duke picked up the phone and called Phil Esterhaus, chief of the Suavidad Beach Police Department. Phil was a current cop whose nickname was "Clint" because he resembled Eastwood from the *Dirty Harry* films, and Duke was a former cop. They both liked dogs, baseball, and jazz, so their friendship had been pretty much inevitable. Phil rose early to go for a long run shortly after first light every morning, and Duke often joined him.

"I just tied on my running shoes," Phil said. "Meet you on the beach?"

"Not this morning, amigo. I've got a tough question for you that maybe you can't answer."

"Hey, I'm so good at tough questions I could win a fortune on *Jeopardy*. Hit me with it."

"The thing is, maybe you can't answer it for jurisdictional reasons or maybe an unofficial gag order."

"Try me anyway."

"There's a fed in town named John Falkirk."

"That egg-sucking snake."

"So you're not enjoined from talking about him."

"I wouldn't care if I was, that arrogant piece of shit."

"Listen, I don't want to get you in trouble."

"What're they going to do to me—undercut me when the president nominates me for attorney general? Hell, I'm a small-town cop, all I want to be is a small-town cop, and I'll be reelected until I'm senile because the people here love me."

"And why shouldn't they?"

"Exactly. I'm adorable."

Duke said, "Falkirk is in town with a team."

"Twenty other domestic black-op assholes with a collective IQ of eighty, National Security Agency credentials, but if they're the best the NSA has to offer, even Belgium could take us in like a one-week war. Twenty! Plus choppers and drones and military ordnance out the ass."

"They're after a guy named Harkenbach."

"What—are these goons staying at your hotel and bragging at the bar each night?"

"I have my sources. I'll tell you later. I don't want to hold you up from your *Chariots of Fire* moment on the beach."

"This Harkenbach guy is some kind of rogue scientist."

"There can be such a thing as a rogue scientist?" Duke asked.

"Falkirk says Harkenbach sold national security secrets to a foreign power. But that sleazeball lies even when he doesn't say anything."

"You think Harkenbach is really in town?"

"Maybe not now. But seems he was hiding out, doing a hobo thing at the deep end of Shadow Canyon. Falkirk and his clown posse are running some kind of operation up there—we don't know what. We're told to stay out, so we stay out, because after all we're just one step up from mall cops and we have great respect for our brothers and sisters in all the fabulous bureaus of federal law enforcement."

"You *are* damn confident of reelection."

"Ellen and I are grooming Phil Junior to run for mayor on the illustrious Esterhaus name like thirty years from now. So tell me, why're you interested in Falkirk and Harkenbach?"

"I have some friends who've gotten caught up in this through no fault of their own. They live on Shadow Canyon Lane, and Falkirk has some stupid idea that they befriended this Harkenbach."

"Is there something I can do?"

"Maybe, maybe not, I'm thinking about it. Listen, let's you, Ellen, and me have dinner tomorrow night. We'll discuss it then."

"Who's paying?"

"Do you ever pay?"

"Neither do you when it's at the hotel."

"Every job has its perks. You get to wear that cool trooper hat," Duke said, and he hung up.

===== 71

At Ed's direction, Michelle quickly hacked off his glorious white mane with scissors and shaved the stubble with her electric razor until his noggin was as smooth as her legs. Strangely, his bald head seemed half again as large as when he'd had hair, so he resembled a 1950s sci-fi movie's idea of what an evolved human being of immense intelligence would look like if he traveled back in time from ten thousand years in the future.

He took off his bow tie and adjusted his shirt collar. "There. My own mother wouldn't recognize me."

"Well, I guess if she was blind," Michelle said.

"Trust me, during my time as a fugitive, I've learned that the best disguises require not an entire makeover but merely one or two strategic changes."

Ed oversaw Michelle's makeover by having her tie her hair in a ponytail and wear a baseball cap. He also insisted that she change out of her pullover sweater into a baggier blue sweatshirt that had belonged to Jeffy. She'd saved it all these years because she had given it to him as a birthday gift and he'd especially liked the words imprinted on the chest—FRODO LIVES! The sleeves extended past her fingertips, and even after she rolled them up, she looked like a lost waif searching for her mom, rather than a woman in search of her lost daughter.

"My own mother wouldn't recognize you," Ed declared.

"Your mother never knew me."

"Exactly."

With Ed in the front passenger seat, whistling a tune that he identified as from Mozart's concerto K. 453, Michelle drove her Ford Explorer into town and slotted it in an automated two-story parking structure a block off Pacific Coast Highway. She fed a few dollar bills into the permit machine and placed the printout prominently on the dashboard. If when they ported back to this timeline they needed to make a quick getaway, she didn't want to discover that her SUV had been towed.

In an alleyway alongside the building, Ed dared to take the key to everything from his coat and activate it. This early in the day, when most people would not head to work for another hour or two and when tourists were still sleeping off the previous night's excesses, the chance was slim that someone would happen on them in the instant when they vanished from this sad timeline where Jeffy and Amity had died seven years ago.

The onshore flow was scented with cinnamon and warm pastry dough from a bakery just opening for the day. The breeze chased scraps of litter along the alley and rolled before it a ball of red yarn. Such was Michelle's state of mind that the unraveling scarlet filament, so vivid against the blacktop, seemed to be an ominous symbol, a thin spill of blood or a lit fuse burning toward her.

"Where do we go when we get there?" she asked.

"Are there people in town who were friends with you and Jeffy back in the day, people that he might have remained friends with in that world, after you walked out on him and Amity?"

"Not me. I never did. That was the other Michelle. Yeah, I can think of a few friends from then who're still in this town and maybe still in the one we're going to. Jeffy was true blue. He never gave up on anyone."

"Then we'll check them out and hope that he and your girl have gone into hiding at one of their houses."

He pressed RETURN, and after passing through a blizzard of light, they arrived in the world where there was hope, however fragile, of a family reunion.

====== 72

No sooner had Duke spoken one last time with Andy Taylor and left the hotel than his cell phone rang. He paused at the crosswalk on the west side of the highway and took the call as light morning traffic grumbled past.

Chief Phil Esterhaus said, "I'm not even to the beach yet to start my run, I get a call about Falkirk. He was shot five times."

"Dead?"

"No. He was wearing Kevlar. Four rounds were stopped, but one took him in the left thigh. He's in the hospital, no doubt making the entire staff wish they'd never pursued a career in medicine. You know who shot him?"

"Not me."

"I didn't think you. If I thought you, the first thing I'd have said is, *I'll pay for dinner, after all.*"

"So who shot him?"

"Two hulks in his goon squad were stationed across the street from where it happened. They're raising hell with my people, as if they never told us to back off. They want arrests made yesterday.

Anyway, it was dark, but they had night-vision gear, so they saw a little. They say it was this traitor Harkenbach and some woman. The perps got away, which makes no sense to me, with Falkirk's crew of numbnuts right there and armed to the teeth."

"Who do they want you to arrest?"

"Well, Harkenbach and the woman—"

"What woman?"

"They don't know. The kind of law these guys enforce, any woman might work for them, plus they want the guy who owns the house."

"Who owns the house?"

"Well, that's the thing I find most interesting. It's a guy named Jeffrey Coltrane, lives there with his daughter, Amity. Would those be the friends of yours you mentioned, the ones who live on Shadow Canyon Lane and got 'caught up in this through no fault of their own'?"

"I've heard of them," Duke conceded.

"Is Coltrane a killer?"

"Is Mary Poppins?"

"I wouldn't vouch for anyone these days," Phil said. "Listen, these guys with Falkirk are like *The Sopranos*, but they have for-real legal authority and a desire to abuse the hell out of it. If the shit hits the fan, I can't pull the plug for you."

"Thanks for the heads-up. See you for dinner tomorrow night."

"I love the lobster bisque."

Duke terminated the call and crossed the street against the light, holding up one hand to stop the traffic, with which he had more success than King Canute did when he commanded the sea to be still.

=== 73

In this timeline, no breeze issued off the ocean, no ball of red yarn appeared, but Michelle's sense of an impending shock did not diminish.

She glanced left and right, thinking, and then told Ed, "Jane and Larry Barnaby. They had a daughter, Keri, the same year Amity was born. We went through that sleepless first year together, babysat for each other. I've stayed friends with them since Jeffy and Amity died. He would have, too, after I . . . after the other Michelle walked out on him."

"Where do these Barnaby people live? If they're still in this town at all."

"Quickest way is out to Pacific Coast Highway and turn south. It's maybe a ten-minute walk."

As she and Ed started west along the alley, a man turned the corner ahead and approached them at a brisk pace. Tall and barrel-chested and broad-shouldered, he might have been a guy who earned his living breaking knees or necks or heads, whatever was wanted of him. Even though he wore a suit and tie, though he carried himself with his spine as straight as a knight's lance, an air of menace clung to him.

Michelle moved to the right side of the alley, as did Ed, giving the stranger a wide berth. The man glanced at them, seemed disinterested, but then did a double take and changed course, crossing directly to Michelle.

"Mrs. Coltrane?"

She strove to suppress her surprise. "What? No. You've mistaken me for someone else."

As she tried to sidle past this stranger, he blocked her.

Ed eased one hand under his coat, to the pistol in his belt holster.

Without looking away from Michelle, his bottle-green eyes decanting pure suspicion, the big man said to Ed, "Cool it, pal. Don't make me break your hand. You don't need a gun, anyway."

"Really," Michelle said, "you're making a mistake. I don't know any Coltrane."

He snatched off her baseball cap, and she gasped, and he said, "You're older, of course, but you look the same as those photos in your daughter's wallet that she's so proud of. She showed them to me not two hours ago. You don't even need to put your hair down. You're Michelle, all right."

Oddly enough, a sudden breeze, scented with cinnamon, stirred litter along the alley. Later than in the world they recently left, the ball of red yarn came rolling past them, unraveling as it went.

This time the scarlet filament didn't call to mind a thread of blood or a lit fuse. Instead, she dared to think of it as a marker that, like Hansel and Gretel's white pebbles in the fairy tale, was meant to lead her through the dark forest of her life and home to family.

Unsettled but also exhilarated by the way this encounter was unfolding, she said, "You know where Jeffy and Amity are?"

"They're at my house." He seemed to have transformed from ogre into friendly giant. "I'll take you to them."

Astonished, she looked at Ed, who beamed back at her and, as if this had been his plan all along, said, "The Ed factor. Things tend to happen around me."

"You're Harkenbach?" the stranger asked.

Ed rubbed his bald head with one hand. "In my sadly depilated condition, I may not look like him—"

"I don't know what he looks like," the stranger said. "I've never seen a picture. I only met Jeffy and Amity this morning, and they didn't much describe you. So you're Jeffy's friend."

"Actually, that's quite another Ed, the Ed of this world. I'm the Ed of this Michelle's world, a braver specimen of myself, I'm happy to say. I know I sound as though I'm talking gibberish—"

"I get you," the big man said. He smiled at Michelle. "You're not the mother who walked out on the girl. Maybe like they've been hunting another you, you've been hunting another them. You must have a damn good story to tell. Best save it till we get to my place, so you don't have to repeat it for your husband and daughter. My name's Charlie Pellafino, by the way. Friends call me Duke, and I'm pretty damn sure we're going to be friends."

As Duke escorted them eastward along the alley, Michelle said, "You met them only this morning?"

"Yes, ma'am. Your husband is a stand-up guy, and your girl is a charmer. She called me Uncle Duke."

"But how could you know all that you know . . . how could you have come to *believe* it if you met them only a few hours ago?"

"Seeing is believing," Duke said. "I accidentally got myself sent to hell with your daughter. We just about got carved up by this scary-as-shit bug-form robot in a version of the hotel that won't ever again turn a profit."

Ed Harkenbach said, "Earth one point seventy-seven. I've been to some worse, but not many."

The ball of yarn had entirely unraveled. As Michelle hurried along with Ed and Duke, her bright excitement was tarnished somewhat by the fear that this might not be a direct route out of the dark forest of her life, as she'd thought. The moon-white pebbles dropped by Hansel didn't help him and Gretel find their way safely through the woods, nor did the bread crumbs with which he later marked a trail. Ahead might lie a wicked witch with a warm oven and a taste for cannibalism. Or something worse.

====== 74

Almost as much as he hated English teachers, John Falkirk also hated nurses, whether they were dressed in white uniforms or green scrubs or were naked in a porno film. Just because they knew the difference between simethicone and simvastatin, could recognize the early symptoms of numerous diseases, could change the bedsheets with the patient in the bed, and could give injections without causing an embolism, they thought that they were superior to their patients, as though they didn't also empty bedpans. Bustling here and there with annoying self-importance, not one of the nurses at Mercy Hospital could have pulled off the execution of a Supreme Court justice with a secretly induced heart attack or would have had the nerve to put a bullet in the head of an influential political activist who made the mistake of believing his party actually adhered to the principles that it espoused. In an overpopulated world, nothing was noble about nursing back to health and saving the lives of those people who were not essential to the function of the state, which were maybe 90 percent of them.

The only medical personnel whom Falkirk hated more than nurses were physicians. The one who treated him was Dr. Nolan Burnside, a thirtysomething whiz kid who looked like a TV doctor and had the so-cool breezy manner and the knock-'em-dead smile of an actor who knew he was destined to be the number-one box-office star in a year or two. He supposedly injected a local anesthetic to block the nerves carrying the message of disaster from the wound to the brain, but the torment did not relent. In fact, as Burnside disinfected the torn flesh, stopped the bleeding, and sewed twenty-six stitches by hand, the pain increased, so Falkirk broke into a sweat that seemed as thick as hot gravy, cursing both the God he didn't believe in and the Devil he knew to be real. Burnside, evidently a graduate of the Quackery School of Medicine at the University of Humbug, had the impudence, the *brass,* to subtly imply that the local anesthetic was effective and that the pain must be psychosomatic. This insolence earned him a death warrant, which would be served as soon as Falkirk obtained the key to everything and amassed the power that would make him untouchable. Oblivious of the truth that his days were numbered, Burnside joked with the nurses, who were all charmed by the bastard. He probably banged the prettiest of them, standing up in a supply closet, while his patients died in agony of sepsis.

The bullet passed entirely through Falkirk, tunneling the flesh, missing major arteries and veins and bones. Had it been an inch to the left, the results would have been devastating. A half inch the other way, the round would have done nothing worse than score the surface of his thigh, requiring no other attention than a bandage. The wound didn't need a drain. Burnside applied the bandage and scheduled him for discharge the following day, but Falkirk refused to stay overnight. He wanted a prescription for a painkiller that would leave him clearheaded, a cane, and immediate release.

"As an NSA agent," Dr. Burnside said, "you may have authority from coast to coast and border to border, but in here, Mr. Falkirk, I am in charge."

Throughout the procedure in the ER cubicle, Vince Canker—who thought he had some psychic ability and that his mother, who'd died a week earlier, had recently been trying to reach him from the Other Side—stood in one corner. He was dressed in black for the Shadow Canyon operation, as was Falkirk, and he wore a sidearm in plain sight. With his flat, hard face and eyes the color of burnt butter, he was of such disturbing appearance that both Burnside and the various nurses had pretended that he wasn't present, as if on eye contact his drilling stare could take a core sample of their souls.

Now Falkirk asked Canker to bring in Louis Wong from the corridor, where he was standing guard outside the cubicle. Louis's father was Chinese, his mother Irish. He had the dreamy face of a Buddha shrine and the clear, green eyes of a Killarney choirboy. He was dressed in black as well, and with a sidearm; but neither the doctor nor the nurses would think that his stare could skewer their souls. Rather, he had the air of a sly man who would do you with a knife.

Louis brought with him a fresh pair of black pants that another agent had delivered to replace the torn and blood-soaked pair that Falkirk had been wearing. In the ICU cubicle, he closed the door and blocked it, while Vince Canker moved to the foot of the bed to stare more pointedly at Burnside.

The physician's handsome face didn't pale. His posture remained loose limbed and confident. Although the curve of his matinee-idol smile didn't appear to change, it didn't really qualify as a smile anymore.

"A bottle of painkillers, a double prescription," Falkirk said. "And a cane. Now."

Burnside was a proud man. "Even if I wanted to oblige, there are hospital protocols—"

"Fuck the protocols, Nolan." Falkirk sat up on the edge of the bed. "I noticed you wear a wedding ring. What's your wife's name?"

Burnside hesitated to answer, and then said, "I don't see what that has to do—"

"You don't need to see what it has to do," Falkirk interrupted. "I assure you, Nolan, if you don't answer me, you'll wish you had."

Another hesitation. Then: "Cynthia."

"Do you and Cynthia have children?"

"Two. We have two children."

"What are their names and ages?"

"Jonathan is four. Rebecca is six."

Falkirk nodded. "Sweet. A nice little family. Hostages to fortune. Very brave of you to have a family. A man alone has much less to lose."

Burnside met Falkirk's stare for a long moment. Then he glanced at Vince Canker and quickly away. "You're not NSA agents."

"Our ID is genuine, though our true employers operate from far deeper in the state than the National Security Agency. Do you want to test me, Nolan, and discover just how deep?"

Although the physician said, "This is outrageous," his voice was marked more by fear than outrage, more by resignation than by fear.

"Think of me as a troll, Nolan. A troll who lives far down in the deepest of deep caverns. Trolls take whatever they want from your world, whatever treasures, whatever pretties, and no one ever follows them down into their caverns to retrieve what they've taken, because no one believes trolls exist."

As if time must be flowing at a different rate in the cubicle than beyond it, Nolan Burnside seemed to have aged noticeably in but a few minutes.

"I'll get the pills and the cane."

"Call a nurse and order her to bring them," Falkirk said. "I need you here to help me get into this clean pair of pants. You'll put on my socks and shoes for me, too. And kneel down to tie the laces."

75

Jeffy enjoyed mundane work like mowing the yard, cleaning the house, doing laundry, preparing meals, and polishing Bakelite radios to restore their luster. When engaged in tasks of that nature, he seemed to have two minds. One remained focused intently on the chore before him, and the other floated free to contemplate or to search for inspiration. His contemplation involved the purpose of his life, the meaning of the world, what he had done wrong, and what he might yet do right. The inspiration he sought always involved thinking of things to make Amity's life more fun and interesting, to keep her spirits high and help her fulfill the potential she possessed in abundance. When Amity was very young, Jeffy's free-floating mind wrote funny poems and stories about magical animals to entertain her. By the time she was five, he gave much thought to how best to homeschool her, which continued to occupy his mind year after year. He had daydreamed of teaching her to surf, and she had learned how to thrash the waves. Now they had the joy of the sea to share. Recently she'd been learning to sail. For him, work was pleasant because it was also a chance to dream, and when work was done, the day was theirs for living out those dreams.

Now, in Duke Pellafino's kitchen, as Jeffy measured coffee into the filter of the brewer, he wondered if he would ever again be able to lose himself in the common tasks of everyday life and allow part of his mind to float free as before, or whether what he now knew of the multiverse would always weigh his mind down with worries about what might be happening in those infinite elsewheres. He could try his best to protect Amity and ensure her happiness in this world that she shared with him. But what of all those other Amitys in so many timelines? Scores of Amitys? Hundreds? Thousands? Inevitably, in some places, she was orphaned, and he was not there to look over her. In still other worlds, she might be ill or lost or tormented in any of the myriad ways that indifferent nature allowed her children to suffer in a fallen world. He loved this child more than he loved life itself, but it seemed to him that his love must be bestowed on all the Amitys who were without him elsewhere, if it were to be a true and worthy love.

That was madness. He couldn't possibly be father to a thousand now fatherless Amitys, or to a hundred, or even to fifty Amitys in different worlds. If they survived their current predicament, he would somehow have to be father to this version of her, as if she were the only one, and put from his mind what travails and horrors other Amitys might be enduring, though at the moment, he was unable to see how this could be done.

These thoughts troubled Jeffy as the coffee began brewing in a fragrant rush and as he took a package of bacon from the freezer, which was when Duke Pellafino entered the kitchen from the hallway, accompanied by a man at once strange and familiar.

"Spooky Ed," said Amity.

At the same moment, Jeffy recognized the scientist. The shock of this development was sufficient to distract him from wondering how the old man had come to be with Duke. In spite of their year of camaraderie on the front porch, a flush of anger warmed his face, and he confronted Harkenbach. "What the hell's wrong with you, Ed? How could you call yourself my friend and yet leave that gismo with me, knowing Falkirk might land on me with both feet, knowing I might have to use the damn thing?"

Harkenbach held up one hand as though to sue for peace. "You've got me all wrong. I was never your friend, Jeffrey. I never left it with you."

"What's the point of denying it? We both know exactly what you did. There's no point in denying it, Ed." Jeffy took a deep breath. "What happened to your hair?"

"I thought baldness and no bow tie constituted an effective disguise. Apparently I was wrong. I seldom am. It's humbling. But I'm *not* wrong about the key. That was another Ed, another me who's less responsible than I am. I was never your friend. I'm her friend in a different world and now in this one."

"Her? Her who?"

Michelle entered the kitchen.

For seven years, Jeffy had hoped for a reunion before finally dissolving their marriage. When the key to everything had thrown his and Amity's lives into chaos, he'd known that if stability returned, he would recklessly risk renewed chaos by using the key to search for her in a world where she needed him. Love was not an act of reason, but a leap of faith, a belief that some mysterious meaning must lie behind existence and that two particular lives were fated to be one; love was an expression of trust in the truth of the heart's yearning and the mind's keen intuition. In the absence of love, the heart might be deceitful above all things, but profound love was an antivenin that cured deceit. Although Jeffy had long dreamed of this moment, dreamed of it while asleep and awake, though he'd so often thought about what he would say and do if ever she were returned to him, he was not able to speak or act, as if to do so would reveal her sudden appearance to be an illusion.

Amity was the first to move. She crossed the room to Michelle and, without a word, put her arms around her mother.

Michelle's eyes filled with tears. As she smoothed Amity's hair with one hand, she met Jeffy's gaze and said softly, "You died."

"You left," he replied.

"We're here," Amity said. "We're here."

 76

Although Falkirk had popped a painkiller, it hadn't kicked in yet, and the local that Dr. Burnside supposedly administered to his thigh before closing his wound didn't help much. His badly bruised chest hurt like a sonofabitch, because Kevlar could stop a slug but couldn't fully diffuse the power of its punch. Nonetheless, he caned himself out of the hospital to the waiting Suburban, spitting curses as he went, and climbed into the back seat, relying on Vince Canker's assistance.

As they drove away with Louis Wong behind the wheel and Canker riding shotgun, Falkirk's phone rang. Jason Foot-Long Frankfurt, the hacker's hacker, was calling.

"How're you doing, boss?"

"I was shot. How do you think I'm doing?"

"We were all so pissed off when we heard."

"Pissed off that I was hit once or that Kevlar stopped the other four?"

"Good to hear you've kept your sense of humor through it. I've got something that'll cheer you up."

"Don't bet on it."

"Philip Esterhaus received two calls this morning from this guy named Charles Pellafino. He's head of security at Hotel Suavidad, an ex–San Diego cop. They're friends."

Chief Phil Esterhaus was one of those straight-arrow small-time cops who chafed at the bit when any federal agent jammed one in his mouth and claimed the right to operate freely in his jurisdiction. Falkirk encountered their type all the time, and he despised them almost as much as he despised English teachers. He looked forward to the day when all law enforcement was federal, when the Esterhauses of the world were packed off to reeducation camps and had their nuts chopped off. As usual in cases like this, Falkirk's crew had installed an unauthorized telecom mirror line on the police chief's official and personal phones, so that Esterhaus's every word was reflected to Foot Long's computer.

Now Jason said, "Pellafino is asking the chief about you, what you're doing here. He knows about Harkenbach. He says he's got some friends in Shadow Canyon that got 'caught up' in this, he's trying to figure out what they should do. It's obvious these friends of his are Coltrane and his brat."

"What did Esterhaus say to him?"

"He wasn't discreet. He called you an egg-sucking snake and an arrogant piece of shit. Just so you know."

"Thanks for sharing."

"He also said you're a sleazeball and that the rest of us are your clown posse."

"You feel the need to tell me all this—why?"

"He also told Pellafino that the collective IQ of your entire team is eighty. That hurt. That cut deep, man. I don't like that kind of nasty shit. He's a cracker-town parking-patrol flatfoot who's not ten percent as smart as he thinks he is. My IQ alone is one hundred seventy."

Falkirk figured that 170 was as much of a lie as the nickname "Foot-Long."

"What I think," Jason continued, "is that wherever Coltrane and his brat jumped to from the Bonner house, they're now back in this timeline, and they're hiding out at Pellafino's place."

Having reached that conclusion even before he'd been told that Esterhaus had called him an egg-sucking snake, Falkirk said, "You have the address?"

The hacker gave it to him. "Coltrane has the key to everything, so we'll have to ghost our way inside and come down on him like a ton of bricks before he knows we're there, blow off the fucker's head before he can port."

Jason Foot-Long Frankfurt was a workstation keyboard guy who spent every operation on his ass, but he seemed to half believe he was a boots-on-the-ground participant when he said "we" and "our" and talked tough about blowing people's heads off.

"So," he continued, "you want us to haunt the street, quietly slide the neighbors out of collateral-damage distance?"

When a building harbored a heavily armed lunatic or a cluster of terrorists, with the likelihood that hundreds or even thousands of rounds of deep-penetrating ammunition might be expended and pass through the walls of nearby homes, neighbors were often secretly extracted through back doors and side exits before a hard-core SWAT assault was launched against the structure. Although this usually could be done without alerting the targets about what was coming, there was always a possibility of doing just that. In this case, because Coltrane had the key and could port out of this world with as little as a twenty-second warning, they could not take the chance that he or his daughter or this Charles Pellafino might look out a window at the wrong moment and see an evacuation taking place.

Anyway, Jeffrey Coltrane didn't have an arsenal, at most merely a single pistol that he'd bought years earlier. The firefight, if it occurred, would be one-sided and brief. Maybe this Charles Pellafino had a gun, being a former cop, but that was only one more shooter to worry about, and he wasn't likely to be armed with a fully automatic carbine with a drum magazine. Falkirk's crew would do reconnaissance and then hit the residence suddenly and hard. In less than a minute, maybe a lot less, there would be three dead—Coltrane, Pellafino, and the girl—and the key to everything would be his.

"You just sit tight," he told Jason. "I'll organize the hit."

Falkirk terminated the call and brooded for a minute or two as Louis Wong piloted the Suburban on a random tour of town, waiting for instructions.

Before Falkirk seemed to lie a one-lane straight-as-a-ruler highway to success.

There were only two wild cards.

He had already figured out that the Edwin Harkenbach who'd shot him was not the Ed of this world, but a version from elsewhere.

And the Michelle Coltrane who'd been with the physicist had not been the woman who walked out on her family seven years earlier. She also was from elsewhere.

Evidently, the Ed from elsewhere was engaged in matchmaking or was trying to do one small good thing to atone for all the damage he had otherwise inflicted on multiple worlds. Or maybe his motive was something else altogether. Who knew how the hell the old guy's mind worked? In Falkirk's estimation, most geniuses were idiots with one special talent, and they made less sense than the people whom they thought less intelligent than themselves.

Regardless of his motivation, the Ed from elsewhere had been scouting out the Coltranes on this world and probably on others.

After being surprised by Falkirk and shooting him, Harkenbach and the bitch ported back where they came from. Most likely, they were shaken by what happened and would be hesitant to come here again anytime soon.

But there was no guarantee. They might already be back in this version of Suavidad Beach, trying to find Coltrane and his daughter.

That was not necessarily a bad thing. It meant that there were now two keys to everything in this timeline, the one possessed by Coltrane and the one used by the Ed from elsewhere.

Falkirk would be satisfied with either key. However, if by some stroke of luck, he wound up with two, with his adversaries dead to the last, all the trouble that he'd been through would be worth it twice over.

As they cruised along Forest Avenue, he placed a call to Lucas Blackridge, his SWAT specialist, and discussed the takedown of the Pellafino house.

=== 77

No one knew how to act, really and truly, because this was a miracle, and miracles left you totally awestruck, gobsmacked. All they could do was hug and touch and be amazed. They knew what to say, but they couldn't seem to find a way to say it, not at once. There weren't just seven years to get caught up on; they needed to tell the stories of their *lives* to one another. Amity and her father maybe knew Michelle better than they knew anyone else in the world, and she maybe knew them better than she knew anyone, yet in a strange way she didn't know them at all, and they didn't know her. It was like freaking weird, but in a good way, a wonderful way. They knew what they felt, or at least knew *most* of what they felt, but the situation was without precedent, so they also had feelings they would need some time to understand.

Then there was death. Mother—*this* Michelle—had seen them dead, had overseen their burial, had grieved for them until her grief had eventually become a settled sorrow. Now here they were before her, alive again. Or alive *still*. If it was a miracle, then really and truly, from Mother's perspective, it must have seemed a little spooky, too.

So while they were trying to figure out what to do and say, and how exactly to feel—other than happy and amazed—they set to work making breakfast, with Ed and Duke, which seemed kind of strange but felt entirely natural. Soon the five of them were sitting around the kitchen table, chowing down right in the middle of a miracle.

In the most secret room of Amity's heart, of which not even Daddy knew the existence, she'd dwelt with the probability that the mother who walked out on them seven years earlier was dead. Long dead. If two private detectives hadn't been able to find any trace of *that* Michelle, then something terrible must have happened to her; she never had a chance to follow her music and all, because soon after she set out on her new life, someone purely evil had taken her and done something horrible to her. Such grisly stories were in the news every week. Faces of the missing showed up on posters and true-crime TV programs. Later, bodies were found discarded like trash. This was that kind of world. In Mother's case, no body was found. The lack of a body didn't mean there might still be hope; it only meant that the killer buried the corpse well or was so seriously sick that he kept it in his basement as a memento. This was that kind of world, too, and even a girl of eleven knew about the dark side of human nature and all, so that such scenes evolved in her imagination, though Amity always forced herself not to dwell on them.

At first, as they ate, no one talked about what to do next or about the immediate threat, as if to do so would bring evil down on them the moment they spoke of it. The bad guys couldn't know where they were. They were safe for now. They needed a breather, a short rest from all the craziness they had been through: just a typical breakfast in an ordinary kitchen, during one hour when life seemed normal. Maybe eating with people who were known to have died and now were alive would never seem entirely normal, but minute by minute, it seemed less bizarre.

78

When Phil Esterhaus returned from his dawn run on the beach, his wife, Ellen, was already off to their daughter's house to help with the new grandbaby, Willy.

Now Esterhaus was in the shower, and John Falkirk relaxed in an armchair in the master bedroom, waiting for the opinionated chief of police to put in an appearance.

The draperies were drawn at the windows. One nightstand lamp with a pleated amber-silk shade provided minimal and restful light, and the prevalent shadows seemed to be a palliative purple instead of harsh black, as if the light and shadows conspired with the capsules of Vicodin to soothe a wounded man's troubled mind.

The susurration of falling water was reminiscent of the sound the unborn hear in the womb, the rush of the mother's blood, which lulls with a sweet promise of eternal safety and peace. A false promise. A damn lie. Not that Falkirk actually remembered what he had heard in the womb. The thought came to him as a consequence of having taken a double dose of the prescription painkiller on top of multiple caffeine tablets, as well as Zantac to deal with the acid produced by the excess of caffeine. He'd had some brandy as well, Esterhaus's brandy, two shots that he'd mixed with part of a can of Coca-Cola, which he was drinking now as he sat in the wombchair, the armchair, waiting for good old Phil to appear with his hair wet and a towel around his waist and snarky quip on his tongue.

Anyway, Falkirk hated his mother, who died and left him to the mercy of a stepmother so greedy she probably *ate* money in secrecy. His real mother hadn't dropped dead in every timeline, but what did that matter if she'd been thoughtless enough to die in this one? Somewhere there were John Falkirks who received their inheritances because there had been no stepmother to steal it from them. The existence of happy versions of himself did not please him. Indeed, he hated those other John Falkirks and would have liked to track them all down and kill them.

As the armchair cushioned him like an amniotic sac, as the shadowy bedroom snugged around him like a uterus, he felt no pain because even a quack of Dr. Nolan Burnside's caliber could provide useful medication when you threatened to carve up his children.

Correction: He felt no *physical* pain, but he was in emotional pain for several reasons. The biggest reason was that he had been shot for the first time in his life, and it had been a close thing, and he could have died.

Maybe because of the painkiller and massive amounts of caffeine and the brandy, he was having thoughts he never had before, insights and realizations. Although, in his capacity as a federal agent, he had killed people—always for good reason, always because they were traitors or otherwise dangerous or annoyed him—he had not until now given any thought whatsoever to the possibility of his own death. On some level, he must have realized that he was mortal. However, he never proceeded with his life as if that were the case. Being shot in the thigh had changed everything.

Since childhood, he had known that no one could be trusted, not your mother who would die on you, not your father who would trade a son's birthright for a hot bitch who would sex him to death, not the family lawyer who would strip you of your birthright for a piece of the fortune settled on your stepmother. Now he understood that he couldn't even trust other versions of himself in other timelines, those who had received their inheritances when he had not, for if they knew of him and his bitter animosity, they would surely want to kill him before he could kill them. To be perfectly safe, to have a chance to use the key to everything to exploit the knowledge of the multiverse and make himself wealthier and more powerful than any emperor in history, he would have to secure this timeline as his base, rather than split for a better one, and then he would need to murder as many versions of himself as he could find on other worlds.

This prospect would have seemed daunting, exhausting, if not for the wonder of Dr. Burnside's little pills and the effects of fine brandy. Freed from physical pain, clear of mind, he knew exactly what he must do.

Before storming Charles Pellafino's house and seizing the key to everything, Falkirk needed to frame Jeffrey Coltrane for the murder of Chief Philip Esterhaus. That would justify the death of Coltrane when the SWAT team stormed the Pellafino residence.

Coltrane had to be killed for Falkirk to get his key. In fact, he had to die merely because he *knew about* the key.

Amity Coltrane had to die because she also knew about the key, because she would be witness to her father's murder, and because she was a deceitful little smart-ass.

Charles Pellafino's death could be justified because he had given shelter to Coltrane, who conspired with the traitor Harkenbach and because . . . well, maybe Pellafino also conspired with Harkenbach, and all of them had colluded with Russia on something. The details could be worked out after everyone who needed to die was dead.

After the assault on the Pellafino house, perhaps it would be possible to stage the scene so it appeared that Coltrane, cornered and desperate, had committed murder and then suicide, killing his daughter and then himself. Delicious.

Documents could be forged to prove that Coltrane—a pathetic loser, a struggling radio repairman—had given shelter to the vile traitor Edwin Harkenbach and helped him avoid arrest for selling national security secrets, and that he murdered Chief Esterhaus, who had tumbled to his scheme. At this very moment, Jason Frankfurt was falsifying the history of the weapon with which Phil Esterhaus would be murdered, so that it could be proved that Coltrane had purchased it two years earlier.

Without pain and medicated into a state of supreme confidence, Falkirk found his plan to be flawless, so clever that, contemplating it, he laughed softly and lit a cigarette. After all that he had been through, it felt good to be happy, especially considering that happiness was a feeling he rarely experienced.

When the cigarette was half smoked, he realized that he no longer heard the sound of falling water. He couldn't be sure how long ago the shower in the adjacent bathroom had been cranked off.

That realization led to another of equal importance. If neither Ellen Esterhaus nor her husband was a smoker, firing up a cigarette had been a mistake.

A sudden sense of jeopardy made him wonder if he might not be as clearheaded as he believed, which was when Philip Esterhaus came out of the bathroom.

Falkirk had seen the chief before, more than once, but never when the man had been wearing so little. In only a pair of briefs, Esterhaus proved to be a more muscular and impressive specimen than he was in uniform, as if sculpted out of stone.

"You look like a demigod," Falkirk said, surprised to have made such a statement, though his compliment was sincere.

The chief held a pistol.

The sight of the weapon perplexed Falkirk. How paranoid must a man be to keep a gun in his bathroom?

"What the hell are you doing here?" Esterhaus demanded.

"Smoking," Falkirk replied, passing the cigarette from right hand to left and taking a draw on it. He thought that was a pretty clever response, but he could see it hadn't amused the chief. So he blew out smoke and said, "We need to talk."

"You want to talk? Get your ass out of my house, we'll talk down at the station."

Esterhaus wasn't pointing his gun at Falkirk. He held it down at his side, the muzzle aimed at the floor.

Neither was Falkirk pointing his pistol at the chief. It lay in his lap, but he had let his free hand settle on it when he passed the cigarette from right hand to left.

His lap was in shadow. In fact, lamplight painted only the left side of his face and his arm, and the hand that held the cigarette. He imagined he must be a rather striking figure, like a mysterious character in a movie. He'd always thought he somewhat resembled a young Michael Douglas, although more handsome.

"The reason I intruded on your privacy," he explained, pausing for a weary sigh, "is that I thought, given what I have to reveal to you, that you would rather hear it in a place more discreet than your office. It involves some embarrassing information about your wife and a man named Charles Pellafino."

Esterhaus took another step into the room. "What bullshit is this? You think you can—"

With the cigarette still held somewhat languorously in his left hand to suggest an unthreatening listlessness, Falkirk tried a most unprofessional one-hand shot. He squeezed off three rounds in rapid succession, the recoil foiling his aim, and Esterhaus managed to bring up his weapon and fire once, and each of them scored one hit.

Falkirk took a brutal wallop in the torso. Although the slug, which burned a hole in his shirt, didn't penetrate the Kevlar vest, his field of vision narrowed to the figure of the nearly naked man, the periphery of the room dissolving into darkness, and he couldn't draw a breath. The impact robbed the Vicodin of its power. Pain splintered through his chest, as if his lungs shattered like glass.

Instead of Kevlar, the police chief had only a pair of cotton briefs. Anyway, Falkirk's one useful round took Esterhaus far above his Jockeys, in the throat, blowing out his esophagus, severing at least one carotid artery, and separating his spinal cord from the base of his brain.

The demigod collapsed in a graceless heap, but Falkirk wasn't ready to spring up from the chair and do a victory dance. Perhaps the punch of the bullet wouldn't have been so bad if his chest had not been bruised by the rounds Harkenbach fired at him point-blank earlier in the day. First, his ability to breathe returned, and he gasped for air, but each inhalation and exhalation felt as if it was being forced through a barrier of pulverized bones. After maybe a minute, the pain diminished, and after another minute, the double dose of Vicodin began to work its magic again.

He had dropped his cigarette. A thread of smoke rose from the carpet. He levered himself out of the chair and stamped out the fire before it could start.

After slipping the pistol into his belt holster, he picked up the empty glass that had contained Coke and brandy. He caned himself into the kitchen. He left the tumbler on the cutting board next to the sink. Mrs. Esterhaus could deal with it when she got home.

He had no concern about leaving fingerprints, DNA, or other evidence. Because this murder would be blamed on Jeffrey Coltrane and because Coltrane was part of the Harkenbach case, over which Falkirk had jurisdiction, nothing incriminating him would be found by the federal CSI team that would probe the premises.

Staring at the empty glass, he considered pouring a bit more cola and taking a third Vicodin. However, he quickly recognized this impulse as dangerous, as a consequence of already being much too far under the influence of medication. He didn't need another Vicodin. He felt no pain. He was happy. Happier than he'd been since he'd killed his stepmother in another timeline.

Nevertheless, he continued staring at the empty glass, which was mysteriously compelling. The very emptiness of it began to seem ominous. After a minute or two, he realized that the empty vessel was a symbol of failure. It must be taken as an omen, an urgent warning that the assault on Pellafino's house might go awry, as to some degree had the murder of the chief, which should have been a one-shot kill, without an exchange of gunfire. The SWAT operation might turn out even far worse, end up a catastrophe. Being free of pain and in a rare state of happiness, Falkirk realized that he was so clear-sighted that things he once would have overlooked were now visible to him in their true and over-whelming importance. Like the glass. The *empty* glass. He must take the empty glass seriously. Some power—perhaps Destiny—was advising him through signs and symbols.

In his heightened state of consciousness, he saw the world as he had not seen it before, but as it had been portrayed in certain movies that had enthralled him, movies that were now revealed to have conveyed the essential truth of existence. Great magic and powers of supernatural potency were contained in such things as a sword locked in stone, in rings forged in Mordor, in a key to other worlds that looked like a smartphone. Spirit oracles spoke of the future through crystal balls and Tarot cards and patterns in tea leaves—and empty drinking glasses.

He was scared. He'd never been truly scared before. For a man who believed that nothing had meaning, it was horrific to suddenly perceive that *everything* had meaning. Horrific and frightening, but also motivating. If there were signs and portents all around, he who heeded them would surely never fail.

A standard SWAT invasion of the house, executed even with the swiftest and most overpowering force, had at best a 90 percent chance of success. But it couldn't guarantee that the precious key to everything would be captured, that Coltrane and his daughter would not teleport out to a parallel world.

If Falkirk didn't nail them this time and seize the key, he very likely would never have another chance. If he failed, his future would be as empty as the glass on the drainboard.

He must set aside conventional thinking, abandon the protocols of standard SWAT assaults, and go big, as the Oracle of the Empty Glass had undoubtedly been instructing him. Instead of armored men battering down doors and shattering through windows and shooting everyone in sight as they exploded into the house, a better plan would be to gas everyone inside. Creep up on the house without alerting those within. Introduce a powerful, rapidly expanding gas that would render the occupants unconscious in a few seconds and dead soon after. Coltrane would have no time to use the key to everything.

When the gas dissipated, Falkirk and crew could enter without personal risk. A story could be concocted to explain the gas as issuing from a device that Coltrane had been cobbling together for a terrorist attack. It malfunctioned, taking out its maker instead of the innocent people he intended to kill. Irony. Karma. The press would never question the story. Most repeated as fact whatever was fed to them by a deep-state source with whom they were sympathetic.

79

Duke mainly listened. As a detective, he'd spent a lot of time listening to moral degenerates denying their crimes, spinning their elaborate alibis, and eventually confessing to mayhem and murder.

His guests had eaten breakfast. A fresh pot of fragrant coffee—the third—finished brewing. Everyone except the girl seemed to be flying on a caffeine jag. She didn't appear to need a stimulant to remain hyper alert and engaged, as though her body regularly produced caffeine along with new blood cells.

Everyone had stories to tell, amazing experiences to relate. Not a little of the talking was done by Ed Harkenbach. The scientist had a plan. He kept saying that he could resolve all the problems that his key to everything had caused in the lives of those gathered here. But before he would reveal what needed to be done next, he wanted them to better understand the multiverse—how it worked, why the key to everything was an existential threat to everyone in all the parallel worlds, and how he intended to mitigate or eliminate the threat that he—more times than he yet quite knew—had created when pride rather than reason guided him.

So for an hour and then another hour, Duke listened for lies, for evasions, for any indication that Ed was not giving it to them straight. There were more than a few moments when he felt that he had fallen down a rabbit hole *and* passed through a looking glass to a place where he would never be comfortable again.

Duke Pellafino's life was one of routines and habits. He moved day to day in a pleasant well-worn groove. Successful police work depended on operating according to proven investigative techniques and procedures. Hotel security was more of the same. In his leisure time, he favored activities—golf, tennis, the piano—that required the development of skills, which demanded routine practice. He loved dogs for the reasons that everyone loved them, but also because they were happiest when they rose for the day, were fed, were taken for walks, and had play sessions according to an unvarying schedule. Aside from those rare moments during his years as a cop when bad guys felt compelled to prove their badness, Duke's life involved little drama. And zero weirdness. He had no patience for talk of ghosts, reincarnation, fortune-telling. He believed the world was only what your five senses told you it was; there were no unseen presences or mysteries concealed behind mere veils of reality.

But then Ed Harkenbach said that when someone saw a ghost, he might be seeing a person in a parallel world, when timelines for a moment crossed instead of being neatly lined up next to one another or being wound around one another like filaments in a cable.

And in a strange way, reincarnation was real, though not in the sense that after death you returned in a new identity. However, you were incarnate as yourself in numerous timelines, living many lives.

Fortune-telling? Who was to say? According to Ed and quantum mechanics, all of time—past, present, and future—was complete in the instant of the big bang. Therefore the past and the future were contained in the present. If the future of this timeline was here to be known right now, there might be people gifted enough to see what most could not.

If earlier Duke hadn't been hurled to an apocalyptic parallel world and escaped it with Amity, there were moments during Ed's explanation that he would have gotten up, stopped listening, and washed the dishes, certain that all this was bushwa. Instead he remained at the table with a coffee mug in hand, in front of a plate on which a residue of egg congealed, and gradually he listened less for lies and more like a child sitting with his troop around a campfire in an eerie wilderness.

At last, Ed got to their predicament, for which he claimed to have a resolution. "You," he said to Jeffrey and Amity, "can never go back to your bungalow. They know you have the key. Even if you surrendered it, they wouldn't let you live, because you'd still know the key exists. They'll never tolerate that knowledge being spread beyond those involved with Project Everett Highways."

"I wish I'd never met that other you," Jeffrey lamented. "No offense."

"None taken. In some timelines I can be a quite difficult genius, given to paranoia and borderline megalomania. Even a mad genius in some versions. Although in my defense, I've not yet encountered a me who was a flat-out *evil* genius."

"I'm not a guy who can live on the run," Jeffrey said.

"Might have some cool adventures," Amity said.

Putting a hand on his daughter's shoulder, Jeffrey said, "From now on, the only adventures we need are those in books."

To Michelle, Ed said, "And you can't go home with Jeffrey and Amity to the bungalow in your timeline, because . . . well, you won't be able to explain how they came back from the dead." He glanced at Jeffrey. "Sorry. My condolences."

"*De nada.* I'm not sensitive about being dead in other timelines as long as the me in this one stays alive."

Unable any longer to contain himself, Duke said, "This is the craziest shit I've ever heard, and crazier still is it makes sense."

"But if we can't stay here in Jeffy's timeline," Michelle said, "and if we can't live in mine . . . where do we go?"

Grinning broadly, Ed made fists of his hands and thumped them a few times against his chest. "I'm so pleased with myself. I found the perfect place for you."

"There better not be bug-form robots," Amity said.

"Not a one!" Ed declared. He got up and, carrying his empty mug, went around the table to the girl. He tapped her nose with his index finger, and he said, "Cute as a button," which she clearly did not appreciate. "It's a great world, Amity, a delightful timeline. Best of all, Jeffrey's mom and dad, Frank and Imogene, your much-loved grandparents a few towns north of here—they're long dead in the world you'll be going to, and your father was never born there, and neither were you. Isn't that perfect?" When the reaction around the table was one of baffled dismay, the physicist realized that he needed to explain. "So Frank and Imogene can go

with you under new identities. To your new world. Three generations of Coltranes making a fresh start."

After taking a moment to absorb the increasing immensity of
what Harkenbach was proposing, Jeffrey said, "Dad and Mom love
the life they have in Huntington Beach. They're set in their ways.
They won't want to pull up their roots and go to a parallel world."

Moving to the coffeemaker on the counter behind Jeffrey, Ed
said, "Of course, if they stay here, they'll be murdered. Can I pour
coffee for anyone? No?"

Coltrane appeared to be baffled by the scientist's assertion or
reluctant to believe anyone would really want to kill his parents.

Sharing his experience of the psychology of sociopaths, Duke
said, "If this Falkirk asshole can't get his hands on you, he'll
assume you're still in this world, because he won't believe you've
skipped across the multiverse and left your folks grieving, thinking you're dead. He'll torture them until they tell him where you
are, when you're coming back, or until they die. So they'll die."

Filling his mug with coffee, Ed said, "Anyway, they already
agreed to it."

Coltrane turned in his chair. "They agreed, what do you mean
they agreed, when did they agree?"

"The morning of April eleventh, two days ago. I paid them a
visit and explained the situation. They were so happy you'd have
Michelle again. I gave them a tour of the new timeline, and they
fell in love with it."

Duke never drank in the morning, but he considered setting
aside his coffee in favor of Scotch whisky on the rocks.

Michelle said, "In the world I come from, Frank and Imogene
are huge *Star Wars* fans. They've seen all the movies. They even
collect memorabilia."

"Here, too," Coltrane said. "It was because they were so into science fiction that I went more for fantasy."

"Adolescent rebellion," Amity noted. "But benign."

Adding cream to his coffee, Ed said, "Almost forty-five years of *Star Wars* prepared them to believe. They were very sweet, how badly they wanted me to be a traveler between worlds." He took a sip of the brew, cried out—"Shit!"—and slammed the mug down, splashing coffee across the counter and onto the floor.

For an instant, Duke thought Harkenbach had burned his tongue. Then he realized the man had been looking out the window and had seen something that shocked him.

"They're here," Harkenbach said, and he already had the key to everything in his hand.

80

Ed said, "They're here," and even as the meaning of those two words were registering on Jeffy, something detonated softly— *whump*—rattling the ductwork within the walls. Jeffy was getting up from his chair, reaching for the key to everything, which he'd put on the table, in front of his plate, when a foul-smelling yellowish mist erupted from two vents near the ceiling of the kitchen. The gas must have been released from a highly pressurized container, because it seethed into the room at such incredible velocity that it whistled between the vanes of the vent grills and made them thrum. Jeffy was not yet all the way to his feet before the kitchen was inundated. He realized he shouldn't breathe, but the attack was so sudden that he had already inhaled as the realization came to him. The vapor was ice-cold in his lungs, which convulsed painfully, and he exhaled violently, with a hoarse shuddering wheeze. He avoided inhaling a second time, or thought he did, but already the sedative or poison or whatever was working on him, his eyes flooding with tears, his thoughts blurring as did his vision. His bones seemed to melt in his legs, so that he couldn't support himself, and he fell backward into his chair, almost toppling it.

Someone gripped him by the shoulder. Abruptly the kitchen was swept away by the familiar white blizzard, and though his vision remained blurry, he knew his rescuer must be Ed Harkenbach.

But what of Amity?

PART 7

EVEN THE GOOD DIE OFTEN

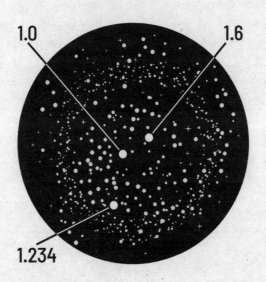

81

Amity was looking at Ed and saw him staring through the window when he said, "They're here," even as he took the key to everything from a pocket of his sport coat, so she knew they were in deepest shit, that he hadn't seen angels descending from on high. Just then something went *whump* hard enough so that you could be sure it wasn't a good development, and things rattled inside the walls.

Instinct, sharpened by hundreds of stories full of adventure, told her to get on the floor, where the bullets would fly overhead if there were going to be bullets. But then the first rush of yellow fog spewed out of the wall vents, and she knew the kind of scene this was going to be, with no bullets involved. So she held her breath, jammed her napkin into her water glass, tore it out, closed her eyes, and covered her face with the wet cloth before drawing a breath through it.

She scooted her chair back from the table and got to her feet, blind because she held the dripping napkin to her face with both hands. Her heart raced like a mouse's heart. She repressed the urge to gasp for breath, warning herself to avoid breathing as long as she could before sucking air through the sodden mask, in the hope that it would filter out all or most of the gas. She was scared, scared so badly that the word had a whole new meaning, more scared than she'd been when the bug-form robot had attacked, because she was unable to see, dared not look. And because no one was shouting or crying out. Which meant they were unconscious or dead. No. Not dead. Not Daddy. Not Mother. Not after all they had endured to be together again. As she turned away from the table, Amity could feel her pulse pounding in her throat, in her temples.

She bumped her father's chair, knocking it against the table, which meant no one was in it. Daddy didn't seem to be on the floor, either, but if he'd managed to get away, he would have taken her with him. He would never leave her behind.

Maybe five or six seconds had passed since she plastered the wet napkin over her face. When swimming, she could hold her breath underwater for half a minute easy, but maybe not as long with her crazy heart pounding so quick and all. She couldn't flee the house, run for open air, because they would be waiting outside. She needed to move, move, move, and she knew where she needed to go, where she just might be safe at least for a short while.

She put her back to the table, took a few steps, and bumped into the counter at the sink, which had been directly behind her chair. She turned left and moved along the cabinetry, repeatedly knocking her right foot against the toe kick to be sure she wasn't wandering off course. After she slipped a little in the coffee that Ed had spilled—Why hadn't he fallen here, where was *his* body?—she reached the corner, turned left. The range with gas burners and stainless-steel hood should be to the right of her. Maybe just twelve freaking seconds, and already she felt as though she was suffocating. Her heart *thundered*. This was a medium-size kitchen but seemed bigger now that she was effectively blind. When she'd set the table for breakfast she'd snooped everywhere, checking out cabinets even after she found everything she needed. She was nosy. Or as the dictionary defined it: unduly curious about the affairs of others. It was a character flaw. She wasn't prying or meddlesome. Just curious. But while curiosity had killed the cat, it had maybe saved her life in this case because now she knew where to go. Her right elbow knocked against the handle on the refrigerator door, which meant she'd made her way past the stacked ovens and the counter space beyond them. Like maybe eighteen seconds, and her lungs already felt as if they would collapse for lack of oxygen or burst with the useless air she refused to exhale, or burst and then *also* collapse. Past the refrigerator was a short section of wall, which she slid along before coming to the door she remembered. Holding the wet cloth to her face with just one hand, she used the other to feel for the knob and turn it. The trick now was to pull the door open only far enough to slip through, and then close it fast, to let as little gas as possible into the safe space beyond. Open, slip into the pantry, slam the door with a decisive bang.

She fumbled for the wall switch, clicked on the light. She let the napkin fall from her eyes, but held it over her mouth and nose as she exhaled and then sucked a first breath through the wet cloth, which was difficult enough to panic her. Well, no, not panic. Truly smart girls didn't panic. But she pulled in such a meager breath of cotton-flavored air that she sucked again and again, as if she were a revived mummy desperate to breathe through its ancient Egyptian windings. The air was in fact much cleaner here than in the kitchen, contaminated by the thinnest of yellow mists instead of a thick cloud. The pantry had no heating/cooling vent through which the gas could be introduced, and the door was tightly fitted. Nevertheless, she kept the napkin in place, because maybe even this concentration of fumes was enough to knock her out.

Although the door was tight in the jamb, there was about a quarter-of-an-inch space between the bottom of it and the threshold. Very little or nothing seemed to be leaking through that gap just yet. One of the things Amity knew from a lifetime of stories was that the tiny particles that made up smoke and many gases were so light that even the weakest drafts kept them airborne a long time, delaying their descent to the floor, where the air usually remained cleaner, at least for a while. Eventually, however, the gas would creep under the door.

Duke Pellafino evidently liked beans a lot. She had noticed this earlier, during her explorations. His pantry had the usual boxed and canned groceries, but there were also soft plastic bags, each holding one or two pounds of dried navy beans, garbanzo beans, pinto beans. Apparently, Duke prepared homemade soups and stews and bean dishes beyond her imagining. She was pretty sure that he must fart a lot, though she hadn't known him long enough to confirm this expectation. Now she used her free hand to snatch the flexible bags of beans from the shelf and jam them against the gap at the bottom of the door to prevent more fumes from entering.

That task accomplished, she stood with her back to the shelves, watching the glittering mist of particles turn lazily through the air and staring at the door, which sooner than later someone would open, probably a humongous thug dressed all in black and wearing a gas mask.

Realizing that it took more energy—therefore more air—to stand rather than sit, Amity settled to the pantry floor. She held the saturated cloth with both hands again, over her mouth and nose. She worried about Daddy, about her mother, about Duke and Ed, about her grandparents, about Snowball in his cage and maybe scared by the strange men in the bungalow, and she wondered if this pantry was one of the many places in which she would die.

82

When they transitioned from the kitchen in Prime to the same house elsewhere, the furniture wasn't configured precisely the same. Jeffy landed not on the chair in which he had been sitting, but beside it, dropping to the floor hard enough to bruise his tailbone.

Apparently, Ed had been sufficiently quick-witted to avoid drawing even one breath when that other kitchen had been flooded with gas. He pulled Jeffy to his feet, shoved him toward the sink, turned on the cold water, and said insistently, "Splash your face. Come on, come on. Take deep breaths, blow them out hard. Splash your face. Keep at it, man, we need your mind clear."

Jeffy's mind cleared faster than he thought possible, which meant that he hadn't twice breathed in the gas, and maybe his first inhalation hadn't been deep. Ed had ported him out of there just in time. He dried his face on a dish towel that the physicist handed him. His vision was no longer blurry. He surveyed the kitchen, which was similar to—but not identical to—the one in which the attack against them had been made.

"Where are we?"

"This is Duke's house, but in the world where Michelle lives alone in your bungalow, where you and Amity were run down and killed by a drunk."

"Where's Duke?"

"If he lives here in this timeline, he's obviously not at home, or he'd be in our face, maybe leveling a gun at us, since he's never met me in this world and probably doesn't know you."

Jeffy pointed to a wall calendar that featured photographs of dogs. "I'm pretty sure he lives here."

"I think you're right."

Like schooling fish, nausea suddenly swirled around and around in the bowl of Jeffy's stomach, a lingering effect of the gas. "I think I'm going to throw up."

"Then do it," Ed said impatiently. "The clock is ticking, we've got work to do."

Jeffy turned to the sink and bent forward, but the nausea passed. "I'm all right. What work?"

Drawing back one panel of his sport coat, Ed revealed the pistol in his holster. "You weren't wearing yours when we ported."

"I put it on the counter, by the bread box, when Amity and I were making breakfast. I never had a holster for it."

"If Duke lives here in this world, he'll have guns somewhere. We need to find them."

"We're going back there shooting?" Jeffy asked.

"If that's what seems necessary when we get there."

"But Amity, Michelle—"

"We'll do our best not to shoot *them*," Ed said, and he led Jeffy out of the kitchen.

In the downstairs hallway, the dark eye of a ceiling-mounted motion detector, part of the home-security system, winked red when they stepped into view. At once the alarm sounded and a stern, recorded voice declared, "*You have entered a protected area. Leave at once. The police have been called.*"

=== 83

Powerful directional microphones were aimed at the windows of the Pellafino house from within a surveillance vehicle disguised as a Roto-Rooter van parked across the street and also from an abandoned house on a parallel street with a line of sight on the back of the residence. With the aid of the mics, those who were about to attack the place had determined there were five people present at that address. One of them was a version of Edwin Harkenbach—almost certainly the one who shot Falkirk at the Coltrane bungalow.

In his heightened state of consciousness, wounded but without pain, *above all pain*, having earlier murdered a demigod without consequences, John Falkirk sat in the back of the Roto-Rooter van, thrilled by the realization that *two* keys to everything were in the house—Harkenbach's and the one that Coltrane had received from another Harkenbach. They were soon to be in Falkirk's possession, the instruments of absolute power.

When the directional mics further determined that all five people were gathered in the kitchen for breakfast, Lucas Blackridge, the SWAT specialist, approached the residence from a direction that ensured no one could see him through a kitchen window. Employing a police lock-release gun, he opened the side door of the garage. The forced-air furnace was located there. Blackridge extinguished the automatic pilot light, to ensure there would be no explosion. He set the timer and inserted the pressurized tank of sedative into the furnace, from which the gas would be distributed through the house ducting to every room.

Falkirk was disappointed that a deadly nerve agent or poisonous gas was not available for immediate use. To obtain either, he would have incurred a wait of between twelve and twenty-four hours while his requisition was sent to Central Ordnance, considered, fulfilled, and delivered to him. For all of its secret power and ruthlessness, the shadow state nevertheless had a bureaucracy of its own and the usual lazy functionaries who felt secure in their positions because the leaders of their union were harder cases than any agents with licenses to kill.

Within five minutes of Blackridge's stealthy entrance to the garage, Falkirk could be certain that the occupants of Pellafino's house were knocked out and waiting to be harvested like fish that had been jacklighted and then blown to the surface with a stick of dynamite by an impatient fisherman. They would remain unconscious for about an hour or more.

At that point, agents swarmed the street in black Suburbans, barricaded both ends of the block, and quickly cordoned off the target residence. When curious neighbors stepped outside to learn the reason for the commotion, they were told to stay in their homes and were respectfully escorted inside if they were polite. However, if they objected to any extent whatsoever or were rude or had the temerity to say, "I pay your salary through my taxes," then they were taught a lesson about obedience to authority that they would not soon forget.

Only a few years earlier, after such a blitzkrieg as this, it would have been necessary for Falkirk and his men to enter the house wearing gas masks and open the windows to ventilate the place. In so doing, they would have risked being photographed by neighbors who would have uploaded their snapshots to the internet, making it more difficult to craft a cover story that even a gullible media and a somnolent public would accept at face value.

If progress had once been the friend of average men and women, these days every advance in technology seemed to give an advantage to those who understood that the masses must be managed, controlled, and encouraged to live in a crafted *virtual* reality where they would be content and confident of their freedom, even though they had none. Now, Falkirk and team benefited from a technological breakthrough that spared them from the need to mask up and enter the house and throw open the windows as if engaged in spring-cleaning.

In the garage, after retrieving the first now-empty tank, Lucas Blackridge inserted a second pressurized container into the furnace. This subsequent round released a high-velocity counterpoising gas that, in chemical reaction with the initial sedative, eliminated every trace of that material and of itself, leaving zero residue of either, returning the air within the home to a normal condition.

Falkirk climbed out of the back of the van. Preceded by two of his men, he caned across the street to the Pellafino residence.

A high-pressure system of dry northern air graced the morning with a meteorological phenomenon known as "severe clear," a totally cloudless sky of an intense blue. The day was warm but not hot, and the air appeared free of all pollution. Hawks swooped wild and high, and other birds sang in the trees.

It was the perfect day to become the emperor of everything and to kill those who conspired against his ascendancy to the throne.

====== 84

In the pantry, Amity heard a second *whump* that rattled things in the walls.

A weariness settled through her mind as she thought, *Now what?* She wasn't physically weary, because she'd slept soundly for a few hours the previous night in the Bonner house, while her father kept a watch on their bungalow. She didn't want to be one of *those* girls, the kind without enough fortitude in the face of adversity. It was always nice, however, in the middle of an epic quest, to have a respite with, say, a kindly retired couple—she having once been a maid to a princess, and he having been a former foundry man who had forged armor for the bravest knights—who would invite you into their cottage in the enchanted forest to share their dinner and then have a pipe and a snifter of brandy by the fire, with two good dogs snoring by the warm hearth. After that convivial evening and a safe sleep in a goose-down bed while the dogs stood guard against witches and warlocks, you were fortified and ready to carry on at any cost.

Instead, what she had was a pantry with canned goods and bags of dried beans that made her want to fart just by looking at them. She was alone and afraid and on the brink of being dispirited.

At least, when she dared to take the wet cloth off her face and breathe without that filter, she found the concentration of gas in the pantry was so low that she didn't pass out.

After the second *whump*, the brief weariness lifted from her because unidentifiable sounds like that always meant something was going to happen. Lord knew what. And whether you were weary or not, you'd better be prepared for whatever was coming.

She got to her feet and took two cans of pears from a shelf, intending to throw them at whoever opened the door.

===== **85**

According to this Ed Harkenbach, who seemed to have more street smarts and be somewhat more balanced than the Ed who had entrusted Jeffy with his key to everything, the security alarm was nothing to worry about.

"A lot of things change from timeline to timeline," he said as he led Jeffy along the hallway to Duke Pellafino's study, "but in those that are at all similar to this world, one of the things you can rely on is that the police will take at least twenty minutes to respond to a security alarm in a private home. We'll have our guns long before then."

"How can you be certain Duke has guns?"

Raising his voice above the wailing alarm, Ed said, "How can I be certain the sun will rise in the east and set in the west? He said he was a detective in the Gang Activities Section of the LAPD."

"He told me, too," Jeffy said. "But he retired from that."

"When you spend years putting hard-core sociopaths in prison, many of them MS-13 lunatics from Mexico and points south, psychos who like to behead people and hang others from streetlamps before eviscerating them, who butcher babies for pleasure, you have to figure if one of them gets out of prison, he might come looking for you. To a guy like Duke, retirement doesn't mean the same thing as it does to your average accountant."

In Pellafino's study, as the house alarm continued to shrill, they found a handsome mahogany gun cabinet. The doors were locked, and the glass in them proved to be armored when Ed tried to shatter it with the butt of his pistol.

"Stand back," the physicist ordered, and with two shots he blew out the lock on the cabinet.

The crash of the shots temporarily half deafened Jeffy, and the screaming alarm seemed to quiet to a mournful wail.

Yanking open drawers in the base of the cabinet, Ed found two handguns, spare magazines, and boxes of ammunition. "A Sig Pro by Sig Sauer. Chambered for forty-caliber Smith and Wesson rounds. Ten-round magazine. Polymer frame but the slide rails are solid pieces of machined steel. Think you can handle it?"

"I've practiced a lot with my pistol."

"This one's more powerful than yours. Expect some recoil, aim low," Ed advised as he loaded a magazine and snapped it into the pistol.

Jeffy took the offered Sig Pro. He didn't want to kill anyone or wound anyone or even point a gun at anyone, but if Falkirk and his goons laid a hand on Amity or Michelle, then he'd do what he had to do. Taking a life in self-defense or to protect the innocent was killing, but it wasn't murder. If he had to kill people in this world, maybe there would be worlds in which ultimate violence was never required of him.

Ed loaded two spare magazines and passed them to Jeffy. Then from the rack of long guns above the drawers, he chose for himself a 12-gauge pistol-grip pump-action shotgun. He clicked a round into the breach, inserted three more in the magazine tube, and loaded his pockets with shells.

"How," Jeffy wondered, "does a renowned physicist and bow-tied academic turn himself into a kick-ass gunman?"

"Necessity."

Ed led the way out of the study and turned left in the hall, heading toward the front of the house.

"Where are we going?" Jeffy asked as he followed.

"Upstairs. When we port back to your timeline, we don't want to pop into the kitchen if Falkirk is there with ten of his goons."

Jeffy's hearing was coming back. The alarm swelled louder.

He said, "What if the house is still full of gas?"

"Then we'll port out before taking a breath, try again in a couple minutes. But there won't be gas. The place will be clear. Falkirk meant to hit hard and wrap up the attack fast."

Ed seemed certain that the assault had involved an aerosol sedative, not a lethal gas, and Jeffy wanted to believe that was the case. After all, he'd breathed it in and survived. But what if he'd inhaled twice instead of once?

The thought of Amity and Michelle dead in that kitchen sent waves of nausea slithering around his stomach again, but it also inspired rage. His spine stiffened and his jaws clenched. The pistol in his right hand felt as if it were a part of him, an extension of his body through which vengeance, if vengeance was justified, would be delivered without hesitation.

As they entered the foyer, Jeffy saw two police officers through the panes of glass in the front door. They were coming up the steps onto the porch. Evidently an ex-cop and friend of the force like Duke warranted a faster response than other citizens.

The cops saw Jeffy and Ed, and the physicist said, "Quick! Up the stairs."

86

Falkirk and his two subordinates entered the house through the garage, where Lucas Blackridge waited for them. The SWAT specialist had already employed the lock-release gun to disengage the deadbolt in the connecting door.

Although the gassed occupants of the house would be sleeping off the dose they'd been given for another hour, Lucas and his two associates preceded their superior with their weapons drawn.

Nothing pleased John Falkirk half as much as the sight of his enemies—or even people who were merely a nuisance—broken and bloody and dead, preferably soaked in urine because terror rendered them incontinent in the last moments of their lives. This world—to one degree or another *all* worlds—was a hard proving ground where no one who reached adulthood cared for anyone but himself or herself, where the only truth was that everyone lied, where the only virtues were envy and ruthlessness, where the only goal worth having was the acquisition of power over others, and where the ultimate power was the power of death. Intuitively, everyone knew the darkest reality of human existence, but Falkirk believed that he was one of very few who could admit it even to themselves: Life was a war of all against all, waged with every weapon from lies and slanders to guns, knives, and bombs.

In the kitchen of the Pellafino residence, he was denied the delight of pooled blood and urine-soaked corpses. But he took some pleasure in the sight of Michelle Coltrane slumped unconscious in a chair at the breakfast table and, opposite her, a giant in another chair, a man who must have been Charles Pellafino.

His pleasure was short-lived when he discovered that these two were the only sleepers in the kitchen. Harkenbach, Coltrane, and the snarky girl were gone. They had all been here during the attack. In the Roto-Rooter van, Falkirk had listened to those fools, all five of them, when the timer on the pressurized tank released the clouds of sleep. No one escaped the house. Considering that the reaction time to the sedative was immediate, no one could have made it into another room. Anyway, gas infiltrated the entire house in seconds, so even if the missing three had fled the kitchen, they would have dropped in the downstairs hall. Through the open door, Falkirk could see no one in that passageway.

The sole explanation was infuriating. The directional mics had picked up Harkenbach asking if he could pour coffee for anyone. He must have been at the coffeemaker near the window. Then he'd said, *"They're here,"* just before the gas was released. He saw someone or something suspicious, and he must have had his key to everything in hand when he did. As the gas erupted into the room, Coltrane and the girl went to Harkenbach, or he went to them, and they ported out to another timeline.

Although there was no chance that the missing three had gotten to another room before succumbing, Falkirk dispatched Blackridge and his two men to search the house.

Fresh vexation now overlaid his more profound, ever-simmering anger.

Alone with the sleepers, he hung his cane on the handle of the refrigerator door, went to Michelle Coltrane, and stood looking down at her. Although things he'd heard through the directional microphones suggested she wasn't the bitch from this timeline, he didn't know with certainty what she was doing here with Harkenbach or why she had been with the old man when he'd shown up at the bungalow and shot Falkirk. When she woke, he would torture the truth out of her.

She was an erotic vision, slumped in the chair, her head tilted back, eyes closed, lips parted as though to receive whatever a lover wished to press between them. He thought of how Philip Esterhaus had appeared in death—throat torn, eyes rolled back in his head, mouth open like this, a dethroned demigod. As he had been in that blood-spattered bedroom, Falkirk was overcome by euphoria, by an awareness that great power was already his, magical power, by virtue of having killed a demigod who had been able only to wound him in return, the wound so inconsequential that it pained him not at all.

Michelle's ripe lips compelled his attention now as had the empty glass on the drainboard in Esterhaus's kitchen. He realized that before him was another sign to be interpreted: a beautiful woman whose open mouth suggested she was whispering, conveying to him some mystery that would transform him. He leaned down and put his mouth to hers and took her soft exhalations into himself, and when he licked her lips, they tasted of cinnamon from the morning roll she'd been eating.

In the heightened state of consciousness that had come to him with two sacramental Vicodin, he understood that whatever mystery she might impart to him would not be one that elevated him, but one that weakened him and turned him away from the acquisition of power that was his destiny. She was Eve, of course, the eternal temptress, as were all women. Whatever she might whisper to him would be a dangerous lie. Everyone deceived everyone else, women and men and children, but in Falkirk's experience, women were the better at it, especially beautiful women. He must not give her the chance to bring him to ruin with false promises.

He took his mouth from hers and straightened up and drew the pistol with which he had killed the demigod. He pressed the muzzle between her breasts. She slept on, oblivious. Slowly he slid the muzzle up her sweater to her throat. He traced the curve of her chin with the front sight of the gun. He pressed the barrel between her lips and let her exhale into it. To save himself from her bewitching deceptions, he must squeeze the trigger before she woke, before she could speak a lie that might corrupt him. Blow all the endless lies out of her lovely head.

One thing and one thing only stayed his finger on the trigger. Not mercy. He didn't believe in mercy or in fact that it existed as more than a concept. Not desire, either. He would have enjoyed being the barrel between her lips. But now that he understood the magical nature of the world, he knew that when he had his pleasure, and she received the essence of him, she would own his soul. He delayed blowing her brains out only because to kill her in her sleep would be to deny him the sight of the terror in her eyes that would be there if she faced death while awake. He must stuff a gag in her mouth and fix it in place with a strip of duct tape to prevent her from enchanting him with lies, and then wait for her to regain consciousness. Only then, when their stares locked and she couldn't speak to cast a spell on him, would *her* power be passed to him, to enhance his own.

He didn't holster the pistol, but instead proceeded to where Pellafino slept at the far side of the round table. Because of his size and his bold facial features, which seemed to have been carved from rock, the big man might have been another demigod, this time clothed. The murder of Esterhaus had been so gratifying and had contributed so much to Falkirk's suddenly deeper under-standing of the nature of reality that he wanted to repeat the experience. After this murder, he might allow himself even greater transcendence with a third Vicodin.

As he pressed the muzzle of the gun to Charles Pellafino's temple, however, he saw past him to a box of pastries on the table, next to which lay the key to everything.

For a moment, he disbelieved his eyes. Then he realized that if the radio repairman and his wiseass daughter had ported out with the Ed Harkenbach from another timeline, this must be the key Coltrane had gotten from the Harkenbach of *this* world, who had eluded Falkirk for so long.

He holstered his pistol and circled a quarter of the way around the table in a state of awe, as if it were an altar, as if the box of pastries were in fact a pyx from which the sacred wafer, the key to everything, had recently been removed. He stared at the pre-cious object, afraid that if he tried to touch it, he would find that it was an illusion.

When he picked it up, the key proved to be real. Although he knew from past experience, before Harkenbach had destroyed the other two keys, that the device was light, it felt much heavier now, as solid as a brick, heavy with the fate of all humanity. The power within this sleek casing would allow him to steal the technology of more advanced worlds and become the godlike ruler of this timeline or any other, the masses his to control like puppets. His wealth and power would be beyond all measurement. Eventually billions of people would honor and serve him to an extent that the subjects of other emperors and dictators had never before in history been required to submit.

Before he had noticed the key, he had wanted a third Vicodin, reckless as such an overdose might be, for he had wished to achieve yet greater enlightenment. But now that the device was in his possession, his quest fulfilled, Falkirk was exalted beyond any level to which any drug could raise him. He slipped the precious object in a coat pocket.

He drew his pistol once more. The others in Project Everett Highways, as well as the consortium of billionaires who underwrote the project when government funds were not enough, could never know he had the key or be given reason to suspect his intent until it was too late for them to stop him.

Anyone with knowledge that the key had been here must not be allowed to live and speak of it. Pellafino and Michelle must be killed before they woke. Coltrane and his daughter and Harkenbach must be shot on sight.

=== 87

Several worlds removed from Amity and Michelle, with the ear-piercing security alarm shrieking as though Hitler's Luftwaffe must have traveled in time and space to conduct a major bombing raid on Suavidad Beach, Jeffy raced up the stairs in another version of the Pellafino house, close behind Ed.

One of the two cops on the porch, watching through the front door, seeing them armed with pistol and shotgun, shouted, "Police!"

"We know, shut up, shut up, we know!" Ed shouted back at them.

This version of Harkenbach seemed to be more tightly wrapped, mentally and emotionally, than the one whom Jeffy had befriended in his world. However, the two versions shared the same genes and many of the same formative experiences, and it was possible, even likely, that under enough pressure, this Ed would crack just as the other one had. Jeffy had not forgotten a single turn of events that had led him from a peaceful dinner in town with Amity, two days earlier, to this mortal and chaotic moment; yet it was incomprehensible to him that she was worlds away, under threat of death, and that their lives were in the hands of an eccentric physicist who shaved his head and took off his bow tie and thought himself transformed beyond recognition.

At the top of the steps, Jeffy glanced back, afraid that the police might force entry, not sure if that was a violation of the standard rules of engagement in a situation like this.

They didn't have to use force. One of them tried the door. Incredibly, it wasn't locked. Maybe Duke's security system alerted him on his cell phone and allowed him to unlock the house remotely for the police.

"They're in the house," he warned Ed as he hurried after the old man, along the upstairs hallway.

He followed the physicist into a bedroom on the right and slammed the door.

"We've got to brace it," Jeffy declared, but he didn't see a straight-backed chair with which he could easily do the job.

"Not necessary," Ed assured him. "They won't burst in on us. They'll take up positions out there and call for backup."

"Let's jump home, let's go, get us the hell out of here."

Frowning, Ed put his shotgun on the bed and began to search his pockets. "You didn't notice if by chance I put the key down in the study, when we were raiding the gun cabinet?"

===== 88

In the pantry, standing with a can of pears ready in each hand, Amity heard maybe three or four men enter the kitchen and express their reaction to the scene with an unnecessary number of casually spoken obscenities. Even though she now occasionally used the word *shit*, and though Duke Pellafino, who was definitely a good guy, now and then used even worse language, it was an article of faith to her that any bad guy's degree of evil could be determined by how foul his mouth was. If that was true, then these bozos were demonic.

She assumed that somehow the gas had dispersed, because none of the intruders sounded like he was wearing a mask. One of them told the others to search the rest of the house, and Amity felt pretty sure that the voice belonged to Falkirk. She tensed and raised the cans of pears, but the searchers trooped out of the kitchen without taking a look in the pantry, their footsteps receding into farther rooms.

Falkirk, if it was Falkirk, stayed behind. Amity listened to him moving around the kitchen, making small noises that she could not interpret. He muttered to himself, but too low for her to make sense of what he said. He sounded like a grumbling troll.

The moment that thought occurred to her, she wished it hadn't. She was reminded of something she read years ago, when she'd been an impressionable child, a story about a troll who stole children while they slept and baked them into pies. It was a stupid story, really and truly, but she'd had nightmares in which she believed she was lying drowsily in bed as Daddy tucked a nice warm blanket around her, only to suddenly realize that the blanket was in fact the top crust of a pie and that she was not in a bed but in a pan, and that Daddy wasn't Daddy.

Maybe it was nervous tension or the faint lingering scent of the gas, or one of the other many smells in the pantry to which she might be allergic, or maybe it was evidence that the devil was real and busily at work in the world, but for whatever reason, she was suddenly overcome by an urge to sneeze. She put down one of the cans and pinched her nose hard with her right hand. The urge didn't go away. The tingling in her nasal passages grew and grew. She put down the second can and covered her mouth because, when you thought about it, the *ahchoo* part came from your mouth rather than your nose. Her effort to repress the sneeze brought tears to her eyes. Gradually the urge subsided. When she could no longer hold her breath, she removed her hand from her lips and breathed quietly through her mouth. Only when she was as sure as sure could be that the tingling was gone and wouldn't come back, really and truly wouldn't, Amity stopped pinching her nose.

The threat of being undone by a sneeze and winding up in the clutches of Falkirk, the troll, so scared her that she was shaking all over. Through everything that this crazy story had thrown at her, she'd remained pretty darn confident and optimistic. Now she understood that confidence and bravery and fortitude weren't always enough, that you needed a little luck as well, or you could be undone by a sneeze, a cough, a fart. Without the pears, she felt more vulnerable than ever. But when she picked up one of those pathetic weapons, her hand was shaking so badly that the can slipped out of her grasp and fell to the pantry floor.

Ed Harkenbach's sport coat seemed to offer more compartments than a magician's wearable portmanteau, as he frantically searched his pockets and patted himself and worried aloud about having left the key to everything in another room.

Pounding footsteps on the stairs revealed that the policemen were boldly pursuing even as the siren of a backup cruiser rose in the distance, a different ululation from the bleat of the burglar alarm.

Jeffy considered dragging a highboy in front of the bedroom door, but a barricade was useless if Ed's key was on the study desk near the gun cabinet. *His* key was on the table in the kitchen of this house in another world. He'd kept it within reach while he'd eaten breakfast, so that he wouldn't need to fumble it out of a pocket in an emergency, but he hadn't counted on being gassed. He also hadn't counted on Ed being one of those forgetful guys who misplaced his keys.

One of the cops in the upstairs hall shouted, "Put down your weapons! Open the door and lie facedown in plain sight, your arms straight out from your sides!"

That seemed to be a wordy and impractical order, and it made Jeffy think they were dealing with a couple of cowboys who might take risks that made no sense.

He didn't want to die here, but he also didn't want to go to jail here for years and years, worlds away from Amity and Michelle, leaving them to fend for themselves, leaving them to die. Never ever would he shoot a cop, not a good and honest officer of the law. But he stepped to one side of the door, took a deep breath, imagined himself as Al Pacino in a gangster movie, and shouted above the shrilling alarm, "I'll fucking kill any shithead who comes in here. I'll blow your fucking brains out!"

Just then Ed said, "Ah, here it is. Why did I tuck it in a hip pocket? I never carry it in a hip pocket."

Jeffy went to him and clutched his arm. "For God's sake, Ed, let's go! They think I'm Dillinger."

"Get my shotgun."

Jeffy snatched it from the bed.

The physicist pressed a forefinger to the home circle on the key. Instead of subjecting them to a four-second wait, the device brightened at once. And there was no period of gray light. The three buttons appeared immediately: blue, red, green; HOME, SELECT, RETURN.

Jeffy said, "Why doesn't mine work this well?"

"Because it was designed by the Ed of your world, and I'm a smarter Ed than he is."

The smarter Ed pressed RETURN.

90

Certain of his immortality, Falkirk stood to the right of the pantry and turned the knob and threw the door open. Bags of beans lined the threshold. Pistol in a two-handed grip, he stepped away from the jamb and saw the snarky girl alone, a can of pears at her feet.

This most perfect day of his life became even better.

"Come out of there," he commanded.

"No."

He trained the gun on her face. "No isn't an option."

The little bitch defied him and sat down on the floor of the pantry.

He was going to kill her. He had no compunctions about killing children. He'd done it before, if only a couple times. He wasn't concerned about what his crew would say, because they wouldn't care that he offed the little bitch. They wouldn't report him to anyone. Doing so would only get them executed by even more ruthless agents of the shadow state. They all knew what the stakes were here, knew what was required of them, and if Falkirk killed her, that was just one less task for them.

However, he didn't want to kill her in the pantry. He needed to get her out of there, secure her to a chair at the breakfast table, where she would wait for her mother and Pellafino to wake. He wanted the girl to watch while he killed Michelle and Duke, wanted her to understand that she had snarked the wrong man. He was a killer of demigods, a man with infinite worlds at his disposal, who could be shot but not stopped, who felt no pain anymore. He had lived a life of pain from an early age, emotional pain. He'd been shit on by everyone: his mother dying on him, his lust-crazed father selling him out for a sexpot second wife, leaving him with no inheritance. To claw his way up in the shadow state and the halls of the überwealthy, he had licked boots and kissed asses and humiliated himself in ten thousand ways, but now those days were done. He had the key now, the only remaining key in this timeline, and it made him free, made him the master of his fate and hers.

He holstered the gun and went into the pantry and shouted at her to get to her feet. She tried to curl up like a pill bug, so he cuffed her hard alongside the head, cuffed her again. He grabbed her by the hair and dragged her, screaming, out of the closet, into the kitchen. She flailed at him vigorously, without effect. He twisted the fistful of hair as though to tear it out by the roots, until her scream became as thin as an electronic squeal. She so infuriated him that he wanted to forget about securing her in a chair to witness her mother's murder, wanted to deal with her now, put a foot in her face, stomp that smart mouth so she'd never be able to smirk again.

91

Jeffy ricocheted from the Suavidad Beach where Amity was long dead, back to the town in which she was still alive, where she had *better be* alive, because the alternative wasn't something that he could handle. He didn't care that there were many parallel worlds in which his daughter remained breathing and vital even if she proved to be dead here, because *this* was the girl he'd loved for more than eleven years. He could love other versions of her— How could he not?—but in the thousands of days of their shared lives, he and this Amity laughed at the same things, sorrowed at the same things, weathered precisely the same vicissitudes of life, and no other Amity could be exactly like the one who'd filled his heart for more than a decade. She was the best thing that ever happened to him. Another Amity, no matter how nearly identical she might be to the one he raised, would not be *his* Amity. The loss of her would be real and devastating. Having failed her, he would dwell in despair all the remaining days of his life, this one life of many, this only life that mattered to him.

When he and Ed arrived in the master bedroom of the Pellafino house, the air was clean, as if the place hadn't been attacked with gas. He half wondered if the key screwed up and delivered them to the wrong timeline. The silence was a relief from the ear-skewering squeal of the alarm in the other world, but such quiet was also a worry because from it he inevitably inferred that Falkirk's work here was already concluded, with no one left to rescue.

Ed whispered, "Shotgun."

As Jeffy handed over the weapon, men laughed somewhere on the second floor, and another man, much closer, called out, "Canker, Yessman—here, now!"

=== 92

With Vince Canker and Roy Yessman, Lucas Blackridge searched the house, bottom to top, though there was no point to it. The gas had been introduced at such high velocity, with so many pounds of pressure behind it, that no one could have had time to flee the kitchen other than with a key that gave him access to the Everett Highways. Besides, there would have been no refuge upstairs, where the gas would have penetrated every corner at most four seconds after the ground-floor rooms were flooded.

He suspected Falkirk just wanted a few minutes alone with the unconscious woman because she was something of a looker. Blackridge knew his boss to be an arrogant ass, knew he hated women in general and pretty women in particular, and suspected him of being a pervert who liked to inflict pain on them. An unconscious woman wouldn't give Falkirk the pleasure of a response to what torment he visited on her body. But maybe he intended to do the damage while she slept and have the gratification of her agony when she woke.

Blackridge had often considered arranging a fatal accident for Falkirk, with an eye toward perhaps moving into his position after the memorial service. However, the sonofabitch was well connected, and getting away with a disguised assassination would not be easy. In his present position with this cockamamie project, he was paid four times what he would have received anywhere else, and he didn't want to wind up back in a civilian police department working more for the pension than for the salary.

They gave the creep ten minutes with the Coltrane woman and speculated among themselves what atrocity he might commit with her.

At the back of the house, as they were ready to turn around and go downstairs, Vince Canker decided he needed to take a piss, and he went into the upstairs hall bath to relieve himself. The urge was apparently communicable, because Yessman decided to wait for his turn in the facilities.

Blackridge continued toward the front of the house. As he drew near the stairs, he heard a sudden insufflation of air. There were no open windows on the second floor, and the sound, though muffled, seemed akin to the *whoosh* that always accompanied transit between timelines. He thought it might have come from beyond the open door to his left.

At the back of the house, Canker and Yessman laughed, being the type who found nothing funnier than bathroom humor.

Blackridge called out, "Canker, Yessman—here, now!"

He hurried into the master bedroom, drawing his pistol as he crossed the threshold, and there was Jeffrey Coltrane, incoming from elsewhere. On arrival, he must have lurched into this timeline and stumbled, which sometimes happened. Having dropped his weapon, he was bending down to retrieve it.

Blackridge said, "Don't touch it."

===== 93

The guy rushed through the open door as Jeffrey pretended to have dropped the pistol. The thug was professional and quick and ready and not stupid, so he realized at once that he made a mistake by assuming his quarry was a milquetoast dealer in antiques and an eccentric physicist with no more street smarts than any tenured Harvard professor. He began to turn his head to the right, but had no time to dodge the blow. Ed stood behind the door, shotgun raised high, and he brought the butt plate of the stock down hard on the gunman's head. Skin split, bone cracked, blood flowed, and the man folded to the floor as if he were wet origami.

The laughing men were still in high humor as they approached along the second-floor hall, evidently unaware that the first man had summoned them to action. Before they appeared in the doorway, screams rose from downstairs. The voice was female, shrill with as much anger as terror. Amity.

===== 94

He was going to kill her.

His eyes were the crazy animal eyes of a vicious predator, cruel and strange. Amity knew there was a real chance Falkirk was going to kill her, and she intuited that the harder she resisted, the greater the likelihood he couldn't stop himself from murdering her in the most painful way he could imagine. But she wasn't able to stop resisting, either. She wasn't being the courageous girl in a story, wasn't fighting back just because that's what she learned from novels. There was something inside her that she had never known was there until now, a ferocious sense of her right to be respected, to be left alone, to *live*. This creep hadn't given to her the right to life, so he had no authority to take it from her. *No one* had given it to her, she'd been born with it, and this life was hers as long as she could defend it. Fighting for your life wasn't just instinct, but also a duty, because life was a gift that came with a mission to fulfill. You were here for a purpose, and you needed to figure out what it was, and to let yourself be killed without a hell of a fight meant you had failed everyone you loved and everyone you might one day have loved. So as this creep dragged her out of the pantry by her hair, she on her back, even though he still held the gun in one hand, she cried out, "Asshole," and reared up and punched him in the balls.

Although her father had taught her the nutcracker technique, resorting to it was of course embarrassing even in these extreme circumstances. She would rather have done something less intimate, like shooting him, but she didn't have a gun. Anyway, although it was an embarrassing move, it was also satisfying and effective. The twist of her hair slipped from his grasp. His face was as contorted as that of a psycho clown, and from him came a combination wheeze and groan that would have been funny if Amity hadn't been fighting for her life.

Her father wasn't here, and neither was spooky old Ed, so she figured somehow they had ported out. They would be back. She had no doubt they would be back. Just maybe not in time.

She scrambled away from Falkirk on her hands and knees, at first with no destination, no purpose other than to put distance between her and him, but then she remembered the gun. Daddy's gun. As they were preparing breakfast, he'd put the pistol on the counter by the bread box. She had never fired a gun before, but it couldn't be that hard. Everyone used them in the movies. In the quick, when either you did the deed or died, the good guy or girl always put a hole in the bad guy or girl.

Abruptly she changed direction, frantically crawling toward the farther end of the kitchen. She almost made it to the bread box. She was maybe four feet from the counter on which her father's gun lay, when Falkirk kicked her hard in the butt and sent her sprawling facedown on the floor.

95

Coming out of the upstairs half bath, Canker and Yessman heard Blackridge call to them from the far end of the hallway, but they didn't hear what he said because they were still laughing about a diarrhea joke that Yessman had told. Yessman always laughed at his own jokes louder and longer than anyone, which was okay with Canker because they were usually damn funny. Besides, Yessman's laugh was infectious.

As Blackridge disappeared into the master bedroom, which they had searched mere minutes earlier, the screaming started downstairs. It sounded like the girl, Amity, which was something of a surprise because both Canker and Yessman had thought Falkirk would have his fun with the woman. Canker didn't care if the boss man got it off with the full-quart beauty or the half-pint, whatever turned him on. Vince Canker wasn't judgmental. *Wrong* and *right* were just words. If it *felt* right, it *was* right. If it felt wrong, you were probably just confused, and if you thought about it some more, then it would feel right.

When Canker went into the master bedroom, with Yessman close behind, Blackridge was on the floor, either dead or waiting for a fast ride to the ICU. Coltrane had a pistol, and Harkenbach had a shotgun, and none of this made any sense to Vince Canker. They had ported out before the sedative gas got them. They were gone and free, and there was no reason for them to port back here fifteen minutes later. They wouldn't have come back for Pellafino. Who the hell was he to them? Nobody. The woman was a looker, but the world was full of lookers. You didn't put your ass on the line for any woman, and the girl was just a damn kid, in a world with too damn many noisy kids causing global warming and wasting government money getting useless college degrees in the literature of Fiji when those funds could better be used to increase the salaries for men like Vince who did the hard work that kept the country functioning.

Canker and Yessman had entered the bedroom with their pistols holstered. They didn't raise their hands high like in old Western movies, but they acted suitably chagrined and respectful, waiting for an opening. Guns weren't the end-all and be-all. They had knives and razor-sharp throwing stars and wicked retractable blades in the toes of their boots. Even at a disadvantage like this, they knew a score of ways to turn the tables and kill their adversaries, and they had done so before. The best thing they had going for them was that Harkenbach was a prissy professor scientist who wore bow ties and ran away from his troubles, while Coltrane was an antique geek with more books in his house than any real man would ever tolerate. Blackridge appeared to be in a bad way, true enough, but the two men who had done that to him were pale faced and sweaty and obviously sickened by the violence they had committed. They didn't have the guts for this, and if you didn't have the guts for the game, you were dead men standing.

"Let's be reasonable," Vince said. "A little negotiation, and we can all be winners here."

The volume of gunfire came as a surprise to him.

===== 96

This wasn't just a fight anymore, this was a living nightmare; she was being attacked not by a freaking nutcase, but by a *thing*, a monster in a human disguise, such an alien creature that it wasn't possible to know what it would do to her before it slaughtered her. Kicked in the butt, knocked flat, Amity tried to thrust to her feet, but Falkirk grabbed her by the seat of her jeans and the back of her T-shirt and plucked her off the floor and turned in place, swinging her in a circle, as her father once played airplane with her when she was little, though there was nothing fun about this. This was vicious, hateful. He was going to bash her head against something. There was no way she could strike out at him, nothing she could do to break free. In time to the two-beat slamming

of her heart, she thought, *Please God, please God, please God . . .*
This man, this diabolic thing, didn't seem to be strong enough
to do what he was doing, especially after enduring a nut busting.
Rage and insanity gave him something like superhuman strength.
As he swung her, he chanted, "Bitch, bitch, bitch, bitch, bitch,"
every repetition more explosive than the last. He was going to
fling her, send her flying. She started screaming again, because if
she landed wrong or slammed into a wall, bones were going to
break. And he let her go.

✳   ✳   ✳

Michelle wandered in a labyrinth with an undulant floor and
stacked-stone passageways, catacombs poorly illuminated by
candles on wall shelves. Reflections of flames licked the stones,
and lively shadows slithered like salamanders over every surface.

The dead lay in niches, wrapped in browning bandages, their
faces concealed. She roamed ever farther into the maze, deeper
into the earth: seeking her mother, who died in childbirth; seeking her father, who was electrocuted in a transformer vault; seeking Jeffy, who died under the wheels of an Escalade, and Amity,
who perished in her father's arms.

Sometimes Michelle carried an oil lamp, although at other
times it was a flashlight. She peeled wet strips of moldering cloth
off face after face. Again and again, she discovered those dead
loved ones whom she sought, and she also unmasked multiples
of herself, preserved in death.

A quiet desperation overcame her as she realized that there
would be no end of searching, that she would never find the final
and true version of mother, father, husband, child, or self.

Just then the silence of the catacombs was riddled by a scream and its many echoes, a child's scream, *Amity's* scream.

Through the lapping light and tongues of licking shadow came the living girl, running for her life, terrified. She streaked past and away, and Michelle set out after her, probing the gloom with the flashlight. As passageways branched off in ever greater numbers, she opened her eyes wider and stared with increasing intensity into each stony corridor—until at last she blinked, blinked, blinked away the labyrinth and saw the kitchen.

Her eyes felt sunken, and tinnitus rang in her ears, and her tongue seemed twice as thick as it ought to be. She remembered the yellow gas gushing from the heating vents high in the walls.

Falkirk raging and capering like a demonic spirit. Amity on the floor, crawling away from him. Falkirk kicking at her and missing, kicking again and connecting with her backside.

Michelle closed her eyes and the labyrinth coiled away to every side, as before. *No!*

Panicked, she opened her eyes and saw the kitchen and the demon and the innocent girl. He swung the child around as if she were only a rag doll. Her head whipped past the refrigerator, missing the long steel handle by an inch. One of her sneaker-clad feet stuttered across a cabinet door.

Where was Jeffy? Nowhere in sight.

Gasping for breath, Michelle tried to press up from her chair.

She felt heavy and slow. Her legs wouldn't work. The kitchen seemed to expand and contract and expand repeatedly, and darkness throbbed at the edges of her vision.

Falkirk flung the girl away from him.

✳   ✳   ✳

Amity was thrown onto the breakfast table and slid across it, sweeping plates and coffee mugs and utensils to the floor. Momentum carried her after that cascade of debris. She crashed into a chair, toppling it, tumbling over it, rolling to a stop in the open doorway to the pantry. Her scalp burned from her hair having been pulled so hard, and her right shoulder ached, and so did her left knee. She'd bitten her tongue; there was blood in her mouth. She didn't seem to have broken any bones or sustained any bad cuts, but her heart was knocking so hard that it seemed about to shake her joints apart—and here came Falkirk. He'd drawn his gun again.

The two thugs didn't have weapons in their hands. However, they were armed, and surely with more than pistols. They were big, hard-looking men with stares as cold and merciless as those of robots.

The shotgun roared twice. Jeffy fired the Sig Pro ten times without hesitation or any expectation of remorse, blasting the two men even after they were down, because maybe they were protected by Kevlar and because, crazy as it sounded, there was something almost supernatural about their deadpan faces and their self-assurance when confronted with imminent death, so that maybe even two point-blank head shots weren't enough to stop them.

Amity was screaming downstairs, and if there were a dozen more of these men between here and there, he would do the same to them if he could. The supreme evil kingdom of Mordor wasn't just a place in Tolkien's imagination. It was real. It always had been real. It was here and it was everywhere men sought absolute power over others. He ejected the empty magazine and snapped a fresh one into the pistol.

Harkenbach said, "Are you all right?"

"No."

✳   ✳   ✳

During seven years of sorrow, ever since the argument and the Escalade, all that Michelle wanted was to have her husband and her daughter back, her family as it had been, and her music even if she never played it for anyone but Jeffy, Amity, and friends. That wish, that miracle, had been granted to her, and she could not bear to see this psychopath Falkirk take it all away.

When Amity was thrown like a rag doll, like a bag of trash, and slid across the table in front of her mother, crashing into and over the chair, two things of importance happened to Michelle. First, she found within herself the power to cast off the lingering effects of the sedative gas. Second, into her lap fell a knife with which she had earlier cut up her breakfast sausage.

✳   ✳   ✳

Amity scrambled to her feet, and the Falkirk thing came at her with the pistol in a two-handed grip, so that she wasn't able to get close to him, couldn't use the nutcracker trick again. Nothing near at hand except the bags of beans at her feet. If she threw those, he'd shoot her, shoot not to kill but to wound, because he wanted to make this as painful for her as he could. His face was twisted with madness but also with savage glee, and all the parts of it were mismatched and wooden, somehow artificial, as though they had been carved for a dozen different marionettes and then hinged together in this one strange countenance. He moved quickly but jerkily, like a figure controlled by the strings of a raging puppeteer. He bared his teeth in a threat that reminded her of Good Boy's killing bite. One of his gray eyes was bloodshot from a burst capillary, as red as a wound, and the other looked as depthless as a painted eye.

She had nowhere to run. She wouldn't drop to her knees and beg for her life, she just wouldn't, and even if she did, he would never treat her with mercy. Every evil person dies many deaths in numerous timelines, but even the good die often. This was a life in which she would die young. She knew it, and he knew that she knew it, and she could see that her terror excited him. When he was an arm's length from her, he thrust the pistol at her, thrust the muzzle against her left eye, so that she could look into the dark barrel and know there was no future for her but the bullet in the breech.

Looming suddenly behind the monster, Michelle raised her right hand high. She held a knife. Face so pale and slick with sweat. She swayed from side to side, still not fully recovered from having been gassed. She fixed her gaze on Amity's right eye. And in that moment, they seemed to be granted telepathy. Amity knew what Michelle—Mother, Mom—was thinking. If she stabbed Falkirk in the back, he might reflexively pull the trigger.

When Amity winked her right eye, her mother returned the wink. They knew what they had to do, take the biggest risk the situation allowed, dare to cheat Death in this world, at least for one day, one hour, one minute.

Falkirk snarled, "You stole my inheritance, little sister, you and your brother and your deceiving whore of a mother. But what's all that money worth to you now, you little shit?"

He was crazy, really and truly, and Amity expected she'd be dead without ever knowing he pulled the trigger—it would be that fast—but she did what she had to do, anyway. With her right hand, she slapped at the pistol, which surprised him, and the front sight of the weapon nicked the skin at the corner of her eye socket, but the muzzle swung wide of her head. Her mother drove the knife down with all the force she could muster, stabbed it deep into Falkirk's back. He squeezed off a shot that went past Amity's left ear, and for an instant that misassembled marionette face looked as if it would come apart altogether—but then everything went wrong.

Michelle was weak and dizzy and nauseous from the lingering effect of the sedative gas. When she drove the blade into Falkirk's back, into the flesh of another human being, her nausea swelled and she thought her trembling legs would fail her. She should have torn the knife out of him and stabbed again, again. But either madness or drugs—he seemed drugged—or the devil himself gave the sonofabitch uncanny resilience. With the knife sticking out of him like some kind of switch handle, he pivoted and struck her with his forearm hard enough to knock her down.

Amity turned to run. Falkirk pivoted again, kicking her legs out from under her. She fell before him, on her back, as defenseless as a sacrifice on an Aztec altar. He pressed a foot to her throat, immobilizing her, while simultaneously warning off Michelle with the threat of crushing the girl's airway merely by bearing down with all his weight.

With his left hand, he reached back to his right shoulder and extracted the dripping blade and tossed it through the open door of the pantry. He pointed the pistol at the girl's abdomen, giving himself two ways to kill her.

To Michelle, as she lay helpless, afraid even to get to her feet lest Falkirk might deal death as he promised, he seemed to have risen out of Hell. He was one of the legions of the damned, unable to be killed because he was already dead.

When Jeffy came through the door from the hallway, armed with a pistol that he dared not use, he seemed to assess the situation in an instant. He held his fire.

More like a malevolent spirit than like a man, as if to tempt Jeffy's soul into despair, Falkirk said, "What kind of father are you that you run out on her and now let her be under my heel? You're even worse than the dirty pig who was my old man. He fucked away my inheritance, but at least he didn't stand watching while I died."

Michelle half wished that the sedative gas had been a poison, that she had not survived to bear witness to Amity being murdered, no matter how many other Amitys might still live elsewhere.

Then she realized that this Jeffy before her had in some way changed since she'd met him only hours earlier. If he was afraid, his fear was not evident in his posture or face. Like the Jeffy she had loved in her timeline, he had been sweet, sentimental; but at the moment, he appeared to be cold and hard. Anger narrowed his eyes, pinched his mouth, but there was somehow a clean quality to it, more wrath than rage.

Instead of responding to Falkirk, he said to Amity, "*A Dragon in New York.*"

Amity stared at him but said nothing, and Michelle sensed that some understanding passed between them.

Jeffy lowered his pistol and put it on the floor. He said to Falkirk, "You win. What do you want us to do?"

✳ ✳ ✳

A calm like none she had ever known settled over Amity. It was the peace that came with an absolute trust in someone, that kind of trust called *faith*.

A Dragon in New York was a fabulous fantasy novel set in the present day. Amity enjoyed contemporary fantasies in real-world settings as much as she liked those crammed full of swordplay and set in mythical kingdoms many centuries earlier. There were life lessons to be learned from both kinds of stories.

What her father proposed was dangerous, but without risk there was no reward worth having, because rewards without risk were just strokes of luck. If you relied entirely on luck, you had better be prepared that as often as it was good, it would be bad.

He put his gun down on the floor and said, "You win. What do you want us to do?"

Falkirk was a murderous sociopath, an apostle of evil. There were two ways such a servant of evil might have reacted to surrender in a case like this, and neither would have been with a respect for life. He might have shot the girl on whose throat he had his foot, and then her father, or the father and then the girl. Of all the things an agent of evil hates, he most hates innocence.

Although he wants to destroy the innocent, he prefers first to have the pleasure of corrupting them and tormenting them until they despair. With Amity's father dead, Falkirk could then kill her mother, kill Duke Pellafino while he slept, order his men to stay out of the house, and have some quality time alone with Amity. That was how a man as sick as Falkirk, in *A Dragon in New York*, had hoped to take full advantage of such a surrender as this, though the girl under his foot was a virgin princess of twenty-six, who was guardian to the dragon, and the man who surrendered was a secret prince, not her father. Now, looking up at this would-be killer, Amity saw that he wasn't the mystery that he had seemed to be, but as common as any villain; not clever, but dull; powerful only until his hatred and obsession caused him to make a decision that exposed his true weakness. He had become so transparent to her that she saw the moment when he made that fateful decision.

He swung the pistol away from Amity, toward her father, but in the instant that he acted, so did she. The moment the muzzle of the gun was not in line with her, but before her father was at risk, she seized the ankle of the foot on her throat and shoved hard with both hands. Even as Amity reached for Falkirk's ankle, Daddy stooped to retrieve the pistol he'd put on the floor. Staggering off balance, Falkirk fired one wild shot, and Daddy squeezed off two. Because a girl couldn't hide from the hardness of the world forever, because she had to grow up sometime, and because Amity was going on twelve, she didn't look away, but saw the head shot, the chest shot, and knew that what had happened was as terrible as it was right and good.

At the table, Duke raised his head and blinked and surveyed the trashed room. He looked confused and said, "What did I miss?"

Mother said, "The final climax, but not the denouement."

Amity wanted to ask what that word meant, but she needed a few minutes to get her breath and to become accustomed to still being alive, like the spunky princess in *A Dragon in New York*.

===== 97

In the blockaded street, where there were enough Suburbans in front of the Pellafino residence to stock a dealership, some of the gathered agents wanted to investigate the reason for all the gunfire in the house. Knowing better than anyone what drove their boss, what his intentions were, what gave him pleasure, and how much he hated underlings who thought for themselves, Louis Wong advised them to wait until Falkirk rang him to order the cleanup of the premises.

A high-pressure system of dry northern air had given them a rare meteorological condition called "severe clear," a vaulting sky of piercing blue, without the least filigree of clouds. The air was mild, the light inspiring. Those who served by waiting in the street had thermoses of coffee and boxes of doughnuts, and they were just as well paid to stand around shooting the shit as they were when they were in the thick of the action.

===== 98

According to Mom, *denouement* was French for *unknotting* and referred to the events following the final climax of the plot, when everything was neatly tied up, or as neatly as could be done without exceeding the patience of the reader.

Thanks to the Ed Harkenbach from Mother's timeline, who loved her as he might his own child and worked so hard to reunite her with her husband and daughter, their denouement was flat-out amazing. It was really and truly humongously more satisfying than Amity would have believed it could possibly be when she was being swung around the kitchen by the maniac Falkirk.

They couldn't go back to the bungalow in Amity's and Daddy's world, because even though Falkirk was dead there, a lot of other equally vicious creeps would be looking for them. They couldn't go back to the bungalow in Mother's world, because Amity and her father were dead in that timeline, and even in this crazy multiverse, the dead did not come back to life.

Ed had found an ideal timeline where neither Daddy nor Mother nor Amity had been born, so there were no other versions of themselves to run into while shopping for groceries.

When working on Everett Highways in his native timeline, Ed had realized that corrupt politicians and bureaucrats were siphoning off several billion dollars from the seventy-six billion in project funding. Surprise, surprise. Unlike the version of Ed who befriended Daddy, this Ed had enough street smarts—and a sense of an impending poopstorm—to line his own pockets with a hundred million, most of which he converted into gold bars, before blowing up the project and destroying all the keys to everything except his own.

Four months earlier, after finding a timeline that was perfect for Michelle, he ported again and again, conveying the gold to that parallel world, converting it into the local currency, establishing himself as an upstanding citizen.

Fabricating a life story and getting ID might have been a butt-busting job, but Edwin was assisted in this new world by yet another version of himself, Edgar Harkenbach. As you might expect, Edgar was a brilliant physicist and highly respected. However, he had been wise enough to realize that, although he could find a way to travel to parallel worlds, doing so would cause endless problems. He restrained himself. Sympathizing with Edwin's predicament and all, Edgar proclaimed him a long-lost twin who had been sent home from the hospital with the wrong family, the way heirs to the throne in stories sometimes wind up being raised by peasants while the real peasant baby becomes king. With a lot of sly and shifty maneuvering and not a little outright hugger-muggery, they not only established Edwin in a new life, but gave him a daughter named Michelle and fabricated a background and ID for her husband and daughter. All this scheming and subterfuge had been completed before Edwin visited Michelle in her world for dinner on the evening of April twelfth, when he told her about the multiverse and convinced her that elsewhere Jeffy and Amity were alive and waiting for her.

So on that severe-clear day with the bluest sky that anyone could remember, the reunited Coltrane family and Charlie Pellafino ported from his house, where four men lay dead and the kitchen was a disgusting mess, and arrived in another timeline where a life had been prepared for everyone except Duke. More shifty maneuvering and hugger-muggery ensued, and an identity was provided for the big guy as well. Within a week, Frank and Imogene, Daddy's parents, were likewise relocated.

They all lived in a compound of five lovely houses purchased by Edwin, on a hill overlooking the sea, in a Suavidad Beach that was even prettier and cleaner than the one in which Jeffy and Amity had lived before they ever heard about the multiverse. Snowball was with them, too, because Edwin, being somewhat of a showboater, ported back to the bungalow on Shadow Canyon Lane and extracted the mouse in the dead of night, right under the noses of the shadow state agents still infesting the place.

The first Edwin they ever met, the one who gave Jeffy the key to everything and told him eventually to seal it in a barrel of concrete and sink it in the sea, who had then disappeared forever, had said that *his* Project Everett Highways had visited 187 parallel worlds. The second Edwin, who had made it his mission to reunite Michelle with her lost family, had checked out 268 worlds, searching for the one in which she might be happiest. He was a different kind of Harkenbach, really and truly.

On the first anniversary of their move to a happier world, the extended family celebrated with an elaborate dinner on the patio at the Coltrane residence. Below them, the storied hills of the town glimmered with magical light, and the starlit sea waited for the moon to rise and play upon its waters. Over the patio were strung Japanese paper lanterns and strings of colored bulbs, and the table was a field of candles in amber-glass cups. The servant robots were efficient, cute, friendly, but not self-aware because artificial intelligence had been outlawed here.

At one point in the festivities, Mother kissed Edwin on his bald head and declared, "You did good, Dad." She could call him Dad because he had adopted her and, of course, he had been as good to her as her late father had been. His head was still as smooth as an egg because he shaved it every day to avoid confusion about who was Edwin and who was Edgar.

He had for darn sure done good, finding them this world. There were, like, so many instances when history here branched away from history on the world where Amity actually *had* been born that she would have needed a hundred pages to stuff it all in a denouement. Some of the most important were that no one here ever took the work of Karl Marx or Friedrich Nietzsche or Sigmund Freud seriously. So there had been no Lenin, no Soviet Union, no communism or fascism; and two hundred million people who, elsewhere, had been killed by those regimes, had not been killed here. No one had ever heard of Hitler or Stalin or Mao. World War II was never fought, nor the Korean War nor any of the wars thereafter. In a world of lasting peace, much more money had been available for research into other than weapons systems, so that medicine and technology were greatly advanced over what Amity had known in her native timeline. In the US, equality between all races had been achieved in 1942.

Daddy was especially pleased that, without the interruption of World War II, the Art Deco period remained at a peak into the late 1950s, and from it had grown new schools of art and architecture so exciting that the soulless buildings of the Bauhaus movement and all that emanated from it were never inflicted on the world.

Although her father continued to collect Bakelite radios, he didn't find the restoration of them fulfilling enough to make that his life's work. Not after their little adventure. He began writing a fantasy novel.

As the years passed, Jeffrey Coltrane became a well-known name on bestseller lists. Although Michelle Jamison Coltrane chose not to become a performer, she achieved considerable renown as a songwriter in this world that was more disposed to her musical style than had been her native timeline. Duke had no further interest in hotel security; however, his experience investigating gang activities and homicides prepared him to be a tough but fair agent for Jeffrey's books and Michelle's songs, which he often played on his piano.

Amity became twelve, thirteen, fourteen, fifteen, under the loving tutelage of her parents. She also had three grandparents—Frank, Imogene, and Edwin—plus one official uncle, Edgar, and one unofficial uncle, Duke. She blossomed and grew wiser; she knew it and thrived on the blessings of the day.

Even in this best of all possible worlds, there were sad times, as when Snowball died, and happy times, like when they got their first golden retriever puppy, Cuddles, but for the longest while, there were no terrible times.

Nevertheless, worlds existed where John Falkirk still lived and sought the key to everything. Evil never dies. It just closes one franchise and opens another elsewhere.

Edwin kept his key to everything as well as the one that had been given to Jeffy and that had, for a short while, been in the possession of Falkirk. The peace of this timeline quickly mellowed him, and he decided against tracking down and killing sicko versions of himself and Falkirk on other worlds. However, he did not destroy the keys or sink them in the sea, for that would leave the family without options if one day another Falkirk ported here with some nefarious purpose.

On the morning of her sixteenth birthday, Amity rose before first light, showered, and dressed. As dawn broke, she took Cuddles for a walk on leash, down through the picturesque streets, through the park, to the shore. A special luncheon was planned and, in the evening, a party, but first she would celebrate with the dog, who loved the sea as if he'd been a sailor in a previous incarnation. Sweet sixteen. She knew that she would remember this day forever, and she wanted Cuddles also to have good memories of it, for she loved him no less than he loved her.

Life was an infinite library of stories, and in every story, a girl such as Amity learned an important lesson, sometimes more than one, whether she was a highborn child of royalty or a milkmaid. She was in fact neither. Her parents were artists, and she found cows too smelly. But she had learned some things, anyway. The biggest lesson that she had learned was this:

Your life in the multiverse was like a magnificent oak tree with a gajillion branches, some of them deformed and some of them beautiful. You made stupid decisions, and tragedy ensued. You made wise decisions, and tragedy ensued. But for every tragedy, there was a triumph, a world where you lived instead of dying, where you found love instead of losing it, where you prospered. Both fate and free will were involved. Everything that could happen to you was known from the big bang, and yet each version of Amity chose the path she wished to choose. In the end, the meaning of your life was the final shape and beauty—or ugliness—of the tree when all branches had grown to maturity. This was a total crazy-ass way to design the multiverse, really and truly. If before her adventure someone had explained this reality to her, she would have called it bullsugar. However, she had experienced the truth of it, and with the passing days, she had come to see great beauty in this infinite forest of oak trees that were human lives in their striving, such beauty that sometimes the contemplation of it left her breathless and humbled.

Pets were allowed on a section of the beach. She took off her sneakers and rolled up the legs of her jeans and freed Cuddles from his leash.

The glorious golden retriever raced across the compacted sand, splashed into the foaming surf, and swam out as if he knew of Japan and meant to get there.

She wasn't worried about him. He never went too far because he couldn't bear to be a great distance from her.

She waded into the waves, which broke around her calves, and she stood watching Cuddles challenge the low swells.

This creation, the multiverse, was a construct of uncountable second chances, and although it permitted evil and death, it also permitted good and life, and made endless allowances for each person, which meant that at the heart of the mechanism was infinite mercy.

Here, now, the warm morning and clear sky and the spangled sea and the joyful dog and the wonder of existence made her heart race and her eyes shine as if all the light of the world came from within her.